DAINDRETH'S TRAITOR

By

Elisabeth Wheatley

For Christian

I think you are Daindreth brought to life, but we can tell everyone you're Thadred if you want to.

CHAPTER ONE

Amira

The Istovari archers surrounded them on all sides in a vanguard. Amira walked close beside Daindreth, her hand clutching his.

The Istovari had taken their weapons and had wanted to shoot Daindreth on sight. Sairydwen, the sorceress whose life they'd saved, had convinced her brother, Tapios, not to kill the archduke. At least not for now.

Tapios appeared to be the leader of the small band, which was odd. Among Istovari, it was the women who led the clan. They were the ones who could pass magic onto their children, after all. Yet Tapios commanded young girls and even a few women among his ragtag troops.

They were all Istovari, but none of them appeared to have any significant amount of magic as far as Amira could tell. All the same, she'd learned the hard way that a well-trained sorceress, even a weak one, could be dangerous. She'd had her arm dislocated by Sairydwen's cleverness back in Lashera.

These Istovari might not be imperial soldiers, but they kept her and Daindreth at arms' length, never within reach, and moved with a trained proficiency.

Worst of all, they treated Amira and Daindreth like enemies.

Amira's only consolation was that the Istovari hadn't killed them yet and her name seemed to mean something to them.

Amira Brindonu—daughter of Cyne Brindonu and Renner of Hylendale, now King Hyle. Though Amira hadn't seen her mother in over nineteen years, Cyne had been the daughter of one of the clan leaders. It had been part of the reason she'd been married to Hylendale's heir. Cyne had been a princess in her own way, Amira supposed.

Though many things had changed, Amira had to wonder just how much had changed. Who led the clan now? How many sorceresses had survived the fall of the tower? No one really knew for sure. How many of their families had made it into the

1

wilderness?

There were rumors and legends of sorceresses living in grand cities within the Cursewood. Then again, just as many claimed they roved in fur pelts, eating animals raw.

Two young men dragged Iasu, the Kadra'han sent by Empress Vesha. His mission had been to kill Amira and take Daindreth home. Thanks to the Istovari, the imperial had been struck in the thigh by an arrow. Blood from the wound dripped down his knee and stained his leg. Unlike Daindreth and Amira, the imperial's hands were lashed behind his back.

He caught Amira looking and glared at her.

Iasu and Amira had studied together years ago as children. Her father had been clever enough to know that a knight's training wouldn't be the best use of her abilities and had shuffled her off to distant Kelamora, where Kadra'han were taught.

How he'd managed to broker that deal, Amira still didn't know. She suspected Cromwell, her father's lawyer, steward, and right-hand man. Usually, if something unexplained happened in Hylendale, Cromwell could be blamed.

"How much further?" Daindreth asked, looking to Tapios.

"No questions!" snapped a young girl on Daindreth's other side. She shifted the bow in her hands but didn't move to raise it.

Amira studied the girl. There was a half-mindedness to the way she held her bow and the way she moved over the forest floor. At the same time, tension made her movements jerky and shaky.

The girl might be used to the forest, but she wasn't used to strangers.

"Soon, archduke," Tapios responded, not bothering to look in Daindreth's direction.

"I told you, Thadred is still out there," Daindreth said. "The kelpie—"

"No one survives a kelpie." Tapios paused long enough to cast the archduke a look that might have been sympathetic or might have been condescending. Amira didn't know the man well enough to tell. "Your friend is dead."

At Tapios' side, Sairydwen spoke. "I'm sorry." The

2

sorceress's sentiment was soft and sorrowful as she drew further into her brother's cloak.

Amira and Daindreth both glanced at Sairydwen. When they'd found Thadred with the sorceress, he had had tried to protect her from the attacking kelpie.

Before that, she'd taken Thadred as her hostage. Yet according to Sairydwen, Thadred had helped her escape the Kadra'han and the Kelamora assassins after being taken captive.

Taking in her mangled hands, it would have been almost impossible for her to use spells. It seemed believable the two formed some sort of alliance or bond during their time together.

They trudged on through the forest and Amira kept watching the Istovari. They were untested as best she could tell. Maybe used to patrolling the forest for beasts and other threats, but they were too uneasy. She guessed the Cursewood didn't get many visitors.

A stench tickled Amira's nose. Was it another trick of the forest or bog? Then the air shifted and the unmistakable stench of rot, urine, and burning flesh stung her nostrils. Amira stifled the urge to gag.

Daindreth coughed, covering his mouth with his sleeve. "What is that?"

Even the Istovari winced. A few of them coughed, too.

"Gah," one of the young men muttered. "We approached from the wrong side."

It took Amira a moment to recognize the smell. It seemed out of place in this wild labyrinth of the Cursewood.

"A tannery." Amira couldn't help but be surprised. It was a such a mundane and *normal* thing. "They're tanning leather."

Despite the unpleasant smell, Tapios and the Istovari archers showed no sign of turning around. They pressed on, a few of them holding their sleeves to their faces.

The stench only worsened. Their group pressed through a line of moss-covered stones. As soon as they stepped through, the *ka* rippled in the air around them. It shimmered like a curtain and slid through Amira's body. A worming sensation went through her like a thousand tiny snakes, but it distracted her momentarily from the reek of the tanning vats.

The sun slapped Amira in the face, and she had to squint.

3

Looking up, she found herself peering between the boughs of solid, towering oaks. They were natural trees without the Cursewood's taint—healthy and strong, with green buds just coming into their spring foliage.

Bright grass bent under her feet. The air was lighter, even if it still held the stench of the vats. All around her, she could feel the spark and shimmer of *ka* in the air, tantalizing her with its presence. The poisonous taint to the air was gone.

Looking back, Amira could see the Cursewood tangling behind them, but she couldn't quite sense its power from here.

How had the Istovari sorceresses done that? It was almost as if the Cursewood didn't exist from where she stood and yet she could see it.

Dozens of boys and girls used poles to stir the contents of massive cauldrons. Nearby, several older boys were hard at work with curved blades, scraping fat, flesh, and hair off slippery pelts.

A yelp sounded, followed by the excited cry of a child. "The rangers are back!"

The sight of the Istovari had most the children dropping their tools and running across the open ground, their aprons flapping, their arms and faces stained with the gore of their work.

Something was off, but Amira couldn't place it. The unknown nagged at her, irritating as a splinter under her fingernail.

"Stay back!" Tapios held up a warning hand.

The children stopped a few paces away, but that didn't stop them from crowding around or letting loose a slew of questions.

"You found her?"

"Mother Sairydwen, are you alright?"

"Who are they?" asked another, pointing to Amira and Daindreth.

"She's pretty!" a girl said, looking to Amira. "Where did she come from?"

"Who's that? Is he hurt?" Another girl's brow furrowed with concern as she noticed Iasu, head hanging as he stood supported by two Istovari.

"Not now, children." Tapios' words dripped impatience, but not quite anger. "Later. You'll hear of it later. Now back to

4

work."

A chorus of displeased groans sounded all around.

"You'll ruin the hides!" Tapios insisted. "Back to work, all of you." The young man shooed them away, swatting at several like unruly lambs.

The children raced back to their work. Several of the cauldrons that had indeed begun to bubble over, but hardly any of the children took their eyes off the adults as they passed.

"I can help!" cried one of the boys, probably no more than fifteen.

"Yes," Tapios agreed. "And right now, you can help by tanning those hides."

"Give it time," said one of the Istovari archers as their small group shuffled past. The young man couldn't have been more than a year or two older than the other boy. "You're not ready for man's work yet."

"Hey!" cried the younger. As he spun around, Amira noticed they had the same freckles and the angled jawline. Brothers, if she had to guess.

"I'm just as good with a bow as you!" the younger shouted, waving the tanning knife.

"Enough!" Tapios spun to his Istovari, gesturing for them to keep up. "Let's go."

As they made their way through the bubbling cauldrons and the children, Amira realized what was wrong—none of the cauldrons had fires underneath them and there was no smoke, only steam.

Ka pooled at the bottom of each cauldron, flickering and pulsing as if it were flame, but it wasn't. The children nursed the pools of *ka,* guiding and shaping them from moment to moment.

It was so…strange.

Amira didn't realize she was staring until one of the Istovari archers shot her a hard glare and Daindreth tugged her hand. She cleared her throat and faced forward, fighting self-consciousness.

Amira had been an assassin for years, hunting and killing men as vile as they came. She was a princess, if a bastardized one. She was betrothed to the heir of the greatest empire the

5

world had ever known. She had fought cythraul and won, and she had entertained the most powerful people on the continent. In her relatively short life, she had seen things most people only imagined in their wildest dreams and worst nightmares.

Yet she turned into a gawping fool at the sight of a little thermal magic. Literal child's play.

They moved past the line of oaks and large stone mounds came into view. At first, Amira thought they were cairns like those that had once been used for the burial of the wealthy, but then a woman in a brown wool kirtle exited one. The woman carried a basket on one hip and as soon as she spotted Tapios and the others, she dropped it, spilling wheels of cheese on the ground.

Ignoring her cargo, the woman gathered up her skirts and raced toward them. "Sairydwen!" she cried. "Sairydwen, we thought—oh goddess." She caught the other woman and wrapped the battered sorceress in a tight embrace.

The stranger's *ka* shimmered over her in a thin veil. She was a sorceress, too. Not a minor or middling one like those who were in Amira and Daindreth's armed escort, either. This woman was stronger than Sairydwen, though it was hard for Amira to know by how much.

The two women exchanged words, but Amira couldn't catch them. Within moments, another woman emerged from the stone mound, much younger than the first.

That girl let off a cry and soon men and women were flocking from the surrounding houses, running to Sairydwen, calling out to the archers, laughing, asking questions, trying to catch Tapios' attention.

Every single woman was a sorceress, and more than half of the men had signs of the gift, too. *Ka* roped and sparked around them like vines. Many of them even had spells running through their clothes, though she couldn't tell what the purpose of the spells were.

None of them looked like what she remembered sorceresses to look like. Instead of the long red, burgundy, or black gowns, these women were in dark woolen kirtles belted with rope or sometimes leather belts. The men were dressed similarly, their

6

dark trousers gathered at the tops of their boots. Their clothes were well-made, and they all appeared to have shoes, but other than that they didn't look any better than the serfs in one of Hylendale's farming villages.

These people were mud-stained, callused, and stank of sweat and hard labor. They were nothing like the groomed and coiffed elites from Amira's memory.

Amira turned in a half-circle, still holding Daindreth's hand. The entire settlement was woven with spells, veins of *ka* crafted into the strange houses, the nearby well, and even parts of the ground itself. *Ka* had been threaded into complex, seemingly decorative designs, invisible to the naked eye and yet not seeming to serve any purpose.

That seemed the sole part of this settlement dedicated to beauty. The low mound houses were covered in greenery and judging by the sheep pens and gardens between them, this place was built first and foremost with practicality in mind.

"This way," Tapios prompted, leading Amira and Daindreth onward into the village.

Four of the archers stayed close behind them as they ventured deeper into the settlement. The rest dispersed, two of them taking Iasu into one of the low mound houses. Amira noted which house it was in case she had to find the bastard later.

As best she could tell, several generations lived together in each house. There were children of all ages and even some elders. It wasn't quite a city, but by all appearances, it was a thriving community.

Amira pulled closer to Daindreth, squeezing his hand tight. "If we're separated, don't tell them anything," she said. "Refuse to answer until they bring us back together."

Daindreth kissed the top of her head. "It will be alright."

Amira wasn't so sure, but she didn't contradict him.

Their small group rounded another one of the mound houses, just like all the others. A tall woman came into view, her silver-streaked hair pulled into a tight plait and a lamb in her arms.

The assassin froze. Dread pooled in her gut mingled with fear, rage, and...something else. Something halfway to hope from that foolish, childish side of Amira that still didn't quite believe this woman would hurt her.

The woman's face was thinner and there were more creases around the edges of her eyes. Her frame was less sturdy, as if the past nineteen years had aged her by twice that much.

The archer at her back ordered Amira to keep moving, but then Tapios noticed the woman with the lamb and stopped.

"Elder Mother." Tapios inclined his head in a bow. He looked to Amira, for the first time appearing awkward and uncomfortable.

"Who are they, Tapios?" the Elder Mother asked, her voice smooth, silky, yet carrying the force of one who has been obeyed without question for a very long time.

"We found them in the Cursewood. He saved my sister's life, Elder Mother." Tapios inclined his head again at that, as if he expected the Elder Mother to be upset.

"And why do you say that like a little boy who was just caught with his hand in the breadbox?" The Elder Mother set down the lamb and let it race to its mother.

"It has created exceptional circumstances," Tapios said, glancing to the archduke and Amira.

The Elder Mother's sharp gaze turned to the two of them. She surveyed them with fresh interest—hard, calculating.

"The archduke," the Elder Mother said without hesitating. Her expression turned cold, and Amira wished she had at least one of her daggers.

The assassin edged closer to Daindreth, glancing between the archers. Would the Elder Mother try to have him killed here?

"Please." Daindreth stepped forward, keeping hold of Amira's hand. "We came to seek your help."

The Elder Mother looked to Tapios. "You were supposed to stop them. Instead, you bring them here?"

"Yes, Elder Mother, forgive me. As I said, they asked permission to petition you and the others."

"There is nothing to petition. It is decided." The woman spoke with the ferocity of a hissing badger, but when she looked to Amira, her expression changed. "Princess Amira?" She spoke as one might to a frightened colt. "Is that you?"

8

Amira had often thought about what she would do when she saw the woman again. She'd expected rage, fury, maybe fear. But now that they were face to face, she felt…nothing.

The Elder Mother didn't take offense at Amira's silence. She looked to Amira and Daindreth's joined hands and her mouth twisted ever so slightly.

"If you want to hurt him," Amira said, keeping emotion from her voice, "you'll have to kill me first."

That might not have been the wisest thing to say. Ultimatums were rarely helpful in real negotiation, but Amira didn't want to leave any room for doubt.

The Elder Mother cocked her head, anger knotting her features as she looked back to Daindreth. "Brought her as a shield, did you?"

Daindreth pulled Amira closer, angling her behind him. "I came to speak with you."

"She's already in this," the Elder Mother said. "Is this your idea of petition, archduke? Using her like your dog?"

"Amira is more precious to me than you can imagine," Daindreth shot back. "She is not my hostage."

"Elder Mother," Tapios interjected. "Whatever else he may be guilty of, he saved my sister's life at great personal risk. She vouches for him. I promised him an audience before the full Motherhood."

"You owe us that much!" Amira snarled, her voice rising to a shrill pitch. Then, lower, she added, "You owe *me* that much."

"Owe you, child?" The Elder Mother sounded genuinely confused.

Anger simmered, hot and viscous, in Amira's chest, mixing with a child's blind fear. Daindreth squeezed her hand, and she fought her feelings down.

"Please," Daindreth said. "We come with no threats, no army. Just ourselves and our request."

A tense silence stretched among them. The archers glanced between them all, but none spoke.

The Elder Mother inspected Daindreth closely, as one might a stray cat suspected of being diseased. She looked to Tapios and the two exchanged a silent look.

"We will give you the audience," the Elder Mother said

finally. "But," she pointed to Daindreth, "repeat these commands to your Kadra'han."

"No!" Amira shouted and she didn't have to pretend outrage. The curse of the Kadra'han no longer bound her, but they didn't know that and if they wanted Daindreth to give her commands... She grabbed his sleeve. "Daindreth, don't."

The Elder Mother was unmoved. She never took her attention off Daindreth. "Give her these commands, exactly as I say, or we will kill you where you stand."

Amira's heart beat faster as a hundred scenarios went through her head. If they wanted Daindreth to give her commands, then they would need to keep him alive to make sure the commands remained binding.

Daindreth looked to Amira. "I'm sorry," he whispered.

She was aware of Tapios and at least thirty others staring, watching their exchange. Whispers flitted around them, buzzing like flies around a bowl of buttercream, but no one dared interrupt the Elder Mother.

Amira's mouth pressed into a hard line, but she didn't argue again.

"Repeat after me," the Elder Mother ordered. "'Go with the Elder Mother. Speak only truth to her and all in this village. Do not try to find me and do not try to escape.'"

Daindreth hesitated and Amira picked up that his reticence was more than an act. Finally, he echoed the instructions, looking straight at Amira. She squeezed his hand tight, concentrating on the words. Now that the curse no longer bound her, she'd have to memorize the commands if she wanted to pretend.

The Elder Mother continued. "'Listen to whatever they have to say. Do not try to harm any of the Istovari, their servants, their homes, their belongings, and do not seek to spy on their secrets or in any way do them harm.'"

Daindreth finished the orders, still holding Amira's hand.

She spun on the Elder Mother. "Am I to be your prisoner, then?"

"My guest." The Elder Mother sounded serious.

"I want to stay with my fiancé."

10

The Elder Mother extended a hand. "Come, child."

Amira was more than twenty summers old. She'd killed men and fought monsters and survived things that would have ended lesser warriors. Yet here this woman stood, telling her to come to heel like an unruly pup.

"We came to throw ourselves on their mercy," Daindreth said, speaking into Amira's ear. "I guess this is where we find out how good a bet that was." He kissed her hair. "I would never ask you to go with them if I thought they'd hurt you. Do you trust me?"

Amira swallowed. This had been her plan as much as it had been his. Now he was the one reassuring her. "I'm not afraid for me," Amira whispered.

The Elder Mother kept her attention on them. "Now, archduke."

"I'll be fine, Amira." Daindreth sounded far more certain than he should have, all things considered. "Go."

It took Amira a moment to remember that she had to obey. She ripped away from Daindreth, getting it over with.

She shuffled to the Elder Mother. The older woman reached for her hand, but she yanked it back.

"Is that anyway to treat your grandmother?" the older woman asked.

Amira stiffened, a thousand outraged retorts, curses, and accusations aching to come spilling out of her mouth. Instead, she clenched her hands into fists at her sides and glared into the other woman's eyes.

"Where's my mother?" Amira clipped, speaking the word like a curse. "Is she dead?" The assassin let her tone be as flippant as she could, just to make sure they knew she didn't care

"No," the Elder Mother answered. "She's assisting with a birth this morning. She'll be glad to see you."

No one seemed to care that Amira wasn't particularly glad to see any of them. All the same, she was supposedly under compulsion to go with the Elder Mother and not cause problems.

"Come, child," the Elder Mother said again, more finality in her tone this time.

Amira looked back to Daindreth.

11

He nodded to her once, putting on a brave expression.

"Secure the archduke until the Mothers can be assembled," the Elder Mother ordered. "Come see us when you are finished, Tapios."

"Yes, Mother," Tapios said with a bow.

Amira had no choice but to watch as Tapios and the other archers led Daindreth away. Her last glimpse of him was his reassuring smile before he was dragged off.

"Whatever happens to him," Amira said, watching where Daindreth disappeared, "I will do to you and worse."

The Elder Mother seemed unimpressed, even though Amira supposedly could speak nothing but the truth under Daindreth's commands. The silver-haired woman surveyed Amira from head to foot, a gleam in her eye that was far too tender for the assassin's liking. "After all these years," she sighed with a smile. "You've come back to us."

"I've come for your help," Amira answered.

The Elder Mother studied Amira closer, her eyes sparking.

The crowd that had surrounded them stayed looking on, curiosity and fear in their faces. Some followed after Daindreth and his guards, but most of them seemed far too interested in the assassin and the Elder Mother.

"Amira Brindonu." The Elder Mother spoke loud enough for all gathered to hear. "My lost granddaughter."

Then she embraced Amira. In front of at least thirty villagers, with the grime of the Cursewood and the muck of the sheep pen covering them both, the leader of the Istovari sorceresses embraced Amira like a prodigal child.

Amira stood rigid and didn't return the embrace. Did the woman just expect her to pretend that the tower had never happened?

CHAPTER TWO

Daindreth

Daindreth had expected them to separate him from Amira. That had given him time to brace himself and remain composed, but it did nothing to soothe the raging fear once it happened.

The Istovari weren't gentle, but nor were they cruel as they herded him to a low mound near the central portions of the village. At first, he thought it was a grave, but then one of them swung open the door on the side, revealing a narrow shaft that could loosely be described as a staircase. The smell of damp earth and roots came from below.

"Down," Tapios ordered, gesturing into the darkness. "And don't try any tricks."

Daindreth didn't move. He wasn't bound, but Istovari hemmed him in on all sides. He faced the other man. "Where is the Elder Mother taking Amira?"

"Somewhere safe," Tapios said. "Now down." The grizzled man jerked his head toward the darkness.

"How soon will I see her?" Daindreth pressed.

"When the Elder Mother deems fitting." Tapios' jaw tightened, his patience wearing thin. "You're not in a position to negotiate, Highness. Get in the cellar."

Two of the younger Istovari grabbed Daindreth's arms and shoved him down. The shaft was narrow and the floor uneven. Daindreth could barely make out the shape of the steps in the dark.

At the bottom, his eyes adjusted. He was in a root cellar stacked with casks and barrels and sealed jars. It was impossible to guess what was inside, but since most of the barrels sat empty in neat stacks, he guessed that this was the village's winter storehouse. Or at least one of them.

Thick logs supported the ceiling. Layered stones lined all sides, but roots showed between the cracks, snaking their way through.

"Are you going to leave me down here?" Daindreth asked

flatly.

"You have somewhere else to be?" one of the Istovari boys replied without hesitation..

Daindreth glanced the boy up and down once. He probably wasn't more than sixteen, jumpy and cocksure at the same time. Even in his limited experience with fighting, Daindreth knew those were the most dangerous types of fighters, the sorts who knew just enough to get themselves and other people killed.

Tapios jerked his head to another young Istovari. "Juliander, the rope."

Daindreth stiffened at that. The last time he'd been bound, he'd been strapped to a silver chair and had nearly lost control of his own body forever.

Here, especially in the village of the people who had placed this curse on his family, was the last place he wanted to be bound again. But what was he going to do? They had Amira, and while he doubted they would hurt her, he wouldn't put it past them if they thought it would make him more compliant.

One of the young rangers, presumably Juliander, stepped forward. He had two lengths of knotted twine in his hands. He watched Daindreth with wide eyes, like he was unsure whether to attack or run.

"Your hands, archduke," Juliander barked.

Daindreth exhaled. He understood why they weren't letting Amira see this part.

He held out his wrists and the young Istovari attached a length of rope to either one, working the knots with expert efficiency. For all his nervousness and hesitance, he knew what he was doing with rope. Daindreth tried to follow the loops and twists of the cords, but lost track. Amira would have probably been able to spot the weaknesses, but he couldn't.

They tied Daindreth against the wall between two support beams, spreading his arms apart.

"How long to you plan to leave me here?" Daindreth interjected.

"As long as we have to." Tapios didn't sound cruel, but nor was there any room for argument in his tone. "That's up to the Mothers. I assume they will speak with Sairydwen and the

14

princess and then make their decision on speaking with you."

Daindreth wasn't worried about either of those women speaking for him. Sairydwen had vouched for him once already and Amira was…well. If there was anyone who had proven she would do anything for him, it was her.

On second thought, Amira might lose her temper and smash the Elder Mother's head through a wall.

The Istovari sorceresses had left Amira for dead. That wasn't something that someone, especially Amira, could just forget. He'd seen glimpses of her rage before. He didn't blame her for hating these women, but if she wasn't able to control it, that might be a death sentence for them both.

Hello.

Daindreth stifled a groan as Caa Iss slithered awake in his thoughts. He hadn't heard from the creature since Lashera, but now it seemed that Amira was far enough away.

Did you miss me, archduke?

A sharp throb pierced Daindreth's skull, painful enough to send bright flashes across his vision.

Look what you've done now. Captured by the Istovari! Who want you dead! Are you really this stupid?

Daindreth's eyes watered as the headache intensified, but he blinked back tears of pain to focus on Tapios. "The other assassins in the forest."

"They can only come here if they've been here," Tapios said. "Or been shown here by someone who has."

Inside Daindreth's head, Caa Iss was fairly shouting into his thoughts.

All that time fighting me to keep yourself and your woman safe and now look—you got yourselves captured and cornered all on your own! You literally walked into this!

"What about Thadred?" Daindreth gasped.

"Who?"

"My cousin. He saved your sister's life according to her. Will you be going back to find him?" Daindreth was very nearly blinded by then next throb of pain through his head, but he kept his chin up and fought to keep from wavering.

Stupid, stupid boy, Caa Iss admonished. *Got your cousin killed. He died trying to save you. Just like Taylan. How many more must die for*

15

your futile resistance?

"No one survives falling into a river with a kelpie." Tapios shook his head. There was a finality to his tone when he said, "Your friend Thadred is dead."

CHAPTER THREE

Thadred

Thadred was in a hurry, but that did him little good when he had no idea where he was going. He'd last seen Amira and Daindreth being pursued upriver, so assumed that was the best place to look.

All the same, that path took him through twisting riverbeds and in some places the stream slowed to a narrow trickle, far too shallow to have carried him and the kelpie.

Yet he had no better plan than to keep moving forward. He couldn't quite understand this place, but it seemed to shadow the rules of the natural world, even if it didn't quite follow them.

The kelpie carried Thadred along the riverbank in some places and through the river in others. Lleuad, as Thadred called the black stallion, was as surefooted on the rocks as any deer.

Every so often, Thadred would glance down to the animal's algae-stained mane just to be sure that this really was happening, and he wasn't dreaming.

He still had no idea how he'd managed to not only survive the creature, but put a bridle on it and ride it, but here they were. And though Thadred's hip, lower back, and bad leg ached incessantly, at least he didn't have to walk.

Lleuad didn't move like the destriers and palfreys Thadred was used to riding. The stallion lifted his hooves higher and was quicker on his feet, which made for a lithe and swift swamp animal. It also meant that Thadred had to cling to Lleuad's mane for dear life more than once. At least no one was here to see him struggling.

Lleuad snorted, jerking to a halt. Without a saddle, Thadred could feel the muscular horse go tense. Lleuad shuffled his hooves and lowered his head, snorting.

Thadred cocked his head, trying to listen, but heard nothing. "What is it, boy?" Thadred whispered, stroking the stallion's neck.

Lleuad raised his head to one of the nearby branches. The Cursewood's tangled vines hemmed them in on all sides and

Lleuad reached for one of the nearest inky branches. He snapped it off in his teeth and there was a crunching sound like breaking glass.

Lleuad kept chomping and swished his tail, head bobbing as he snorted and plodded along.

Thadred cringed, but couldn't help chuckle when the stallion's tongue lolled out and smeared over the horse's lips. "Does it taste bad?"

Lleuad snorted.

"Then why did you eat it?"

The horse, naturally, didn't reply. Lleuad carried Thadred onward and along the path of a trickling stream.

Cursing, Thadred considered his options. Getting to the Haven seemed his best bet at safety. That was where Amira and Dain would go, anyway. But the sorceress Sair had told him that the Haven could only be found by those who had been there before.

Regardless, he had no idea how to go about contacting the Istovari on his own. As much as he might have mixed feelings about the clan of traitorous sorceresses, being their captive seemed like a better option than starving and freezing in the forest.

On cue, Thadred's stomach rumbled and reminded him that he hadn't eaten since that morning when he'd been a captive of the Kadra'han.

Thadred looked up at the black trees with their drooping black leaves wrapped in black vines just like this black horse. Everything was black. Black like the pitch used to seal the hulls of the great galleons in Mynadra's harbor.

The stallion stopped again and this time the kelpie's ears perked up, swiveled toward the trees to their left. It looked like just another collection of bushes and brambles to Thadred, but in this place, one could never be sure.

"What do you hear, boy?" Thadred murmured, glancing in that direction.

The kelpie knew this forest better than anyone else. If he was interested in something, it was worth listening. The stallion chuffed and lowered his head again.

18

Thadred nudged the horse forward with his heels and the stallion snorted irritably. It took Thadred a second to remember that this was a wild animal, not one of the carefully trained palfreys of the palace. Lleuad would assume Thadred was just kicking him. While Thadred tried to think of how to go about this, the kelpie stepped forward.

Lleuad crossed the shallow stream, hooves scraping on the rocks. For an animal that spent half his life in the water, he had impressively solid hooves.

Thadred held onto the makeshift reins, not sure why he'd bothered anyway. It wasn't like he had hope of controlling the untrained man-eating beast.

Lleuad crossed the river, nostrils flaring and ears twitching. His head lowered and he moved slower.

Thadred tightened his grip on the animal's mane just in case. If Lleuad decided to attack something or bolt, he just hoped he'd fall onto soft mud or at least somewhere without rocks or roots.

The forest was always dark, but it had started to get darker. Soon Thadred expected that it would be too dark to see in front of his face, the way it had on the past few nights here in the Cursewood.

Could the kelpie see in the dark? Probably. That seemed like something a water-dwelling, carnivorous, possibly magical horse would be able to do.

Lleuad crossed the stream and continued into the trees on the other side. For a moment, Thadred feared the kelpie would get them lost, then remembered that they were lost anyway, or at least Thadred was. The kelpie was choosing their path at this point and Thadred accepted it.

Lleuad carried him farther and farther into the trees. The horse's ears twitched with interest.

Whatever it was, the kelpie seemed more curious than aggressive or afraid. Nonetheless, Thadred still remembered the attack on the Kadra'han and their horses. This animal was fully capable of explosive violence.

Lleuad stopped in the dark, ears twitching again.

Thadred glanced around, searching. Then he caught just the faintest whiff of something familiar. Hope and alarm coursed through him at once. It was a sharp smell and it stank.

"Demred's balls."

He couldn't understand why any animal would want to go *toward* that, but Lleuad seemed interested. The kelpie snorted and lowered his head, then turned and plodded off to circle around the smell.

"What *is* that?" Thadred could swear he smelled tanner's vats, but that made no sense in the middle of the wilderness. Thadred pulled on the makeshift bridle. This time Lleuad heeded him, turning to the side and continuing. The little horse made his way through the branches and the inky brambles, not seeming to notice when they scraped along the thick hair of his legs.

"We need somewhere to rest for the night," Thadred said. "Can you understand me?"

Whether Lleuad did or not, Thadred couldn't tell, but the muscular animal plodded back into the forest. Thadred scratched at the horse's neck.

"Good boy."

Lleuad ignored him, black tail swishing. The ground shifted and the kelpie went on, carrying Thadred up a hill slick with mud.

Near the top of the hill, Lleuad slipped, hooves skidding out from under him. But just as soon as he had lost his footing, Lleuad regained his balance and plodded on as if nothing had happened.

Thadred gasped in relief. He hadn't realized he'd taken the stallion's mane in a death grip until he let it go.

This horse had lived his whole life in the swamp. He knew what he was doing.

Lleuad crested the hill, and a rocky outcrop came into view, not unlike the one that lined the river from yesterday. Thadred glanced up, unable to see the peak of the outcrop in the dark.

In front of him, there appeared to be pits of darkness—caves, he would guess. Stones rolled under the kelpie's hooves as he carried Thadred toward the dark.

"Well." Thadred shrugged, though there was no one to see it. "It's better than nothing."

The kelpie stopped, whole body rigid. He raised his head and

20

snapped at the air with his teeth.

"What is it, boy?" Thadred crouched lower as best he could with his sore hip. The horse shuffled his feet and sidestepped.

Thadred glimpsed light then. For an instant, his heart leapt, then he noticed three figures crouched by a fire near the mouth of the cave. It took him a moment to recognize them, but as soon as he did, his heart sank.

And here he'd been hoping they were dead.

The Kadra'han appeared battered, bloody, and far, far worse for the wear. They had only one horse left and all three of them were bandaged in some way.

The one called Fain, the leader, crouched beside the one called Venner. It appeared Venner's shoulder was injured, and the older man was working either some spell or medicine over it or perhaps both.

Contrary to what Sair said and what he'd been able to do with her help, Thadred still couldn't sense magic the way Amira or any of the other sorcerers could. He wasn't fully certain that the Kadra'han even had their own magic, but it was possible.

Thadred counted in his head. Where was Iasu and the other Kadra'han?

He glanced around but couldn't see a damn thing in the dark. Was one of them going to return from scouting and catch him?

If there was one thing for sure, Thadred had no intentions of being taken captive by them again. "Good job, swamp horse."

Lleuad ignored him, ears flicking.

"We should go back," Venner said, voice strained. "Meet the reinforcements from Svitmorga."

Thadred had never hear of Svitmorga. He wasn't sure he could even pronounce it correctly.

Fain didn't speak for a time, focusing on wrapping the younger man's arm.

The third figure across the fire shifted. "We might still be able to get inside," said the third. "We can remove the girl before they arrive."

Thadred found himself straining to hear, heart beating faster. The girl? Did they mean Sair?

"We might," Fain agreed. "But she could be under protection from sorceresses by now."

21

"Are we afraid of women?" scoffed the figure across the fire.

"Sorceresses," Fain corrected, tying off Venner's bandages. "I saw them in the Battle of the Tower. They leveled entire battalions and the hills under them, too." He inhaled and stretched his own neck from side to side.

"They've been weakened since." The figure across the fire shifted. "Their power is gone."

"We don't know that," Fain argued. "We've assumed that because they didn't attack the empire, they couldn't. But we've had no reliable intelligence on the sorceresses since they established the Cursewood."

Thadred cocked his head to the side, forgetting his own physical pain and the closeness of his enemies in the moment.

Sair had made it to the Haven? But it didn't make sense for them to be talking about Sair. They'd had the chance to kill her already and hadn't, which probably meant...

"They might kill the archduke," the third Kadra'han warned. "We have orders to return him unharmed."

Fain's voice turned sharp. "I know!" As a Kadra'han, he wouldn't need reminding. His curse would force him to do everything possible to see that the commands were carried out.

"Then..." The Kadra'han let those words hang for a long moment. "We can't wait. The archduke could be in danger."

"I don't believe that the Istovari girl would let him be harmed."

Istovari girl? They must mean Amira.

"She could have been working with them from the start," the third figure argued. It annoyed Thadred that he still didn't know the guy's name. "That might have been why she abducted him from the palace."

Thadred's brows shot up at that. *Abducted* was a funny word for it. How exactly did they think that one girl had *abducted* a grown man from the middle of an imperial palace? She might be an Istovari, a trained assassin, and scrappy as a dockside bouncer, but no one was that good, not even Amira. She couldn't have gotten Daindreth out if he wasn't willing.

"I have considered it," Fain agreed.

Thadred grinned in excitement despite everything. They *were* talking about Amira. That meant she found the Haven, Daindreth too.

They were safe, at least for now. Unfortunately, it sounded like their safety was in question from several sides.

"The Svitmorga forces will be here by nightfall tomorrow," Fain said. "Now that Jumer knows the way, he can bring them straight here. As soon as he arrives, we will act."

"The archduke could be dead by then." The unnamed Kadra'han added something that sounded like a curse.

"Yes," Fain agreed. "He might. But we'll most certainly be dead if we try to save him on our own." Fain slugged Venner in the shoulder as if to make the point. The other man winced. "Venner can't use his shield arm. And both of us have lost blood, too."

The Kadra'han across the fire cursed.

"I don't like it either," Fain said.

The three of them kept talking in circles with the third Kadra'han pressing that they should try to get inside the Haven and *rescue* Daindreth while they had the chance.

As Thadred listened, more and more became clear. The Kadra'han had found the Haven somehow, or rather been found by Istovari whom they had escaped and then followed to the Haven.

Thadred's joints ached more and more as he watched, but he stayed as he was, listening. He should have fled already, he knew that. It was dangerous to be this close and wait this long, but this might be his only chance of not dying in this gods-forsaken wilderness.

Oddly, Llewad didn't try to attack the Kadra'han or their surviving horse. Thadred wasn't sure why, but that was par for the course at this point.

As Fain came close to raising his voice at the younger Kadra'han, it began to rain. Just a light sprinkle, but Thadred was guessing, with his luck, that it would turn into a downpour at any moment. He couldn't hear the voices of the Kadra'han over the sound of the rain anyway and he certainly couldn't risk getting closer.

"Well, boy," Thadred sighed. "I guess we need to find another place to crash for the night."

He let Lleuad have a loose rein and hoped the stallion would take him somewhere dry.

CHAPTER FOUR

Amira

The scene didn't look like something out of her nightmares, but Amira kept having to remind herself that she wasn't in one. The last time she'd seen this woman had been in those dreams, when she relived the horror of the Battle of the Tower. In those dreams, the Elder Mother was strong, tall, and at the height of her power.

She seemed lessened now. She wasn't quite frail, but nor was she as formidable as Amira remembered. The assassin watched the Elder Mother pour tea into two small teacups.

The two of them were in the large central mound at the middle of the village, which had proven to be more of a complex unto itself.

According to her grandmother, this complex had been the first living quarters for the sorceresses when they had come to this place, hence its many rooms and chambers. The building was an odd mismatch of stone, thatch, and living roots that knotted and tangled through the inside like ivy on the outside of a house.

A brazier lit by glowing stones warmed the hearth and Amira could see a spell binding the heat within the stones. She remembered nothing like that from her childhood.

The floor was packed dirt and tidy like the rest of the mound. It was a different kind of cleanliness than the spotless palace of Mynadra. This was a kind of ordered chaos, like the trees and the roots and the stones had been politely asked to mind the furniture.

It was strange, yet comforting, in an odd way. Amira might have liked it if she'd been in different company.

The Elder Mother passed Amira one of the teacups and sat across from her by the worn table.

Amira lifted the steaming mug to her lips and inhaled deeply. It was black with a subtle sweet smell. "How did you get this?"

The Elder Mother replied with a gentle smile. "The cups? Iona across the village is most skilled with a potter's wheel."

"The tea," Amira said, deliberately. "Imported black tea infused with vanilla and bergamot—commonly known as Imperial Brew. It's shipped in from the Spice Islands and only under special charter from King Hyle."

And it was massively expensive. Amira knew because a few years ago, several smugglers had begun bringing bootleg Imperial Brew into the harbors, costing Hylendale a small fortune in lost taxes. Her father had sent her on a swift mission to handle the smugglers and end their operation.

The Elder Mother shrugged her narrow shoulders. "We have our ways."

Amira's eyes narrowed. "You've had contact with the outside world."

"I would think you'd know that by now. Didn't Sair tell you anything? Didn't your friend Cromwell?"

Amira bristled at mention of the lawyer, squeezing her teacup tighter. "He's not my friend."

"No?" The Elder Mother sipped her own tea. "My mistake. He always spoke very highly of you."

Amira almost threw her teacup but stopped herself. Daindreth had ordered her not to hurt anyone and she had to pretend to still be bound by her curse.

The Elder Mother set down her teacup and smiled at Amira. "I'm sure you must be very tired."

It was barely midafternoon by Amira's reckoning, but unfortunately, the other woman was right. When they had reached the mound, the Elder Mother had ordered one of the young girls who followed her around to have a room made ready for Amira and fresh clothes, too. She'd have been lying if she claimed she wasn't eager to sleep in a real bed, but she had more pressing matters on her mind.

"When do I get to see Daindreth again?" Amira didn't expect a straight answer, but she did plan to pester them until they gave in or she found a way to see him regardless.

The Elder Mother pursed her lips tighter. "Your liege lord?"

Amira raised her chin. "He's my liege lord, yes."

The Elder Mother's eyes flashed so quickly Amira barely caught it—anger—but she wasn't sure if it was directed at her or something else.

"You were fine to leave me leashed to my father for years," Amira spat. "Having me do his dirty work in the shadows. Kill for him." Her lip trembled and she stopped herself, blinking quickly.

"We had no way to get to you," the Elder Mother said. "By the time we learned you had survived the tower, you'd already taken a Kadra'han's vows. There was nothing we could do."

"I survived *you*, you mean." Amira imagined what it would be like to punch the old woman.

The Elder Mother was silent for a long space of heart beats.

Amira resisted the urge to shift in her seat. Had the plan been to just ignore that small detail? That the Elder Mother and the others had tried to kill Amira, but failed? Had they really thought she'd just forget that?

"I am sorry for how things played out," the Elder Mother said finally. "It's not what any of us wanted."

"You tried to kill me," Amira said, her voice hard. "I have the scars to prove it."

"You know nothing," the Elder Mother shot back.

Anger rising, Amira gripped the edge of the table. She could feel a tingling along her scars, reminding her of just what had happened that day so many years ago. "I know you took a knife and slashed it across both of my arms. I know you left me bleeding out on that floor and it was only because Emperor Drystan's Kadra'han found me that I lived."

The Elder Mother shook her head. "Now is not the time to discuss this."

"No?" Amira's voice trembled as she struggled to stay under control. She reminded herself that Daindreth was their prisoner and she needed to pretend that she was bound by his command *not* to harm the Elder Mother.

"I cannot begin to explain to you what we went through in that tower. What we are still going through."

Amira forced herself to remain seated with one hand gripping the edge of the table. Inwardly, she recited every curse, obscenity, and insult she knew. "Daindreth," she said shortly. "When do I get to see Daindreth?"

"You're very concerned for him," the Elder Mother

remarked,

Amira bristled at that. "I *am* marrying him," she retorted, with just an edge of venom to her voice.

"Your father gave you away to him," the Elder Mother said. It wasn't a question.

"I'd think you'd be pleased. Who wouldn't want their granddaughter to be an empress? Their great-grandson to be an emperor?"

The Elder Mother's nostrils flared. She took just a moment too long speak again, but when she did, some of the tension left her shoulders. "You're not pregnant."

Amira cocked her head to one side. She thought about lying but guessed the Elder Mother had ways of knowing. "Not yet. But it's just a matter of time. I plan to give Daindreth as many little archdukes and archduchesses as he wants."

"You are a sorceress of the Brindonu line." The Elder Mother stiffened. "You are not a broodmare for that cursed dynasty."

Amira's eyes narrowed. "You want to speak of their curse? Fine. Let's speak of their curse. How do we break it?"

The Elder Mother shook her head. "Amira, you don't know what you're talking about."

"Don't I?" Amira clung to composure, fighting to keep her bubbling anger contained. "I know that you bound Caa Iss to his father. I know he hears that thing day and night, and I know that thing wants to take him over. I know that the curse passed to Daindreth when he was eleven. What I have wondered is how you meant to control Caa Iss. I know you must have had a way or at least some bargain."

The Elder Mother shook her head resolutely. "You don't understand any of this."

"Then make me understand!" Amira almost shouted. "Tell me why you set a cythraul on the throne of the empire, Elder Mother."

The Elder Mother stared at Amira for a long time. "We made a mistake, Amira."

Of all the things that the Istovari matriarch could have said, that was among the most shocking. Amira had never expected

28

to hear an admission of guilt at all.

"We thought we could control Emperor Drystan through the cythraul, but the creature found a way around our bargain. As they do."

Amira brimmed with questions, but she didn't dare interrupt, not while the other woman was talking.

"We tried to turn him into our savior, but we created our own destruction." The Elder Mother shook her head sadly. "We don't know how to break the curse. But if the bloodline ends, there will be no one for the cythraul to inhabit."

Amira was shaking her head before the Elder Mother finished. "If you touch Daindreth—"

"I will do nothing without the consent of the entire council," the Elder Mother said. "It was a mistake we all made and one we must agree on how to fix." The Elder Mother's expression fell, the creases in her face deepening and her shoulders drooping, as if they suddenly held a great weight. "What we did to you was one of our mistakes," she said. "But we can't change it now."

Amira shook her head. "Why?" Her voice was small, almost childlike as she asked the question. "Why did you do that to me?"

The Elder Mother shook her head sadly. "It takes power to summon a cythraul."

It took a moment for her to process the words and when she did, Amira could feel the color draining from her face.

"Even all of us together weren't powerful enough. We needed a sacrifice." The Elder Mother didn't weep, but her eyes shone. "We thought you could save us."

"I was the sacrifice." Amira didn't know what else to say. It made sense. She'd assumed she'd been the sacrifice to erect the Cursewood, but now, thinking back...the sorceresses had still been trying to win when they had sacrificed her.

"Yes, Amira," the Elder Mother said softly. "Don't think we haven't all regretted it, because we have. Your mother wouldn't speak to me for months after. Not until we received word that the Kadra'han sorcerers had saved you."

Amira looked away. That her mother had regretted it was one thing, but that didn't change that she had allowed it in the first place. Amira had been a child, but she still distinctly remembered her mother standing by as the Elder Mother cut her wrists, watching, and doing nothing.

"I don't forgive you," Amira spat. "I don't know that I ever will."

The Elder Mother nodded. "I don't expect you to."

Amira glanced down to her still untouched tea. "What happens now? When will the Mothers meet?"

"Soon," the Elder Mother said. "We'll want to hear from Tapios and his rangers. You, too, of course. And from the archduke." The contempt in her voice at the mention of Daindreth was hard to miss.

"He can't help that you cursed him." Amira just stopped herself from adding an obscenity. "Just like I can't help that you abandoned me to become a Kadra'han."

The Elder Mother shook her head. "You don't understand what that thing is, Amira."

"I've faced him before," she countered. "Twice. Both times I fought him. Once with daggers and once with my spells. Both times I won." More specifically, she and Daindreth working together had won under special circumstances, but those details weren't helpful to her case at the moment.

"You know nothing," the Elder Mother said. "If you'd faced the demon, the real demon in his raw power, you wouldn't be as arrogant and rash as you are now."

Amira fumed. In the back of her mind, she knew it, but frustration, rage, and a touch of desperation drove her to keep pushing.

"You owe me this," Amira hissed, leaning over the table. "After all you took from me, after all you did, you *owe* me!"

The Elder Mother blinked at Amira, unmoved. When she finally did speak, she had the imperious tone of someone dealing with a spoiled child. "You are asking for the moon on a platter, Amira." She ignored Amira's sputtered insults and went on. "Death is the only way to break the curse."

Amira's nails sank deeper into the table, leaving half-moon marks. "If you touch him, I will make what happened to the Istovari at the Tower look like a lover's tiff."

30

"Really?" The Elder Mother was still unimpressed. "You'd kill innocents for the sake of your revenge?"

Amira spoke without thinking. "Why not? You did."

The Elder Mother studied Amira for a long moment. "You will make your case before the Mothers, and they will decide."

"You are the Elder Mother," Amira protested. "You can decide now."

"I cannot be objective," the Elder Mother explained. "You are my granddaughter. I will be there, but I will leave the decision to them."

"You *have* changed," Amira said. "When I was a child, you at least had the courage to wield the knife yourself."

"You know nothing of me, Amira," the Elder Mother said. "Nothing of what I have been through. Our people have been through. The sacrifices that were made to protect our clan. We were revered once, in case you forgot. We were princesses and queens in the land, with first pick of husbands among the sons of the Northern Reaches."

Amira wasn't in the mood for a history lesson. She scoffed and folded her arms across her chest.

"Emperor Drystan feared us when he conquered the North. With connections to every house with a drop of noble blood, it would take but a few of us with the right allies, banded together to topple his regime," the Elder Mother continued. "So, he set out to exterminate us or bind us in a Kadra'han's oaths. A few of our sisters relented and they were ordered to fight against us. We had to kill them."

Genuine sadness weighed the Elder Mother's face then. This time, Amira didn't interrupt.

"You had an aunt. Do you remember her?"

Amira didn't, but the Elder Mother didn't wait for a response.

"Her name was Aeffenwy. My youngest." The Elder Mother smiled sadly. "She was barely seventeen when the war broke out. Married to the son of a border baron who was one of the first to pledge allegiance to the empire. Aeffenwy took a Kadra'han's vows because she couldn't bear to leave her husband." The Elder Mother shook her head.

Amira could guess how this story ended.

31

"She died in the assault of our Tower," the Elder Mother said. "I found her body after." She shook her head. "Half her face was burned off, leaving nothing but scorched meat and bone underneath. The ground was churned where she had writhed in agony for Eponine knows how long." The Elder Mother's eyes focused and she turned hard. "So if you think our revenge against the emperor was too harsh, if you think we overreacted to being thrown from our homes, hunted like vermin, and forced to kill our own daughters, sisters, and friends, I want you to ask yourself if you could live in the same world as the bastard who did all of that."

Amira didn't want to think of anything but the injustice of what had been done to her and Daindreth, but just for an instant, she saw Fonra. Sweet, kind, delicate Fonra.

What would she do to someone who hurt her sister? She honestly didn't know.

"Emperor Drystan did what he did. You did what you did." Amira inhaled a long breath. "He's dead now, you're not. You've won." She swallowed.

"Have we?" the Elder Mother asked softly.

"Yes! The emperor is gone, and his son came here to beg your help." Amira waved her arm wildly in the direction she'd seen them take Daindreth. "You can negotiate new terms, new protections. If you help him, you won't have to live in hovels inside a cursed forest."

The Elder Mother exhaled. "We can't help."

"What do you mean?" Amira's jaw tightened and her hackles raised, not sure whether to be angry yet or not.

The Elder Mother gestured to the root walls. "We survived and built the Cursewood to protect ourselves, but at great cost. Much of our power was drained to create this place. Even the most powerful among us have but a whisper of the magic we once had."

Amira didn't want to believe it, but she could feel it for herself. The Elder Mother's power was there, present, yet it was little more than a whisper to Amira's own.

"We summoned the cythraul, yes, Amira. But when we were all at the height of our power and with a sacrifice of the greatest

32

possible value." The Elder Mother smiled sadly. "The power to summon and banish demons, the power you came to seek, no longer exists."

Amira shook her head. "That's impossible. Every curse can be broken."

"Yes," the Elder Mother agreed. "Just as every knot can be untied. But that doesn't mean that *you* can untie it or that you will."

"You're lying," Amira insisted. "There has to be a way."

"To banish a cythraul, you must draw it out with the same amount of power used to bind it. You must also open a portal to the Dread Marches—with all the risks involved with that— and put the demon back. If the demon is separated from their host and not banished back to the Dread Marches, it will be free to roam and find a new host. A much easier way is to kill the host."

"What's different about killing them?"

The Elder Mother let off a long-suffering sound she had no right to make. "When a person dies, their soul passes from this world to the next. The Dread Marches lie in between and so the cythraul will be dragged back as the result of their bond."

"It won't just end up in the Celestial Reaches? Say the Halls of Demred?"

The Elder Mother blinked at her as if she were an idiot and the answer was obvious. "Cythraul cannot pass to the Celestial Reaches."

Amira ignored the condescension in her tone and continued. "Emperor Drystan was killed, and it passed to Daindreth."

"Because we bound the cythraul to their bloodline. Daindreth is the last of his line," was all the Elder Mother said. "The last descendant of Drystan."

Amira shook her head, not liking where this was headed. "No."

"For all his other faults, Emperor Drystan had no bastards." The Elder Mother spoke academically, like a scholar presenting an interesting anecdote, not someone advocating the death of an innocent man. "Whatever else the emperor might have been, he was reasonably faithful to his wife."

"There's another way," Amira insisted. "I know there is."

"If you've really met the demon, you know how bad he is," the Elder Mother said, her voice flat. "You know he can't be allowed to stay in the world, and he certainly can't be permitted to have new hosts."

"Stop it!" Amira ordered, bolting out of her chair. "Daindreth is a good man. The best man I've ever known, and if you think I'm going to let you—"

"Amira?" a woman's voice startled her from behind.

Amira spun around and faced the newcomer, anger still twisting her features. She didn't recognize the other woman at first. It had been years and the former Queen Hyle also seemed lessened now. She was gaunter and not quite as tall as Amira remembered.

Her hair was a disheveled mess and there were dark rings under her eyes. She was pale and her arms were bare, sleeves rolled past her elbows.

"Cyne," the Elder Mother greeted her daughter with an odd tone, not quite pleased, but not quite angry. "You heard news of our guests, I take it."

"Sairydwen's son came to tell me and I..." Cyne trailed off, not taking her eyes off Amira.

Amira didn't move. She didn't know what to do.

For just an instant, Amira forgot the lifetime of abandonment, the betrayal at the tower. She forgot that her mother had let her be sacrificed and then never sought her out once over the years that followed. For just an instant, she was a little girl again, running to her mother to show off a new set of ribbons from Cromwell or seek help with a skinned knee.

"Mama," Amira said, still not rising from her seat across from the Elder Mother.

Cyne let off a choked cry and ran to Amira, wrapping her arms around her daughter while choked sobs wracked her whole body. She smothered Amira in an embrace, stroking her travel-stained hair and kissing both her cheeks.

When Amira didn't reciprocate, Cyne pulled back, her tearful eyes sweeping over Amira with just a hint of accusation.

"Amira?" She smoothed back Amira's hair, sniffling as she looked her daughter over from head to foot.

"I…" Amira's whole body had locked, as stiff as an icicle. She didn't move. Couldn't seem to find it in her to push the woman away or pull her closer. She blinked at Cyne, not even sure what she should think.

"You found us," Cyne whispered. "I've begged Eponine to return you to us, but I never thought she would."

Amira's chest clutched. Those words soothed the childlike part of her that still ached for her mother's arms. But another part…

"What's wrong, darling?" Cyne asked, her voice soft. Something about that tone—the same tone she had used to comfort Amira during thunderstorms and console her when she'd stubbed her toes—made the assassin bristle.

Amira trained her face into a stony mask. "I haven't returned to you," she said coldly. "Not in the way you want, at least."

"Amira is still a Kadra'han and still bound by their curse," the Elder Mother said, her voice calm, cautious, even.

Cyne looked to her mother and then back to Amira. "Your father sent you?"

Amira shook her head. "He's not my liege lord anymore."

The Elder Mother wasted no time in delivering the bad news. "The archduke Daindreth Fanduillion was found with her. He holds her oaths, now."

Cyne looked between the Elder Mother and Amira again. If it was possible, she became paler. "We heard that you were betrothed to him, but…" She shook her head. "No. No, it can't be."

"It's not what you think," Amira said, not sure why she felt the sudden need to explain things to her mother. "He's never hurt me, Mama. He's good to me. He—"

"Can we break the bond?" Cyne asked, looking to her own mother.

The Elder Mother shook her head sadly. "A Kadra'han's curse is permanent."

"Every curse can be broken," Cyne said, repeating what Amira had heard her say so often.

"Exactly what I tried telling her just now," Amira clipped.

Cyne faced the older woman. "Mother," she began. It was hard to know if she was using the woman's formal title or addressing her out of their relationship. "We can't leave her like this. We can't—"

"The Mothers will decide this," the Elder Mother insisted. "Her archduke came to beg our help. Tapios brought him here under truce."

"Why?" Cyne demanded. "The rangers should have killed that monster when they had the chance."

Amira shot a sharp look to her mother. She'd started to get her hopes up that she might be able to count on help from Cyne. That was clearly an idiot's optimism.

"No!" Amira shoved back her chair to stand. "If you raise one hand against Daindreth, I swear by Eponine, Moreyne, and all the gods who can hear that I will do to you whatever you do to him and worse!"

"Peace." The Elder Mother didn't stand, but she spread her hands in a placating gesture, like one who was used to solving quarrels. "The council will decide, as I have said. The archduke saved Sairydwen's life in the Cursewood. She vouched for him."

Cyne shook her head vigorously. "Sairydwen was too young. She doesn't remember."

"She is a full sorceress, the mother of a child, even if he is a boy, and has the right to vouch for anyone, regardless of how long or short her memory is," the Elder Mother said. "The archduke will be heard."

Amira couldn't believe that the Elder Mother now seemed almost on her side. Despite already having the outcome of the trial decided, she appeared to be quite set on observing the rules of the clan.

Cyne shook her head vigorously. "Every hour that he is in this village—no, every moment that he is *alive,* he is a threat to our people and the whole world if he isn't stopped."

The Elder Mother never got to reply. Shouting in the hall outside sounded over the pleading voice of the Elder Mother's young assistants. A male voice grew louder and then the door burst open.

Instantly, Amira was on her feet, forgetting she was supposed to be unable to hurt any of the Istovari.

"Bardaka," the Elder Mother began, her voice stern.

The man on the threshold was a little over average height with a square jaw and one unusually pale eye peering out from his tanned face. The other eye—or at least its socket—was covered by a black patch. Dark brown hair hung over his ears and bristled across his cheeks in a thick beard and mustache. Facial hair always made it harder to guess ages, but Amira would say he was in his thirties, old enough to remember the Tower. An anxious acolyte tugged at his sleeve, still pleading for him to turn around.

"Tapios has endangered us all!" the man roared.

"Bardaka." The Elder Mother stood, veiny hands spread across the table. "You will remember your place."

"Is it true?" Bardaka demanded. "Did my cousin bring the host of a cythraul into our midst?"

The Elder Mother was silent.

Amira studied the man carefully, but there was nothing much to be learned. As far as she could tell, he was unarmed and there was nothing to distinguish him from the other men within the village.

"Your cousin and his rangers brought someone into our midst who will face judgment before our council," the Elder Mother said. "The Mothers will decide his fate. Not you." The Elder Mother glared to Cyne to emphasize her point. "Now leave."

Bardaka shook his head. "The risk is too great."

"I gave my word." The Elder Mother didn't sound particularly pleased to admit that. "To your cousin, to the archduke, and also to my granddaughter."

Bardaka finally seemed to notice Amira, then. His one eye flicked over her like he would a strange dog. "Your granddaughter?"

"Amira Brindonu," the Elder Mother said. "Daughter of Cyne Brindonu and King Hyle."

Bardaka actually inclined his head in what might have been a bow before looking back to the Elder Mother. "You more than anyone knows the risk. My mother was ripped apart by that thing."

Amira's brows rose and she shot a glare to the Elder Mother. Just how much more to the story was there? Not that it mattered.

Amira would fight to the death for Daindreth either way.

The Elder Mother cleared her throat, ignoring Amira's insistent attention. "We've all suffered because of that thing," the Elder Mother said. "And our suffering will end, but not before we do things properly."

"Properly?" Bardaka pointed furiously toward the northeast.

Amira made a mental note. Was that where they were keeping Daindreth?

"That thing found us! You should question it to find out if more are coming and then send it back to the Dread Marches."

"It is not that simple, my son," the Elder Mother said patiently. "We will address this later. Properly."

Bardaka tried to keep arguing but was wrestled out the door by the acolyte and the door slammed after him, leaving Amira alone with Cyne and the Elder Mother once again.

"I won't let you take Daindreth from me," Amira said, whirling on the other two women as soon as the doors closed. "I'd kill a thousand Istovari before I let one touch him."

The Elder Mother was unimpressed. Why should she be? As far as she knew, Amira was still bound by her curse.

"You're a foolish girl." Cyne's hands clenched in her threadbare skirt. "You'd throw it all away for some man?"

"What exactly am I throwing away, Mother?" Amira demanded. "A life of indentured servitude to my father? The privilege of groveling before the women who tried to murder me?"

Cyne shook her head. "You don't know what you're talking about."

The Elder Mother interrupted Amira's response, hot and roiling and enraged as it was, that was probably a good thing. "I'd save my strength if I were you. You may be a great warrior and a strong sorceress, Amira. But you are untrained in your power and there are hundreds of us." She let that sink in for a moment. "You'll have to appeal to the council." She straightened, all softness and maternal welcome gone, replaced with cool detachment. "I suggest you address them with more respect than you have addressed your mother and I."

CHAPTER FIVE

Thadred

Thadred was cold, tired, wet, and hungry. His hip ached, his spine ached, and pretty much every other part of him ached from either the cold or his fall or just…everything.

He had wandered the Cursewood aimless for what felt like forever, carried by Lleuad. The kelpie had taken him to a copse of trees that seemed to be a regular hideout for the horse, judging by the packed earth and the worn moss. When they had first stumbled into the copse, Thadred had been too tired to complain. Now he had the strength to complain and even more things to complain about.

The stallion was nowhere to be seen, having disappeared earlier that morning. Thadred stumbled outside the copse to relieve himself and was greeted by another cloudy morning. Dark brown marsh grass and the black branches of the Cursewood crowded as far as the eye could see.

"Lovely." Thadred reached for the laces of his trousers.

When he was finished, he limped in a slow circle around the copse, keeping his eyes out for anything suspicious. As best he could tell, the kelpie was an apex predator and generally avoided by other animals in the forest. Hopefully, the horse was coming back and not planning to leave Thadred stranded here.

There was no sign of life in the surrounding marsh grass or in the trees beyond. Nothing but—

"Don't move!"

"Shit!" Thadred cursed, throwing up his hands.

A man slid out of the marsh grass, bow and arrow nocked and trained on Thadred's neck. At first glance, Thadred thought he was a Kadra'han, but his clothes were too worn, his weapons too few, and his accent too northern.

"Who are you?" the stranger demanded.

"Thadred Myrani," he blurted, not seeing any point in lying.

"How did you get here?" the stranger pressed. His cowl hid his face, making Thadred nervous. He didn't like not seeing people's faces.

"I…do you mean *here* specifically or the Cursewood in general?"

"Just answer the question!" the stranger ordered, pulling his bowstring back farther.

"I was a prisoner!" Thadred admitted. He didn't know who this man was, it could be one of the reinforcements the Kadra'han were counting on, for all he knew.

The stranger paused for a long moment. "You're a Kadra'han."

Thadred squinted, peering at the stranger curiously. "What makes you say that?"

"I can see your oaths," the stranger said.

Movement from behind made Thadred turn, and he was able to make out the shapes of several more archers. All wore the same thick wool cloaks of varying shades of brown.

The first archer lowered his bow—unnecessary now that there were three more trained on Thadred—and pushed back his cowl.

He was a sturdy-looking man with a bristling beard that would have looked boorish back at court. His pale eyes flicked over Thadred the way one might inspect a stray dog caught gnawing at salt pork crates.

"Who took you prisoner?" the stranger pressed.

"The first time or most recent?" Thadred glanced to the archer to his left, looking for some clue as to who the hell they were. Of course, he couldn't outwit them for long in any case, but…Thadred frowned at the archer to his left. "You're a girl!"

"So what, imperial?" the girl shot back. The derogatory way she spoke the name was all the confirmation he needed.

"Istovari!" Thadred turned back to the leader. "Look, there's a sorceress somewhere in this forest. She's injured. Her name's Sairydwen. We were separated, but I think she's with two friends of mine so she should be safe."

The Istovari glanced to each other. For a moment, Thadred thought they didn't believe him, but then the leader spoke.

"You're the one who fell into the river." The leader sounded a bit impressed.

Thadred dared to hope. "You found them?"

"We found them."

"All three of them?" Thadred wasn't sure how much he should be telling these people. Something seemed off in the way they studied him and the way they still hadn't lowered their bows, but he was willing to risk it.

"A man and a woman were with Sairydwen," the leader said. "They are both safe."

Thadred could have whooped with joy. "Well, that's some good news." He grinned despite himself. Then again, he wasn't sure why he'd doubted Amira.

"Sairydwen said you were attacked by a kelpie," the female archer said.

Thadred's grin broadened. "Technically, I attacked him."

"Where is he now?" the leader demanded. "We thought we were tracking a mounted scout, but the hoofprints led us here. How did you survive him?"

Thadred had been wondering the same thing. "I have no idea. Lleuad seems nice enough now, though."

"Who?"

"The kelpie. That's his name."

The leader shot a glance to one of the other scouts. "How do you know his name?"

"He told me." It sounded as ridiculous out loud as it sounded in his head, but Thadred didn't know how else he was supposed to explain it. He hadn't known the thing's name, then he did.

"You're coming with us," the leader said.

Thadred gave a martyred sigh. "And here I had plans to drink sherry in the parlor."

"What?" demanded the young female archer. Archeress? Thadred wasn't sure what she'd be called.

"He's jesting with us," the leader clipped, annoyance edging his tone.

Under these conditions, Thadred was owed far more credit for his cheery attitude.

"Did you find the imperial Kadra'han?" Thadred asked. "There were three of them around here somewhere."

The leader shook his head. "The only one we've found is

you."

Thadred considered that for a moment. "Well, they're here. I promise. I followed them to a cave up on that ridge last—" Thadred pointed in the direction he'd come from and let off a curse.

Where there had most certainly been rocks and crags last night was now covered in an endless expanse of trees and swamp as far as the eye could see. There was no sign of the craggy outcrops that had been there the night before.

"That's the Cursewood for you," one of the Istovari, a man, chuckled. "Never the same way twice."

Thadred half-expected them to try binding his hands, but after the leader conducted a quick search to make sure that Thadred was indeed unarmed, they set out through the marsh.

Their going was slow with Thadred's bad leg, and he wished Lleuad would come back. Limping along, he stifled his curses in the beginning for the sake of the females in their group. As he stubbed his toes or caught his boot or stepped wrong or otherwise stumbled again and again, he became more generous with his curses.

The ground was slick and muddy, spotted by heads of crab grass. It would have been hard going under the best of circumstances, but with Thadred's handicap, it was that much more miserable. He cursed his way forward, his escorts watching him as much as they watched the surrounding Cursewood.

"With all the noise you're making, you're lucky if the whole forest doesn't know we're here," the leader growled.

"I'm sorry." Thadred glared at the man. "Would you like to hike through this hell-slush with one and a half legs?"

"Be quiet. Or at least try."

"Why? At least if we manage to call the Kadra'han to us, you can kill them first." Thadred doubted the Kadra'han were within distance to hear, especially with the shifting topography of the forest, but the taunt was hard to resist. "Imagine that? Retrieving a lost nobleman and finishing off Vesha's assassins, all before supper."

"There are worse things in this forest," the leader chided, voice tight. He looked to one of the other archers. "Caenos, help

42

him."

A younger man of probably less than twenty stepped up to Thadred. From his expression, he wasn't excited about the prospect of playing human crutch, but he swung his bow under one arm to obey.

"Give me your arm," the youth ordered.

"Finally, a gentleman," Thadred sneered. He imagined he didn't like needing help any more than the youth liked giving it, but neither of them had much say in this situation.

Had Lleuad brought him through a swamp last night? Thadred couldn't remember. He was fairly certain the stallion hadn't, but by now, that was no surprise. Direction was an illusion in this place.

The earth gave a squish as his boot went down and it made a sucking sound when he pulled it free. A glob of mud clung to his boot and made him slip the next time he tried to step on a head of marsh grass.

Thadred cursed, no longer caring that there were women with them. He let off a string of profanities worthy of a Mynadran dockworker. The girl archer actually giggled while the boy supporting Thadred's arm blushed.

Thadred took a deep breath and continued to hobble along. There was no end to the marsh in sight, but the Cursewood was like that. It would seem to be unending in all directions and then suddenly change without a moment's notice.

"How's Sair?" he asked offhandedly, trying to distract himself from the general pain in his whole body.

The leader visibly stiffened. "My sister is none of your concern."

Sister? Interesting.

"I damned near died trying to save her," Thadred shot back. "I'd say she's at least some of my concern."

He still wasn't sure why he'd done it. Sair had abducted him and made it perfectly clear she meant to kill Daindreth. All the same, it had seemed wrong to leave her to the mercies of Vesha's Kadra'han. Thadred hadn't been able to do it.

After they'd escaped in the madness of the kelpie's attack, they'd hidden in the crags along the riverbed and shared…Thadred didn't know what to call it.

43

With Sair's help, Thadred had used magic for the first time in his life. That had meant something to him, something deep, personal, and intimate in a way he would have never imagined before. Their souls had touched in that exchange, and it wasn't something he could just forget.

"She's fine." The leader interrupted Thadred's confused jumble of thoughts. "Alive, well, and recovering."

"Good," Thadred grunted, dragging his foot out of yet another puddle. "I hate your home, by the way. I can't believe anyone would live here on purpose."

"Silence," the leader clipped.

"Touchier about insults to your swamp than your sister? Your priorities seem a bit—"

"Silence!"

Thadred noticed then that the other man had drawn his bowstring back and several of the others had drawn their weapons as well.

"I heard it, too," said Caenos, the young man supporting Thadred.

Something rustled the marsh grass to his left. He turned in time to see a patch of brown fur disappear into one of the deeper puddles.

"What was that?" one of the archers asked, also a young woman, though Thadred hadn't noticed before. "A pond eel?"

"It was too big to be a pond eel," one of the men said back with a grim tone.

Something rattled to Thadred's left and he turned in time to see motion, but nothing else.

"They're surrounding us, whatever they are," the leader assessed.

"Delightful," Thadred grumbled. "Just smashing."

Caenos let go of Thadred to draw an oversized knife that looked like a cross between a dagger and a cleaver with a single sharp edge. The youth tensed like the others.

Thadred wondered if he could count on this boy and the ragtag group of strangers to protect him. Might it be wise to start considering escape plans? Not that Thadred would be running anywhere.

"There!" someone screamed.

A shape flew out of the mud and dozen more swarmed after it. The ground turned into a writhing mass of dark brown shapes with flashes of claws and teeth. Dozens of the creatures sprang up from under the marsh, no bigger than rabbits. But what they lacked in size, they made up for in numbers.

The Istovari put aside their bows and drew knives like the one Caenos had. They hacked and slashed at the shapes and splashes of red stained the brown mud. Squeaks and squeals of pain rent the air, but no sooner had one of the shapes been slashed aside than three more were rushing forward to take its place.

"What is this?" Thadred demanded.

"Swamp shrews!" Caenos shouted back, slashing madly with his weapon and stomping on the animals that came too close.

One of the shapes hurled at Thadred and latched onto his good leg. It was some sort of rodent with a conical snout. Massive claws edged its webbed feet and beady red eyes glared up at Thadred.

Thadred batted it off, but two more rushed up to take its place, biting, clawing, and scrambling over each other in their hurry to attack.

"It's a warren!" one of the female Istovari shouted. "We're in their warren!"

"Tapios!" one of the archers screamed. At least twenty of the little vermin rushed him at once, piling over each other in their race to knock him down. The archer lost his footing and fell.

The shrews were on the boy in an instant, attacking his face, his arms, his neck, anything they could get at. The other Istovari rushed to his aid, including Caenos.

Without a weapon, Thadred was left to stomp and kick and hope he didn't lose his own footing. More shrews came at him, and he cursed with every bite.

One of them got its claws into his trousers and ripped. Teeth sank into his shin and Thadred let off a yell of pain and rage. He went to shake it free, but another grabbed his ankle, throwing his weight off.

He saw what would happen an instant before it did and got

in one final profanity. He hit the mud with a wet smack, landing on top of several shrews. They squished under him, but the next instant at least thirty swarmed him.

They bit his face, clawed at his clothes, and tore at anything they could reach.

Howling, Thadred covered his face with his arms as they shredded his clothes and then his skin underneath. He tried to throw them off, but more bore down on him as soon as he did. He tried to punch at them, but no matter what he did, more came. He curled into a ball, but the shrews were undeterred. They bit and tore at his back like they were trying to burrow inside.

A squeal split the air and a snort. Someone screamed. The Istovari leader's voice shouted above the madness.

A shadow blocked Thadred's vision. Heavy hooves struck the ground and teeth snapped. Bones crunched and mud splashed.

Just like that, the shrews fled.

Thadred laid still for a few moments, arms still over his face, bad leg drawn up as close to his chest as he could force it. He looked up to find a long black head looming over him.

"What took you so long?" he muttered.

Lleuad chomped on the remains of a shrew, its deflated body limp in his massive jaws. The stallion's teeth cracked bone like it was easy, turning the carcass into a mangled mass of fur and blood. He dropped the mutilated shrew in front of Thadred's face.

The knight grimaced, squinting up at the swamp horse. "Charming."

The kelpie snorted and sniffed at Thadred's bloody back. He licked at the wounds like a dog and pawed at the ground.

"Does it look as bad as it feels?"

If Lleuad's nervous lipping was an answer, Thadred had to assume it was.

"Great." Thadred forced one arm under himself. He was covered in equal parts blood and mud and more scratches and bite marks than he cared to inventory. If he'd thought everything hurt before, he was wrong. Everything hurt now and it hurt

46

worse than before.

"That's a kelpie," the Istovari leader said, a bit louder than necessary.

Thadred glanced over to where the Istovari stood gathered around their friend who had fallen. Whether they'd just abandoned him or if they'd retreated when they saw the kelpie, he couldn't tell.

"You tamed a kelpie," the leader repeated, eyes wide as he stared at the black stallion.

"I told you so," Thadred grumbled back.

Lleuad nosed at Thadred's bloody shoulder and ran his tongue over the bite marks. He swished his tail and snorted, nuzzling at the tears in Thadred's sleeve.

"How?" The leader just stood there, staring like an idiot.

"No idea." Thadred looked up at Lleuad. "How did I do it, boy?"

Lleuad responded by dragging his tongue over Thadred's face.

"Gah!" Thadred spat into the mud. "Are you a horse or a dog?"

"He's a kelpie," one of the Istovari girls said.

"Do you people always say the obvious? I can see he's a kelpie!"

"No one has tamed a kelpie in generations," the leader said.

"What can I say? I'm special." Thadred shot a look to the leader. "Look, are you just going to leave me here? In case you hadn't noticed, I'm a bit challenged in the legs department." Lleuad had helped him to stand before, but Thadred's arms were too sore to reach that high.

"Will your kelpie cause problems?" the leader asked.

"Lleuad?" Thadred glanced to the kelpie. "These are friends," he said, trying to sound as stern as possible. "Friends. Got it?" He had no idea if the animal understood or not or how he'd react to having strangers so close, but the kelpie snorted and seemed compliant enough.

The leader singled out two of the Istovari youths and they hesitantly came toward Thadred and the black horse towering over him.

Lleuad snorted and shifted when the two young men each

grabbed one of Thadred's arms and hoisted him upright. The sudden motion yanked all Thadred's sore muscles and made every cut and wound throb. He grunted in pain, resisting the urge to double over since that would only make it worse. The kelpie snorted and snapped his teeth in the air, pinning his ears.

"Easy, boy," Thadred groaned. "It's alright."

The kelpie's ears swiveled and flicked. Pale eyes fixed on Thadred. He didn't seem to care about the Istovari. Why should he? He was the top predator, after all.

Lleuad stomped and snorted. He lowered his head and sniffed at the dead swamp shrews at his hooves.

"We...should be moving," the leader said at length. "Let's go."

With two Istovari helping him this time and the kelpie off to the side, Thadred was able to move in a straight line without fear of being attacked by some other swamp fiend.

The Istovari kept eyeing the kelpie, but not one of them raised their bow to him. Maybe they knew Lleuad would stomp them to death if they tried.

"How did you do it?" asked one of the young men, eyeing the kelpie anxiously.

"I told you. I don't know."

"The kelpies are descended from Eponine's own mounts. If you were allowed to tame one, you must have her favor."

Thadred chuckled, pain making him lightheaded. "Yet another woman who can't resist me."

CHAPTER SIX

Amira

Amira hated prisons, even if they were called *home*.

The Elder Mother and her servants treated Amira better than she could have asked for. They prepared her a warm bath and got her clean clothes. For supper, she ate a full meal of lamb stew washed down with berry wine.

After, they took her on a short tour of the barrow and its rooms that spread out like a rabbit's warren. There were kitchens, smoking rooms, a cheese cellar, and even a small feasting hall that was now being used as a workroom for processing piles of sheep fleeces.

Cyne had disappeared. It seemed that after their unsatisfying reunion, the former queen was choosing to avoid her daughter.

The Elder Mother and the others eventually took Amira to one of the burrow-like rooms with a narrow bed in it. They didn't seem to trust her—with good reason—but at least they gave her privacy. Amira laid awake for a long time after they shut the door, mind racing. She sensed the *ka* of several others nearby, along with a weaving of magic through the entire barrow. She couldn't determine the spell's purpose, but it seemed benign, at least for now.

She wondered where Daindreth was. If he was being cared for or if they had caged him like an animal. She tossed and turned for hours before exhaustion finally won out and she collapsed into sleep.

When morning came, she was taken to a breakfast with the Elder Mother and a collection of girls, boys, and a few adults with missing limbs or other deformities who seemed to be the matriarch's personal staff. They were all respectful of Amira and gave her space. Cyne still didn't return. The Elder Mother insisted she was with the new mother and child that had been born yesterday, but Amira didn't believe it.

"When will the Mothers meet?" Amira did her best to keep her tone soft and respectful.

The Elder Mother's face tightened, much like one who has

had to tell a toddler "no" too many times already. "They all have their own duties with their own households. They will be here this afternoon before the evening meal."

"Have you sent word to them?" Amira pressed. "Have they received summons?"

The Elder Mother's longsuffering look wavered and for a moment, it seemed she might snap. "Yes, Amira. They have received summons and they know what has happened."

Amira swallowed and looked down to her bowl of pottage. It was bland and humble compared to meals she'd eaten in Lashera and certainly in Mynadra, but not bad after starving in the forest. "When do I get to see Daindreth?"

"Soon enough," the Elder Mother replied.

Amira almost screamed at that. "I want to speak to him before the meeting."

The Elder Mother inhaled a long breath. "Why?"

Amira blinked at her. A thousand reasons came instantly to mind along with a thousand curses. She thought about saying, *at least he never tried to kill me,* then thought better of it. "I've told you he is precious to me." Amira had shown as much, but something about saying it made her feel vulnerable.

"And he will receive a fair trial," the Elder Mother said.

"Fair trial?" Heat writhed in Amira's chest and rippled through her body. *Ka* shivered in the air, responding to her anger. "Like you gave me a fair trial?"

"Amira!" The Elder Mother raised her voice for the first time, slamming her hand down on the table.

At that, several of the invalids and children around the table paused, looking to Amira and then the Elder Mother.

Realizing their stares, the Elder Mother schooled her face into calm composure. "All will be revealed in time," she said. "You have been here less than a night and a day. Have patience."

"You won't even tell me where he is."

"Safe. As you are."

"At the bottom of a ravine?" Amira shot back. "Safe in a kelpie's gullet?"

"You would do well to remember your place, child."

Amira stiffened. She had seen over twenty summers, killed

more men than she could name, faced a cythraul and won, and stolen an archduke from the heart of the imperial palace. "Child" was the last thing she should be called. Her anger made her forget wisdom and she opened her mouth to say as much, when the kitchen door flew open.

A flush-faced boy swept in, dirty cheeks bright from the morning chill outside. "Tapios and the rangers have come back!" he said.

"Already?" the Elder Mother asked, concern in her tone.

Amira hadn't even known the rangers had gone out again. At least the Istovari seemed to be taking precautions against the imperial Kadra'han.

"And they found someone!" the boy added.

Amira's attention was fully diverted then along with everyone else at the table. "Who?" she demanded, echoing the questions of the others.

"I don't know," the boy shook his head, making his unruly curls bounce around his face. "But I think he's hurt. It looks like he can't walk. Tapios said they're bringing him here."

Amira rose, having to lift her heavy wool skirt to step over it. "Can't walk?"

The boy shook his head. "Caenos and Brunner are carrying him between them."

"Let's see!" screamed one of the girls, popping off her place on the bench. Her eagerness set off a chain reaction and every one of the children leapt up after her. Like a gaggle of ducklings headed for a pond, they streamed for the door and into the hall.

Amira ran after the gaggle of curious children, ignoring the Elder Mother's voice. They led her straight through the maze of the barrow and to the main hall. The doors were open and already she could see Tapios striding through.

The lead ranger was covered in mud from head to foot and already looked exhausted despite the early hour. Had he slept at all last night?

She noticed fresh tears in his clothes and those of the Istovari rangers who followed after him. She stood still, dreading what she was about to see, fearing—

"Nice place." Thadred limped through the door between two Istovari.

51

He was bloody, bedraggled, and had dark circles under his eyes so deep she mistook them for bruises at a first glance. His clothes were torn, almost trailing off his body. He looked like he had been drowned, fed to a horde of starving tomcats, and then half-resurrected, but it was him and he was alive.

"Who is he?" asked a little girl, the first one who had jumped up in the kitchen.

"Where did he come from?" asked another.

The children crowded around, and the rangers shooed them back, shushing their questions.

"Easy," Tapios said. "Later, little ones. Later."

"Thadred!" Amira had never thought she'd be as happy to see him as she was in that moment.

Thadred whirled to her, and his eyes went wide. "Amira! You *are* alive!"

Amira laughed. "*I'm* alive? You're the one who tackled a water horse into a river."

"Yes, well, about that. It's a funny story." Thadred grunted as the Istovari helped him down several steps into the main level of the hall. "Where's Dain?" he asked, looking over her shoulder and then around them as if perhaps the archduke was hiding amid the faces of gawking children.

Amira shook her head. "They won't let me see him."

"You're the other Kadra'han." The whole hall went silent at the Elder Mother's voice. The old woman had appeared at the entrance to the hall, her hands folded before her.

"Elder Mother." Tapios bowed to her. "This is the man who helped Sairydwen."

The Elder Mother nodded. "You're also bound to the archduke, then."

Murmurs went through the adult Istovari in the room, grumbles that didn't quite have words. Amira watched closely, trying to read their body language or catch something intelligible. She didn't.

"What commands does he have on you?" the Elder Mother asked.

Thadred shook his head. "None."

The Elder Mother didn't look convinced. "You're telling me

that he's had you as his bondling for decades and has never given you a single command?"

"Not quite decades," Thadred grumbled. "I'm not that old."

"Answer me," the Elder Mother clipped.

"He's released me from them all," Thadred answered.

"Since when?"

Thadred huffed. "Why don't you ask him?" He glanced around again. "Where is my cousin, anyway?"

"None of your concern," snapped one of the Istovari rangers, a young woman.

Amira tried to remember the precise command that the Istovari had made Daindreth give her. The words didn't bind her, but the Istovari needed to think they did. There had been something about honoring the will of the Elder Mother and not trying to escape or find Daindreth. Also, something about not hurting any of the Istovari.

But surely she could get away with more general questions?

"You know where he is?" Amira pressed, casting the young woman a hard look.

The Istovari looked down her freckled nose at Amira, mouth stiff and chin up. "I don't answer to you."

Amira frowned at the disdain in the woman's tone.

"You look like you're in need of a hot meal and a good bath. Probably some clean clothes, too," the Elder Mother said, fixing her attention on Thadred. "You were right to bring him here," she added to Tapios. "Ella, get some pottage from the kitchen. Lews and Foren, go heat some water for a bath."

"A bath sounds splendid," Thadred admitted.

The Istovari helped him to sit down on one of the many benches in the hall, one of the few not covered with sheep fleeces. The knight sat, groaning and wincing the whole time, but not speaking.

Amira sat across from him, not sure how she could help, but not wanting to abandon him. It seemed that the Istovari knew more about tending injured people than she did.

"How did you survive?" Amira asked, shaking her head. Thadred looked awful, but still far better than she would have expected. "That fall alone, not to mention the kelpie…"

"Ah yes," Thadred chuckled. "The kelpie. My new best

friend."

"What?"

"He turned back at the border of the Haven. Wouldn't come into the settlement itself."

"It's warded to keep his kind out," Tapios interjected.

"That would explain it," Thadred agreed. "Anyway…"

"What are you talking about?" The Elder Mother shook her head. For once, she and Amira had the same question.

"The knight tamed a kelpie," Tapios said.

The Elder Mother's eyes went wide as several of the other Istovari rangers nodded their agreement.

"We all saw it," agreed the freckled girl. "Before our very eyes, the beast came to rescue us when we stumbled into a swamp shrew nest."

Amira could only look at Thadred in confusion. "Tamed?"

The knight shrugged, cracking a layer of mud on his clothes as he did.

"Then you are blessed by Eponine," the Elder Mother said, her voice solemn, almost reverent and…was it Amira's imagination or was that fear in her tone? "Welcome home, my son," she said.

Thadred blinked at her with bloodshot eyes. "There's more Kadra'han and imperial troops coming. They found the Haven and they're going to lead an attack force here to extract Daindreth."

Whatever respect or deference the Elder Mother might have shown for Thadred evaporated in an instant. Whirling on the younger Istovari, she shouted, "Children, out!"

The gaggle of younglings looked up at her in confusion. "I said *out!*" She shooed at them with the long sleeves of her robe. "See to your morning tasks. Go!" She spun on Thadred as soon as they were trotting out of sight.

Thadred rolled his eyes. "It's true. I found their camp with the kelpie's help. It seems they followed this lot," he jerked his thumb to Tapios and the rangers, "when they captured Amira and Dain. They know where the Haven is, they can find it again, and they're bringing the empire's wrath with them. Tonight, from the sound of it."

Tapios shook his head. "Even if they knew the way, they'd lose hundreds of men bringing an army through here."

"They'd gladly lose thousands if that's what it took to get their archduke back." Thadred looked to Amira. "They're Kadra'han. Vesha's Kadra'han."

Amira's mouth tightened and her hands clenched into fists atop the table.

"You were delirious," said the freckled archer. "The Cursewood can play tricks on an unsuspecting mind."

Thadred leveled a flat look toward the girl. "Do you want to try saying that again? Maybe with less shaking in your voice this time?"

Amira made eye contact with the knight. "They're planning to give Daindreth a trial tonight." She didn't dare say what she meant out loud, not with the Istovari here.

"Trial?" Thadred balked. "For what?"

"That's what I said." She cast a pointed look to the Elder Mother. "They claim they can't help him."

"Have they tried?" Thadred demanded.

Amira glared at her grandmother as the older woman took Tapios aside, speaking with him in low tones. "No."

"Well then." Thadred exhaled a long breath, shifting and adjusting his leg on the bench. "It sounds like we're thoroughly buggered, aren't we?"

"A bit," she sighed. They were no longer in a stalemate with the Istovari. If the imperial army was coming, there would be a reckoning and much sooner than the sorceresses would like.

"How long?" she asked. "Before the army comes?"

"They said tonight." Thadred flashed a wan smile.

"How can they get men that fast?" Amira shook her head.

"They said they were getting men from a place called Svitmorga."

"That's an imperial garrison along the coast," Amira said. "It might be able to raise a few hundred men, but they'll need more than a day to do it."

Thadred shrugged. "It's possible that Fain was over-optimistic."

"Fain? You spoke with him?"

"Not *with* him, no," Thadred admitted. "Lleuad took me to

55

his camp. We listened to them from the shadows for a while."

"Lleuad?" Amira cocked her head at the strange name.

Thadred grinned. "Yes. My very own swamp horse. Always wanted one."

Amira shook her head. "How? What happened?"

Thadred's eyes widened as one of the girls returned bearing a giant bowl of hot pottage with a bun. Thadred accepted it as if it were the grandest feast he'd ever laid eyes on. He gladly began mopping the dense bun in the broth.

Over Thadred's shoulder, Amira watched as the Elder Mother and Tapios kept speaking in low tones, apart from the others. A few of the Istovari rangers spoke amongst themselves, but several stepped outside. If the voices beyond the hall entrance were any indication, there were more than a few onlookers drawn by the strangers.

"We're prisoners, aren't we?" Thadred spoke barely above a whisper, his face angled carefully into his pottage so only Amira even saw his lips move.

"Yes. They're keeping one of the imperials alive, too."

Thadred's eyes flickered up briefly, but he gave no other reaction.

"Iasu," Amira said softly, pretending to examine the sleeves of her grey wool dress. "He was injured and they took him to one of the houses. They separated Daindreth and I yesterday. I haven't seen or heard of him since."

Thadred didn't respond, but his uncharacteristic silence was all she needed to know.

CHAPTER SEVEN

Daindreth

Daindreth was fairly certain that if he hadn't already been dehydrated when he was tied up in the cellar, he would have pissed himself by now. As it was, his throbbing skull kept time with the beat of his heart.

It would serve you right if they left you down here to die, Caa Iss sneered.

After extracting his revenge on Daindreth's mind for hours last night, the cythraul was still recovering. Caa Iss had extended himself too far and now had to rest. He couldn't send the pains and overwhelming visions he sometimes did, but he could still nag at Daindreth's thoughts.

Your whore is dead by now, you know. The Istovari would have never allowed her to live. Not after she was tainted by you.

Daindreth squeezed his eyes shut, but it made no difference. He was already in total darkness. No one had come to see him since they had locked him inside.

All alone, Caa Iss purred. *With just me. As it was always going to be.*

Daindreth exhaled a long breath out his nose. His arms and wrists had gone numb except for the occasional sharp pain. His neck ached from being in one position too long, but no matter which way he turned his head, it still ached. His skull seemed too tight, and a constant pain settled through his bones.

How long had it been since he'd drank water? He didn't know. They'd been in the Cursewood for at least two days before the Istovari had found them. Hadn't they finished their water on that first day?

Overhead, he heard voices. He tried not to get his hopes up. Daindreth had heard voices pass by, but nothing had come of them.

You should show me more respect! Caa Iss's voice turned loud and insistent enough to make Daindreth recoil. *I am all you have. I am all you will ever have in the end.*

Daindreth didn't respond. It never ended well when he

responded to the creature's taunts.

Something scuffled outside and scraping rasped from the door.

What's this? Caa Iss sounded almost excited.

Several thuds came from overhead in the direction of the stairs back up to the surface. Something creaked and a sliver of light pierced the dark. It was barely anything, but Daindreth shrank back. After so long in the pitch black, it was blinding.

I guess they aren't leaving us to rot in here after all.

Male voices clamored and the tramp of boots descended the narrow cellar steps.

"What is this?" clipped a familiar voice. It took Daindreth a moment to recognize it as Tapios, the ranger who had brought Daindreth and Amira here. "I ordered you to look after him."

"We did," stammered a younger voice. Daindreth couldn't see the speaker with his eyes still blinded by the brightness.

"You left him trussed up in the dark like a bundle of kindling. What—" Tapios cleared his throat. "Get him some water and a bucket to piss in."

Footsteps came closer and Daindreth was still blind. He did his best to pull himself upright, but his arms and legs wouldn't quite cooperate.

"Archduke?" Tapios asked.

"Istovari," Daindreth responded. Squinting against the sunlight, he could just make out the ranger's dark silhouette.

Tapios was quiet for a moment. He stepped over to the nearest post that had Daindreth's wrist tethered to it. The rope slackened and Daindreth's arm fell to his side. With his weight no longer suspended by the bindings, he staggered, trying to catch himself.

"Easy." Tapios caught Daindreth's free arm, steadying the other man.

Daindreth blinked at him, eyes still not adjusted to the light.

"They weren't supposed to leave you like that all night," Tapios said in a short tone.

Oh, I've played this game, Caa Iss crowed. *One captor plays the tormentor and then another plays the savior. They're softening you up. Just wait for the questions.*

Daindreth had been thinking that even before the demon had said anything. Perhaps Amira was wearing off on him.

The archduke's eyes adjusted as Tapios unbound his other wrist and helped him sit on an overturned barrel. Daindreth didn't resist, rubbing his chafed wrists and trying to think over the cythraul's chatter.

They want to negotiate with you. But they want information first. These Istovari never make any big decisions without the input of all the Mothers. This son of a bitch must be their spy.

Daindreth was finally able to see and get a good look at Tapios. He was a little surprised to find that the other man was covered in mud and looked as if he hadn't slept at all. Bloody scratches marred his face, and his skin was sallow as if from lack of sleep.

"Where is Amira?" Daindreth coughed, his voice hoarse.

Above, he could hear the younger Istovari returning with water. He licked his lips at the thought but didn't want to appear too eager.

"She's fine," Tapios said.

"But where is she?" Daindreth persisted. He used the deep, level tone he used with unruly envoys back home. While it didn't cow Tapios as it might have a foreign dignitary, the other man shifted his weight, showing unease.

He's scared of us. Do you think it's me he fears more or you? I'm betting it's me.

Even though he towered over Daindreth from where the archduke sat, Tapios hesitated. Daindreth couldn't tell if it was feigned or not.

"Tell me what you want, sorcerer," Daindreth said. "I don't believe you came to see after my comfort."

"Is there an army coming?" Tapios asked.

Daindreth paused a moment to consider the question. It was blunt, a bit too blunt. Either Tapios had no skill with this, or he was extremely skilled and was trying to lure Daindreth into a false sense of superiority.

Don't underestimate these sorcerer whelps. We can't trust them.

For once, Daindreth agreed with the cythraul, but he had no leverage. He was their captive, they had Amira, and they had rescued him from the Cursewood. No one could come for him who didn't already know the location of the Haven and as far as he knew, there was no one who could.

"I don't know what you mean," Daindreth answered honestly.

Behind Tapios, a young boy appeared carrying a water skin and the bucket the older man had ordered. Daindreth forced himself not to stare as it came closer. He supposed they could drug him, but trickery made little sense at the moment.

"We found your other Kadra'han," Tapios said.

Daindreth froze, schooling his face and his body into the cool, collected composure he had practiced for a lifetime. "My Kadra'han?"

"Thadred Myrani."

Daindreth felt his eyes widen despite his effort to show nothing. "Thadred? He's alive?"

"He's fine." Tapios answered a little too quickly for Daindreth's liking.

"How is that possible?" Daindreth didn't dare believe it. Didn't dare get his hopes up.

"It seems Eponine favors him," Tapios said, offering an unconvincing shrug.

Daindreth's eyes narrowed on the Istovari. "You're lying."

Of course he is! Caa Iss agreed. *You think even Thadred the Unkillable could survive a fall with a man-eating swamp horse?*

"Istovari don't lie," Tapios shot back, seeming offended. "Your friend says there's an army coming, led by your Kadra'han."

Daindreth shook his head. "Amira and Thadred are the only Kadra'han I have."

"That's not what Myrani says."

"Then you're lying, and you don't have my cousin." It was not the most diplomatic response Daindreth had ever given. Perhaps he should have been more careful, but he didn't understand what the Istovari stood to gain by dangling the lie of Thadred's survival in front of him. "I've played many games, Tapios of the Istovari. With courtiers, kings, and commoners. I'm willing to play many more." Daindreth fixed Tapios in a hard glare. "But don't think you can use my family as pieces."

Tapios' nostrils flared. "I'm not lying. He's in the Elder Mother's hall with your woman."

Daindreth inhaled a long breath. "Then bring them to me."

Tapios worked his jaw for a moment before replying. "The Elder Mother has forbidden it."

Ha! Caa Iss laughed.

"How convenient."

"They're demanding to see you, too," Tapios said.

"That I could believe," Daindreth answered.

The boy with the water had stopped a few paces away and observed the two men hesitantly, like he didn't know what to do next. Daindreth resisted the impulse to snatch the water. Even if he was in the weakest negotiating position of his life, appearing desperate could make it worse.

"What?" Tapios glanced between the archduke and the child. The boy hesitated, hanging back.

The child's lower lip trembled. "My brother says that he's a—"

"Here." Tapios snatched away the water skin and handed it to Daindreth.

Daindreth took the water skin and unstopped the top. He didn't want to appear weak, but he hadn't had anything to drink for days. Much longer, and he wouldn't be able to function or move.

"Slowly," Tapios cautioned as Daindreth began to drain the skin. "You'll make yourself sick."

The archduke forced himself to take slow, careful pulls of water. It crashed into his throat like a spike of ice, but also the sweetest relief he'd ever felt.

"Will an army come for you?" Tapios repeated the question.

"You tell me," Daindreth said between sips. His hands trembled despite his best efforts to hold steady.

"No one can find the Haven who hasn't been here," Tapios said. "And no one you brought with you has been allowed to leave."

"There you have it, then," Daindreth said.

No one that they know of, Caa Iss snickered.

Daindreth hesitated at the cythraul's words. Surely the demon didn't know anything that Daindreth didn't. They shared the same body, after all. Sometimes Daindreth wondered if Caa Iss didn't also have a connection to somewhere *else*. There were times he seemed to know things he shouldn't but most times he just pretended in order to toy with his host.

Vesha's Kadra'han are as devious and cunning as your own. And hers don't get captured by defanged sorcerers.

Daindreth's mind caught on that word—*defanged.* He mulled it over, wondering if it was nothing or if it was one of those rare times when Caa Iss accidentally revealed something he knew that Daindreth didn't. Caa Iss might be limited by the body of his host, but he had inhabited Daindreth's father before infecting Daindreth.

Tapios made a frustrated sound. "Does the empire know you're here?"

"You just said no one has been allowed to leave," Daindreth countered. "But if you mean to ask if my mother knows I came here, I would say yes. She has probably known where I was headed for weeks."

Tapios hesitated. He did a better job of concealing his expression this time, but his pause betrayed uncertainty. "The empress…you're not here with her blessing?"

Caa Iss cackled in Daindreth's mind. *He has no idea.*

Again, Daindreth and the cythraul agreed on something. Now that was an unsettling thought. "No," Daindreth answered. "She tried to stop me."

Tapios shook his head. "Why?"

Daindreth wasn't sure how much he should reveal to this man. He drained the rest of the water skin and reached out to pass it back to the boy. The child shrank away. Tapios took it and shoved it toward the child.

"You're subverting the empress by being here? You're admitting to treason?" Tapios didn't sound convinced.

Daindreth tried to read the ranger's reaction but didn't know him well enough. "If you want to call it that," he said. "Yes. I am."

Tapios deepened his frown and looked to the young rangers behind him, but they offered no insight. The older man made a frustrated sound. "You and your cousin saved my sister's life," he said at length. "She has reminded me of that at every opportunity."

How odd, Daindreth mused. A few days ago, Sairydwen had been ready to see him beheaded and burned.

War makes strange bedfellows, Caa Iss purred.

War? Again, Daindreth paused over the cythraul's word choice, then ignored it.

"The Mothers will decide your fate," Tapios said, finally. "But protecting the Haven is my duty. My people have been through too much for us to suffer another slaughter from the empire."

Daindreth looked up to Tapios, then. The ranger didn't strike him as an evil man. Quite the opposite. But he knew as well as anyone that it didn't take evil men to do evil things.

Slaughter is no better than they deserve, Caa Iss sneered. *Treating an imperial archduke worse than an animal. You'd be right to kill them all, you know.*

"I have no desire to see anyone slaughtered," Daindreth answered the ranger calmly. "I came to see your people for one thing and one thing only."

"And what's that?" Tapios demanded.

"I want this parasite removed," he said, letting venom color just a little bit of his tone. "I want my mind back. Do you know what it's like to live with the voice of a demon in your head, Tapios of the Istovari? To never have a moment's peace? To see visions born of his perversion? His fantasies of what the world should be?"

Tapios hesitated, but only for a moment. "Our people had no other defense against—"

"I never attacked your people," Daindreth said, voice flat, final, imperial. "A man I barely remember did. A man who ordered his own Kadra'han to kill him when it became too much."

Tapios shifted, visibly uncomfortable at that. "We were facing extermination. If we could do anything to stop the tyrant's advance, we had to."

"Look to your own Mothers," Daindreth growled. "Your own Elder Mother tried to kill Amira when she was a child. How do you justify that? They left her for dead, bleeding on the floor of the tower."

Tapios inhaled sharply. "Those were desperate days. We all did things we aren't proud of."

Caa Iss chortled. *Ah, so he's ceded the moral high ground! Finally. I thought he'd never give it up.*

"And how many other things will you do that you're not proud of?" Daindreth pressed. "After you slit my throat and toss my corpse in the swamp, will you throw Amira in after me?"

"You don't know what you're talking about," Tapios said. "You have no idea what's at stake here."

"Don't I?" Daindreth inhaled a long breath as his head spun. Perhaps he'd drank the water too fast. "You have Amira." He swallowed and released his breath. "I am ready to die if that's what it takes to defeat the demon."

Idiot! That turned out so well last time, didn't it?

Daindreth fixed Tapios in a hard look. "But I won't leave her at the mercy of you or the empire or anyone else."

She could be dead already, for all you know. They tried to kill her before. Why not finish the job?

"I told you, she's safe," Tapios insisted, sounding impatient. He didn't strike Daindreth as someone who was questioned often. If he had really lived the past nineteen or so years in this place, only venturing into the surrounding Cursewood to scout, then he probably wasn't questioned very often at all.

"Let me see her," Daindreth pressed.

Tapios stiffened and his spine went a little straighter. "She's not yours!"

"Yes, she is," Daindreth countered. "And I'm hers and if you think you can keep us apart, I can point you to a trail of dead men who thought the same."

"Are you threatening me?" Tapios demanded, anger coloring his tone.

"No," Daindreth said, taking on a conciliatory tone. He didn't want the Istovari too upset, just unsettled enough to ask questions. "I want you as a friend, Tapios. You and all the Istovari. But friends need to understand that there are some lines that shouldn't be crossed."

"You are in no position to bargain with me," Tapios said.

"And the decision to grant you death or life lies with the Mothers."

Daindreth didn't believe that, not completely. Too often, he had heard nobles and ambassadors deny responsibility only to have them produce miraculous results after the right promises. Still. He didn't press the issue. It never did any good to do that.

"Then I hope we can at least understand each other," Daindreth said. "You will do anything to protect your family and I will do anything to protect mine."

Your mother is your family, Caa Iss countered. *Look how you've treated her.*

Tapios blinked at him for a long moment. "If an army comes, will you be able to turn it back?"

"No," Daindreth answered honestly. "Not if they're led by Kadra'han."

"Bardaka," Tapios singled out one of the Istovari, a young man with only one eye. Yet that one eye glared hard enough for two. Tapios didn't seem to notice. "See that he's cared for. Properly, this time. I want that door to stay open and light in that cellar. Also, no tying him to the wall again. And make sure two men are watching him at all times." With that, Tapios stormed out of the cellar.

Daindreth leaned back against the wall, his head still throbbing and hot with dehydration. His wrists ached, his elbows, knees, and joints ached. He closed his eyes, trying to think.

That went well.

It was hard to tell if the cythraul was being sarcastic or not.

Trying to make a new friend?

Daindreth inhaled. He didn't know how much of the Istovari's words could be trusted, but the other man had still revealed much. The Istovari were afraid and at least some of them had to be hoping Daindreth could help. Tapios' vehement insistence that Amira didn't belong to Daindreth told the archduke that there had to be at least some protectiveness toward the assassin. That was encouraging.

As for Thadred...Daindreth wanted Tapios to be telling the truth. He *wanted* Thadred to be alive, but who could have survived that fall?

The archduke closed his eyes. He didn't weep, he was still too dehydrated for tears, but he wished he could.

CHAPTER EIGHT

Amira

"They're coming," Thadred insisted. "I'm telling you, they're coming."

"How do you know?" Amira asked.

"Because it's the worst thing that could happen and that's just how our lives have been going," he said, running his hands through wet hair. The Istovari had provided Thadred with a hot bath after his meal.

"Fair point." Amira exhaled and folded her hands in her lap. Having someone to talk to, someone who was on her side, had helped her calm down considerably.

Despite their efforts to keep composed outwardly, it seemed that his allegations had caused quite a stir with the Elder Mother and the rangers. After leaving Thadred in the care of her acolytes and forbidding Amira to follow, the old woman had disappeared.

Not only that, but their meeting with the Mothers to discuss Daindreth's fate had been postponed. Tapios had taken several rangers into the forest, presumably to scout. Amira suspected that the coming army was being taken more seriously than the Istovari wanted to admit to her and Thadred.

Thadred had been stashed in another alcove room with barely enough space for a bed, a chair, and a small table for a candle. A window had been created from a large piece of broken glass with roots and earth packed around it. Natural light filtered through the makeshift window, telling Amira that it was around mid-afternoon.

Amira sat beside Thadred, sure that there was an Istovari somewhere, somehow listening in on them. She kneaded the fabric of her woolen skirt, feeling as helpless and defenseless as that day months ago when she had discovered Daindreth held her tether.

"What should we do about it?" Amira asked quietly. "If the army is coming for him and we don't know where he is, and the Istovari have no army…" She gestured to the length of Thadred.

"And you're in no condition to do more than rest."

Thadred huffed. "Well, I must admit you're right on that. I don't think I've been this sore since my fall on the mountain."

Amira knew which mountain he was talking about—the one where his horse had rolled over him and left him maimed for life.

"In summary, we are trapped, captive, and have no idea where the most important person in our lives is being held." Amira clenched her skirts tighter. "Delightful."

"You're not captives," said Cyne, appearing at the entrance of Thadred's small alcove. She had to duck to enter.

Amira turned. She'd felt the woman approaching down the hall, but hadn't thought this was her destination. "Pardon me, then," she snipped. "What would you call us? Involuntary guests?"

"You walked into the Haven of your own free will," Cyne said.

Amira inhaled deliberately. "Yes, because the alternative—"

"I don't believe we've met," Thadred interrupted, flashing Cyne his usual charming smile. "Thadred Myrani, at your service. You'll have to pardon me if I don't bow."

Cyne studied him for a heartbeat too long. "The sorcerer who saved Sairydwen."

Thadred pshawed. "I wouldn't say I'm a sorcerer, but I did help her out of some tight spaces."

"Tapios says you tamed a kelpie," Cyne continued.

Thadred grinned at that. "A bit, yeah."

"What was your mother's name?" Cyne asked.

"Sorry, remind me who you are?" Thadred pressed.

"Cyne Brindonu," Amira answered for her. "Former Queen of Hylendale and my mother." Try as she might to keep the contempt from her tone, some of it seeped through.

Thadred shot a quick glance to Amira. "Oh."

Cyne stepped closer to the edge of Thadred's bed. Amira had the impulse to reach for a knife, then remembered she didn't have one.

"Thadred Myrani. Myrani is an inland name," Cyne said.

"Mother's maiden name," Thadred clarified. "She's married,

now." He made a waving motion as if prompting Cyne to fill in the blanks. "She was Zeyna Myrani."

Cyne blinked slowly. "The empress's sister?"

"Oh come on," Thadred scoffed. "It was no secret. You would have still been queen then. I'm sure you heard the gossip."

"Forgive me," Cyne said. "It's been a long time and I never paid much heed to gossip."

Cyne sat on the edge of Thadred's bed without asking, studying him intently. "Zeyna Myrani, then?"

Thadred swallowed awkwardly. "Yes."

It wasn't like Thadred to get nervous, especially around women, but Amira's mother visibly unsettled him. Not that the assassin could blame him. The woman unsettled her, too.

"Did she ever mention your father?" Cyne pressed. "His name? Perhaps where he was from?"

Thadred blinked at Cyne like she had just asked something incredibly stupid and in a way, she had. "My mother left me with a wet nurse before I learned to speak. I don't remember her, and I haven't seen or heard from her since."

Cyne pursed her lips tightly. "Well, then. That does complicate things. But we might be able to find a way around it."

"What are you talking about?" Amira interrupted, protectiveness surging in her chest. "Whatever you're scheming to do with him, you'll have to go through me first."

Cyne cast Amira a disinterested glance. "We need to know which family he belongs to."

"He belongs to no one." Amira bristled, shifting closer to Thadred. "Certainly not any of you."

Cyne looked back to Thadred. "Sanydwen has asked for the rights to you if we cannot determine your father's surname. Since she was the first to discover your power and her brother was the one to rescue you in the Cursewood, she has a valid claim."

Thadred pulled back. "Hold on, what?"

"You are a man," Cyne said, sounding almost disappointed. "But you have power and that your father passed his magic on to you is proof that you could pass it on to your issue."

"Stop right there." Thadred held up his hands. "What are

69

you talking about? We didn't come here to stay. We—Amira and I—we're inlanders. We serve Daindreth. Once this is all over, we're going back to Mynadra with him." He narrowed his eyes at the sorceress. "Assuming he's alive like you people keep swearing he is."

"It doesn't matter," Cyne said, dismissively. "He can offer neither of you a future. We can."

"So that's your plan?" A hot sensation simmered in Amira's chest as rage threatened to boil over. "Keep us captive and breed us like pedigreed hounds?"

Cyne shook her head. "That isn't how it is at all."

"Then how is it, Mother?" Amira asked, her voice turning shrill at the last word. "You women are already fighting over Thadred. Is there a bidding war for me, too? Are Tapios and the others already fighting over which of them will get to share my bed?"

Amira hadn't forgotten the Elder Mother's rage when Amira had mentioned bearing children for Daindreth. Nor had she missed that the Elder Mother had sounded relieved when she realized Amira wasn't pregnant yet.

Cyne paused for a moment. "Forgive me, I realize that this could have been taken the wrong way." She looked to Thadred. "Word has spread that you tamed the kelpie. Many of the Istovari women are assuming that you will stay in our village. Few of our men survived the war and even fewer with magic."

"Oh gods," Amira swore, smearing a hand over her face. "You want him as a stud."

Thadred grimaced at that. "While I'm not what one would call a puritan, I still find this idea unsettling."

Cyne shook her head. "I am explaining it poorly. Men among our people must have a mother or sister to answer to. She speaks for them in the clan meetings and takes responsibility for their training, if they have the ability for it."

Amira had always known that the Istovari clans were matriarchal, but she'd never really had to consider what that looked like. Her mother had mostly adapted to the imperial way of life during her marriage to the king, and Amira had been too young to remember anything strikingly different about the way her mother and her mother's people did things.

"I bring this up now, because…" Cyne looked between them. "There is to be a feast tonight in the main hall. The Elder Mother wants to present the two of you to the rest of the village."

Amira bristled. "What about Daindreth?"

"His trial is being delayed," Cyne said. "There is still more information that needs to be gathered."

"What does that mean?" Amira demanded.

Cyne hesitated, no doubt wondering how much she should divulge. "I mean that there have been new discoveries surrounding the archduke. We want to make sure we explore them before he is held to account."

"Held to account?" Amira hardly believed what she was hearing. "He's done nothing wrong!"

Cyne turned to face Amira, hands still folded in her lap, looking as composed and proper as the queen she had once been. "And we want to make sure that when we rule on his fate, we make the best decision."

"We?" Amira cocked her head to the side. "You're one of the Mothers?"

"I sit on the council, yes," Cyne confirmed. "As do five others and my own mother."

Amira took a deep breath, fighting to control herself. This woman was a stranger. A stranger who claimed to love her. Nothing could be more dangerous than someone who thought they were doing the right thing. "Fine," she said, breathing out. "Fine. I'll do what you want, just…the Elder Mother promised me I could see Daindreth."

Cyne waited several heartbeats to respond, like she knew what Amira's reaction would be and dreaded it. When she finally did speak, her words were no surprise, but no less infuriating. "The Elder Mother does not believe that would be wise at this time."

Amira bolted to her feet. "Have you killed him?" she demanded. "Is that it? Because if you have, I will tear this place apart until—"

"Amira!" Thadred grabbed her arm and yanked her away from her mother.

She hadn't realized she'd been advancing on the woman until she was jerked back. Only then did she recognize the faint swirl of *ka* around her mother, of the other woman gathering the power for a spell.

Thadred cast a grin to Cyne, still not letting go of Amira's arm. "Forgive my impetuous friend, but trust is the bedrock of any relationship." He sounded every bit as cordial and polite as he had back in Mynadra when facing down scores of scheming nobles. "We've given you every reason to trust us and asked for one thing in return. You can understand why it would be upsetting if we're denied that."

Cyne glanced between the two of them, studying Amira closely. Cyne appraised Amira the way Vesha had—like she was facing down a rival. Amira was surprised to find that, even after everything, even when she was sure she didn't care what that woman thought, seeing her mother look at her like the enemy stung.

"The archduke is dangerous," Cyne said. "More dangerous than either of you knows."

Thadred huffed. "I think you underestimate how much we know."

Cyne's nostrils flared. She looked to Amira. "We made a mistake, Amira," she said. "With cursing the emperor. We thought…" She turned away, blinking quickly before she turned back. "Amira." Her face softened. "You weren't the only thing sacrificed that day."

"I'm sure." Amira didn't particularly want to discuss *that day*.

Cyne continued. "No, you need to understand…your blood summoned Caa Iss, but the Cursewood…we used our own power for that." Her face fell. "That was the price."

Amira glanced to Thadred, sure she was missing something.

"We weakened ourselves," the former queen said. "Each sorceress gave seven-tenths of our power to the curse in exchange for seven-tenths of these mountains to be covered in an impenetrable forest."

Amira's mind whirred. "You gave your power to the Cursewood?"

Cyne nodded. "And the Cursewood will stand until every

one of us who gave it our power is gone. Maybe a few years after, but not too long."

Amira considered the implications of that, remembering how weak she had thought Sairydwen and the Elder Mother to be. How magic infused this village and yet there were no great sources of it. Power was threaded like cobwebs, sparing and strategic.

"We still have many tricks, but none like our former glory," Cyne said. "But we thought it was worth it to spare our clan. Until we came here. Until the first children were born."

Amira had seen many youths and toddlers in the village and there certainly seemed to be quite a few judging by those who populated the Elder Mother's table.

"Every adult and youth with an ounce of strength to spare gave to the spell," Cyne said. "Not just the Mothers. We thought it would only affect us, but all our children since have also had lessened power."

Amira's gut churned as several things made sense at once. The Elder Mother's comments about Amira's children, the Istovari's apparent interest in Thadred.

"That's why you want Thadred and I," Amira said. "We're good breeding stock?"

Thadred had still been holding Amira's arm, but let go. "Not in a thousand years," he said. "You're a fine woman, Amira, but I'd sooner be a monk and I have never said that about anything before. No, no, just no."

Amira found herself pulling away from Thadred at the same time, fuming. "You can't—we're not—no!" she shouted, glaring at her mother. *"This,"* she gestured between herself and the knight, "isn't happening!"

Cyne exhaled. "Don't hear what I'm not saying, Amira. Please. We were talking about the cythraul."

It didn't escape Amira that her mother hadn't denied their allegations, but she let it pass for now. "Daindreth's curse?"

"All magic requires sacrifice," Cyne said softly. "As do curses. The difference between a curse and a spell is that while a spell can be unraveled, it can also be performed with a regenerative source."

Amira blinked. "Forgive me. My magical education was cut

short rather abruptly when I was four." She'd had some tutoring and learned some by trial and error, but she preferred to use the jab at her mother anyway.

"Strength is a regenerative resource," Cyne explained. "As is a sorceress's power, most of the time." She cleared her throat. "To open a portal to the Dread Marches, extract a single cythraul, and bind him to the emperor, we needed an unregenerative sacrifice."

Coldness washed over Amira as she realized what she was hearing. "Something with power in it," she said softly.

Tears filled Cyne's eyes, but they didn't fall. "Yes," she quietly confirmed. "You were the sacrifice to bind the cythraul, Amira."

Amira didn't question it. The answer made sense. It explained why she could suppress Caa Iss—she had been the original tether that called him out of the Dread Marches and bound him to his first host. Being near her made the binding stronger, like a cage tightening around a tiger.

Amira was quiet for a long moment. "So if my life is bound him…" Her mind whirred, conclusions jumping at her from every angle. "If I died, would that unbind Caa Iss? Would that free Daindreth?"

"No," Cyne said, finality and a rebuke in her voice. "You were meant to die. Caa Iss was supposed to take over Drystan completely and stop the army's siege, but it went wrong. You survived and Drystan maintained control. If anything, your death now would only make the demon stronger."

Thadred shrugged. "Explains why he hates you."

"What?" Cyne looked sharply to the knight.

"Nothing," Thadred said. "The cythraul hates Amira."

Cyne's hawklike expression flicked between the two of them, but she didn't press the issue. "Both of you have served as Kadra'han," she said. "It has made you stronger. I can see it." Her gaze lingered on Amira, hesitating. "You have served the archduke well." She grimaced. "*Very* well. I can see his aura in your power."

"You could grow stronger, too," Amira said, not sure herself if she was serious or not. "Take oaths to Daindreth, serve him,

74

and you could regain your power."

"Death first," Cyne said. Her voice was calm as a summer sea, but there was a storm beneath it to threaten a hurricane. "After what his father did to our daughters and sisters who took the oaths? After all we did to remain free? You think we would collar ourselves to a master?"

"Daindreth is a good man," Amira said.

Cyne's wrath deflated at that. "Good men do as much evil as bad men," she said softly. "Perhaps more. Look at your father."

Amira hadn't planned to defend that son of a bitch, but she wasn't about to let her mother take the high road. "I don't know. He *did* beg Emperor Drystan to spare my life when they found me in the Tower." Amira folded her arms across her chest. "After you left me there."

Cyne didn't defend herself, didn't refute the accusations. "I'm glad he did," she said softly.

Amira looked to Thadred, then back to her mother. "Help us," she pleaded. "You helped cast the curse. How do we break it?"

Cyne shook her head.

"But you put Caa Iss in the emperor." Amira wasn't ready to give up. "Surely you can find a way to get him out of Daindreth."

"I told you, Amira," Cyne said. "Seven-tenths of our power. Even at the height of our strength, we were barely able to do it. There is no hope that we would be able to manage it now."

Amira refused to believe it. "You have to," she said. "There has to be a way!"

"There isn't." Cyne cast her daughter a sympathetic look. "You can't free him, Amira. And you certainly can't bear him children to carry on the curse."

Amira's head spun as more thoughts whirred through her head.

"It's like a Kadra'han's curse," Cyne said. "It can be broken, but only by death."

That was wrong. Amira had broken her curse. She almost screamed that at her mother but stopped herself just in time. The Istovari couldn't know, not yet.

75

"There's a way," Amira said, voice lowering to a growl. "I know there is."

Cyne inclined her head. "Perhaps. If we had a thousand sorceresses and a thousand years, we could find a way. Perhaps if you could trick the cythraul into breaking their bargain, we could find a way. But today, there is none."

"Trick the cythraul? What do you mean?" Amira might not be a master schemer, but that could be their best chance.

Cyne shook her head. "You would have to force him into violating the terms of his contract. That would break it."

"Can I see the contract?"

"We kept nothing from that tower but ourselves."

Well, Cyne was clearly not going to be helpful.

Amira's mind went to work, thinking of alternatives. If the Istovari couldn't help, they needed another powerful sorceress.

There were dozens of magical colleges and academies scattered through the known world, but few had progressed beyond alchemy. With so many of the sorcerous bloodlines killed off in the Erymayan war, unbroken maternal lines of sorceresses were nearly extinct.

The only other powerful magic user Amira knew of was Vesha. That had obvious problems, but there might be a way to get the empress's help.

What if they could force Vesha to take a Kadra'han's oaths? Amira had no idea if that would even work, considering that Vesha had no real magic of her own, but it was worth considering. Then again, what of Darrigan and the other Kadra'han who served in Vesha's personal circle? What if they could find a loophole that allowed them to help free Daindreth?

The captain of the guard had said that it was in Vesha's best interest that Daindreth be killed, because of the demon. What if Amira could recruit him to do away with the cythraul by other means?

"What about the army?" Thadred said, interrupting Amira's train of thought.

Cyne stood, brushing off her skirt as she did. "Tapios has sent scouts into the Cursewood. To be safe."

Thadred grunted in approval. "Good." He glanced to Amira.

"I think I like that guy. A bit uptight and strange, but not a bad fellow, overall."

Amira sniffed and looked away. Tapios didn't seem like a bad man, but he was an Istovari loyal to the Elder Mother. Along with the rest of the clan, he seemed ready to knife Daindreth in the chest. Amira was mentally preparing herself to kill Tapios and whomever else if she had to.

Cyne turned to leave and stopped at the threshold. "Sairydwen should come to see you soon, Thadred," she said. "She wishes to speak with you."

"If she's planning on putting a leash on him and turning him into her pet knight, she'll have to go through me first," Amira spat.

Cyne was unimpressed. "Taking ownership of him yourself, are you?"

Amira's hackles rose. "How dare you—"

"Amira, it's fine," Thadred said. "Let it go."

Cyne inclined her head to Thadred. "I will see you both tonight if not sooner." She left, then, and her footsteps receded down the hall.

Amira sat back down and stifled several curses aimed at her mother, the Elder Mother, and the Istovari in general. "I hate them," Amira whispered, hoping no one was listening, but at the point where she desperately needed to say it. "I hate them all."

"I believe you," Thadred said. "But it's like in Mynadra."

"What?"

"Do you remember Dame Rebeku and her marzipan foxes?"

It took Amira a moment to remember. The subtle snubs and passive-aggressive slights of the palace seemed like a lifetime away. "Yes."

"It's like that. These women are politicking. The whole Istovari clan is. Can't you tell?"

"Yes," Amira agreed. "But I'm tired of it. This is Daindreth's life. Our lives."

"And their lives," Thadred agreed. "Don't you see? They're as afraid of us as we are of them. They know one wrong move here could mean death for them all."

Amira inhaled through her nose. "You're right," she conceded. Cromwell had taught her better than this. "I need to be more composed. I just..." She scrubbed at her eyes. "Daindreth."

"I know." Thadred flopped back on his pillows with a deep sigh. "I know, Amira. I'm afraid, too."

It was a bit strange to hear Thadred admit that. "Afraid?"

Thadred smiled wanly. "Shocking, isn't it? But yes. These people are frightened. And frightened people do the stupidest things."

Amira had to agree. That did nothing to make her feel better.

CHAPTER NINE

Daindreth

"**O**n your feet," the Istovari youth ordered.

By the torchlight, his face was hard to make out, but Daindreth sensed fear in his tone.

Afraid of you? Caa Iss sounded far too amused. *Really?*

"Where are we going?" Daindreth still hadn't left the cellar since arriving.

True to Tapios' commands, the Istovari men had kept Daindreth under constant watch. They still hadn't fed him, but his head no longer ached with dehydration and the last time he'd relieved himself, his urine was no longer brown.

"To get you cleaned up. Come on." The boy waved impatiently. His companions looked to each other.

How old were they? The oldest couldn't be more than seventeen. A man, but barely.

They carried large blades that were still little more than glorified knives. They were children with sticks. Frightened children who had been raised on horror stories of war and still didn't know the first thing about facing it themselves.

You know, Caa Iss mused. *I bet that you could kill that skinny one there before the others even knew what was happening.*

Daindreth rose to his feet and exhaled. "And just what does getting me cleaned up mean, young man?"

"The Mothers want to see you. But Tapios wants you cleaned up first."

Daindreth wasn't sure why they would suddenly care that he was covered in mud and filth from head to foot. Nor was he sure that the boy was telling the truth, but he exhaled and nodded. "Lead the way, Cymogan."

The boy jumped a little at his name, probably not realizing Daindreth had caught it earlier.

The makeshift guard surrounded him as soon as he stepped out of the cellar. The cold evening air blew in his face and he shivered.

Finally. I thought we'd never get out.

The Istovari settlement was different at night. It was quieter, calmer, a dreamlike version of itself.

Woodsmoke scented the air along with the smell of freshly cut grass. It reminded Daindreth of a village he and his entourage had once stayed in overnight when they'd been traveling.

That had been during the Maying and there had been sacrifices to the gods along with dances, songs, more wine than even the royal guards could drink, and beautiful girls with flower crowns. Daindreth hadn't joined in, but Thadred and some of his men had. The next morning, Thadred had been hungover as a sailor after his first night ashore. He still grinned like an idiot every time he talked about that night's exploits.

Thadred.

Daindreth swallowed a lump in his throat. He might weep over his cousin soon. An ache had settled in his chest and stayed there. For now, Daindreth could distract himself with the need to find Amira, but as soon as that was gone, he expected to weep good and hard.

They're taking you to your death. Whether they want you cleaned up first or not, it doesn't matter. They'll kill you as soon as they get the chance. Are you really going like a sheep to slaughter?

Daindreth glanced up to the sky, a little surprised to find it clear. After so many nights in the Cursewood, with nothing but the pitch black of the dark above, it was a welcome relief.

Yes, archduke, Caa Iss sneered. *The sky is still there. Now will you focus on keeping us* not *killed?*

Daindreth kept staring anyway. How strange to miss the sky. It was something he had always taken for granted. How odd that after just a day and a half underground, it became so much more beautiful.

This is a trick. The cythraul's tone changed in pitch. *I'm telling you, this isn't good. We—*

Caa Iss's voice snapped off. Just like that, he was silent.

Excitement spiked through Daindreth. His heart sped up just a little and he glanced around, looking for signs of Amira. Everything was dark, but she was close. She had to be.

"Where is Amira?" Daindreth asked the boys. It was the same thing he had been asking for hours, but now it took on fresh urgency. "I need to see her."

"Princess Amira is with the Elder Mother," Cymogan said.

The Elder Mother had to be close then, or else Amira had sneaked away. Daindreth wouldn't put that past her. Was she watching them? Was she close? He just hoped she wouldn't kill any of these boys while trying to get to him.

The boys herded him around a corner of a large barrow and from the smell, he guessed that they were near a sheep pen. Then again, much of the village seemed to smell that way, so perhaps it was nothing.

They rounded a corner and trudged over a low hill to an empty paddock. The boys shuffled him inside and then toward the barn.

It was empty. The stalls for donkeys and sheep were stocked with hay, but the residents were nowhere in sight.

For a moment, he thought that perhaps this was meant to be his new prison, but then Daindreth noticed there were no lights. Something was wrong. For once, he should have listened to Caa Iss.

Daindreth stopped at the threshold of the barn and the boys at his back nearly ran into him. "You could have murdered me back in the cellar, you know," he said. "There would have been less chance of witnesses back there."

It was dark, but Daindreth thought the younger boy gulped. "We're not murderers," Cymogan said, even as he reached for the sizable blade at his hip.

"No?" Daindreth stalled for time, thinking. Amira was close, but he wasn't sure how close. He had no idea if she knew where he was, if she was watching, or…

What if they'd already murdered her and her body was lying somewhere around here?

No, that wasn't it. If she was repressing Caa Iss, she had to still be alive.

"No," the Istovari lad insisted.

His friends shuffled.

Daindreth was unarmed, but he had been trained as a knight, he was several years older and about thirty pounds heavier than any of these boys. He could probably overpower at least two of them before the others got close enough.

He might be able to take a hostage, but with the hesitant and untrained way they held their knives, they were just as likely to hurt themselves as him. It would be messy, and it would scare them even more. Scared, foolish boys with weapons rarely made good decisions. Hardly ever, in fact.

"Listen," Daindreth said. "I'm guessing Tapios didn't tell you to do this." Daindreth chose each word carefully, calling to mind every interaction and hint at dynamics he had seen within the Istovari. "I'm also guessing that whatever you're planning, you don't want anyone else to know. Am I right?" Daindreth made sure to keep his tone gentle, almost paternal.

"Don't threaten us, imperial." An older, tougher voice barked from Daindreth's back.

Torchlight washed over their little group and Daindreth's hackles raised.

It was Bardaka, the young man missing an eye. He moved with a stiff gait that belied other injuries, old wounds that hadn't healed properly. "You're going to tell us where the army is coming from, how many there are, and how to stop them."

"As I told your leader, I don't know," Daindreth calmly answered, keeping his tone as neutral as possible.

"Tapios isn't our leader," Bardaka scoffed. "He's just someone the Mothers have in charge of the rangers."

Daindreth glanced at the nervous faces around him. Time was on his side. The longer he stalled, the more likely that someone would come by who would tell Tapios. Despite what Bardaka said, the secrecy and the way they had all responded to the ranger told Daindreth that the other man had some authority.

"You don't want to do this," Daindreth said calmly. "Whatever it is you're planning." He shook his head. "I don't want to go back to the empire," Daindreth said. "The empress isn't my ally in this. I don't know what you've heard, but if anyone is your enemy, it is Vesha, not I." He spread his hands in a gesture of peace. "I didn't come to hurt your people," he continued. "I came to ask the Mothers for help and that's all I want." Daindreth turned to include all the boys in his statement. By the torchlight, he was reminded of how young they were. Besides Bardaka, there wasn't one among them who could have been more than sixteen. They wouldn't have even been alive during the war.

In some ways, that might be worse. They would have been raised on stories and legends of the Tower and the horrors of the Empire.

"Let's talk about this," Daindreth said calmly.

"You think I'm stupid?" Bardaka demanded. "You think I'm fooled by your words like Tapios is?"

"I think you want to protect your family," Daindreth said, sensing that the situation was devolving. "I think you're frustrated and angry and I understand. I would be, too."

"You know nothing about me!" Bardaka roared. "Your soldiers stormed our home, killed our mothers, and took our sisters."

Daindreth didn't think it would be helpful to point out that it had been his father's soldiers, not his.

"We just wanted to be left alone," Bardaka continued. "Just left alone in this miserable corner of the world, but no. You had to follow us here."

Daindreth stood his ground, keeping his voice calm and gentle. The young Istovari man in front of him was as angry as a speared boar and might charge at any second. "If I have caused any danger to your people, I am sorry," he said. "And I will do everything in my power to make it right, but you must believe me, and you must trust me."

"Grab him!" Bardaka ordered.

Cymogan looked to Bardaka. "If Tapios finds out——"

"You follow Tapios now?" Bardaka sneered. "You follow the ranger? That glorified woodsman?"

"The Mothers trust him," Cymogan said. "He protects us."

"From kelpies and stiltfoxes, not imperial soldiers," Bardaka shot back. "Are you men or cowards? Grab the imperial."

Daindreth had nothing to bargain with, nothing to reason with. If he had known more about the dynamics of the village, more about who ruled and who had authority and what these people believed, he might have been able to think of something.

As it was, with him outnumbered and weakened, they had the upper hand.

Cymogan was the first to move. He grabbed Daindreth's arm in a viselike grip, surprisingly strong for his lean frame.

"Cymogan." Daindreth made eye contact with the boy, but didn't resist. "Anything that has to be done in secret shouldn't be done at all."

Cymogan hesitated, but the five or six other boys were already grabbing Daindreth's wrists and arms and the back of his shirt.

"Bring him!" Bardaka ordered, marching away into the empty barn.

Daindreth gulped, searching the darkness for pitchforks or ropes or anything he could use to create a distraction and break free. But even if he broke free, what would he do?

Finding Amira seemed like the obvious thing, but how was he going to do it? Shouting for her also seemed obvious, but if she came to him right now, he expected that she would end up killing Bardaka at the very least.

Right now, with the Istovari already so volatile against them, that was the last thing they needed.

While he was still trying to think of an escape route, they dragged him to the back of the barn and the water trough. Daindreth's heart beat faster, adrenaline coursing through his veins. His senses sharpened even as his mind started racing, thinking less and less beyond fighting or fleeing.

"Kneel," Bardaka ordered.

Daindreth wouldn't have obeyed, but the boys were forcing him down before he could think about it. The five of them together overpowered him and slammed him to the ground in front of the water trough.

Their hands shook and Daindreth could hear their breathing coming faster, too. Jittery and anxious as young hounds, all of them were losing rationality faster with each passing moment.

Bardaka secured the torch to the wall and came stalking back. "You're going to tell us how many soldiers are coming, when they are coming, and how we turn them back."

Daindreth shook his head. "I don't know any of that."

"Don't lie!" Bardaka roared. "I'm not stupid! I haven't forgotten the imperial bastards who took my eye." He jabbed a finger at the patch on the side of his head. He ripped it off, exposing the mangled socket underneath. Even by the dim torchlight, Daindreth could see it had not been a clean wound. The flesh around the socket was puckered and pale, ridged with a map of scarred flesh.

Daindreth shook his head, forcing his voice to remain level, calm. "I'm sorry for what was done to you. It shouldn't have happened."

"Your soldiers did this!" Bardaka cried. "And slit my sister's throat after they had their way with her."

"Listen to me," Daindreth said. "We can't change the past. I wish we could, but we can't. All we can do is—"

Bardaka's fist slammed into Daindreth's jaw. The archduke's head snapped back, and he would have fallen over if the boys hadn't been gripping his arms so tightly.

Before he could recover, a hand shot out and grabbed his hair. Daindreth's head yanked forward, and his face plunged underwater.

Daindreth struggled instinctively, reason and logic flying from his mind in an instant. He fought and managed to yank back. His head tore free, and he gasped air, still fighting.

"Enough!" Daindreth yelled.

"You wanted water?" Bardaka shouted, voice rising over Daindreth's shouts and the protests of the Istovari youths. "Is the water here not to your liking, imperial?"

"Bardaka—" Cymogan spoke up, but the older man whirled on him.

"Are you afraid of him?" Bardaka demanded. "You should be. Do you know what these bastards did to your mother, boy? What they did to all our mothers?"

Daindreth sputtered and coughed. "The demon hurt my mother, too."

"Shut up!" Bardaka slammed Daindreth's head back under the water.

Daindreth tried to calm himself, tried to get under control, but he couldn't. He felt like he was drowning. He *was* drowning.

He ripped his right wrist out of the grip of the boy to his

side and tore his arm free. Slamming his elbow back, he knocked free enough to blindly grab the edge of the stone trough and shove back.

Bardaka had pressed down too hard on Daindreth's head. As soon as Daindreth yanked out from under him, he found himself careening headfirst into the trough. Daindreth ripped free just as Bardaka stumbled and fell in sideways.

Cursing, Bardaka yelled at Cymogan and the others, but Daindreth was already slamming his elbow back into the boy at his left and grabbing for the gangly neck of another.

No time to catch his breath, Daindreth staggered to his feet while the others were still confused. He grabbed Cymogan and dragged the boy in front of him.

Locking an arm around Cymogan's neck, he positioned the boy between himself and the others. Cymogan struggled, writhing and twisting in Daindreth's grasp, but the archduke held firm.

"Stop it." Daindreth sounded more like an angry Thadred than he cared to admit. "We're all going to calm down now," Daindreth said. "And we're going to think about this."

Cymogan reached for his knife, but Daindreth squeezed the boy's neck tighter with one arm and wrested the blade away with the other. He tossed the knife into the darkness of the barn.

"None of that."

One of the other boys reached for his own knife and Daindreth let off a sharp warning. "Don't you dare," he growled, forcing Cymogan between them. "Now listen, all of you."

Bardaka crawled out of the water trough, sputtering and raging mad. "Let him go, you son of a bitch!" Bardaka ordered.

"I will," Daindreth said. "When you go get someone reasonable for me to reason with."

"You have no right to demand anything!" Bardaka shouted, voice rising to a bellow. "You come into my home and take hostages of my brethren—"

"After you tried to drown me," Daindreth shot back. "If you think I'm putting myself at your mercy again, you're wrong."

"Bardaka?" one of the younger Istovari boys said, looking to the older man. "I don't think—"

Bardaka let off a roar of fury and disappeared into the shadows of the barn. That couldn't be good.

Daindreth looked to one of the younger boys, the one he had elbowed, standing to the side. The lad was glancing between his friends, Cymogan held hostage by Daindreth, and Bardaka clanging through the dark of the barn.

"You should get help," Daindreth said. "And quickly." There was a risk that more witnesses would make this worse or that they would join in, but Daindreth was willing to bet that Bardaka was out of line. "Go, boy!" Daindreth ordered.

The boy hesitated, shaking.

"Go!" Cymogan shouted. "Ganner, go!"

The small boy was the first to break, running out of the barn as fast as his thin legs would carry him. The rest of the pack broke next, tearing out as fast as they could.

"Cowards!" Bardaka roared, coming back into the light of the torch with a shovel in hand. "Sniveling milk-drinkers!"

But the boys were long gone, already fleeing to tell their fathers, mothers, or whomever else Istovari children ran to when they were in trouble.

"Bardaka," Daindreth said, regaining his composure. Water still clogged his nostrils and throat, but he managed to speak calmly. "This isn't going to help you, your people, or anyone else."

Bardaka adjusted the shovel in his grip, jaw clenched.

The archduke kept Cymogan between himself and the other man, shaking his head. Cymogan writhed and fought to claw Daindreth's arm off. The boy was strong, but he was no warrior. Daindreth locked his arm tighter around the lad's neck until he was forced to stop struggling.

"Don't!" Daindreth repeated, using Cymogan as a shield.

Bardaka didn't even seem to register the hostage. He let off a savage cry and swung straight for Cymogan.

Daindreth shoved the boy aside in time to keep Cymogan taking the full force of the blow upside the head. Ducking, Daindreth kicked Cymogan away to make sure he was clear of the strike.

Daindreth retreated, but not fast enough and the shovel slammed into his shoulder. White-hot pain shot through his

87

entire left side. Daindreth covered his head with his arms and cowered.

He staggered backward in the dark as Bardaka swung again with another cry of rage. Someone else was shouting and a crack rang through the dark.

The shovel came back around and connected with Daindreth's back. The force slammed him to the ground and Daindreth knocked into a wooden fence.

Bardaka swung too wide the next time and smashed into the fence instead of Daindreth. Wood splinters rained in all directions and Daindreth had to curl into a ball to protect his face.

As Bardaka raised the shovel again, Daindreth kicked out and caught the other man in the ankle. Bardaka stumbled, but swung again and his shovel smashed down on Daindreth's forearm.

Something cracked, but Daindreth barely felt it. He scrambled to get away from the fence and away from the corner, but Bardaka blocked him. The other man swung with the shovel again and Daindreth barely managed to shield his head as the next blow fell.

Daindreth's only advantage over the shovel was how far Bardaka had to swing back. The next time the other man raised the shovel, Daindreth lunged.

He wrapped his arms around Bardaka's waist and tackled him to the ground. Bardaka cursed and kicked, but Daindreth smashed a fist into the other man's gut in a move Thadred had taught him.

Bardaka's breath wheezed out of his lungs and Daindreth didn't give him time to recover. Scrambling upright, he landed another punch to Bardaka's face.

Bardaka's head jerked. Daindreth straddled the other man and pummeled the Istovari in a flurry of blows that would have made any tavern brawler proud.

Something flew at him from the side and smacked into Daindreth's head. His whole body jerked sideways and the world spun. Heat washed through his skull and pain sent black splotches over his vision. Up was down and down was up. He scrambled to reorient himself, but a heavy wood shape smashed into his back.

Bardaka had grabbed a wooden bucket and he wielded it like a flail, smashing and bashing at Daindreth. He let off a mad cry and Daindreth was reduced to shielding his face and head again. Bardaka kicked blindly in the dark, boots striking Daindreth's back, ribs, legs, and arms. Screaming in fury, Bardaka snatched up the shovel again and came back at Daindreth.

Daindreth's head pounded and his mind whirred as he desperately tried to spot an opening, any opening. He kicked at Bardaka's legs again, but the other man wasn't to be caught by that trick twice. He skirted back and smacked the shovel down into the side of Daindreth's knee.

The archduke cried out and Bardaka used the opportunity to kick a boot into Daindreth's jaw. His head flew back and smacked into the barn wall at his back. Dazed and with blood pouring down his mouth, Daindreth had a good view of Bardaka raising the shovel over his head for a massive strike.

Bardaka was going to kill him, Daindreth realized. The other man was too angry to stop. The Istovari swung down, the metal head of the shovel flying straight for Daindreth's face.

"Bardaka!" shouted a male voice, deep and authoritative and familiar. "Bardaka, stop!"

A shape flew out of the darkness and tackled the other man into a heap of straw. Bardaka went down with a bellow of rage and swung at his new attacker, but the other man yanked away Bardaka's shovel and tossed it across the barn.

"Enough! What do you think you're doing?" The other man loomed over Bardaka. It took Daindreth a moment to recognize the man through the blood pouring into his eyes, but Tapios was unmistakable with his huntsman's habit.

Bardaka screamed, writhing to get free from under Tapios. "They took everything from us! They will take everything from us again."

"Silence!" Tapios shot a glance back to the entrance of the barn.

There were at least ten onlookers, several of the boys from earlier along with a few adults Daindreth didn't recognize. One of the boys leaned against an older woman, who was fretting over the welt on his cheek. Daindreth wondered if he was responsible for that.

Crawling upright, Daindreth found that he couldn't move the fingers in his left arm. He had a new headache, one that throbbed and burned. His knuckles hurt, too, from pummeling Bardaka, and pain pulsed through him from head to foot. The Istovari's blows had landed well along the entire length of Daindreth's body. It hurt now, but Daindreth shuddered to think what it would be like tomorrow.

"This isn't how we do things," Tapios said, shaking his head. "This isn't..." He let off an exhale. Tapios stepped back and marched over to Daindreth. He crouched just out of arm's reach, surveying the other man. "Archduke, are you well?"

Daindreth leaned back against the wall of the barn, keeping his left arm carefully cradled in his lap. "I've had worse," he lied.

Tapios surveyed the damage with a grimace and glowered at Bardaka. "Come," he said, reaching out a hand to the archduke.

Daindreth didn't move. His left eye was swelling and several cuts on his face bled, making it even harder to see. It hurt to lean against the barn wall, but moving threatened to be even worse. His back, ribs, legs, and joints throbbed along with his head. He paused to decide the least painful way of standing.

Tapios pulled and helped him to stand, but pain shot up Daindreth's shin and he stumbled. Tapios caught the archduke, slinging Daindreth's good arm around his shoulders.

"Move," Tapios barked to the onlookers.

Daindreth leaned heavily against the other man, fighting not to groan in discomfort. He wasn't sure if he could trust Tapios, quite the opposite, but he wasn't about to gain anything by rejecting help at the moment.

Even if it was part of an exceptionally elaborate ploy, it was one Daindreth would have to ride out to the end.

"Back to the cellar?" Daindreth asked.

"No," Tapios grimly answered. "Cymogan, grab that torch. Lead the way."

"Where are we going?" the youth asked, looking suddenly very young and confused.

90

"My house," Tapios said without hesitation.

The boy opened his mouth at that, then shut it. He trotted over to fetch the torch Tapios had indicated.

"Guin," Tapios said to another of the boys. "Run ahead and tell my sister we're coming."

"You're making a mistake!" Bardaka croaked, leaning heavily against a center brace. His face was swollen and bloody from Daindreth's fists, his lip split and bleeding. But the archduke was too sore to gain any satisfaction from it. Anyone who looked at the two men could see which of them had taken the worst of the fight.

"Silence, Bardaka," Tapios growled. "You've done quite enough for one night."

With Cymogan leading the way, Tapios helped Daindreth limp out of the barn. The small crowd of onlookers parted, watching the archduke and the ranger with wide eyes.

"He's a threat to us as long as he's alive!" Bardaka shouted.

"That is for the Mothers to decide!" Tapios shouted back. "Not you."

As they left the barn and climbed up a short path toward the center of the village, Daindreth searched the darkness for any sign of life. There were several barrows surrounding them in all directions, smoke rising from a few. Several hundred paces off, he spotted a large structure at least three times the size of the other barrows. He couldn't make out much of it in the dark, but light spilled out two large double doors.

Even from this distance, he caught snatches of voices and laughing and the patter of drums and the whistle of flutes. Was that a party? It seemed an odd thing to have a celebration at a time like this, with an invading army supposedly on their doorstep.

The cold night air made Daindreth's wet hair and clothes feel like ice against his skin. He shivered involuntarily and that made his many bruises and sores shudder.

"Where is Amira?" Daindreth asked. She was close. The silence in his head attested to that.

"You'll see her soon," was all Tapios said.

"It's been more than a day," Daindreth said, his voice flat. "I want to know that she's alright."

"You'll have to be patient," Tapios said, not looking at Daindreth.

"If it was your woman, would you be patient?" Daindreth countered.

Tapios kept marching toward a barrow with light spilling out the front. They staggered through the door and into a bricked inner chamber with wood planks for a floor, a burning hearth at the edge, and several round doorways leading off into other chambers.

Sairydwen was already waiting for them at the entryway, a small boy who couldn't have been more than five or six clutching at her skirts. Her hands were bandaged, but she was cleaned up and had color in her face, looking far better than she had a day ago. Or was it two days by now? Daindreth had lost track of time.

"What happened?" Whether this was a ruse or not, her shock looked genuine when Sairydwen saw Daindreth's bloodied face and torn clothes.

"I'm getting to the bottom of it," Tapios answered. He shuffled Daindreth toward one of the chairs by the hearth. "He needs food and…" Tapios looked over the other man, hesitating. "He needs tending. Should I call Cyne to help?"

Sairydwen looked Daindreth over. "Rhisiart can help me." She looked to the child at her side.

Tapios nodded as Daindreth sat in the offered chair.

"Thank you for your hospitality, madam," Daindreth said. Thadred would have been able to turn that into a charming statement, but Daindreth thought his own words came out as more of a wheeze. More pitiable than charming.

Tapios glanced between the archduke and his sister. "I'll have one of the rangers join you."

"Perfect," Sairydwen said, her expression neutral.

The barrow was earthy, but clean, humble, but well-cared for. It reminded him of the village homes he'd seen passing through Hylendale.

Daindreth closed his eyes, a sense of relief washing over him even as his whole body ached. Sairydwen and Tapios were good people, he believed that much. They wouldn't let him be harmed in their home.

The fire was pleasantly hot, and a warm, meaty aroma filled the barrow. He inhaled and exhaled slowly. Glancing down with his one unswollen eye, he was able to see that he was covered in dirt and blood from head to foot.

Tapios stepped to the door and barked a series of orders outside. Whether he was a simple woodsman or not, he was a leader. Daindreth could recognize one when he met them. The ranger kept one foot inside the barrow and his body half-turned toward the archduke even as he spoke to those outside. He might have brought the archduke into his home, but it was clear Daindreth still had a lot of work to do before he earned trust.

Sairydwen slid in front of Daindreth, her hands hovering at waist height and bandaged. She studied him critically, with an eye like a woodcarver about to get to work.

Daindreth took another breath and grimaced. Pain shot through his ribs. A few of them might be broken, now that he considered it.

"Amira?" Daindreth asked. "She's close, isn't she?"

Sairydwen shook her head. "You don't want to see her like this," the sorceress said. She looked to the boy at her side. "Rhisiart, can you fetch me the wash basin and a terrycloth from the kitchen?"

The small boy trotted away, large eyes watching Daindreth as he did.

A young woman with freckles slipped into the barrow, vaguely familiar. She and Tapios exchanged a few brief sentences, and then the older ranger stepped outside and shut the door. The girl eyed Daindreth suspiciously, but went straight to Sairydwen.

"Mother Sairydwen?" she asked. "Your brother said you needed help."

"Yes," Sairydwen confirmed. "I need your help tending our guest."

"Guest?" Daindreth asked, making an effort to keep the sardonicism from his voice. "Not your prisoner?"

Sairydwen shook her head. "You may see this however you like."

Rhisiart returned with a washbasin almost as big as he was

and a white cloth.

"Thank you, darling," Sairydwen said. "Ellia, fetch the wine and oil. Rhisiart, can you help Mama with this?"

Daindreth sighed and submitted to the tender ministrations of the Istovari woman.

They were right about one thing—neither him nor any of the Istovari wanted Amira to see him like this. If she did, Bardaka was a dead man.

CHAPTER TEN

Amira

Amira felt like the fatted calf being paraded through town before the spring sacrifices. She sat at the table at the front of the hall with Thadred at one side and the Elder Mother to the other.

The assassin studied the mass of faces, wondering which of them might know where Daindreth was and how she might pry it out of them.

"Nice party." Thadred sipped his wine. The cup was clay, rough and plain like most of this settlement. Yet Thadred held it as gingerly and delicately as if it were a silver chalice.

At least thirty Istovari gathered in the room. The piles of wool had been moved to make space, but the dim light still made it feel crowded. A few candles flickered from the walls, but most of the light came from the central fire at the middle of the large chamber.

"See anyone interesting?" Amira mumbled out of the corner of her mouth.

"That man by the door. The one who keeps glancing this way."

Amira waited a moment and then glanced to the open double doors in front of them. Sure enough, one of the rangers stood by quietly, arms folded across his chest, making a poor job of watching inconspicuously. These people knew the forest well, but when it came to fighting and outwitting other people, they had a lot to learn.

"I didn't think he was your type," Amira said, voice flat.

Thadred chuckled a little at that. "They're nervous. The Istovari."

"Wouldn't you be?"

"Of you? Yes." Thadred inhaled and exhaled before shifting his bad leg. "The Elder Mother told me that Tapios sent scouts to look for the army. Which means they either haven't come back yet, haven't found anything, or they're not coming back at all."

Across the room, a middle-aged woman missing a hand raised a cup of wine to toast the Elder Mother. The room hushed and even the music stilled as everyone turned to face the speaker.

"Elder Mother, I want to extend my deepest congratulations at the return of your granddaughter, Princess Amira, whom we thought lost to us." The one-handed woman inclined her head and the room let off a smattering of applause. "May she be the first of many stolen children returned."

More cheers erupted around the room.

"May it be so!" the Elder Mother agreed, her voice as loud and strong as a summer gale.

The speaker downed her cup of wine, and the singing and dancing went back into full swing.

On the Elder Mother's other side, Cyne watched quietly. She didn't speak and she barely acknowledged when another sorceress led a second toast to her.

No one directly approached the head table. From the way people kept glancing in their direction, Amira wondered if that was customary or not. Had the Elder Mother ordered the others to keep their distance? It certainly seemed like something she would do.

"It's getting late," Amira mused to Thadred. "You think the army will actually attack tonight?"

The Elder Mother was speaking with Cyne in low voices and the noise of the hall covered their words.

"If they're here? I don't know." He chewed his lip. "These are imperial Kadra'han. They weren't trained by assassins like you. They were trained by knights."

"We need to speak to Iasu." Amira pasted on a smile as the one-handed sorceress raised a third toast, this one to her. She barely heard what the woman said, and she didn't care. "The Istovari wounded and captured Iasu when they caught me and Daindreth. I think they're holding him somewhere in this village, too."

Thadred snorted. "These people like collecting dangerous pets, don't they?"

"Look at them." Amira resisted the urge to point. The adults in the room glanced their way and kept glancing back. The children outright stared, wide-eyed with mixtures of fear and curiosity. "They haven't seen strangers in over a decade."

"Fine fix this is," Thadred grumbled. "Just *fine.*"

Amira had a pleasant buzz from her wine and was grateful. If not, she would have probably screamed. They were stuck here with people who would rather party and wait to see what would happen than take action and save their own village, Daindreth, and possibly the world.

Then again, perhaps this was the Mothers' efforts to protect their clan. There were rangers on patrol and by bringing people into the center of the village, they would likely be more protected. That the Elder Mother had not warned her people was still inexcusable to Amira.

Dozens of people danced and made merry and sang like nothing was wrong. Beyond the barrow, Amira could feel the cords and webs of magic woven like so many threads. This entire village was alive with magic, soaked with it like oilskin. She was tempted to pluck at the magic, just to see what would happen, but thought better of it.

Sources of *ka* flickered here and there. Closing her eyes, Amira could sense a thick cluster of it that was probably sheep. Not too far away was a less dense cluster sprinkled through a tree—roosting chickens, if she had to guess.

Bodies gathered beneath thin blankets of *ka,* people in their grass-covered homes.

Gods, this entire village was alive. Between the living wood beams and supports of the barrows and the net of magic that covered the entire settlement, Amira almost expected it to breathe. This place was its own organism.

Not too far away, she sensed another cluster of bodies, moving quickly and grappling together. She wasn't sure how to place it or even where they were for certain, but she kept reaching out across the village, mesmerized by the sheer amount of power. She could reach so far, sense so much.

For the first time, this place overtook her with wonder. It was incredible, this home that the Istovari had made. It wasn't much to look at, but sorceresses didn't use just their eyes to see.

"Amira?" As if from far away or underwater, someone called her name. "What are you doing?"

Amira kept reaching, curious to see how far she could go. She stretched out her consciousness, following the webs of magic that wove through the village. She passed over more barrows with more people inside, dogs beside sheep pens and pigs rooting in the *ka*-rich garden beds.

Amira could sense the walls of the Cursewood hemming them in on all sides, pressing against the Haven. It was then that she realized the Cursewood didn't just surround the Haven, it gnawed at it. The spells woven through the settlement were to keep the Curse out.

Considering this information, Amira felt along the boundary of the Cursewood's miasmic pressure. It lapped against the Haven like waves against a wharf, a wolf's tongue licking hungrily at the fence.

Amira mused on that, the magnitude of both the curse and the spell that countered it. If the Cursewood could be held back by magic, why couldn't a demon?

She considered this for a long moment.

"Amira?" a second voice called.

Amira ignored them both, sinking deeper into her thoughts. She already countered the cythraul and it sounded like she did that by the binding magic that had been tied to her. If her blood had been the sacrifice to shackle Caa Iss, could he possess Daindreth's heir if that heir shared her blood? Or would the cythraul simply be bound permanently, shackled and mute within his next host's skull?

Amira needed to think more on this. If they couldn't excise the demon, perhaps they could—

At the edges, something rippled. Shapes of *ka,* richer with *ka* than any of the sorceresses Amira had met here, slipped through the boundary and into the Haven.

Amira stiffened, her hands gripping the table in front of her. For a moment, she thought that the shapes might be rangers returning from patrol, but then they split up. As Amira waited, they broke off into pairs and trios, circling the village.

That was wrong.

Amira's eyes flew open, and she bolted to her feet before she knew what she was doing. "They're here," she gasped.

"Amira?" Thadred and the Elder Mother spoke at once.

Amira whirled on Thadred. "They're in the village." She spun to the Elder Mother. "The imperials are here."

The Elder Mother stiffened, shooting a glance to the Istovari gathered in the hall. She leaned toward Amira, voice a harsh whisper. "That's impossible."

"They are," Amira hissed back. "They're circling the village."

No doubt, they would be searching for her and Daindreth— to kill her and abduct Daindreth. Amira needed a weapon and she needed to get to the archduke.

"We've heard nothing from the scouts." The Elder Mother remained outwardly calm, but her voice wavered. "No one can get inside the Haven who hasn't been here before.

"Well, they're here now," Amira snarled.

Thadred was already climbing to his feet, leaning on the table for support. "Amira. What's happening?"

"Someone has breached the Haven," Amira panted, breathless as her heart raced.

"Who? How do you know?" Thadred frowned at her.

"I just know," Amira said.

That seemed good enough for Thadred. He nodded and straightened.

Cyne stood and blocked Amira's path. "It's probably the rangers returning from a patrol."

"They split up and are circling the village," Amira countered. "At least fifty of them."

Cyne hesitated at that. All four of them knew that the Haven didn't have fifty rangers to send out on patrol at once.

"It could have been an illusion," Cyne said, but her voice was soft.

The Istovari had been prepared to be hunted, but they must not have thought that the imperials would actually make it to the Haven so easily.

"The Kadra'han said they would be here tonight," Thadred said. "I've been telling you."

Around the room, people had started noticing the disturbance at the head table. People looked in their direction, a few of them whispered to one another.

The Elder Mother shook her head. "They can't—"

A pulse of *ka* shot through the air and darkness flooded the hall. The fire went out along with the handful of torches.

Thadred was the first one to speak. "Bollocks."

Amira dropped into a crouch as voices clamored inside the hall. She pulled Thadred down beside her so that they were under the head table.

"What is this?" the Elder Mother demanded.

"Get down if you want to live," Amira snarled.

This time, the Elder Mother listened to her, crouching beside Amira under the table.

At least one imperial Kadra'han was close enough to work magic. Most of them had very little magical skill or ability on their own, so there was either a single man with a device or tool to help him, or there were several of them working together.

Amira's mind raced. If the imperials were here, they might know where Daindreth was. They might not. They might know where she was, or they might not.

"Amira," Thadred whispered. "How would you recommend we go about killing them first?"

Amira bit her lip. She wanted to reach out and see what she could piece together from the movement of *ka* in the village, but she dared not close her eyes that long.

Voices began shouting in the hall, people panicking and with good reason. Mothers called for their children and husbands called to their wives.

"Peace," the Elder Mother called. "Peace. Can anyone light another fire?"

There came the sound of people fumbling in the dark for flint and steel, but Amira suspected it would be no use.

"Where is Daindreth?" Amira demanded, spinning on the Elder Mother. She found the other woman in the dark, relying on the outline of *ka* to guide her.

The Elder Mother was unmoved. "That's hardly—"

Amira had stuffed a knife up her sleeve at the start of dinner. Now she slipped the knife free and pressed it against the Elder Mother's inner elbow. As her eyes adjusted to the darkness, she saw her grandmother's eyes widen. "Tell me where he is, or I will give you scars to match mine."

Amira heard the Elder Mother open her mouth to speak, then Thadred cried out from behind her.

"Amira!" The knight tackled Amira to the floor just as a flash of silver jabbed for her torso.

Someone screamed and Amira and Thadred fell to the ground in a tangled heap.

The Kadra'han struck for Amira again, his blade flashing in the dark. Thadred kicked out with his good leg, boot knocking the blade away.

Flipping away from Thadred, Amira grabbed the first thing she could get her hands on, a chair. She hurled it at the attacker, and he knocked it aside easily.

Amira cursed. She'd dropped the knife when Thadred had tackled her and now she couldn't find it.

"Amira!" Cyne called out this time and Amira ducked just as a second attacker stabbed for her back.

She dropped down to one knee and jabbed backwards with her elbow into his gut. Her elbow slammed into a leather-armored torso and a metal stud struck right on her nerve.

Yelping, Amira kept moving, rolling out of the way of the next strike.

The second man stomped down on her skirt, stopping her from rolling to her feet. He swung, short sword in hand.

A woman's voice cried out and a flash of red nearly blinded Amira for an instant. The attacker staggered back with a web of red splattered across his face. By the glow, Amira could see that his head was unarmored and exposed and now covered in glowing veins like spider webs.

Cyne stood with an empty wine goblet in one hand and the other outstretched, face pinched in concentration.

Amira rolled onto her feet, disentangling herself from her skirts. It was dark and bodies pressed all around her. She couldn't see beyond the red glow of the magic web on the other assassin's face. The *ka* in the room was a churning, confused mass of bodies. The imperial clutched at his face, screaming and writhing on the ground.

Another shadow swept for Cyne and the former queen turned, but not fast enough. The killer's blade came up and then the Elder Mother stepped between them.

Amira heard her grandmother speak a sharp word that sounded like spitting. The Elder Mother's *ka* swelled, and the old woman splashed wine on the attacker.

Amira couldn't see what happened in the dark, but she heard sizzling and the imperial's screams made it plain enough.

She'd have to get them to teach her that trick.

Groping in the darkness, Amira found Thadred. She seized the front of his shirt and between the two of them, they dragged him upright. "We have to get out of here," Amira said, her voice all but lost in the screams and cries that filled the hall.

"And find Daindreth," Thadred agreed.

Amira grabbed Thadred's hand and followed the shapes of *ka* toward the exit. Everything was confusion and Amira couldn't tell if more Kadra'han were in the hall or not.

Bodies clamored for the exit of the hall, Istovari fleeing into the dark. Outside, the fires had been extinguished and the dark had overtaken the settlement.

Amira's heart raced, her breath turning white in the frosty night air. She held onto Thadred's hand, afraid to lose track of him in the dark.

They burst out into the open night air. Shapes streamed in every direction and the dark only made it worse.

A child screamed and Amira made out two figures to their left. One of the assassins had a small girl by the wrist. He clamped a hand over her mouth and scooped her into his arms.

The girl kicked and screamed for her mother and the invader lost his hold. He stooped over to get a better grip.

Amira let go of Thadred's hand and lunged for the Kadra'han. She locked her arm around his neck and yanked him backwards. All three of them—Amira, the child, and the Kadra'han—tumbled to the ground.

Amira wrapped her legs around the man's back. Her skirt bunched around her thighs, but she locked her forearm tighter across his neck and jerked.

The imperial Kadra'han cursed and let the girl go. Still screaming, the child ran into the darkness, sobbing.

The imperial wasted no time. One hand grabbed Amira's arm to pry it off his throat. His gauntleted hands scraped and scratched, but she gritted her teeth and held on. She held his head back tight against her collarbone, squeezing hard enough to bruise them both. She pulled hard at the *ka* in the air, infusing herself as fast as she could. Without the help of *ka,* she would never beat a grown man in a wrestling match.

Choking, the imperial's hand went to his belt. A knife flashed as Amira realized her mistake. The knife came up, headed straight for Amira's face.

"Amira!" Thadred grabbed the imperial's knife hand. He twisted it around and jabbed it down into the man's ribcage.

The blade punched between layers of leather and the imperial's body seized. He let off a gurgling, choking sound.

Thadred yanked the knife free. There was a moment of indecision, probably as he realized that the other man's head and neck were too close to Amira.

With barely a second's hesitation, Thadred stabbed for the other man's unarmored inner thigh. Amira didn't see the strike, but the imperial's body went tight just before the hot wash of *ka* on the ground.

Thadred wiped the knife on the grass as the man's body shook and then went still.

The man was still alive when Amira pushed him off her, but they didn't have time to waste. She groped over the fast-fading imperial's baldric and belt, feeling for weapons.

"Tackle an armed Kadra'han in the dark," Thadred muttered. "While you were unarmed and in a dress."

Amira pulled down her skirt with one hand before setting to unbuckling the weapons on the dying man. She scowled at Thadred even though he couldn't see it in the dark. "It worked, didn't it?"

"Only because I was here to keep him from making you one-eyed."

"Dagger or sword?" Amira asked, doing her best to feel at the weapons without cutting herself.

"Sword," Thadred scoffed. "Honestly, I'm not sure why you had to ask."

Amira shoved the sword at him, still in its sheath.

"Huh." Thadred looked down the length of the blade. "Not quite what I'm used to. His is smaller than mine."

"I've dropped men with smaller blades than that," Amira said. "If you need me to deal with the killing tonight, that's fine."

"It was a joke," Thadred said.

"What?" Amira blinked at him in the dark.

"A joke. Smaller…you know?" Thadred cleared his throat. "Never mind."

That was the best suggestion Amira had heard all night. She took the dagger. She didn't bother to keep the sheath for herself. She slung the baldric with its few throwing knives over her shoulder. There were only four left, as far as she could tell. But that was four more than she'd had a few minutes ago.

There were at least ten slots for knives on the baldric, which meant that there were probably badly injured if not dead Istovari back in the hall.

Amira paused just long enough to reach with her consciousness and feel for *ka*. Power was smudged and spattered all over the hall. Blood was everywhere inside and it made her throat tighten. Reaching out over the village, it wasn't as bad, but Amira could feel where the imperials had attacked and left bodies in their wake. She didn't have the time to sort through details, but…

"Why do you think he wanted the girl?" Amira asked.

Thadred's tone held a note of bitterness when he replied. "Why does any invader want a girl?"

"No." That had occurred to Amira, but Kadra'han wouldn't be so easily distracted. Not when the archduke was unaccounted for along with the two presumed targets for death—herself and Thadred. "You and I are still alive, which means that at least part of their mission is unfinished."

Thadred glanced around. In the moonlight, his dark hair looked like black water. "You mean they're not doing anything for fun right now?"

"We have to find Daindreth." Amira scrambled to her feet and reached back a hand for the other Kadra'han.

Thadred took it and stood with a low grunt.

"Are you good to move?" she asked.

"Let's just find Daindreth," Thadred said. "And quickly."

CHAPTER ELEVEN

Daindreth

"What's your name?" Rhisiart hadn't stopped staring at his mother's guest since he'd arrived.

"Daindreth," the archduke answered.

The boy's nose wrinkled. "That's a weird name."

"My friends call me Dain."

"Dain. That's easier. You come from the woods?" Rhisiart asked, eyes wide.

"More or less," Daindreth answered. His jaw hurt and it was painful to speak, but the child hadn't stopped speaking.

Sairydwen didn't discourage the boy, though she had to have noticed that Daindreth was taking a long time to answer the child's questions.

The archduke sat in front of the family's fireplace, stripped to the waist. That exposed most of his injuries to Sairydwen's view, but there were still plenty of other bruises and cuts on his lower body. Daindreth wondered if she planned to tend those, too.

"Your face looks funny," Rhisiart said, peering closely at the archduke.

"Those are bruises, Rhisiart," Sairydwen said. "That's why his face looks like that."

"Oh," Rhisiart said. "Why?"

"That's how our bodies respond," Sairydwen said. "*Ka* collects at the site of injury to heal us faster."

"Why?" Rhisiart scurried to help his mother with one of the terrycloths, holding the bowl for her while she wiped blood off Daindreth's jaw.

"It's just how our bodies work," Sairydwen answered.

"How did you get hurt?" Rhisiart asked.

"He made someone angry," Sairydwen quickly put in, not giving Daindreth the chance.

Rhisiart's already large eyes widened even more. "What did you do?"

105

Daindreth looked to the sorceress, but she didn't answer this time. "He thought I wanted to hurt his family."

"Oh." At his mother's prompting, Rhisiart fumbled with a spool of bandages. "You wouldn't hurt our family, would you?"

"No," Daindreth replied, trying not to watch Sairydwen's response as he did.

In truth, Amira was more likely to hurt someone here than he was. That she hadn't yet torn the village apart trying to find him made him that much more anxious to find her.

"But someone else thought you would?" Rhisiart asked.

Daindreth took a shallow breath. "Yes."

"Why?"

Daindreth might have laughed if his ribs hadn't hurt so much. The child seemed to be a bottomless pit of curiosity.

"Rhisiart," Sairydwen said. "Can you get me the saint wort from the pantry?"

Rhisiart trotted across the room to a collection of cupboards and shelves lined with pots, baskets, bags, and jars. "Which one is that, Mama?"

"The one we used for my hands earlier." Sairydwen didn't look up as she spoke, carefully studying the cut along Daindreth's jaw.

The cold air brushed along his back, making the tiny hairs stand on end. He fought a shiver as it made his whole body tense and that made his ribs hurt even more.

"You took a good beating." Sairydwen glanced down to his hands and knuckles still bloody from connecting with Bardaka's face. "Did you give one back?"

Daindreth thought that sounded like a trick question. His first impulse was to respond that she should see the other man, but he needed to be careful. He wanted to be neither the helpless victim nor the aggressor here.

"I fought back," Daindreth replied, keeping his tone neutral. "Like anyone would."

"Mama, is it this one?" Rhisiart called from across the room.

"Yes, darling," Sairydwen said. "Bring that here." Even with her hands bandaged, the sorceress seemed able to move far better than she should have just two days after having her hands stabbed through.

Rhisiart trotted back with the jar, small feet pattering on the dirt floor.

"No running," Sairydwen admonished.

Rhisiart slowed down. "Yes, Mama." He reached her and held out the jar.

"Open it for me," Sairydwen said.

Rhisiart set to freeing the lid of the jar, face pinched in concentration as he worked the clasps holding it in place.

"That's good. Now set it down there." She gestured to a stool that had been serving as her worktable.

Outside, a dog began barking. Daindreth looked to the door. It sounded close.

Hovering in the shadows by the door was the ranger woman, watching him like she was thinking of putting an arrow through his eye. She probably was.

No one else seemed troubled by the dog. Sairydwen and Rhisiart went about their business, the ranger by the door remained there, silently brooding.

Another dog joined the barking. Then another.

Daindreth looked to Sairydwen. "Is that normal?"

"It's probably just one of the rangers coming back from patrol late," Sairydwen answered.

Daindreth looked to the ranger. "Is there a patrol out tonight?"

Dogs were always barking at something, day or night. And yet…

He remembered Tapios' question from earlier that day. The ranger had been so interested in an attack that was alleged to happen tonight.

Even if it hadn't been Thadred, Tapios had to have a reason to think they were in danger. Somehow, Daindreth had the feeling that Tapios was the kind of man who needed a reason for everything.

He looked over to the ranger by the door again. "Were any late patrols sent out?"

The ranger stiffened. It was the first time he had directly addressed her. "None of your business."

These people seemed to have little guile. The closest to it he had seen was with Sairydwen and the Elder Mother. Most of them seemed too sheltered or too young to have had any use for it.

Voices clamored outside. Faint at first, but quickly growing louder.

Sairydwen straightened.

By the door, the ranger shook her head. "If this is some sort of trick—"

"It probably is some sort of trick," Daindreth cut her off. "But it's no trick of mine."

The Istovari slung her bow off her shoulder, though Daindreth didn't see what good it would do her in the dark.

The ranger reached for the door just when the door smashed into her face, kicked in from the outside. The ranger staggered back.

Two dark shadows swathed in black burst into the room. The first jabbed for the ranger's torso. She instinctively blocked, but the blade passed by her in a blur. She staggered back and the shadowed figure kicked her into a shelf of clay pots.

The ranger smashed into the shelf. Pottery exploded and she fell into a heap of broken clay, seeds, and blood.

Daindreth bolted to his feet just as Sairydwen pulled her son back.

"Eponine save us," Sairydwen gasped.

Daindreth blocked the path of the two intruders on instinct. He grabbed the poker from beside the fire and swung it at the nearest one.

The intruder caught it in one hand and made to jab Daindreth's exposed torso with a knife. He was expecting Daindreth to be as unprepared as the Istovari girl, but was met with a nasty surprise.

Daindreth grabbed the intruder's knife hand, but instead of trying to wrestle the arm like most men would, he jerked it forward and past his own body.

The other man overbalanced and stumbled sideways. Daindreth drove a knee into his side and the intruder skirted back, drawing a second weapon.

Daindreth had caught him by surprise the first time, but that advantage was gone.

Both the intruders came at Daindreth at once. If they were Kadra'han as he thought, they didn't know who he was. They would kill him and then the others in the house unless help came and soon.

"Get out!" Daindreth yelled to Sairydwen. "If there's a window or a back door, get out and get help!"

The sorceress didn't need to be told twice. She grabbed the small boy at her side and fled into the other room. Daindreth only hoped there was a way out from there.

Aching and half naked, Daindreth almost wished he could unleash Caa Iss. If there was one thing the demon and Daindreth could agree on, it was *not* dying.

But if Caa Iss was silenced, that meant Amira had to be close. Daindreth needed to get to her and make sure she was safe. If agents from the empire were here, she'd be at the top of their list.

"Did the empress send you?" Daindreth breathed as deeply as his cracked ribs would allow. All the training in the world couldn't change the fact that he was injured and outnumbered.

The intruders didn't answer. The first came for him, curved knife in hand.

Daindreth snatched up a chair and blocked, thrusting the legs at the man's face. The intruder ducked and tried to circle around Daindreth, but the archduke slammed the chair at his head.

The second attacker circled, trying to flank Daindreth from the right.

Daindreth gritted his teeth and tried to turn to face the second intruder, but the first came on hard. The first drew a backup knife and stabbed at Daindreth, forcing him to defend.

The second man skirted around easily and Daindreth saw a flash of motion out of the corner of his eye. The second intruder prepared to strike and Daindreth scrambled for a counterattack.

The second man stumbled and fell, revealing Sairydwen with an iron skillet in her bandaged hands.

"The child got away," the first intruder shouted, a rough, smoky voice with a foreign accent. How he knew that Rhisiart was gone, Daindreth couldn't guess. "Let's go," he said.

The first intruder turned and sprinted back for the door. The second followed and the two of them disappeared into the darkness outside.

"Where is your son?" Daindreth set down the chair and leaned against it, breath coming in increasingly painful gasps.

"I sent him out the window," Sairydwen said, voice shaking. "You don't think they—?"

"See to her," Daindreth ordered, pointing to the bleeding Istovari ranger by the door. He didn't wait to see Sairydwen's reaction before he stumbled for the darkness outside.

"But Rhisiart!" Sairydwen cried, grabbing his arm. "I told him to run for the Elder Mother's hall. He's outside!"

"I'll find him," Daindreth promised. "I'll find him." He pointed to the bleeding ranger. "She needs your help."

Beside the door, the Istovari ranger's eyes had become glazed and unfocused. She didn't seem to see the others in the room or know what was happening.

Sairydwen knelt beside the other woman and Daindreth didn't stay to see what happened next.

He staggered up a few steps and out into the cold night air. The cold sent a shiver through him, but at the same time soothed his cuts and bruises.

Outside, the world was chaos. Screaming came from all directions. Dogs barked everywhere. There were no fires or torches lit. Darkness and madness reigned.

Daindreth fumbled his way out. Damp grass beneath his feet reminded him that he was barefoot. He turned as his eyes adjusted, shapes and figures coming into focus.

"Rhisiart," the archduke called.

If the intruders had known that Rhisiart had fled, they probably had a way of knowing where he was. Magic? Amira had used magic that way.

Rhisiart would be fleeing toward the Elder Mother's hall. Daindreth didn't know where that was and directions wouldn't have been especially useful in the dark. He took off toward the loudest screaming, what he hoped was the middle of the village.

Would Rhisiart still go that way if it sounded like bloody murder? Daindreth had no better ideas.

Stumbling through the dark, he had time to think. Why did the Kadra'han want children?

He stubbed his toe and almost fell. Cursing to make Thadred proud, he kept moving toward the screams.

"Rhisiart?" he called, a little louder as the cries rose higher. "Rhisiart!"

"Dain?" A voice called back, but it wasn't a child's voice.

"Rhisiart!" Daindreth shouted again.

"Dain!" This time, it was a child, and it came as a scream. "I want my mama! I want—"

The boy's voice broke off into silence, but Daindreth was already charging through the dark toward the sound.

"Rhisiart!"

"Dain!" the boy screamed.

"Dain!" someone else yelled.

Two shapes flew at him from the dark. He couldn't see much of their features, but he caught the glint of weapons in the moonlight and skidded to a stop. He raised his fists defensively, not sure what he planned to do with his bare hands.

"Daindreth!"

The first figure reached him and grappled him in a hug. Weight slammed into his broken ribs and nearly knocked him over. He wheezed and made to throw the attacker off, but stopped as red hair and a familiar scent slapped him in the face.

"Amira?" Surprise, excitement, and relief flooded him an instant before he gasped in pain and Amira took a step back.

"Oh goddess," she looked him up and down in the dark, probably feeling his *ka* the way sorceresses did. "What have they done to you, Daindreth? Who did this?"

"Amira." Daindreth wheezed a cough, his side throbbing and stinging.

"I'm so sorry," Amira said, feeling gently along his side. "I didn't realize. I should have been gentler."

They were under attack, and he had never been sorer, but a part of Daindreth's mind savored the feel of her touching him. She didn't seem embarrassed by his partial nakedness, her fingers skimming over his sides, chest, and abdomen. She hesitated near his bruises and his cracked ribs, probably feeling the distorted *ka*. She was gentle, but shameless.

111

Merciful gods, he liked her touching him. It was a good thing it was dark, and he didn't have to look her in the eye.

"Well damn. You pissed someone off, didn't you?" Thadred's voice brought the archduke back to focus. So his cousin was alive.

Daindreth shook his head. "No time to explain. They took the boy."

"What boy?" Amira glanced over her shoulder to Thadred. "I don't—"

A child's voice cried out and Daindreth bolted in that direction.

"Daindreth!" Amira leapt after him and Thadred let off a shout before stumbling after them.

Daindreth swerved around a low house to find a kicking and flailing shape caught between two dark figures. He almost ordered them to let the boy go, then stopped himself. Best not to ruin the element of surprise. He could—

Then a knife was flying for his face, and he was forced to duck. A hand grabbed his arm and yanked him back behind the barrow.

"Damn it!" Thadred panted, leaning against the earthwork. "Trying to get yourself killed?"

"They have Rhisiart!"

"Hold on," Thadred said.

"Where's Amira?" Daindreth demanded. He and the knight were alone behind the barrow.

"Ah," Thadred smirked, teeth flashing white in the moonlight. "You keep forgetting what your woman is, don't you?"

"I—"

A thud from the other side of the barrow interrupted and Daindreth didn't wait for more of Thadred's explaining. He leapt out from behind the shelter of the earthwork.

Amira had rammed a wheelbarrow into the knees of one Kadra'han. He stumbled back while the other struggled to keep a grip on the flailing shape of a boy.

The Kadra'han Amira had rammed recovered himself and drew a gleaming sword. He leapt over the wheelbarrow and

112

lunged at her just as she brandished her own short blade.

"Dain!" Thadred tossed his sword into the air and Daindreth caught it by the hilt.

Adrenaline pumped through his body and his senses narrowed, focusing in on the imperials in front of him. He charged the man closest, the one holding Rhisiart.

The man saw him coming and spun around, one hand keeping a grip on the boy and the other reaching for a weapon. "You just don't quit, do you?" the Kadra'han growled. He drew another throwing knife, but Rhisiart yanked to the side with a scream, jerking him off balance. The knife skittered off into the dark.

The Kadra'han dragged the boy away from Amira and the other imperial, now exchanging a flurry of blows. Amira held her own, which was no surprise, but Daindreth could have sworn she glowed.

Her skin was pale as the moon itself and her eyes caught the light, burning gold. She was using magic—she had to be.

From the corner of his eye, Daindreth saw Thadred come tearing around the earthwork wall, limping as fast as his bad leg would let him. Without missing a beat, Thadred grabbed the discarded wheelbarrow and slammed it right into the legs of Amira's attacker.

The imperial Kadra'han went down, and Amira was on him in an instant. It was a quick death.

The Kadra'han holding Rhisiart threw another knife, but that missed, too. Hitting one's target in the dark whilst holding a screaming child was near impossible. Even for an imperial Kadra'han.

Daindreth ducked and swung, but the Kadra'han retreated a step, yanking Rhisiart in front of him.

Daindreth heard a thud and a cry from behind, but he didn't dare turn around.

"None of that!" A flash of steel showed the knife that the imperial pressed to the child's neck. "Stop fighting, Istovari brat," the man snarled. "Drop the weapons or the boy dies!"

"Are you so sure?" Amira's voice was barely recognizable, heavy with a dare and something akin to a taunt.

Daindreth spun around, chest tight.

Amira knelt over the body of the other imperial Kadra'han, her sword dripping red. This time he wasn't imagining it, she definitely glowed. The man wasn't moving, but she jerked his head back by his hair and sawed open his throat. She dipped her fingers in the gory wound, eyes on the Kadra'han who held Rhisiart.

"I mean it," the second imperial repeated. "I'll kill the child. You'd best believe me!"

"Haven't you heard?" Amira's voice turned cold and detached, like it had been the first time Daindreth met her when she had thought he wanted her for revenge. "Killing children is nothing to Istovari."

"Amira." Daindreth shook his head.

Amira ignored him. She stood, one hand stained dark by the blood of the corpse at her feet.

The Kadra'han shifted Rhisiart in front of him. "These are precious to you," the imperial Kadra'han said, adjusting his grip on the knife. "I know they are. You have so few and—"

"Would you like me to take your hands?" Amira tilted her head like she was genuinely curious. "Or would you prefer to lose your feet?"

"You don't have the power," the imperial Kadra'han snapped. "Not since the creation of the Cursewood. You're too weak."

Amira flexed her bloodied fingers. She exhaled out her nose. "A part of me wants to try it anyway. Just to see if I could." She stepped over the body of the dead man.

Daindreth, Thadred, and the surviving imperial Kadra'han watched her. Daindreth felt that none of them, not even Amira, knew what she was going to do next. "Amira…" he began, not sure what to say.

Amira ignored him, her attention still on the other Kadra'han. "I'd tell you to let the child go, but you'd never let it be that easy." She shrugged. "So, I won't waste my time." She raised her bloody left hand toward the Kadra'han. "I've never tried this before. I'm a bit excited to see what happens."

For a moment, nothing happened, but Daindreth knew better. Amira's eyes sparked just the faintest glint of copper. By the moonlight and the glow of her skin, he could see her expression harden.

The imperial Kadra'han gasped. He pulled back, tightening his grip on the boy in front of him. "Stop," he ordered. "Stop right now."

"Release the boy," Amira said. "You'll be no use to your empress if I keep going."

Daindreth couldn't see what was happening, but the imperial Kadra'han shook his head frantically. "She ordered us to take them!"

"Then find another!" Amira shouted. "She never commanded you to take a specific child, did she?"

The imperial Kadra'han gasped, doubling over, but still holding onto Rhisiart.

Amira's voice rose, unyielding. "You'd best make up your mind quick."

"Stop!" the imperial Kadra'han pleaded. "Stop, please!" He shook. Still, Daindreth couldn't see anything wrong with the man.

"Release the child," Amira ordered again.

"I can't! My oaths—"

"Don't give me that!" Amira roared, voice rising and genuine anger coming through. "Find a loophole in the curse. Another way to obey Vesha."

"Please!" the Kadra'han begged. "Mercy!"

"This *is* mercy," Amira snarled. "Think of another way to serve her. Now!"

"Amira." Daindreth reached for her, but she yanked away, bloodied hand still outstretched toward the screaming man.

"Pull yourself together!" Amira ordered. "Drop this boy and find another. There's no reason your curse shouldn't accept that."

"I—" The Kadra'han clung tighter to Rhisiart as his voice broke.

"I'm giving you a chance!" Amira bellowed.

"I can't!" the imperial cried.

"Daindreth, the boy!" Amira shouted.

Daindreth took the cue and lunged. He grabbed the man's knife hand and wrenched it back. Rhisiart leapt free, diving into

115

Daindreth's arms. The archduke dragged the boy off while the Kadra'han's hands went to his face.

The imperial's eye sockets burst into flame, popping like embers. The stench of burning flesh filled the air and the man's scream rose in a blood-curdling screech.

Daindreth shielded Rhisiart, turning the child away as the cries grew louder. The boy clung to him tight, as if they'd known each other all their lives.

Molten heat glowed from inside the imperial's skull and burned out with a red-hot intensity. Fire consumed the man's eyes, leaving blackened holes where they had been.

The man collapsed, hands clutching at his face and mouth still open. He struck the ground and went still.

Daindreth panted, staring in mute horror at the charred body. Rhisiart shook against him, small and trembling and frightened.

"I want my mama," Rhisiart mumbled, sniffling. "I want my mama."

"Shush, we'll take you to her," Daindreth promised. "It's alright."

The boy cried, clinging tight to Daindreth's chest. "I just want my mama," he repeated, softer this time.

Patting the boy's head, Daindreth looked to Amira.

She stared at the body of the mutilated Kadra'han with an expression he couldn't quite read. Her lip was curled slightly, almost contemptuous, but at the same time, he thought there were tears in her eyes.

"Why didn't you fight it?" Amira said to the corpse. Her bloody hand hung limp at her side as she watched the body. "You could have found a way out. I gave you a way out!"

"Amira." Thadred grabbed her arm.

The assassin jumped and shot him a look, as if she'd forgotten he was there.

"It's over," Thadred said. "You saved the kid, and you killed the son of a bitch."

Amira turned to Daindreth. "Are you alright?"

"Yes," Daindreth panted, only then realizing he was out of breath. "You?"

She nodded and looked to the boy, still hugging Daindreth's waist. "We should get out of here." Amira jerked her chin toward the village. "There are still more of them."

"Can you sense them?" Thadred asked.

"Some of them," Amira said. "It's...strange. They're leaving."

"That makes no sense," Thadred said. "Why leave?"

Amira looked pointedly to Rhisiart. "I'm guessing they got what they came for."

CHAPTER TWELVE

Amira

Amira flexed her hand, the blood of the first imperial drying on her fingers. She could still feel the hot *ka* she'd pulled from his body, coursing through her veins and sparking like lightning bugs.

She stared at the corpse of the second man, the one whose eyes she'd burned out of his skull. She wasn't quite sure how she had done it, but she'd known that she could.

She'd focused her anger on him, her rage and her frustration with a million different misfortunes and ill chances. Wrath like fire had burned through her and she'd focused it on him, pooled it in his eyes.

When she'd been doing it, she'd barely considered it, but now…did she regret it? She wasn't sure. The man had probably deserved it. And if other Kadra'han chose to bow and scrape to their curses, she couldn't help them.

It suddenly made sense to her why no other Kadra'han had managed to break their curse. Too many accepted that the commands were foolproof. That they couldn't be subverted. Amira knew better.

"Amira?" Daindreth came toward her, the small boy still clinging to his side. "Are you alright?"

Amira started, glancing his direction. "Fine." She looked back to the burned-out body. "I just…" She shook her head. "He didn't have to die, but he wouldn't—"

"Release the child!" a familiar voice shouted. Tapios rushed around the side of a barrow with half a dozen others on his heels, their bows nocked and aimed straight for Amira and Daindreth.

Amira's lip curled and she stepped closer to Daindreth. "Tapios! How good of you to join us."

"Avva!" cried the small boy at Daindreth's side. The child dove for Tapios and the ranger stooped to catch him.

"Rhis?" The ranger looked the boy over. "Are you alright? What happened? Did they hurt you?"

Amira clamped her jaw shut, angry enough to scream. Did the ranger really think she of all people would stoop to hurting children? Maybe he assumed she took after her grandmother.

Daindreth edged her behind him. It was subtle, but clear enough what it meant. "Ask your sister what happened," the archduke said. "She's back in her house."

"The bad men grabbed me," Rhis said. "And I told them I wanted Mama, but they wouldn't listen and then Dain and his friends came, and they were fighting and the bad man grabbed me and he started screaming and then Dain grabbed me." Rhis's small frame shook. "I want Mama. Avva, I want Mama."

"Shush," Tapios hugged the boy. "It's alright, Rhis. It's alright."

"Tapios," said one of the rangers, still keeping her bow trained on Amira. "Look," she pointed to the bodies.

The ranger took in the charred eyes of the Kadra'han at Amira's feet and paused. Even by the poor torchlight, Amira could see the horror on his face. "What happened?"

"I told him to release the boy," Amira said. "He didn't."

"She burned out his eyes, Avva," Rhis offered helpfully. "Can you burn out people's eyes?"

Tapios turned the boy away from the corpse, shielding him from the sight. "Don't look, Rhis."

"What did you do?" the female archer demanded.

"It's as the child said. The Kadra'han took the boy captive. I told him to release the child or else. He chose *else.*"

"Take them to the Elder Mother's hall." Tapios singled out a few of his rangers. "All three of them. Keep them there until I return."

"The Kadra'han are fleeing," Amira said. "There isn't much to find."

Daindreth reached behind and caught her hand in the dark. It was the bloody hand, the one stained with a dead man's blood, but he twisted his fingers through hers. "Amira," he said quietly. He didn't give a command, but he didn't have to.

She forced herself to be quiet.

"Surrender your weapons," the female ranger said.

"Seriously?" Thadred scoffed. "After all that?"

"Just take them to the Elder Mother," Tapios repeated.

"And quickly." He handed his nephew to another of the rangers. "Fannin, Hadrian, you go with Mylva. Take Rhis. The rest of you come with me."

Three of the rangers, including the woman who had originally told them to surrender their weapons, stayed behind while Tapios led the others into the darkness. It wasn't enough to properly guard the archduke and his two Kadra'han, but numbers were not a luxury the Istovari had.

"You heard him," the woman, presumably Mylva, said. "To the Elder Mother's hall with you."

Thadred muttered under his breath and began limping in that direction.

Amira stepped up beside Daindreth, still holding his hand. "Are you alright?" She could feel the heat of *ka* leaching out his skin, usually a sign of bruising or open wounds. "What happened?"

Daindreth shook his head. "If I told you, you'd kill them all."

Amira wasn't sure whether to laugh or be angry.

"Come on." Daindreth tugged on her hand lightly. He limped after Thadred, steadying himself with her hand. Whatever had happened to him, he'd been beaten within an inch of his life.

"Did Tapios do this to you?" Amira pressed.

"No," Daindreth answered.

"The Elder Mother told me you were being treated fairly. If they let this happen—"

Daindreth pulled her to him and swung his arm across her shoulders. "I'd rather not have to defend what happened," he said, leaning on her just a little. "But if you must know, it was one man who was the ringleader. The rest were just boys."

Amira's eyes narrowed in the dark as she considered it. "Who was it?"

"Amira…" Daindreth let off a slow sigh.

"Fine." Amira tossed a stray lock of hair back from her face. "Protect the bastard. But I will find out."

"I know," Daindreth agreed. "I just can't deal with it right now."

Amira held onto her bloody blade in her free hand, searching the darkness for *ka* or any other signs that they were about to be attacked. People scurried through the village. Women cried out and male voices shouted. Animals brayed and several barrows had caught fire, though the blazes seemed to be contained.

The three rangers escorted them into the main hall. The main fire had been re-lit and the hall had become an infirmary. People with bleeding heads, gashes in their arms, and stab wounds sat or laid on the floor and on the benches. Most of the wounds weren't too serious, but a few bodies already lay with their faces covered.

Amira and the two men were herded to one side of the room. Rhis clung to the neck of one of the rangers, looking around at the blood and human suffering with wide eyes.

It occurred to Amira that the child had probably never seen anyone from outside his village before today. Now strangers had come and turned the great hall into a charnel house.

In the light of the torches and central fire, Amira took a good look at Daindreth. He was covered in bruises, just as she'd thought. His bared upper body was scored with cuts and dark welts. Her face tightened as she studied the wounds.

She fingered a cut on the side of his head. Someone had begun cleaning it. She could smell the spices and there was salve on several of his wounds, but whoever had been tending him hadn't finished.

His forearms were covered in defensive wounds where a series of blows had rained down again and again. There were similar marks on his shoulders, back, and ribs.

When she got ahold of the man that did this…

But there would be a time for that later. Right now, Daindreth looked like he needed comfort, not retribution.

"You're hurting," Amira said. "You have to be." She slipped her hand up and cradled the back of his neck, one of the few places she didn't see any wounds.

"Less now," Daindreth said, closing his eyes and leaning toward her. "Sairydwen gave me something for it."

"Sairydwen was tending you?"

Daindreth nodded. "She's Rhis's mother."

From Daindreth's other side, Thadred looked to the boy at that. "Your mother is Sairydwen?"

121

The ranger—Amira thought it was Hadrian—had set down the boy to let him stand on the ground. Peering out from behind the man's legs, the child nodded. "I'm Rhisiart, son of Sairydwen."

Thadred looked at the boy a little differently. "Huh," he said. "Small world."

"You're my mama's friend?" the boy asked. He stepped closer to Thadred, curious.

The ranger watched him and Thadred but didn't move to stop the child.

Thadred chuckled a little at the boy's question. "I hope we're friends. If not, I went through a lot of trouble to still be enemies."

Rhis's small face darkened. "My mama came home hurt."

Thadred nodded. "Yeah. But she's better now?"

Rhis's large eyes took in Thadred. "You're Dain's friend."

"Yes," Thadred answered.

"Dain is Mama's friend. So, you're Mama's friend," Rhis said.

"Alright then." Thadred chuckled. "I'm your mama's friend."

"Good." Rhis smiled shyly.

For a child who had just been taken captive and was surrounded by pain and panic and suffering, he was being easily distracted.

Amira feathered her hands along Daindreth's side, studying one especially large bruise to one side of his back.

"Inspecting me?" Daindreth asked. It had probably been intended to sound playful, but with his pained voice, it was just strained.

"I'm trying to see if your ribs are broken." Amira could sense the *ka* pooling under his skin, usually a sure sign of injury.

"They are." Daindreth made a wheezing sound as she touched a darker bruise. "Or else they're bruised badly enough to feel like it."

"I'm sorry." Amira kissed his shoulder. His skin tasted of salt. "We'll get the rest of your wounds tended and get you somewhere you can rest."

Daindreth lowered his head. "There's others who need help more than me."

"Not like any of them would accept my help."

"Probably true," Daindreth admitted.

Thadred and the small boy were still talking. "Where's your papa? Is he with the rangers?"

Rhis shook his head. "My papa's gone." He said it neutrally, matter-of-factly.

"I'm sorry," Thadred said. "Do you miss him?"

Rhis nodded solemnly. "When I was little, he was here."

"What happened to him?" Thadred asked. Amira noticed that the knight's tone was surprisingly gentle, but maybe that was just how Thadred was with children.

"He got sick," Rhis answered. "I got sick, too, but I got better."

"Amira," a familiar voice called.

The assassin shifted to get between the archduke and the newcomer.

Cyne emerged from the chaos of the hall to stand in front of them. Her sleeves were rolled to her elbows and blood stained the front of her skirts.

Amira thought to herself that the woman just couldn't seem to keep the stuff off her.

Cyne looked to the three rangers watching over Amira, Thadred, and Daindreth. Something in her expression demanded an explanation.

"They killed two Kadra'han who tried to take Rhisiart," said Mylva, the female ranger.

"The bad men tried to take me," Rhis said, looking up to Cyne. "But Dain and his friends stopped them."

Cyne's gaze locked on Daindreth.

Amira bristled, something possessive and protective surging in her chest. She edged sideways, ensuring her mother had no direct lines of attack toward the archduke.

Daindreth shot Amira a glance, then looked back to Cyne.

"This is him?" Cyne clipped.

"I don't believe we've met, my lady," Daindreth said, his tone far too formal for a shirtless man beaten bloody and covered in bruises.

Cyne ignored him and looked to the rangers. "Why is he in this hall?"

"It's rude to ignore the crown archduke, Mother," Amira said, ice in her tone.

Cyne shot her a glance for just a second, then looked back to the rangers. "Well?"

"We had orders from Tapios," Mylva answered. "He's going to meet us here."

"And you thought it would be a good idea to bring *that* into a hall full of our weak and wounded?" Cyne's tone turned hard.

Daindreth only closed his eyes and leaned forward to rest his head on Amira's shoulder.

"Look at him," Mylva clipped. "Does it look like he'll be hurting anyone any time soon?"

Several voices raised around the room as men and women called the names of their children, mostly boys. Voices raised and panicked cries came from all directions as some parents ran outside to search the village or ran inside in the vain hopes their children had come here.

Their weeping and calling made the assassin go cold inside. All these parents calling for their lost little ones even though she knew it was pointless. If they really had been taken as she suspected, the Kadra'han would have gotten them far away by now. There was nothing she could do to help them and it wasn't like these Istovari would be likely to want her help anyway. She'd done what she could. She'd saved the one she could. Rhis was fine and now Daindreth was back with her even if he was hurt.

Amira carefully pulled Daindreth closer, trying to find places she could touch him that weren't injured. "I'm sorry," she whispered in his ear. "We'll get you somewhere you can rest soon."

"I don't think any of us are going to be resting for a while," Daindreth whispered back.

"Rhis!" Sairydwen burst in through the front door, shoving past the flow of people in and out of the hall. "Rhisiart!" Her hair flew in stray whisps around her face and her apron was crooked. Mud splattered the hem of her skirt and her injured hands hovered carefully in front of her.

"He's here!" Thadred shouted, raising one hand in the air and turning Rhis around with the other. "Go to your mother, kid."

Sairydwen spun around just as Thadred pointed her out for Rhis.

"Mama!" The child took off like a rabbit, leaping through the crowd and charging for her across the room.

Sairydwen dropped to her knees, and the child flung his arms around her neck as she embraced him. It was hard to see from this distance, but it looked like the Istovari sorceress was crying.

Around her, similar reunions took place as loved ones were found. But there were also cries of anguish as searches proved futile.

Sairydwen was still clutching her son when Tapios came marching in after her. A handful of rangers followed him as he made a straight line across the hall. Amira didn't notice where the Elder Mother sat bent over a young woman's injured arm until Tapios stopped in front of her.

"Elder Mother," the ranger said.

"Tapios. What's happening?" The Elder Mother's whole attention was on him.

Amira strained to hear and as she did, the whole hall hushed as others did the same. As she'd noticed before, Tapios was the closest thing this village had to a constable. Even if he was used to fighting things that came from the Cursewood, everyone looked to him in times of trouble.

"Elder Mother..." Tapios looked around the room. "They've left."

"What do you mean they've *left?*" demanded one older sorceress with a scowl that could frighten a badger.

The Elder Mother raised a hand for silence. "What do you mean, my son?" she asked gently.

"They've fallen back. We don't know where." Tapios shook his head. "They...they've taken a number of the children with them. We're not yet sure how many."

All around him, parents and grandparents wailed. Even though many had already known their children were missing, it seemed that hearing it from the ranger's lips only confirmed their worst fears.

125

"We've secured the village," he said, "but they could attack again at any time."

"You brought this on us!" shouted a woman with pale yellow hair and a pinched face. "You brought them here and the empire's wrath with them!" She pointed an accusing finger at Amira and Daindreth. "You saved your nephew, but our—"

A man with an arm that ended in a stump at the wrist stepped up beside the woman and spoke in her ear. She pushed away from him but said nothing else.

"Tapios could not have foreseen this," the Elder Mother said. She looked back to the ranger. "Find out who was taken. Make sure that the village is guarded."

"It would be easier to protect everyone if they remain gathered in the central buildings," Tapios said.

The Elder Mother replied to that and then the room was clamoring with voices again.

People argued with one another and over each other while others still desperately called for their children and others tossed accusations at Tapios, the Elder Mother, and some at Amira and the two men with her. No one seemed to know who to blame or what had happened.

There couldn't have been more than a hundred people in the hall, but it was a rancor of fear, anger, and grief.

Through it all, Daindreth kept his eyes closed, still leaning against her. She thought he might be dozing off until he spoke. "The Kadra'han won't hurt the children," he said. "They're too valuable. Both as hostages and as new recruits."

"Yes," Amira agreed.

He exhaled. "My mother knows me too well."

Amira kissed the top of his head. "She knows you won't abandon children to the Kadra'han any more than you would have abandoned Thadred."

"Yes," he said.

"You're too good, my love," Amira whispered.

Daindreth didn't answer.

The assassin looked to the Elder Mother. "I'm taking Daindreth to our room," she said. "I don't see what I can do out here."

There was a great deal she could do, actually, she just doubted that the rangers would allow her to do it. She'd need weapons for that and they still thought she was under the compulsions of Daindreth. They wouldn't trust her.

Then again, they might not trust her even if they knew she'd broken her curse.

"Go," the Elder Mother said dismissively, already turning to address someone else.

Amira wasted no time. "You heard her," she said to their ranger guards.

"Amira…" her mother began.

Amira shot the woman a glare that would have made Vesha proud. "Come along," she said to the rangers. Then, more gently to Daindreth, "Come, my love."

"Our?" Daindreth leaned on her as he stood from the bench. "You and Thadred are sharing a room?"

"Not really. You'll see."

With Amira on one side, Thadred on the other, and the rangers trailing behind, they made their way out of the hall and into the warren of tunnels and passages. It took Amira a moment or two to remember the correct route, but she found her way.

Inside, they eased Daindreth onto the bed Thadred had occupied earlier. Thadred shuffled to light the candles while Amira helped Daindreth to sit. No sooner had he sat down, than someone filled the doorway at their backs.

"You saved my son." It was Sairydwen, Rhisiart at her side.

Amira glanced up, bristling, but the woman wasn't looking at her, she was looking at Daindreth.

The archduke shook his head. "Amira and Thadred did most of the work."

Amira caught one of Daindreth's hands, then noticed his knuckles were bloody. Her man had a lot of explaining to do.

Sairydwen looked to Amira only briefly before her gaze fell on Thadred. "You did?"

Was Amira imagining it or did Sairydwen's face soften when she looked at Thadred?

Thadred shrugged, then grimaced. "It was nothing, really."

"They grabbed me from the bad man," Rhisiart said, all his previous fear and timidity gone now that he was safe with his mother.

Sairydwen looked back to Daindreth. "I looked you in the eye and said you should die. My people did...*this* to you."

By *this*, Amira wasn't sure if Sairydwen meant the beating Daindreth had taken or his curse. Either way, it was a fair statement.

Amira picked up Daindreth's hand and kissed his bloodied knuckles. "He's a good man."

Daindreth looked to her, meeting her eyes as she knelt in front of him.

"He's the best man there is," Amira said softly.

Sairydwen stepped into the room, Rhisiart close at her side. "Let me finish tending your wounds," she said.

Amira arched one eyebrow and looked to Sairydwen. "Finish?"

"My brother brought him to me after Bardaka beat him," Sairydwen said.

Amira knew that name. She turned ever so slowly back to Daindreth. "So. Bardaka?"

Daindreth squeezed her hand. "Don't, Amira."

The assassin didn't argue, but she made no promises, either.

"Don't you have others to tend?" Daindreth asked. "Many looked to be in a bad way out there."

Thadred eased down in the chair beside the narrow bed, groaning. Amira had forgotten that he'd had a few rough nights as well.

"The others are being tended," Sairydwen said. "And this is the least I can do."

"I don't know if you've noticed, but your hands aren't especially useful at the moment," Amira clipped.

Sairydwen was undeterred. "You can be my hands, then," she said. "Unless you know how to tend wounds as well as give them."

Amira choked back a retort. The truth was that aside from a few tricks she'd learned from getting injured herself, the things she knew were meant to tide one over until a real physician could be found. She knew next to nothing about actual medicine.

Swallowing her pride, she nodded. "Tell me how to help

him."

CHAPTER THIRTEEN

Daindreth

Daindreth woke with his fingers tangled in Amira's hair. He didn't remember how they'd gotten like that, but when he opened his eyes, she was still asleep, kneeling next to his narrow bed with her head pillowed on her arms.

Thadred slouched in a nearby chair, leaning against the wall with his feet propped up on an overturned wash bucket. A thick blanket covered the knight, his arms tight around his torso.

Light was just streaming through a slat in the ceiling sealed by a crooked piece of glass. Daindreth could hear the waking village around them. Low voices spoke from just outside their room, probably what had woken him.

Daindreth lay still, watching Amira. She looked different when she slept. Her face was softer, innocent.

A sharp pain cut through his side, and he was reminded that his rib was broken. His head throbbed—had his head been struck? His sides, back, and legs hurt along with his shoulders and most of his arms.

Wincing, he still watched Amira. The desire to kiss her awake and the desire to let her go on sleeping pulled him in conflicting directions. Also, it hurt to move and even the small effort needed to lean over and touch his lips to hers seemed monumental.

He curled his fingers tighter in the fiery strands of her hair. He loved her. Was intoxicated by her. He wanted to drown in her until nothing else existed and yet...

A stirring at the door caught his attention. Female voices conversed lowly, and a male voice responded. He couldn't quite recognize any of them, but he thought the male voice might be Tapios.

Amira shifted and glanced toward the door. She was on alert almost right away despite the dark circles under her eyes. She straightened, flexing one shoulder as if it were sore. Her hair was still caught in his hand, and he tugged it hard enough to get her attention.

"Good morning, love," Daindreth said.

Amira whirled her attention back to him. "Daindreth." Her expression softened instantly. "How are you feeling?"

"I've been better," he said. Daindreth twisted the ends of her hair tighter around his fingers. "But I've also been worse."

Amira leaned over and pecked his lips.

"Amira." Queen Cyne filled the doorway. Should he still think of her as the queen? She was the former queen. The deposed queen.

The assassin straightened and Daindreth let go of her hair. She didn't stand, but she faced her mother like a fox ready to fight an intruding badger.

The former queen looked over Daindreth and Amira with something like disgust in her face. She jerked her chin to her daughter. "The Mothers will see you in the hall in one hour."

Daindreth forced himself onto one elbow. "Who?"

"All of you." Cyne's lip curled just slightly as she glanced to Daindreth. If he hadn't been trained by a lifetime of courtly social cues, he might have missed it. "Be ready."

"What?" Thadred's eyes flew up. "Who?"

"We've been summoned," Amira said, not taking her attention off Cyne. "It seems that the Mothers are finally blessing us with an audience."

"An audience?" Daindreth asked. "Or that trial I was promised?"

"Be ready," was Cyne's unhelpful response.

Amira grumbled several curses under her breath as she clambered off the ground, a little stiffly. Spending a night kneeling on the floor was no easy thing, even for one as fit as Amira.

Daindreth groaned as he fought to get upright. Amira leaned over to help him.

Thadred cursed as he shifted his legs off the bucket. "Damn, that hurts."

Daindreth chuckled despite himself, looking to his cousin. Laughter devolved into wheezing coughing as pain shot through his ribs.

131

"What's so funny?" Thadred demanded.

"We are," Daindreth choked. "Look at us. We can barely get out of bed."

"I didn't even have a bed," Thadred grumbled. "You took the bed."

Amira shot Thadred a glare. "And I took the floor. What are you complaining about?"

"You're not crippled or wounded like we are," Thadred whined, unabashed. "Must be nice. Having four working limbs."

Amira made a rude gesture in his direction and hooked her arm through Daindreth's to help him stand.

"Do you think I could get a shirt?" Daindreth asked, leaning on Amira for balance. His ribs were bandaged, and his cuts had been cleaned by Sairydwen last night, but he was otherwise still naked from the waist up.

"I'll steal one for you if I have to," Amira said flatly.

Daindreth gripped the roots splayed through the ceiling. "Careful, love," he grimaced. "We might be about to beg for our lives."

That wasn't quite true. They were about to beg for his life. Thadred and Amira had told him as much as they knew last night about how the Istovari wanted to keep them because of their ability to use magic.

Amira squeezed his arm tighter, her fingers digging into his bicep. She swallowed. "I won't let them...I *can't*..."

Daindreth realized his mistake and patted her hand. "It will be alright," he promised her, even though he had no way to guarantee that. "It will."

Amira took a deep breath and kissed his right hand, now bandaged. "Come on."

"Archduke." Sairydwen appeared in the doorway. She looked even worse than she had the night before, almost as bad as when Daindreth and Amira had found her in the Cursewood. Dark half-moons sagged beneath her eyes and a good portion of her hair had escaped from her braid. Blood stained the front of her dress and it appeared that the wrappings on her own hands had bled through again. "They've sent me to help get you ready."

Daindreth glanced briefly to Amira. "Ready?"

Sairydwen nodded. "You need to be properly clothed, for one."

"Oh good," Daindreth said, hoping to alleviate some of the tension radiating from Amira. "At least my fiancée won't have to steal clothes now."

No one laughed.

◆◆◆

It was amazing how much longer simple tasks took when one was injured. Daindreth had never been in this much pain in his life. He'd thought the beating had been bad, but it was nothing compared to the day after. As he relieved himself, cleaned his face in a washbasin, and let the two women make him presentable, he began to consider asking Sairydwen for an analgesic.

He'd never known how much he moved his torso until he experienced stabbing pain every time he did.

"Is this what it's like for you?" he groaned to Thadred as the two of them sat outside on overturned buckets while Amira and Sairydwen helped them shave. "Always in pain?"

"No," Thadred said, for once not being dramatic. "It's not usually this bad."

Amira didn't speak, but she kissed the side of Daindreth's neck as he said that. If there was one enjoyable thing in all this, it was her attention.

Daindreth closed his eyes, focusing on the feel of the early morning sun on his skin and the clean motion of the razor along his jaw. Amira might not have had much practice shaving men's faces, but she knew knives well enough.

Dew coated the grass, and the chickens and geese of the village were just waking. The place seemed quieter than it should be and not many people were in sight.

"It's a pity," Amira said softly, almost in a whisper. "I kind of like you unshaven. Makes you look roguish." She ran one finger along his cheek. "Though smooth is nice, too."

Daindreth opened his eyes. "When we're married, I will shave as often or rarely as you like. Or never at all."

"Hmm." Amira finished and moved to the other side of his

133

face. "I will hold you to that."

It was easy to talk about when they were married. As if there wasn't the question of whether or not the Mothers would let Daindreth survive today. Then if there was indeed a way to remove the cythraul from Daindreth without killing him.

Amira and Thadred had repeated everything that Cyne had told them about the cythraul—including that they were no longer powerful enough to help. Daindreth wasn't sure he shared the Istovari's certainty, but he didn't share Amira's optimism, either.

When they had spoken, Amira had been sure there still had to be another way. Though none of them had said it out loud for fear of being overheard, if her curse could be broken, why not his?

All the same, Daindreth doubted it could be so simple. Things rarely were.

Sairydwen sent a young girl to fetch fresh clothes for Daindreth. Amira helped him put on a too-large shirt he suspected of belonging to Tapios.

By the time the hour had passed and the three of them were ushered toward the great hall by their ranger escorts, Daindreth could at least stand on his own. Some of the stiffness had been worked out of his muscles, even if the soreness remained. Amira held his hand, but he no longer needed to lean on her to keep from collapsing.

Thadred hobbled after them, making use of a rowan staff that Sairydwen had provided. The sorceress walked beside him, her expression grave.

"Will you be on your best behavior?" Daindreth asked Amira, only half joking.

Amira squeezed his hand tight between them. "I will try." She offered a smile that was more a grimace.

"It will be alright, my love. I will see to that," Daindreth said, not sure how he intended to keep that promise.

"I won't let them hurt you, Daindreth," she said quietly. "It's not right and even if it was...I can't lose you."

Daindreth smiled wanly at that. "Don't worry. You won't be getting rid of me that easily."

"Daindreth…"

They came into the main gathering hall. It looked far different than it had by the light of bonfires last night. The great doors at the end were open, letting in natural light. The remains of broken furniture were still being cleared away by a handful of younger children, but Daindreth noticed that none of them appeared any younger than ten. That might have been because the job was too difficult for younger children, but a sinking feeling in Daindreth's gut told him otherwise.

Near the large hearth at the dais near the front, nine thrones had been lined up. They were all the same middling size, and all appeared to have been grown from wood instead of carved. From what Daindreth could see, each one was made up of thousands of tiny branches and vines that had been grown and twisted together. All nine of the thrones were empty.

"Are we late?" Thadred gestured to the thrones.

"No," Sairydwen said. "We're on time."

"Then?" Thadred jerked his chin at the empty seats.

"You wait for the Mothers," Sairydwen said. "They don't wait for you."

Daindreth was tempted to be annoyed. Not only was he sore and standing was requiring unreasonable effort, but as archduke, he was usually the one people waited for. Then again, he supposed that was the point.

Thadred came to stand on Daindreth's other side, leaning on the staff Sairydwen had found for him.

"You look like an old man," Daindreth jibed.

"And your face looks like raw pork roast," Thadred clipped back.

"You're right. We both look awful. I think Amira's the only one who looks good this morning."

Amira seemed surprised at first, but that did earn him a small smile.

Thadred scoffed. "She always looks good. Especially to you."

"She does," Daindreth agreed.

Amira watched them both. Despite their circumstances, mischief glinted in her eyes. "It's not my fault you lost a fight with a pony, Thadred."

Thadred wagged a finger at her. "It's pronounced *kelpie*. And need I remind you that I won that fight?"

They were joking, trying to take some of the edge off before the Mothers came to interrogate them. It was laughing in the dark, the way he and Thadred had done for years when things had seemed hopeless.

Stirring at the back of the hall caught their attention. Several older women filed in, the youngest being perhaps in her forties with a tight press of braids around her head. The oldest was the Elder Mother who still managed to look regal as she ascended the single step up to the dais.

The sorceresses took their places, most of them not bothering to look at Daindreth and his companions.

Sairydwen stepped to the side, settling herself on a nearby bench. The rangers also stepped back, but they remained within easy reach.

The Elder Mother took her place in the middle throne. Cyne took the one to her left.

"I thought you two weren't objective enough to judge him," Amira said, looking to her mother and grandmother.

"Amira." Daindreth squeezed her hand in warning.

"You will speak when spoken to, princess," Cyne said.

Amira inhaled a sharp breath and Daindreth feared she might reply, but she didn't.

Thadred swept a bow, or as close to one as he could manage. "My ladies. Good morning."

That greeting had also probably been out of line, but the Mothers let it pass. Several of them nodded to the knight in turn.

From what Amira and Thadred had said, Thadred had tamed a kelpie—though none of them was quite sure what that meant—and the Istovari were somewhat in awe of him. There was also the matter that Thadred apparently had magic. Daindreth still didn't fully understand the ramifications of that, but it seemed for once his cousin was held in higher esteem than he.

"Archduke Daindreth Fanduillion," the Elder Mother began. "We finally meet properly."

Daindreth inclined his head. "Forgive me if I don't bow," he said, hoping he sounded sincere. "My broken ribs make it hard to stoop at the moment." It was true enough. He also didn't want to give them the illusion that he would grovel.

If the Istovari had said they could help him, things would have been different. But these women had already given up. If they were going to be persuaded to share the secrets of the cythraul—so that perhaps he and Amira could find another way—then he needed to be strong.

"When we heard of your plans to visit Hylendale to fetch the girl Fonra as your bride, we sent word to our friends there," the Elder Mother said. "We made sure that the king was advised to take swift action. We can see that he did, but there were…complications." The Elder Mother looked to Amira.

The assassin stood close beside Daindreth. She wasn't quite glaring, but she watched the other woman like a cat ready to spring its claws.

"You survived, and we thought perhaps you would remove Fonra from the line of succession. Perhaps we would one day have an Istovari on the Hylendale throne."

Daindreth grimaced. What they meant was they'd hoped his cythraul would kill the other girl somehow and leave Amira as the only surviving heir.

"But then you took Amira." The Elder Mother still did not look away from her granddaughter. "Naturally, we assumed the worst. We gave her up for lost then."

"Imagine our surprise when Sairydwen spotted you in Lashera," said another of the mothers, a woman with brown feathers pinned in her hair. "Without your entourage, traveling in secrets as best we could tell."

Daindreth wasn't sure what they wanted him to say, so he asked what he wanted to. "Is Cromwell loyal to you?"

The Elder Mother's mouth tightened. "Cromwell is loyal to Cromwell."

Daindreth sensed he touched on a wound there.

"That's fair enough," Amira conceded.

"You took our daughter," the Elder Mother went on, still addressing Daindreth. "You made her your Kadra'han. Claimed her as your woman."

Daindreth ground his teeth together, a lifetime of courtly

etiquette and discipline coming in useful. "I've done no dishonor to your granddaughter." Though, he'd often wondered if Caa Iss hadn't been an issue, perhaps he might have.

Even with the fear of Caa Iss that had plagued him for most of his life, it had been hard not to give in. Amira had made it clear that she was willing. They loved each other. He wanted her and she wanted him.

The Elder Mother didn't argue that point. The others seemed skeptical.

"Am I on trial?" Daindreth asked, raising his chin so that it was as high as it could go without forcing his head back, a pose he'd learned as a child. "If so, for what crime?"

"You are not on trial," the Elder Mother said, looking to her counterparts.

Amira looked to her mother and then her grandmother. "You said you wouldn't sit in judgment of him."

"This is not a judgment," the Elder Mother said. "And that was yesterday."

Daindreth searched the women in front of him, trying to read them, trying to pick up on the subtle cues that courtiers sometimes gave. They were agitated. They looked tired. Most of them had probably not slept at all last night.

"The Kadra'han have taken twenty-six of our children," the Elder Mother said, her voice wavering just enough the archduke noticed.

Daindreth looked to Amira who met his gaze with wide eyes.

Had the Kadra'han made a demand? Did they want Daindreth and Amira in exchange for the children?

"They sent a messenger with their terms of ransom." The Elder Mother motioned to a scroll on one of the nearby tables, left as if it had been thrown aside in anger. "They want you, of course."

"But we are not fools," growled another of the women, one with a scar splitting her mouth that turned her face into a perpetual scowl. "They will take our children whether we hand you over or not."

Daindreth had to agree with that.

"We are offering you a deal, archduke," the Elder Mother

said. "If you can bring them back, we will spare your life."

Daindreth stayed perfectly still, letting a heartbeat pass before he responded. He wanted no surprise to show on his face.

"Spare his life?" Amira demanded. "He's committed no crimes!"

"Amira." Daindreth tugged her back. "My lady is right," he said. "I am hardly in physical condition to rescue your children. Furthermore, my life means little to me if I have to share it with a cythraul."

Amira muttered something angry at that, but Daindreth ignored her.

"As we have told the princess, we have no way of reversing that," the Elder Mother said.

"I am archduke of Erymaya," Daindreth said. "When I reclaim my throne, I will have limitless resources." At least, that was mostly true. "Whatever needs to be done to change your situation, I can make happen."

The Elder Mother inhaled a long breath.

The woman with the brown feathers shook her head. "You cannot undo our curse. The curse of this forest."

Daindreth charged on. "Then here is what I want from you."

The nine women before him visibly stiffened.

Daindreth focused on the Elder Mother, not interested in what the others had to say. He understood that they all needed to agree, but this woman was their leader, Amira's grandmother. She'd been the one to slit Amira's arms open and he suspected she still felt guilt over it—rightly so. She was the one he stood the best chance with.

"We get your children back," Daindreth said.

Thadred coughed. "Dain—"

"We don't even know where they are," Amira hissed in his ear. "They could be in Mynadra for all we know."

"Trust me," Daindreth said, not taking his attention off the Elder Mother. "We return all twenty-six of them alive."

Amira rankled at his side.

Daindreth knew he was taking risks. It was a huge promise to make for even one, but to assume that all twenty-six would be alive and able to be rescued…he knew he was gambling.

But these children had nothing left to lose and neither did

139

he.

"In return, you will truthfully tell me the answers to everything and anything I ask about the cythraul and this curse for so long as it ails me," Daindreth said.

The Elder Mother breathed unsteadily out her nose.

"That will be your entire life," the scarred woman said.

"Then you will answer my questions for my entire life," Daindreth replied, fighting to keep the bitterness from his words. "Next, my friends and I walk free from this place."

There didn't seem to be any opposition to that.

"Finally, you give Amira your blessing to marry me," Daindreth said.

Amira was quiet at his back, which told him she was surprised.

At his words, the Elder Mother stiffened. Cyne's nostrils flared and several of the other women shifted on their wooden thrones.

"No," Cyne said, her hands clenching on the armrests of her seat.

"Absolutely not," agreed another of the women, one who had not spoken thus far.

Amira moved closer to Daindreth and pressed against his shoulder. He couldn't see her expression, but he guessed that she was glaring, taunting them, daring them to try and stop her.

He spoke before she could. "King Hyle signed the marriage contract as did the empress and both of us," Daindreth argued. "She comes to me of her own free will. Our betrothal is as legitimate as any."

"Amira will not go to you," said Cyne.

Amira inhaled a sharp breath and Daindreth spoke quickly before his fiancée could tear into her mother and make things worse.

"Those are my terms," he said, doing his best to sound like a king on equal footing, not a captive archduke. "If you want me and my Kadra'han to return your children, I want your help in ridding myself of this cythraul, I want our freedom, and I want Amira."

"You think you can just demand my only child that easily?"

Cyne leaned forward, looking ready to leap to her feet in rage.

"I've seen her scars," Daindreth said. "You were willing to sacrifice her once before. I don't see how it's so different to sacrifice her again."

Amira went stiff at Daindreth's side. She didn't move. She barely breathed.

Daindreth worried for a moment he'd upset her, but she didn't make so much as a sound.

Cyne bolted to her feet. "I should have you—"

"Cyne!" the Elder Mother cut her off. "Peace."

Cyne's mouth snapped shut, but she whirled a glare on the Elder Mother. "You would let him have her?" The former queen's tone was calm again, almost eerily so. "After everything?"

The Elder Mother looked back to Daindreth and Amira. "Archduke, command Amira to speak truthfully."

Daindreth tensed. He didn't like the sound of that. Even if Amira wasn't bound by the oaths of obedience, he hated the idea of even trying to force her into anything.

"I need to ask her something," the Elder Mother said. "And I need to make sure you haven't commanded her on what to say."

That seemed fair enough, but Daindreth still didn't like it. He looked to Amira.

Her eyes were wide, and her anger seemed forgotten, but she nodded. If they asked a question she'd rather not answer, Amira was experienced enough with subterfuge to give a misleading answer.

"Amira, answer your grandmother truthfully in this meeting." Daindreth added the caveat to make it believable. If she'd still been bound to obey him, he would have never ordered her to outright always tell her grandmother the truth.

Amira looked to the Elder Mother. "Yes?"

"Do you choose to be with this man?" the Elder Mother asked, motioning to Daindreth.

"Yes," Amira said without hesitation.

"You were under no compulsions when we spoke of him two days ago? Those were your true feelings?" the Elder Mother pressed.

Amira took a deep breath and let it slowly out her nose before continuing. "I want to marry him. I want to bear his heirs. He hasn't forced me into anything. I love him and I won't leave him."

The Elder Mother looked to Cyne. "It's decided, then."

Cyne turned and stormed out of the hall. She left the way she had entered, refusing to look at her daughter, her mother, or anyone else.

The Elder Mother glanced up to watch her go, then returned her attention to Amira.

No one else acknowledged Cyne's departure. Several glanced after her, but none spoke.

"Bring back our children, archduke. Then you can have Amira."

Daindreth tried not to show anything. "If I'm going after the Kadra'han, she's coming with me."

The Elder Mother nodded, not looking away from Daindreth. "I would expect nothing less."

CHAPTER FOURTEEN

Thadred

"Y ou know it's a trap, right?" Thadred said as he tightened his horse's girth.

"Yes," Dain answered, not looking up from his own horse's bridle. "But what choice do we have?"

Amira looked to Thadred, grimacing. "The Kadra'han are expecting us. Vesha, too."

"I know," Dain exhaled, patting the neck of his sorrel mare.

Amira and Dain's horses had been found by the rangers not long after they'd found Thadred. The rangers had conveniently failed to mention it until this morning, but they were overlooking that for now.

At least Thadred's cane sword had been in their horses' things. Thadred was grateful to have that again. Even if he had been managing without it.

Thadred had to saddle a sturdy mountain pony like the rest of the group they were taking with them. The small animal rolled a testy eye in his direction, as if daring him to try something.

Tapios and some twenty or so rangers were at work saddling horses around them. Thadred suspected that most of these people hadn't been outside the Cursewood since its formation. All the same, they saddled their horses with expert efficiency, taking only what they needed to survive in the forest.

Amira had asked Tapios how they kept several dozen horses fed on top of hundreds of sheep. Tapios had said that the animals grazed in the Cursewood most days. That provided more questions than answers, but Thadred had bigger things to worry about right now. They all did.

The Istovari had mastered the Cursewood, learning how to survive in it and even subsist from it. They'd adapted to conditions that would have killed most other people, but Thadred had his doubts these people could stand up to the imperial Kadra'han in full force. He was sure they were doomed, actually.

Thadred had spoken to Amira and Dain for a good two

hours last night solely about how they could help the Istovari rangers survive a full-on encounter with the imperial Kadra'han. So far, they hadn't thought of anything particularly brilliant.

Most their plans boiled down to keeping the rangers out of a direct confrontation. No one liked their chances.

"Is that everyone?" Amira called to Tapios as another pair of cloaked archers arrived, leading their saddled ponies.

"Almost everyone." Tapios jerked his chin toward the barn entrance.

Iasu came limping with hands tied in front of him and a ranger on either side. His thigh and calf bulged with bandages beneath the leg of his trousers. He was pale and seemed thinner than he had been a few days ago.

Amira ducked under her mare's neck and marched up to him. "Brother."

"Little sister."

Thadred almost laughed. Amira was around average height for a woman and Iasu was a full head shorter than her.

Iasu cocked his head, eyes bright even as his face was drawn and pinched with pain. "I hear we're taking a short journey."

"Correct." Amira grabbed his hands, studying the ropes.

As she'd instructed, the rangers had left his hands tied in front, where it would be easier to lash them to the pommel of his horse's saddle. She inspected the knots carefully, making sure they were secure.

Good. Thadred didn't see the rangers as being particularly experienced in keeping prisoners.

Amira dropped his bound hands and stepped back.

"Do you think I'm going to be of any use to you?" Iasu said, condescension in his tone. "I couldn't tell you anything of importance, even if I wanted to."

Thadred caught his meaning. He'd been ordered to secrecy by Vesha, like almost all the Kadra'han were.

They could torture and interrogate him for eternity, and he still wouldn't be able to divulge his liege's secrets. It was one of the many reasons Kadra'han were so prized as servants.

"Bold to assume we need your cooperation in order to use you," Amira smiled back.

Iasu didn't speak, but there was a flicker of doubt in his eyes.

"Put him on that pony over there," Amira said to the rangers, pointing to a small dun horse. "He'll ride between the two of you."

The two rangers obeyed, leading Iasu over to a pony near Thadred's.

Iasu's attention fell on Thadred. Recognition flickered across his face and his lip curled. "Brother."

Thadred smirked back.

"Sorry about the rest of the family abandoning you," Thadred said, not sure if he meant it or not. "Dozens of Kadra'han were crawling over this settlement, taking children left and right, and yet they left you."

Iasu's smirk remained firmly in place, frozen as tight as the face plate of a knight's helmet.

"They left you for dead, Iasu," Thadred said. He looked down to the other man's bandaged leg. "If I were you, I might start thinking of ways to help the people who were keeping me alive."

"You know that's not how it works."

Thadred shrugged. "Every curse can be broken," he said, even though he was getting tired of hearing the words himself.

Amira had done it, though it was a unique situation. She and Thadred had discussed it and she still believed beyond a shadow of a doubt that others could find a way to do the same. Thadred just wasn't sure how.

Not that they could tell Iasu any of that, of course. It still suited them to let the Istovari think Amira was bound. They also weren't sure if even Vesha and Darrigan knew she'd broken her curse.

"Thadred."

Thadred turned at the sound of Sair's voice.

She was wearing a light blue dress today, one that gave her a splash of color and made her eyes look brighter. Sair stood with her hands hovering in front of her, their bandages clean and fresh.

"How are your hands?" Thadred asked, reaching under his pony for the saddle girth. That motion tugged at sore muscles and made his aching back throb.

145

Behind him, he glimpsed Amira helping Dain do much the same.

"They're fine," Sair said.

"Good," Thadred nodded, buckling the pony's girth, and moving to the saddle bags. A fluttering feeling shivered in his chest. What was wrong with him? He kept his attention on his work, not looking up. "Rhis?"

"He's fine," Sair said. "He's worried about his friends, but otherwise fine."

Thadred nodded. "Good." He cleared his throat as he finished with the saddle, patting the pony's neck.

The little horse glared at him as if to say, *Don't think I'll be won over that easily.*

Not able to put it off any longer, Thadred made eye contact with her.

Sair stood watching him, but he couldn't read her expression. It wasn't the hard way that Vesha or the Istovari Mothers looked at him. Nor did she wear the coy smirk of a courtier. There was an...openness and honesty to her expression. Maybe even vulnerability. Fear.

Was she afraid? He wanted to tell her everything would be alright, that he would find a way to get the children back and keep her and her family safe.

Sair swallowed and Thadred realized he had been staring without speaking. Thankfully, she broke the silence. "Do you think you will be able to find them? The children?"

"Only one way to find out," Thadred said. "Tapios insists he and the rangers can track through the Cursewood." Tapios had also given several qualifying statements to that, leaving Thadred confused.

What the knight gathered was that Tapios and the others could make educated guesses but weren't entirely *sure* about the answer.

Sairydwen grimaced. "It's not quite that simple, but if intent is there, they should be able to find the children."

Thadred barked a laugh. "Nothing is straightforward in this place, is it?"

Sair didn't smile back. Her voice dropped to a whisper, soft so those nearby wouldn't hear. "You believe you can rescue them?"

Thadred shrugged. "We have to try, don't we?"

Sair exhaled, looking over the group of rangers before looking back to Thadred. "I attended the births of at least half those children," she said softly. "They are precious to me. To all of us."

Thadred couldn't have said he understood. He didn't have children or any close friends who had them. Children were often employed as hall boys, scullery maids, and for other menial work in the imperial household, but that was different.

Still, he nodded. "We're going to do our best, you know," he said. He offered a resigned grin. "The Mothers are going to kill us if we don't."

Sair glanced to where Amira and Dain stood, finishing the final work of saddling up the archduke's horse. "No," she said softly. "Not all of you."

Thadred didn't want to think that through. If the Istovari knew what was good for them, they wouldn't touch Dain while Amira was alive. If they hurt him, the knight had no doubt she'd kill those responsible in gruesome and creative ways.

If it came to that, who knew? Thadred might even help her.

"Is Rhis up to the task of keeping you safe while I'm gone?" Thadred asked.

Sair frowned. "What?"

"Well, with Tapios coming with us, someone has to keep you out of trouble."

Sair inhaled, looking to where her brother was speaking with several of his rangers. "The boundaries of the Haven have been sealed. Nothing will be getting in that we don't want in."

"That's some comfort." Thadred checked the length of his stirrups, letting them down a few notches so his legs wouldn't be scrunched up when he got on the horse.

"Be careful." Sair's words were soft, barely audible. She shifted and for a moment, he thought she would take a step toward him, but she stayed where she was.

Thadred arched one eyebrow. "You almost sound worried."

Sair looked down to her bandaged hands, shifting them awkwardly.

"You *are* worried." Thadred stifled a laugh. It was strange to have a woman worried for him. Especially one as respectable and wise as Sair. "Never fear, my lady. I know men are in short supply for your people these days, but this one has no intention of dying."

"Good." Sair nodded curtly. "I'm grateful," she added, her voice low. "You're a good man, Thadred Myrani."

"Careful." Thadred winked at her. "You don't know me *that* well." Had he just winked at a sorceress? He hadn't wanted to give her the wrong idea. He didn't think of her like that, did he? She was an Istovari, a respected leader in her community and he was…well. He was Thadred Myrani.

Sair cleared her throat and this time she did take a step toward him, then another, closing the distance between them. "Come back safe."

"I will," Thadred said, his voice full of a confidence he didn't feel. "But only if you stay safe. Agreed?"

A smile quirked at Sair's lips. "Agreed." Next thing Thadred knew, she wrapped her arms around him.

Thadred took a few heartbeats to realize what was happening before he returned her embrace, squeezing her back. She felt nice, pressed up against him. She was soft and warm and…gentle. He'd always been welcomed in the arms of his women, but touching Sair was different. Touching her felt like quiet, like the crackle of a hearth on a winter's night.

"Does this mean—?"

Sair pulled away before he could finish his question. "Farewell, Thadred. Until we meet again."

Thadred opened his mouth, then closed it again. Deciding he would never understand women and trying to ignore the feeling of missing her warmth, he settled on, "Farewell."

Sair nodded curtly and spun away from him. She headed straight for her brother, not looking back.

Thadred watched her go, a little bemused. He wasn't sure what to make of that exchange, but that was true of most his interactions with the Istovari.

If she were a palace debutante, he might think she liked him. But she was a widowed sorceress with a son to consider, and she

148

had been his enemy a few days ago. He'd hated her guts then, or at least had thought he did.

Their group mounted up not long after. Amira and Daindreth rode side by side with Thadred directly behind them. A ranger rode to his left, one of the young women. Under normal circumstances, he wouldn't have minded that, but this particular one kept scowling at Dain while the archduke's back was turned.

She was probably thinking how she'd like to put an arrow through his imperial highness's spine. Thadred didn't like that.

Their horses filed out of the barn and through the village in a dark grey and green parade under an overcast sky. It wasn't raining yet, but Thadred guessed that could start at any moment.

The Cursewood loomed ahead of them like a great black beast. The horses snorted as they entered, uneasy.

The green grass of the Haven grew right up to the shadows cast by the infected trees. There it stopped as if it had struck a wall, blocked by the ring of the curse's power.

Amira shuddered as their horses stepped over the boundary.

"Are you alright?" Dain asked.

"Fine," Amira answered.

"You look green," he said.

"I feel green." She shook her head. "It's the *ka* in this place. Like I told you, it's rotten."

Dain watched her for a few moments but said nothing more.

Thadred couldn't rightly tell the difference. Even though he had channeled *ka* and was apparently a sorcerer, the Cursewood only felt more humid to him. The air was heavy, like the breeze on a hot day by the sea.

Their column wended through the forest with Tapioo in the lead. He stopped every so often to check their surroundings, though Thadred wasn't quite sure what good that would do. Didn't the Cursewood shift and evolve, sometimes minute by minute?

Several other rangers spread out around them. A few dismounted to inspect the ground as their group moved onward, searching for tracks.

"Are we sure they came this way?" Thadred called, reining in his stocky pony beside Daindreth.

"We lost their trail up here," Tapios shouted back. "Last night, it was dark."

Thadred looked to Amira. "Could they be using portalstones the way Sair did back in Lashera?"

Amira shook her head. "I asked my mother about it. She said they only existed in the cities. There are no reliable rock veins here in the Cursewood. It's constantly shifting by its nature."

Thadred grunted his annoyance. "Of course it is."

One of the rangers shouted and came jogging up to Tapios' horse.

Thadred nodded, trying not to sound impressed. "Sounds like they've found the trail."

Sure enough, the ranger handed something to Tapios before returning to his own horse and remounting.

The leader nodded his approval and held it up for the rest of the group to see—a torn scrap of light blue cloth. "From one of the children," Tapios said. "They found it over there with some skid marks. One of them tried to flee."

"This way," one of the rangers called from up ahead. "More tracks."

They plunged deeper into the Cursewood, the rangers spreading out around them to track through the trees.

The tracks ended not long after.

Thadred and Amira indulged in a round of curses, but none of the rangers seemed surprised. They said this was the way the Cursewood worked and that they should pick up the trail again soon.

It began to rain not long after, but no one suggested they stop. Everyone pulled their cloaks up and kept on riding. Thadred's hip began to ache, but it was nothing he wasn't used to. Changes in the weather bothered him all the time.

They continued, though it was hard to know for how long. There was no sun to judge the time thanks to the thick overhang of branches and brambles.

There was no new sign of tracks from the Kadra'han or their gaggle of child prisoners. The hours wore on and Thadred began to wonder if the Istovari actually knew what they were doing.

"We've never had to track someone *from* the Haven before,"

Tapios admitted to them as they stopped for a brief rest.

"No?" Amira sipped on a water flask before passing it to Dain.

"No," Tapios confirmed. "None of our enemies have ever made it inside. And no one from inside has ever tried to leave." He exhaled, looking up to the dark canopy overhead. The low murmur of the rain could be heard striking the black branches above. "These storms haven't let up for weeks."

Dain, Amira, and Thadred looked to each other at that. They'd been distracted, but as soon as Tapios mentioned it, Thadred remembered a conversation the three of them had on the road.

Vesha had made a deal with the cythraul for the empire's prosperity. That had included fair weather, good harvests, and an end to natural disasters. In exchange, Vesha was supposed to provide the cythraul with a host for Caa Iss to one day rule the empire.

When Amira had freed Dain from the palace and made it impossible for Vesha to keep her end of the bargain, the deal—according to Caa Iss—had been broken. Thadred hadn't given much thought to it since Dain had shared that with him and Amira. The demon said a lot of things, after all. What was one more speculation and supposition among thousands?

A look passed between Thadred's cousin and the assassin, something beyond words. Amira gave a slight shake of her head.

Thadred sighed. Amira and Dain became closer every day, but that often left him feeling like the outsider. Amira was first in Dain's confidence more and more. He went to her with problems, fears, and strategy questions first. It was annoying.

The horses shifted. Several of them kicked at the trees where they were tied. One of them whinnied uncomfortably.

Thadred looked to Tapios as the ranger went tense along with all the others. He noticed the warriors reaching for their bows and arrows, glancing around the shadowy forest.

"Is everything alright?" Amira asked, not moving anything but her eyes as she searched the Cursewood around them.

"I don't know," Tapios answered. "Probably, but…"

"Argh!" one of the rangers cried.

Tapios spun around with his bow drawn, string pulled back

to his ear.

"Kelpie!" another man shouted.

Thadred straightened. "Kelpie?"

Dain was already on his feet and held out a hand to Thadred. The knight took it, limping toward the rangers as soon as he was upright, straining to see.

Sure enough, there stood a little black horse at the edge of their clearing. The stallion surveyed them carefully. He dropped his head, ears forward, watching their group.

"Is it your kelpie?" Tapios asked, keeping his bow trained on the animal as the other rangers did the same.

The horses tied in a picket line whickered uneasily.

"Lleuad?" Thadred took a step closer, a little to the side so that he wouldn't be in the line of arrows if the rangers let loose. "Hey, boy. Is that you?"

The stallion clopped out of the tree line toward Thadred. As he came closer, the knight recognized those huge white eyes, the ones where he'd seen the kelpie's whole life as a flare of sensations, colors, tastes, and smells.

Thadred held out a hand to the kelpie, knuckles first like he would with a dog. The kelpie lipped at his hand, tail swishing. The black horse nickered and his ears flicked.

Thadred patted his neck, grinning back at Tapios, Dain, and the others. "Dain. Amira. Meet Lleuad, my kelpie friend."

Amira hung back, one hand on the dagger at her hip. "It's true." She looked to Tapios. "You weren't exaggerating."

Tapios lowered his bow. "No."

Dain stared, brows raised. "You really did it." He was clearly impressed, which Thadred liked. "How?"

Thadred shrugged as the kelpie stood beside him as mannerly as any imperial carriage horse. "Not sure, but I did."

Amira looked to Thadred. "The kelpie can track things through the forest."

Thadred considered that for a moment. Come to think of it, Lleuad had shown several times that he could track quite well in the Cursewood. "Why yes. Yes, he can." He looked to Lleuad. The stallion seemed content to just let Thadred scratch his neck and shoulder. It was hard to believe this little animal had attacked and killed two mules not that long ago.

"He's a creature of the Cursewood," Tapios said, though no one had asked. "Likely foaled and raised here. He isn't affected by it the same way we are."

The horse probably knew where the Kadra'han had taken the children, but how was Thadred supposed to ask him to show them? It wasn't like he had any kind of training.

Thadred petted Lleuad's glossy neck, thinking. The stallion's coat was thicker than a regular horse's, but sleek. It was like petting an otter. "Dain, come help me up."

"What?" Tapios interrupted.

"I have an idea," Thadred said. "Dain, come give me a leg up."

Dain hesitated but came over to Thadred and the kelpie.

"He won't hurt you," Thadred said. "Will you, boy?"

Lleuad, naturally, did not answer, but the kelpie bobbed his head up and down. Thadred could have sworn it was a nod.

Dain came up beside Thadred, cautiously giving the kelpie space.

"Daindreth…" Amira wheezed, like she was choking on a whole litany of protests. "Be careful."

"That thing is dangerous," Tapios said quietly. "Remember that."

The rest of the Istovari rangers looked on with mute horror as Thadred knotted one hand in the kelpie's mane and placed another on his back.

"You can't be serious," Amira said. "You don't want a saddle?"

"Lleuad's never worn a saddle." Thadred motioned to Dain. "Leg up?"

Dain knelt, webbing his fingers together so that his hands made a step. Thadred put one foot on the loop of Dain's hands and jumped. Dain shoved up and Thadred used the momentum to swing one leg over Lleuad's back.

The stallion snorted and stomped.

Tapios and the rangers jumped, raising their bows and arrows again while the kelpie shifted.

"Easy," Thadred said, not sure if he was talking to the kelpie or the rangers. He patted Lleuad's neck. "The trail heads that way, right?" Thadred pointed off into the trees.

"Yes," Tapios confirmed.

"Excellent." Thadred took a deep breath. Lleuad wasn't trained to ride. He wouldn't know any of the signals the way a regular horse would. Thadred thought about it for a moment before shifting his weight forward. "That way," he said, feeling just a little like an idiot. "That way, boy."

Lleuad took one step forward, then another. He plodded in the direction of the tracks, snorting.

Thadred grinned triumphantly as the kelpie marched past the gaping Istovari. They stared as if he had just manifested in a flash of lightning, like he was a legend among them.

The kelpie continued straight past the other humans, their small temporary camp, past the picketed horses, and into the forest. Thadred wasn't entirely sure this was the correct direction, but he had a good feeling.

A very good feeling.

Thadred turned, casting a playful look over his shoulder. "Are you coming?"

Dain was the first to move, heading straight for his sorrel mare. "What are you doing, Thadred? What's your plan?"

"I don't know yet," Thadred admitted, ducking as Lleuad clopped under a low branch. "I'll figure it out along the way."

CHAPTER FIFTEEN

Amira

For someone who didn't know what he was doing—with magic, the Cursewood, or the kelpie—even Amira had to admit Thadred was doing well.

They continued for most of the day with Thadred urging the kelpie along the tracks of the Kadra'han. Sometimes they lost the trail and the rangers had to help them find it again, but after the first few hours, the kelpie seemed to figure out what Thadred wanted.

Tapios explained that kelpies were smarter than regular horses, but Amira already believed it after being chased by one through the forest. Thadred rode ahead of them without reins or a bridle. He seemed fine with the situation, but Amira and Daindreth discussed several times what they'd do if the animal suddenly decided to buck Thadred and attack.

"The kelpie won't harm him," Tapios said confidently. "He's tamed it." The ranger rode beside her and Daindreth, his small brown horse clopping over the obsidian blackbriar roots on the ground. None of the animals could move quickly through the treacherous terrain. Their hooves slid and lost their balance whenever they came in contact with the hardened stones and roots.

Amira looked to Tapios. "You know a lot about kelpies?"

"More than most lowlanders, I imagine," he answered.

Amira's eyes narrowed. "Tamed a lot of them, have you?"

"Obviously not." Tapios shot her a glare, matching the sardonicism in her tone. "But our people have tamed them before."

"And?" Amira pressed when Tapios didn't elaborate.

"Tamed kelpies would do anything for their masters," he said. "They're the most loyal and trustworthy steeds one could ask for."

"When's the last time one was tamed?" Amira asked.

Tapios took a while to respond. He looked in the opposite direction of her, studying the massive oak trees covered in blackbriars around them. "I'm not sure. Generations, at least."

"I see." Amira didn't see. It made no more sense than anything else about this place, but she doubted Tapios understood, either.

Amira looked to Daindreth. The archduke had been silent for some time now, not speaking for the better part of an hour. "Are you alright?"

Daindreth offered her a look that was more a grimace than a smile. "Fine, love."

Amira bit her lip. "You're not fine at all."

Daindreth shook his head. He kept his entire body from the neck down rigid as he did. "I can last until our next rest."

Amira reached over and touched his forehead. Her hand came away clammy with sweat. "Oh, darling…"

"Nothing we can do about it," Daindreth said, his voice almost a rasp. "It's not a fever, just…a little soreness."

Amira's first impulse was to call him a liar, but she didn't want to pick a fight with him right now. He was already tired and in pain, and he was right that there was nothing they could do about it now.

They rode for most of the day. Every so often, Tapios would send scouts to circle around them and make sure that they were still on the trail of the Kadra'han. They were.

Whatever else he might be, Thadred's new pet was tracking their quarry and doing an excellent job.

Finally, it became too dark to see clearly. The white eyes of the kelpie shimmered faintly under the moonlight, but the rest of them needed to stop.

Tapios called a halt after Amira leaned over and—forcing herself to be polite—asked for one. She didn't especially like Tapios at this point and courtesy chafed at her. Still. If she fought with Tapios, Daindreth would have to be the one to keep the peace and she didn't want him to have to deal with that right now.

Tapios and the rangers built a fire while Amira helped Daindreth off his horse. Despite his insistence that he was fine, it took several long minutes for him to swing one leg over and slide off.

Amira saw Daindreth safely beside the fire before she oversaw Iasu dragged off his horse. By unspoken agreement, Amira seemed to have been put in charge of the other Kadra'han.

When they brought him to sit beside the fire, it was she who checked his bonds again. The last thing she wanted was him breaking free during the night.

"I don't know why you've bothered tying my ankles," Iasu muttered. "It's not like both my legs work, anyway."

"I don't want to leave any room for creativity," Amira quipped back.

Thadred had dismounted his kelpie and the little black horse circled their camp just at the edges. It made Amira nervous. Sometimes she would lose sight of the animal completely only to have him reappear on the opposite side of the camp.

Tapios and Thadred seemed convinced that the animal wouldn't harm them. Amira still wasn't sure what to make of it.

She discussed guard placements with Tapios and who would be assigned first, second, and third watch. Though the rangers seemed to think no one could sneak up on them with the kelpie nearby, Amira wasn't so sure. They'd all been certain no one could find the Haven, either.

Supper was oatcakes with jerked venison. Amira saw that Iasu was fed before making her way across the fire to Daindreth.

The archduke sat quietly, back against a blackened oak tree. His eyes were shut, but his breathing was too quick and shallow for him to be asleep.

"Daindreth?" Amira spoke his name softly as she knelt beside him.

He looked up, eyes still half closed.

"I know you're hurting." She reached for his nearest hand, careful not to touch the scabs of his bruised knuckles. "What can I do to make it better?"

Daindreth exhaled out his nose, expression softening. "I don't think there's anything, love."

"But it does hurt?"

Daindreth nodded. "I don't think I can lie—yes. It hurts to breathe, and it hurts to move."

Amira hesitated. "Do you think you would be more

157

comfortable lying down?"

Daindreth frowned, as if taking a silent tally of all his aches and pains. "Yes," he said at length.

"Do you want to lie down?"

Daindreth took a long, painfully slow, breath. "Yes."

"Alright." Amira touched his thigh. It would have been a far more erotic gesture if they hadn't been surrounded by witnesses and he hadn't been nearly doubled over in pain. "I'll make your pallet first. Hold on."

Amira fetched his bedroll from his horse's saddlebags as the rangers made camp. Several of Tapios' men started a fire and set to warming the cold rations while the rest tended the horses. She returned and spread his blankets on the ground beside him.

"You're treating me like an invalid," Daindreth mumbled.

"You want to do it yourself?"

"I'm not complaining."

"Good. Because it's another long day of riding tomorrow and I need you in fighting shape."

Daindreth scoffed, probably at the idea he would be fighting anything by tomorrow.

"Here." Amira held out a hand and helped him shift onto the blankets. He most likely could have done it himself, but he didn't stop her helping him as she took off his boots and helped him lie down.

She left him to rest while she finished tending the horses with the rangers. Her little bay mare had already been unsaddled, but she finished rubbing down the mare's sides and legs before covering her in an oiled horse blanket to keep off the rain.

Next, she moved to Daindreth's sorrel mare. As she rounded the sorrel's haunches, she nearly collided with one of the female rangers, a blonde girl with large brown eyes like a doe's.

"Pardon me," Amira said, stepping around the girl.

The girl only nodded, going back to work on the animal beside the sorrel. They worked beside one another in silence for several long minutes until Amira was blanketing the sorrel and clasping the buckles in place.

"You care for him," the blonde ranger said, "don't you?"

Amira didn't even look up from the sorrel's buckles. "I love him," she said without hesitating.

"Would you still be with him?" the ranger asked. "If you had a choice?"

"I already chose." Amira didn't understand why it was so hard for these people to believe she was with Daindreth of her own free will. Why did they always assume that every act of loyalty was because of some compulsion? Did they really not understand how much better he was than her father? Than the Istovari themselves?

Of her mother, father, and Daindreth, the archduke was the only one who had never tried to dominate or exploit her. He was the only one who had protected her, even risked his own life for hers. He'd been willing to sacrifice his mind to keep her safe. More than once, he had given her the chance to walk away—something no one else had done.

Yes, their relationship had begun with an assassination attempt and a Kadra'han's oaths, but it was more than that now. She was with him because she wanted to be.

After she saw the horses tended, Amira returned to Daindreth. She helped him sit up to eat his oatcakes and venison ration. He didn't eat much, but Thadred heartily gulped down his portion, still speaking with Tapios.

Amira eased down behind Daindreth and slipped her arms around his chest. She was gentle, careful to avoid as many of his injuries as possible. Daindreth leaned back against her and she rested his head against her shoulder.

Kissing his temple, she held him, enjoying his closeness, the smell of him, the feel of him.

"This is nice," Daindreth sighed, closing his eyes. "This doesn't hurt."

Amira was aware of Tapios, the blonde ranger, and plenty of the others casting looks their way. The only one who seemed not to care was Thadred. The knight sat at the edge of camp tossing bits of venison into the air while Lleuad caught them in his jaws.

Daindreth relaxed in Amira's arms and was soon dozing. Amira's left leg went numb, and her shoulder ached, but she didn't move. She enjoyed the weight of him against her. It made her wonder what it would be like to lie like this with nothing but skin between them. What would it be like to touch more of him and be touched in turn?

Thadred came to set up his bedroll beside them not long after. His limp was more pronounced than usual and he moved rigid and tense as an old man, but he was smiling.

"You're in a good mood," Amira remarked, voice down so as not to disturb Daindreth's sleep.

Thadred grinned back. "My boy Lleuad is taking us straight to the Kadra'han," he said. "Glad you brought me along now, aren't you?"

Through the trees, Amira could just make out the shape of the kelpie, hovering a few steps outside the firelight. "You're glad to be useful again," she said.

"Damn right I am," the knight said without a second's hesitation.

Amira could understand that.

◆ ◆ ◆

They rode through most of the next morning with the kelpie leading the way, Thadred on his back. Amira stayed close to Daindreth, trying to keep him as comfortable as she could. The rangers kept in a loose formation around them, silent and alert.

Without warning, a boom shook the earth and lightning cracked across the sky. Amira's mare squealed and animals reared and snorted around her. Daindreth barely held back his own horse.

Torrents of rain poured down on them a moment later. *Ka*—bright, burning, and radiant—pressed in on them from every direction. It was a healthy golden glow, not the sickly miasma of the Cursewood.

Amira cast about in shock as she realized that the Cursewood was at least a hundred paces at their backs. The world around them was forest, living and healthy. The rush of healthy *ka* came so fast, Amira was lightheaded for a moment.

"Where are we?" Tapios quickly asked, looking in all directions.

Amira had been asking herself that same question. She

160

looked left and right, hoping to recognize something.

They were on a grassy noll with aspens and red maple trees all around them. Mountains surrounded them, vague shadows through the rainclouds.

Amira pulled up the hood of her oilskin cloak as did Daindreth and everyone around them.

"Does anyone recognize this place?" Tapios called out.

Amira squinted. It was hard to make out anything in midst of a thunderstorm. Another roll of thunder rumbled across the sky.

"What's that?" someone called, pointing up ahead.

Faintly, through the sheets of rain, Amira could make out the outline of a large stone structure squatting on a mountain ridge above them. It might have been a mile or so off. A road snaked down from the fortress, lined by square, bright red arches.

Iasu laughed. It was a mocking, bitter sound that made the hair on the back of Amira's neck rise.

It was then she recognized what she was seeing.

"We're in Kelamora's lands," Iasu laughed. "Are you ready for a family reunion, sister?"

His words churned Amira's stomach.

"Your swamp horse has led us to Kelamora!" Iasu cackled.

"No," Amira corrected. "He led us to the children." She looked to Daindreth.

The archduke was silent, his hood drawn up though the rain had already drenched his head and shoulders. He met her look quietly, expression difficult to read.

"Something is wrong," Daindreth said.

"Everything is wrong," Amira agreed. She looked behind them to where the boundary of the Cursewood was still visible. "Since when has the Cursewood come all the way across the mountains?" she demanded.

"It's been coming closer and closer every year." Iasu volunteered the information with a smug look. "Why did you think the leaders of Kelamora agreed to help Vesha? Your mothers really should have been more careful with their curses."

Amira wouldn't argue with that. She looked to Tapios. "We should head deeper into the forest that way and set up a base

161

until we can scout the fortress."

Tapios nodded, silent and pensive.

None of the rangers spoke, eyes wide as they surveyed the strange land around them. The land of Nihain was lusher, greener, and often rained more than other parts of the world.

With Thadred still in the lead, their group headed into the thick woods of the surrounding trees.

Amira rode beside Daindreth, hovering close at his side.

"Any clever plans yet?" he asked. His tone sounded halfway teasing, but the humor was lost.

"No," Amira replied.

"We'll think of something."

Amira looked up to the trees. The forest was alive with *ka*, teeming with it. But something was wrong. "Tapios," she said, twisting in her saddle. "Something—"

Lleuad, the kelpie, squealed from his place at the head of their column. He let off a cry of rage and bolted into the trees.

Thadred flew off, landing in a cursing pile. No sooner had the kelpie disappeared into the brush than the snap of branches and the cry of a human voice rent the air.

Shapes burst from the trees, clad in armor and flashing like silver fish from the dark underbrush. Arrows shot down from above and the rangers returned arrows into the trees, but the missiles on both sides skittered off course, striking madly at the surrounding forest.

A rope caught Amira around the waist. Next thing she knew, a hard yank ripped her off her horse. She thudded to the ground, but barely felt it. She snapped up to her knees and had a dagger out the next moment. Hacking through the rope, she tore it off.

"Amira!" the archduke cried.

"Daindreth!" She glanced over her shoulder.

He was still on his horse, but several imperial Kadra'han surrounded him, circling his sorrel with ropes.

She spun around to run to him, but a shape with a sword came swinging for her head. She ducked and retreated as her horse dashed into the forest. All around her, men and women and horses screamed.

She was vaguely aware of the kelpie's enraged whinnies and

162

Tapios shouting orders.

"Amira!" the archduke struggled to reach her, but his horse was surrounded.

"Daindreth!" Fear spiked through Amira. She couldn't let them take him. Couldn't. A fate worse than death awaited him if she failed now.

Amira spun to face her attacker. He was perhaps a head shorter, but knives strapped across his back, chest, and waist. His black and green mottled uniform had blended with the forest. This forest was so alive with *ka* that she'd been too overwhelmed by it to sense him and his comrades.

He had no band of *ka* around his throat, but his life force was strong enough that he might be a sorcerer. It was hard for her to know.

He wore a mask over everything except his eyes, making it impossible to recognize him. He wielded a blade almost as long as his leg, swinging, blocking, and parrying with a dizzying speed. Wielding the shorter weapon, it was all Amira could do to keep moving and avoid being cloven in two.

Out of the corner of her eye, she saw Daindreth torn off his horse. "No!" she screamed. Amira took her attention off her opponent for just one, dangerous instant.

A net fell on her from above. It engulfed her and she went down, tackled by a weight that slammed into her back. She couldn't see and all she could hear was chaos.

Daindreth screamed her name and Tapios shouted to his rangers. The kelpie shrieked and she thought she heard Thadred.

"Daindreth!" Amira cried. "Daindreth! No!"

She dropped her dagger and clawed to get the net off her face even as a knee drove into her back. She was dead now. She knew it. It would be too easy for them to finish her off.

They had no reason to take her alive—did they?

Bundled in the net, they dragged her through the grass. Someone screamed. Amira couldn't see. She fought to grab one of the knives at her side, but her arms were tangled in the net, and she couldn't reach.

They hauled her back through the trees, over rocks and exposed roots and branches. Amira twisted around, fighting and thrashing like a porpoise she'd once seen caught in a fisherman's nets along the coast.

"Watch her!" she heard a vaguely familiar voice say. "Careful. She has other weapons. Don't doubt that."

Someone grabbed her wrists through the rope webbing. Amira tried to gather *ka* to herself, but just as she reached for it, she felt it blowing away from her, streaming away like sand through her fingers.

"Gifted," she heard that same voice say. "I underestimated you before. But you are still untrained with magic."

Amira peered up with one eye through the net and panic rose in her chest. "Darrigan?"

The senior Kadra'han looked her over, his plate armor spattered in mud. "Bind her hands."

Some of the Kadra'han wore full plate armor as he did, and others were in the camouflage scouting gear. The empire had prepared the perfect ambush—light armored men to strike with the element of surprise and then the heavily armored soldiers to smash through the Istovari rangers and break apart their ranks. Assuming one could call what the Istovari had *ranks*.

Amira's hands were dragged behind her and manacles locked around her wrists. Something hard slammed into her lower back and her vision washed white. She couldn't breathe for several torturously long moments.

"Daindreth," she whimpered, looking back through the trees. "Where...?"

"He'll be joining us soon." Darrigan crouched in front of her as two Kadra'han searched her, rifling through her pockets, belt, boots, and vest for weapons.

Amira twisted around, slamming a knee into the nearest warrior. He grunted, then responded with a fist to her gut.

Wheezing, Amira snapped her head forward. Her skull connected with his mouth. She felt a crunch and the strike rattled her head, making her see stars.

The Kadra'han cursed her in a jumble of different languages and dialects, some she didn't recognize. A fist connected with her jaw, snapping her head back. Amira tasted blood and her vison went double for several seconds.

One of them locked another metal cuff around her wrist.

164

Instantly, Amira lost all awareness of *ka* and the world seemed to go dark of magic.

There was nothing she could do.

By the time they finished searching and binding her, she was bloody, covered in dirt, bruised, and her nose bled.

"Be careful with this one," Darrigan said dryly. "She's a handful."

A grunting, shuffling through the forest caught her attention. Through a swelling eye, Amira turned.

Daindreth was held between two Kadra'han, fighting as best he could while battered and outnumbered.

He caught sight of her, and his eyes went wide. "Amira!" He tried to lunge for her, but the Kadra'han held him back.

"Daindreth!" Amira tried to reach for him, but Darrigan's men pinned her to the ground.

They groped Amira from head to foot, stripping off her weapons and tossing them aside. Darrigan stood with his hands on his hips, keeping count as the assorted throwing knives and daggers were tossed at his feet.

Amira could still hear Thadred and the other Istovari fighting the Kadra'han through the trees. Their shouts and screams were muffled, barely audible through the greenery.

Amira looked desperately to Daindreth and he shook his head. He didn't know what had become of their friends any more than she did.

"Let her go!" Daindreth ordered, straining against his guards. Four Kadra'han had to hold him back. "Don't touch her!"

Darrigan ignored the archduke, crouching in front of Amira. His face was slashed by a pale scar where she'd cut him the last time they'd met. He studied her closely, curiosity piqued in his eyes.

The captain jerked his hand toward Amira's guards, and they hauled her upright so she knelt in front of Darrigan. The older Kadra'han watched her closely, his expression unreadable.

Amira thought about spitting in his face but didn't think her swelling lip would cooperate.

Darrigan leaned in, bringing his mouth so close that his breath tickled her ear. "How did you do it?"

"What?" Amira choked, blood streaming down her chin and neck.

"How did you defy the archduke's orders in Mynadra?"

Amira swallowed. Darrigan had once tried to tell her that he was bound to Vesha's orders, helpless to do anything other than what he told her. While Amira believed he genuinely wished to serve Vesha, perhaps even loved her, Darrigan had expressed fears over her association with cythraul. As her Kadra'han, he was unable to save her from herself.

Amira considered her next words carefully. Darrigan might be asking for help, but Vesha might have ordered him to ask this question. "I wanted to serve Daindreth more than the curse wanted me to obey him."

Darrigan was quiet for a moment.

"Service and obedience are two different things," Amira added, repeating the words he had spoken to her all those weeks ago in Mynadra.

"Amira!" the archduke called again. "Amira…"

Darrigan inhaled a long breath. "You make it sound easy."

"It wasn't," Amira whispered back. "I was sure it would kill me. But I didn't care."

Darrigan looked to the guards holding Amira and then back to her. He straightened, hands behind his back. "With what the empress has planned," he said, words spoken slowly, like he selected each one individually before stringing them together. "You may wish it had killed you. And very soon."

Amira did her best to hide a shudder at that.

Daindreth shouted at the Kadra'han captain. "Darrigan, I swear by every god from the Dread Marches to the Halls of Demred that if you hurt her, none of them can save you from me!"

Amira had never seen her fiancé this angry. His face twisted into a snarl and a vein bulged along his forehead. His teeth flashed and she imagined he might even be a match for a cythraul in this state.

Darrigan turned, slight amusement on his face. "Save your threats, Your Highness," he said. "You have greater enemies than I."

"Amira!" Daindreth shouted as the Kadra'han shackled his hands behind his back.

"It's alright, Daindreth," Amira said, lying through her teeth. She looked to the guard captain, still standing in front of her.

"Don't look to me," Captain Darrigan said. "I can't help you." He smiled at her then, but it was all sadness.

Amira cleared her throat. "I'm sorry about your face," she said.

Darrigan brushed the pink scar with his gauntleted hand. "Don't mention it," he said. "Our kind all have to do things we'd rather not."

Amira caught the double meaning. He couldn't help them, no matter how much he might want to.

"Let's go," Darrigan said, rising to his feet.

The Kadra'han forced Amira to her feet and she stifled a groan, her aching head spinning.

"Captain, there are still Istovari in the forest," said a younger man in the armor and uniform of an imperial officer.

"We have what we came for," Darrigan said. "And I don't like to keep the empress waiting."

"My mother is here?" Daindreth demanded, looking between the Kadra'han and the imperial soldiers.

"Yes," the captain answered. "And she is most eager to see you."

The color drained from Daindreth's face. Amira had suspected Vesha was here for some reason, but hearing it confirmed from Darrigan's lips brought a sinking sensation into her gut.

"Daindreth…" Amira wanted to say something, but she didn't know what.

The Kadra'han dragged them through the trees to a band of waiting horses.

They were doomed.

CHAPTER SIXTEEN

Thadred

Lleuad had thrown him off almost as soon as everything had gone to shit. Crawling through the tangled greenery, Thadred drew his cane sword and staggered to his feet.

As best he could tell, they had walked into an ambush. Imperial soldiers swarmed from the front, back, and left side of their column. Horses squealed. People screamed.

Tapios and his archers did their best to return the attacks, but their horses were panicking, making it even harder for them to get hits. Arrows skittered far off their targets and many that did strike attackers hit their armor and bounced off anyway.

Thadred heard Amira and Daindreth shouting, but he didn't know where they were. He could barely make any sense of what was happening between the trees, the ferns, and the chaos of beasts and humanity around him.

Thadred had been trained to fight in formation or in tourneys one on one. This was neither.

He straightened in time to meet the attack of two imperial soldiers lunging for him at once. He had just one second to realize how very *bad* this situation looked. He had no armor, no shield, and these were fully kitted imperial infantrymen. At least Vesha was sending her best.

As he raised his sword into the ready stance, a black shape slammed into the soldiers from the side. Lleuad kicked and stomped at the men, knocking them down before they could land a strike on the kelpie.

His hooves clanked against their armor. Lleuad tried to bite, but his teeth scraped off their plate. Squealing in frustration, the stallion went back to stomping.

Thadred watched, half impressed, half horrified, as Lleuad smashed both men into bloodied, crumpled balls.

The stallion snorted and turned to Thadred, nostrils flaring. One of the men lay unmoving, but the other strained to reach his dropped sword, groaning.

"You don't play around, do you?" Thadred muttered to the horse.

Lleuad snorted.

Thadred limped over to the man who was still moving and finished him off with a swift cut to the neck. "Come on." He beckoned to the horse and turned back to the forest. "Dain?" he shouted. "Amira?"

Thadred limped as fast as he could through the tangle of green at his feet, ducking under low branches and pulling himself along with the sturdier ones.

Lleuad trotted close at his side, not letting him more than a few steps ahead or behind. The stallion hovered around him like an anxious mother hen.

Up ahead, the sounds of battle rang through the air. People shouted and he could make out Tapios' voice above the din.

Thadred stumbled past a tree to find a young ranger kneeling in front of an armored imperial. He raised his sword and charged the man, but Lleuad got there first.

The stallion reared, hooves pawing at the air. The soldier ducked the first few blows, swearing and turning to face the horse.

He slashed his sword, but Lleuad was faster. The stocky animal kicked again. Then the clang of hooves hitting plate rang out. It looked like Lleuad barely touched the man, but he went sprawling backward into the grass.

Thadred grabbed the Istovari ranger while Lleuad stomped on the soldier. "Come on!" he said, hauling the young man to his feet.

The lad was pale with blood streaming from his temple. "Thadred?"

Oh, good. The lad knew who he was, even if he didn't remember the kid's name. "Gather your brothers and sisters," Thadred ordered. "We can't fight them here. We need to fall back."

The boy watched with wide eyes as the soldier lay helpless on the ground, groaning with his armor dented. Lleuad kept kicking, stomping, and biting at the man. Damned hell-horse certainly didn't do things partway.

169

Thadred was reminded how glad he was that Lleaud was on his side now.

"We can't fight them," the boy panted. "How are we going to fight them?"

"We'll worry about that later. Now go! There's a river south—" He paused a moment to remember. "—east. Southeast of here. Grab who you can and head that direction."

The boy nodded, still breathless.

Thadred shoved away from the youth and called to his horse. "Lleaud! Let's go." He didn't bother finishing off the soldier under Lleaud's hooves. From the massive dents in the man's cuirass and greaves, Thadred doubted the man would be a threat to anyone any time soon.

"Amira!" He gripped Lleaud's mane in one hand for support. The stallion nearly dragged him through the thick trees, straight toward the sounds of fighting. Lleaud might be smaller than most mounts, but this was a war horse if ever there was one. "Dain!"

Lleuad leapt into a quick trot, towing Thadred along.

"Bloody hell," Thadred swore, gripping the stallion's mane as tight as he could and doing his best to scramble along beside the horse. "Are you trying to kill me?"

The kelpie snorted and veered around a thick brown maple tree, toward the sound of voices.

Someone let off a yell and next thing Thadred knew, a half dozen arrows were pointed in his face.

"Hey!" He ducked as one skittered off to his left, missing by a good arm's length. "It's me, you jumpy bastards."

"Thadred?" Tapios stood, missing his cloak and clutching a handful of arrows.

"Yes," Thadred said, looking over his shoulder. "What happened? Where did the imperials go?"

"I don't know. They withdrew as soon as…" He looked past Thadred, toward the trees.

"Where are Dain and Amira?" Thadred asked, tightness rising in his throat.

"They were taken," the ranger said, swallowing. "The Kadra'han took them."

Thadred froze for a long moment. For some reason, he felt as if he had already known. "Gather whoever you can find," he ordered. "I've told the others to meet us at the river."

"But if they unleash the archduke's demon—"

"Then we're all buggered." Thadred didn't see the point in lying about it. "But we're no good to him scattered and disorganized. Gather what rangers you can and whatever wounded you can find and let's go."

Thadred turned to head back in the direction of the game trail where they had been ambushed.

"Do you think it's a trap?" Tapios asked. "Are the imperials waiting for us to be exposed before they attack?"

"No," Thadred answered. "They all left."

"How do you know?" Tapios pressed.

Thadred had to think about that. How *did* he know? He shrugged. "They have what they came for. Come on." He beckoned to the rangers. "I expect they'll want to get Dain and Amira back to the keep, but that doesn't mean they won't send hunting parties back to finish us off."

Tapios swore under his breath. It was the first time Thadred had heard him use foul language and it did raise his opinion of the man just a little.

The handful of rangers with Tapios fell into a loose formation behind Thadred and Lleaud, giving the kelpie ample space. Tapios took the lead by unspoken agreement.

Thadred thought it stupid for a commander to take the point where he was most likely to be killed, but now wasn't the time to argue. Also, he was confident that the imperial soldiers and Kadra'han were gone.

Tapios went out first, straight back to the site of the ambush, bow drawn, and arrow nocked. Around the clearing lay a handful of scattered bodies amid churned earth. Most the horses had fled, but one lay groaning on top of its motionless rider—an Istovari ranger with an imperial arrow buried in his throat.

After a few moments, Tapios crossed to the other side of the glade. He completed a fast circuit before motioning to Thadred. "All clear."

Thadred limped out of the trees and the rest of the Istovari followed. Lleaud chuffed and snorted at his side. The stallion stopped to nose at the crumpled body of an Istovari ranger. He opened his mouth and chomped down on the corpse's arm.

"Don't eat that!" Thadred smacked at the horse's neck.

Lleaud's mouth came away bloody, but the corpse looked to still be intact.

"Sylvie!" one of the rangers cried, recognizing the body. He knelt beside the corpse and rolled it over.

The young woman had a sword wound slashed across one side of her face and across her chest. From the brightness of her blood, she'd probably been dead for just a few minutes.

Thadred looked in the opposite direction as the rangers mourned, checking over the corpses and accounting for their fallen. For those unused to war, they were more stoic than Thadred had expected.

Tapios looked on with a grim expression. He turned to Thadred. "We can't leave the bodies here."

"But we can't take them with us." Thadred knew he sounded heartless, but he was more concerned with keeping the living alive than respecting the dead. "These people are out of time, but there's still hope for Dain and Amira. Your stolen Istovari children, too."

Tapios inhaled through his nose, shoulders rising and falling with barely contained…something. But he didn't argue. If there was one thing these Istovari understood, it was that decency was often the first thing sacrificed for the sake of survival.

The knight took a few steps toward the imperial bodies. He noticed that just as many imperials lay dead as Istovari. Some were marked with arrows, others had been felled by blades, likely the work of Amira and Dain.

Thadred knelt beside a small body in the linen of an Istovari. The body lay motionless, not breathing. Thadred pushed the corpse's shoulder to roll it over.

He had just an instant to register the knife before it lunged for his gut.

Thadred batted it away out of reflex, catching his attacker's wrists and slamming them back to the ground.

"Iasu," he grimaced, glaring down at the small man.

Iasu's wrists were still bound in the ropes Amira had lashed to him that morning. It looked as if he had been thrown from his horse and his injured leg had kept him from running.

"The imperials left you behind *again,* did they?" Thadred might have smirked if Dain and Amira hadn't been taken.

Iasu spat and Thadred grabbed the side of the smaller man's head, slamming him to the ground.

Iasu laughed, a strained, wheezy sound. "Beating your captives? How noble of you."

"I get rude when people try to stab me," Thadred quipped back. "But I have good news, Iasu. You had orders to capture Dain and Amira. Well, they've been captured. That means you're released of that command and can help us now."

Iasu snarled. "You're a fool if you think I'll help you."

"Oh, I think you will," Thadred growled back, pressing the smaller man's head harder against the earth. "And where did you get that knife?"

Iasu shrugged from his place pinned to the ground. "One of your dead friends didn't need it anymore."

"Tapios. Someone." Thadred jerked his head and a ranger responded—a young man with golden stubble just beginning to show on his cheeks and chin. "Take his other side."

Thadred would have hauled Iasu up himself, but he and the imperial only had two good legs between them.

"They left him?" Tapios asked, frowning at the sight of Iasu.

"Apparently," Thadred ruffled Iasu's hair as if he were a younger brother. "Consolation prize, I guess."

"Not much of a prize," Tapios responded. "They took the princess and the archduke."

"True," Thadred agreed. "And they still have the children, but!" He cocked his head to one side. "This fine gentleman grew up in Kelamora. He knows it as well as anyone." Thadred grabbed Iasu's face, dragging him around so that they were eye to eye. "And he's going to show us how to break them out whether he likes it or not."

"Death first," Iasu spat.

Thadred grinned at him for just a moment to hide his frustration. He'd hoped that the imperial Kadra'han leaving Iasu behind—twice at this point—would turn his affections, but it seemed this one was a little harder to turn. All the same, he knew enough about interrogation to know he needed to keep up a confident façade in front of his captive.

Thadred jerked his head to the other Istovari. "Take only what you need and let's get out of here." He looked to Tapios. "Can you hide our trail?"

"If you don't leave too many tracks."

Thadred nodded. "We'll try."

Lleaud still hovered nearby. The stallion didn't try to eat any more of the bodies, though he eyed them hungrily.

Several horses had been caught by the other rangers. They slung Iasu aboard one of them and lashed his hands to the pommel of the saddle.

Blood soaked through the bandage on Iasu's leg, but the smaller man didn't let off so much as a whimper of pain. Thadred could respect that, at least.

Behind him rode one of the rangers who had injured her right arm. A gash cut across her inner bicep and it looked bad, but she insisted she could still use her bow. Thadred doubted any of the others believed her any more than he did.

He mounted Lleaud, still without a saddle or bridle. He considered taking gear off one of the dead horses to tack up the kelpie, but had a suspicion that Lleaud might try to bite his arm off if he did.

They made their way to the southeast, toward the river Thadred remembered from his brief time in Kelamora. He was worried the stallion might stray, but the horse seemed eager to head toward the water. Thankfully, he didn't try attacking any of the other remaining horses, either.

Tapios and his rangers jogged around them, quiet and stealthy through the woods. Moving unseen and unheard was one skill they had mastered quite well. Avoiding the monsters of the Cursewood had prepared them for this, at least. They might be rubbish in a fight against imperials, but at least they knew what they were doing when it came to stealth.

Thadred wracked his brain as they headed toward the river. Their goal was to free Dain, Amira, and the Istovari children from one of the most secure fortresses in the world. To accomplish that, he had some two dozen or so demoralized rangers, one murderous swamp horse, and an uncooperative Kadra'han hostage.

One of Darrigan's favorite sayings to new trainees was, "Never believe you are helpless. Always choose how you act."

Amira had freed Daindreth from the imperial palace with a dagger, a chain, and sheer force of will. What Thadred had was an army in comparison.

All the same, he had no idea how he was going to work this out. He glanced up to the cloudy sky, grimacing.

"Eponine," he whispered, hoping no one would overhear. "If you're listening, if you give a damn at all, I'd really appreciate some help right now."

Lleaud snorted and tossed his head just as he finished his prayer.

CHAPTER SEVENTEEN

Amira

Kelamora was different from how she remembered. The red arches were not quite as brilliant and the many koi ponds weren't quite as impressive. The massive stone walls that she had once thought to be godlike in their size and breadth didn't seem so large now.

Perhaps it was because she had seen too much of the world since the last time she had been here. She had seen kingdoms across the sea, fortresses that had been unconquered for a thousand years, palatial paradises, and Mynadra itself. Kelamora was not so intimidating by comparison.

Amira and Daindreth were dragged apart as soon as they entered.

"Take her to the cells," Darrigan ordered, gesturing to Amira. "And search her again before you do."

Panic rose in Amira's chest. "Daindreth!"

"Where are you taking her?" Daindreth demanded, straining against his guards. His hands had been tied, just like Amira's, and he'd earned a few punches himself for resisting their captors.

"She'll be alive the next time you see her," Darrigan said. "Come." He turned toward the main entrance.

"I will find you," Daindreth vowed. "I will get back to you, I swear."

Amira could feel tears welling in her eyes. Failure was all she had to show for everything they had sacrificed, survived, and fought for. "Daindreth, I—"

The Kadra'han hauled her off in the opposite direction before she could finish speaking. The last glimpse she caught of Daindreth was of him straining against the iron grips of his guards.

Amira's tears fell then, anger and grief and hopelessness welling up in her chest at once. "No!" she screamed. "No!" Her voice echoed off the stones. A trio of doves spooked from one of the arches and fluttered away. Amira tried to elbow or kick one of the Kadra'han, but they had already shackled her ankles and any efforts she made were ineffective.

She tried to gather *ka*, but it evaded her. She couldn't even sense it. That cuff around her wrist kept her from using magic. "Daindreth!"

Kelamora had always been a peaceful place. It was oddly serene, despite what went on within its walls. To Amira, it had always struck her as a forest—a place where life and death were played out moment by moment and yet it remained stoically composed.

Her screams ricocheted off the stone. She spotted a pair of white-robed acolytes scuttling out of their path. They passed a courtyard with carefully arranged beds of moss, an elderly man seated in the center with his eyes closed, dark robes fanning out around him. If the old man heard Amira's screaming and struggling, he gave no sign.

Otherwise, she saw no one. That wasn't too surprising in and of itself. Kelamora was not the sort of place where people went on leisure strolls.

The guards took Amira down to a lower level of the fortress, one that smelled of mold and damp earth. They arrived at a long corridor wrapped around the base of the Kelamora fortress. To one side were rows of iron-grated cells. To the other was a sheer drop of at least one hundred feet to the forest below.

From here, Amira could see the edge of the Cursewood. It splayed black and tarlike across the forest, like poison in a wound.

"I will kill you all," Amira swore, still fighting, straining to see past her swollen eye. "I will kill every last one of you!"

The Kadra'han didn't respond.

The two men dragged her into a cell a few doors down and one of them slammed her against the wall. It was lined with some dark metal that had been hammered in sheets, as was the ceiling. The bars at the front appeared to be made of the same metal.

Her two captors staggered for a moment as if they were dazed, too, but they recovered before she could exploit their hesitation.

The second man drew a knife.

Amira's training kicked in. She batted at the one holding her back and he grunted as her knee connected with his groin. But he didn't let go.

The one with the knife grabbed her belt and undid the buckle. He ripped it off and tossed it outside the cell.

"Don't touch me!" Amira screamed.

The Kadra'han grabbed the front of her tunic and hooked the knife inside the collar. He ripped downward, tearing it open. He found a knife tucked in the bandeau around her breasts and cut that off next. The cold air rushed up to meet her skin and gooseflesh prickled over her entire body.

Amira fought and cursed, but she couldn't stop him. She was at their mercy.

The second Kadra'han set to unbuckling or cutting off everything she wore, taking inventory as he did. He unbuckled her boots and dragged them off. Next, he unlaced her breeches and slipped the knife under the waistband to cut those off, too. She struggled and he nicked her thigh. Blood ran down her leg.

Amira tried to focus on that—the tickle of the warm stream sliding down her knee and along her shin—instead of the cold stone against her naked back or the rough leather armor of the first Kadra'han pinning her to the wall.

The Kadra'han with the knife found her hidden weapons one by one. He tossed a handful of small blades and a flint and steel into the pile outside.

Amira's face burned with humiliation as they continued to strip her naked, searching her as they did. She'd never been unclothed in front of men before, much less complete strangers. Their disinterested, businesslike manner made it all worse.

She tried to let her mind go somewhere else, to not think about what was happening. She thought about Daindreth, trying to picture his face. He was on the other side of this. She just had to get through this, and she could have him.

Daindreth would be gentle. Daindreth would be loving. She just had to live.

Amira choked back tears and fought to compose herself. If this was going to happen, she didn't want to cry or beg through it.

Once the second Kadra'han had stripped her down to

nothing but the chains on her wrists, he nodded to his compatriot. "She's clean."

The first Kadra'han nodded, still gripping Amira's wrists. The two of them each took an arm and dragged her to one corner of the cell.

Amira found herself going numb. Should she fight them or should she just let them do what they wanted so that they would leave? That wasn't something she'd ever thought she would ask herself. Of course she should fight them, but—

The two men locked a chain around her ankle. The lock clicked into place, and they let her go.

"Get the cuff," one of them said. "We don't have many of those. She can't use magic in here anyway."

The Kadra'han unbuckled the cuff from around her wrist and she got her first good look at it. Dark, tarnished metal resembling hammered wrought iron—tenebrous steel. They'd come prepared to take an Istovari prisoner.

The two of them stepped back and out of the cell. They slammed the door shut and one of them locked that as well.

"Good luck getting out of that," said the first Kadra'han. His voice was flat, humorless.

The second Kadra'han scooped up the torn pile of her bloody clothes, knives, boots, and belt. "It's going to be a long night for you, princess," he said.

"If you're lucky, you'll freeze to death tonight," the first man added.

"True," the second agreed.

There was no malice in their words nor pity. They were stating only what they considered to be fact and no more.

The two of them turned and marched back out the way they had come. They didn't speak. This was just a task to them.

Amira sat alone in the cold, her naked body shivering. Dirt stuck to her, and she realized the Kadra'han had cut her several times. She was covered in bruises from her beating in the forest as well as the stripping just now.

Her chains rattled whenever she moved. It was impossible to get comfortable. The shackles cut into her ankle no matter how she sat.

She brought her knees up to her chest and wrapped her arms

around her legs. Closing her eyes, Amira fought to compose herself. She needed to think. She needed to focus.

The world around her was still dead. There was something about this cell that was cutting her off from *ka*. It must be lined with tenebrous steel.

Amira couldn't imagine how much it must have cost to line an entire room with the metal. It must have taken alchemists and blacksmiths months to create.

Amira breathed deep, reviewing her situation.

The Kadra'han had confirmed that Vesha had wanted her alive. That struck her as strange. The empress had seemed quite set on her death not too long ago.

Perhaps they meant to use her as a hostage to keep Daindreth in line, but it had to be more than that. She had very little to work with, but she ran through every word, action, and hint from the past hour.

Darrigan had implied he was under orders. He didn't seem to harbor any harsh feelings about his face, so perhaps he was her ally in this after all—or as close as she could hope for one. Then again, he had given the order for her to be stripped naked and chained by his soldiers.

He'd tried to tell her before that Vesha needed to be stopped, for her own good as well as the empire's. Unfortunately, he'd seemed to think killing Daindreth to void the empress's deal with the demons was the only way to do that.

Amira supposed she should be complimented that Vesha had sent Darrigan this time. At least the witch was sending her best now.

Something one of Amira's jailers said stood out in her mind—*If the empress lets her live that long.*

Vesha was here, surrounded by sorcerers, and she had Daindreth. Amira was locked in this cell, completely helpless. Who knew if Thadred and the others were even still alive?

Despair engulfed Amira then. It was a dark, yawning chasm that seemed to swallow her whole. How could she possibly hope to save Daindreth, much less herself, from this one?

They were alone. They were separated. They were doomed.

After everything, Caa Iss would take full possession of

Daindreth. She would be left to the mercy of whatever tortures the demon chose and Daindreth would be forced to watch.

It made everything she had fought and bled and suffered for these past months seem like nothing but an idealist's folly. Perhaps she had always been spitting in the wind. She'd been an idiot to think she could save Daindreth. That she could save herself.

Amira let herself weep then, sobs wracking her shoulders. A faint wind moaned through the corridor. A bird flew past, just outside the massive open side of the jail. Amira kept on crying, giving herself over to the hopelessness and frustration she'd kept bottled up. Always there had been something to distract her from the odds, some goal she could focus on instead of the enormity of their plight.

Now there was no plan, no hope, no goal. There was just Amira, her thoughts, and the time until she met whatever gruesome fate awaited her and the man she loved.

Don't cry, my pet, crooned a hissing, taunting voice.

Amira jumped and almost screamed. If she hadn't already been trapped in a corner of the cell, she would have backed away.

A pale creature blinked at her with fiery red eyes, elliptical slits flicking over her hungrily. When the thing spoke, its forked tongue flickered across its teeth like a snake.

"Saan Thii," Amira gasped. If she had doubted Vesha was in Kelamora, seeing the empress's familiar banished all questions.

How is my favorite troublemaker? the cythraul purred.

"What do you want?" Amira tried to remind herself that the demoness couldn't hurt her. Saan Thii had once tried to attack her in the physical world and failed.

Saan Thii crouched across from Amira, wrapping her tail around herself like a cat. *What do* you *want, princess?*

"Where is Vesha?" Amira pulled her legs closer to her chest. Her first impulse was to take up a defensive stance, but, realistically, how was she supposed to defend herself in this situation against a cythraul of all things?

Not far, the demoness purred back. *She doesn't know I'm here.*

Amira wasn't sure what to make of that last part. "Are you happy?" She glared at the demoness. "You're finally getting the cythraul archduke you wanted."

No, Saan Thii mewled back. *No, I'm not happy at all, actually.*

Amira braced herself as the cythraul's red eyes flickered over her from head to foot, taking her in like she was a meal.

Vesha has everything she needs to unleash my brother on the world. Once she does, he will be archduke and then emperor.

Amira swallowed as another wave of hopelessness overcame her. How was she supposed to fight back against the entire empire and all the hordes of the Dread Marches with them? It was hard to believe she had done it before. That seemed lifetimes ago and it had been under strikingly different circumstances.

"That sounds like your fondest wish," Amira croaked, ashamed to hear her voice crack. "Isn't that what you want?"

Saan Thii hissed. It was an audible sound, not spoken thought as was most the cythraul's speech.

It is what my mother wants, at least partly. It is what Caa Iss wants, certainly. As for me… Saan Thii's elliptical slits ogled Amira once again. *You are a pretty little thing,* she purred. *Scars everywhere, but…* She cocked her head to the side.

Amira forced herself not to cower. "Stay away from me," she growled. A cold wind whipped up then and she shuddered, shivers wracking her whole body. Her chains rattled as she did.

Already, a chill had settled into her hands and feet. Never in her life had she been this exposed.

Now, now, Saan Thii purred. *Don't be afraid, my pet.*

Amira's nostrils flared. "I don't know what you want, and I don't care. Get out of here and leave me alone."

Saan Thii made a throaty, croaking sound that might have been laughter. *But darling, I want what you want.*

"Get out!" Amira shouted. She added several choice curses for emphasis. Saan Thii was unimpressed.

Saan Thii craned her neck so that she was level with Amira, elongated, beaklike face coming closer. *Do you know what's going to happen to you?*

Amira gritted her teeth. Her imagination had run wild over the past hour or so. She'd seen enough and done enough to imagine quite a bit. There were a hundred thousand tortures she had envisioned twice over, and she was sure Caa Iss would think of some that she hadn't even considered.

My brother will take over your precious archduke completely. The man you love will be locked away inside his own body for the rest of his earthly existence. He'll be forced to watch everything my brother does to you...and then to the rest of the world.

Amira swallowed.

That's enough to drive anyone mad, the cythraul chirped, almost laughing again. *It's probably for the best though. Do you know why Caa Iss was the one chosen to inhabit your archduke's body?*

Amira hadn't considered it.

He was the strongest of us, the most ruthless. Saan Thii cocked her head to one side. *When we heard the call of your Mothers from beyond the Dread Marches, inviting one of us to have a body once again, we were ecstatic. But there was never any question Caa Iss would be the one to pass through. He would never have allowed anything less.*

"Why are you telling me this?" Amira demanded. "Are you here to taunt me? Is that it?"

No, my pet. Saan Thii scoffed. *I want you to understand that Caa Iss is not loved in the Dread Marches any more than he is here.*

Amira shifted on the stone. She didn't really care about the demon's popularity with his own kind.

He has many enemies in the Dread Marches. Enemies who would like to see him fail.

"More power to them." Taking a deep breath, Amira looked past the demoness to the view beyond the bars of her cell. From here, she could see the valley and the forest and even the distant waterfall.

He has made many promises to our mother. But he has been delayed for years. If he is delayed much longer, it will cost him.

"Good. I hope your mother tears his eyes out." Amira wasn't sure how one would go about torturing a being that didn't technically have a body, but she trusted that Moreyne would find a way.

Saan Thii licked her lips. *If Caa Iss falls from favor and fails to secure the throne, then it will open the way for another.*

Amira didn't look directly at the cythraul. "What are you saying?"

Your Mothers cursed the Fanduillion bloodline, but...as their daughter, you could alter the bargain.

Amira didn't speak, didn't even move. Was she hearing correctly?

I could help you.

Amira knew better, but she shot a look to the demoness. "Help me do what?"

Right now, your archduke is cursed under the terms of the contract. Saan Thii cocked her head to the side. *But if we alter the terms slightly, you and I could take it over.*

"That makes no sense," Amira said, not caring that she was honest with the cythraul for once.

Everything requires balance, my pet. Her forked tongue slithered over her lips. *To cast a curse requires a sacrifice. The same to break one.* Saan Thii showed her teeth in what might have been a smile.

Amira was instantly suspicious. "What's in it for you?"

Saan Thii stared at Amira hungrily.

A sick, cloying feeling started in the back of Amira's throat and worked its way through her mouth and gut. "Why would you betray your own brother?"

Caa Iss isn't the only one of us to want a body again. We all do.

Amira wanted to shake her head, but she couldn't quite move.

You could take his curse onto yourself—I have authority to allow it. I wouldn't even demand full control. I just...want to feel *again.* Saan Thii sounded wistful. She brushed her claws against Amira's chained ankle, and they passed through, incorporeal and insubstantial. *It would be as Caa Iss and Daindreth are now. You keep control. I just...advise you from time to time.*

Amira shook her head. "No."

Saan Thii's teeth twitched, and Amira thought she must be trying to click her jaws. *Are you sure?*

"Daindreth would never forgive me," Amira said quietly. "Not if I took on a cythraul when he's fought his whole life to be rid of one."

I think your archduke would forgive you much. You've stood beside him when he's had a demon. Why wouldn't he stand by you?

Amira shook her head. "I can't."

If you're worried that he won't have you because of me, I wouldn't be

184

concerned. It's different for the woman. Not like you'll be beating him bloody if you were to lose control. Saan Thii's lips curled in what Amira was starting to recognize as a smirk. *Besides...my tastes aren't as dominant as my brother's.*

Amira swallowed. It *was* different. As much as she knew Daindreth would be horrified that she'd taken on a cythraul, she didn't know what else she could do.

"What about Vesha? Aren't you bound to her as her familiar?" Amira pressed.

Saan Thii made a dismissive gesture in the air. *I can be Vesha's familiar and your mind friend, too.*

Amira paused at that. "Why haven't you offered her this deal, then?"

Saan Thii chortled. *I want someone younger. Someone just now coming into her power. Not someone already beginning to wane.*

Amira stared at Saan Thii, mind racing. Cythraul could lie as much as they liked. According to Daindreth, they were good at it, too. "What do you mean she's waning?"

Daindreth will be emperor soon. We have seen it.

"You cythraul see the future now?" Amira quipped.

Saan Thii ignored the mocking tone in the assassin's voice. *Pieces of it. Possible futures. Too many of them show the archduke taking the crown and not long from now.*

Amira let hope—a single, daring ember of it—glow in her chest.

Not all of them show Caa Iss behind his eyes. Only about half of them. Curious, don't you think?

Amira didn't know what to think. On one hand, Daindreth might not be doomed. On the other...how was she supposed to save him? If her only hope was a jealous demoness who, by her own admission, was ready to sell out Vesha because she saw a better deal come along...

You love your archduke. I can smell the love in you.

Amira turned her head away, looking determinedly toward the open expanse of sky beyond her cell.

But love will not save him this time, little fox. Only cunning will.

She had nothing to say to that. "No one wins a deal with a devil."

Saan Thii's eye twitched. *Not so. You would win. I would win.*

Amira steeled herself and stood her ground. "If I die, I die, but I won't come groveling to the denizens of the Dread Marches."

You will wish you had groveled, Saan Thii seethed. *When Caa Iss has you splayed on a torture wheel.*

"Maybe," Amira clipped back. "My Mothers made deal with your kind, and it has brought them nothing but heartache. Same for Vesha."

It's worked out well for the empress so far.

"And yet you're the one telling me that her reckoning is coming soon." Amira shook her head, speaking with a confidence she didn't feel. "Be gone, Saan Thii."

Saan Thii leapt for Amira, hovering over the assassin. Her snout would have been rammed against Amira's face if she'd been a corporeal being.

Foolish, foolish little girl, the cythraul sneered. *You have doomed yourself, your beloved, your people, and this entire empire.*

"We were already doomed," Amira replied. "So it sounds like we're no worse off than we were an hour ago."

You could have saved them! Everything that happens now is your fault.

"Leave me alone!" Amira roared into the demoness's face.

Saan Thii snarled and whirled around, seeming to fold in on herself. She disappeared into nothingness, only the vague sensation of an echoing growl to show she had been there at all.

Amira rested her head back against the wall of her cell. Everything went silent again.

As soon as Saan Thii vanished, regret flooded Amira's entire mind. What if that had been her only chance to save Daindreth?

Making another deal with a cythraul wasn't a real answer, but it would buy them time. And if it was just Amira who was subjected to the curse, Daindreth could still rule.

A part of her wanted to call the demoness back and say yes, yes she would let Saan Thii have share in her mind and whatever else if it just meant Daindreth could be saved.

But she didn't.

Amira sat alone, naked in the cold, wondering how long before Daindreth was no longer himself. How long before Caa Iss came striding down the corridor of this prison, wearing

Daindreth's face, Daindreth's body?

She wondered what had become of Thadred, Tapios, and the others. Were they still alive? Something told her that kelpie of Thadred's wouldn't let anything happen to him, but what of the rangers? Darrigan had ordered everyone to return to Kelamora to deliver her and the archduke here, but what was to say he hadn't sent out killing parties since returning?

They were almost certainly dead. Everyone was dead. Dead or doomed. Even Fonra, back in Hylendale, wouldn't be safe for long once Caa Iss was unleashed on the world.

It had all been for nothing.

Amira pressed her face against her knees and let herself fall into weeping again.

CHAPTER EIGHTEEN

Daindreth

Daindreth saw Amira dragged away by the two Kadra'han as his own guards held him back. "Where are you taking her?" he demanded, whirling on Darrigan.

"She is to be held in a cell below the temple," the captain answered. "The empress ordered it."

Daindreth strained against his captors. Pain seared through his injuries, but it was nothing to the pain of seeing Amira taken away. "My mother is here?"

Darrigan nodded. "She is."

A sick feeling welled in the pit of Daindreth's stomach at that. He knew full well what that meant. And if Vesha had decided to keep Amira alive...

"Bring him," the guard captain ordered. He turned and marched deeper into the temple, the guards at his back, confident and sure as if he owned the place.

The layout reminded Daindreth of a beehive, built in a labyrinth of corridors that connected galleries, courtyards, and gardens. Of the many gardens, no two were alike.

Daindreth was led through a garden filled entirely with moss-covered rocks arranged into patterns. Another boasted koi ponds not unlike his mother's. One appeared to have nothing but thorn bushes, all arranged neatly and in an orderly fashion.

"Welcome to the Kelamora Monastery," one of the Kadra'han at his left said.

Daindreth had never heard it described as a monastery before, but he supposed it made sense.

They took him through another one of the gardens and up a set of steps to a sliding door. Darrigan pushed the door back and steam billowed out. The Kadra'han followed with Daindreth, escorting him into a stone room.

"Girls!" Darrigan shouted into the room. "Girls, where are you?"

A pair of young women answered and bowed to Darrigan. "My lord," they said, almost in unison.

They were both slight and slim with black braids swinging down their backs. Their frocks were modest, but Daindreth supposed they were pretty.

"Bathe him," Darrigan said, jerking his head at Daindreth. "Tend his wounds and get him fresh clothes. The empress is impatient to see him."

"Yes, my lord." The girls bobbed into bows, once again in unison.

"Time grows short," Darrigan said, looking straight at the archduke. "You should take all that you can."

Daindreth studied the other man, looking for some subtle clue or double meaning. Both he and the guard captain had been raised in the scheming and intrigue of the palace. They knew how to spot duplicity and how to read hidden meanings behind innocuous phrases.

Amira had shared that Darrigan had tried to talk Vesha out of her deals with cythraul. Daindreth had found it hard to believe, but the more he spoke with Amira about her own curse and how Darrigan had managed his own, it seemed more and more believable.

What was Darrigan trying to say?

"Bring Amira back." Daindreth didn't expect his orders to work on the guard captain, but he tried anyway.

Captain Darrigan was unmoved. "You will see her again soon."

"Alive?" Daindreth demanded. "What are you doing with her?"

Darrigan's nostrils flared. "She is alive, archduke. And in one piece. Now you need a bath before you see the empress."

Daindreth knew Amira was alive. His demon was still silenced, but that told him nothing about how long she would be alive or what they meant to do with her.

"Cooperate with them," the guard captain said, nodding to the two girls. "If I hear you aren't, I will have them whipped until you comply."

Daindreth frowned at that. "What?"

Captain Darrigan pointed to the two girls, who looked

189

impossibly delicate in that moment. "I will have them whipped."

It took Daindreth another moment to understand. "You sick son of a bitch."

Captain Darrigan shrugged, not reacting to the insult. "It was your mother's idea."

Of course, it was. He looked to the pair of men still gripping Daindreth's arms and barked a short set of orders. With that, the older Kadra'han turned and marched out of the bathhouse.

Daindreth was left with the Kadra'han guards and the two girls. One, the slightly taller of the two, curtsied awkwardly.

"Right this way, Your Highness," she said, her voice soft and delicate as a spring breeze.

Daindreth didn't know anything about these two girls, but he didn't want to see them whipped for him. He complied, stepping after them and sitting on a low stone bench.

He eased down stiffly, trying to keep his upper body as motionless as possible. As soon as he sat, the girls went to work. One knelt to remove his boots while the other set to unbuckling his belt.

"What are you doing?" Daindreth asked sharply, grabbing the older girl's hand as she touched the buckle.

"We're to bathe you, Your Highness," she answered, not quite making eye contact.

Daindreth hesitated. "I'm not sure—"

The girl bowed her head. "If I may."

Daindreth let her hand go, not knowing what else to do.

She unfastened the belt around his waist and began carefully undoing the wooden toggles at his neck.

Daindreth shifted uncomfortably, heat creeping up the back of his neck.

"You are injured?" the older girl looked to the dark bruises along his jaw and temple.

"Few days ago," Daindreth admitted. The ministrations of the Istovari and Amira had helped, but he was still sore.

"We will be gentle."

The girl at his feet finished unfastening his boots and pulled them off. She tossed them aside and then reached for his arms and the leather hunting bracers he'd gotten from the Istovari.

They pulled his tunic over his head, slowly. Daindreth didn't resist, but nor did he do much to help them—partly because he couldn't raise his arms comfortably and partly because this felt...wrong.

The two girls inspected the bandages around his torso and the dark welts that had been hidden by his tunic. The younger of the two mumbled something Daindreth didn't understand and the elder nodded, responding in an indistinct phrase. Were they speaking Nihainite? He thought so, but the dialect sounded off.

The two girls peeled off his bandages next, exposing red cuts and old poultices beneath. They tossed those aside and then moved down to his trousers.

Daindreth stood when they prompted and waited awkwardly while they unlaced him and finished stripping him down. His face flushed, but neither of the girls seemed to mind his nudity and neither did the guards.

The younger of the two piled his clothes into a heap along with the discarded bandages and tossed them to the nearest guard. The Kadra'han knelt and began rifling through the discarded garments, looking for what, Daindreth couldn't be sure.

The elder girl took Daindreth's hand, a gesture that made him flinch. "Step into the water, archduke. It's purified and will help cleanse your wounds."

Daindreth had already committed to obedience, so he let the girls lead him to the edge of the nearest pool. He stepped in, finding steps led down from the edge.

"Sit," the elder girl said.

Daindreth obeyed, sitting down by the pool's edge. The water was deliciously warm, flowing over his cuts, bruises, and aching muscles. It smelled of sweet spices and perfumes and made him think of the baths at home.

Once he sat, the older of the two girls untied the front of her long robe.

Daindreth stiffened. "What are you doing?"

"I'm getting in with you," she answered, speaking as if they were discussing his choice of soap.

Daindreth coughed. "I don't think—"

She sloughed off her robe, revealing that she wore an undyed linen kirtle and tunic underneath. Without further ado, she slid into the water beside him.

Daindreth had reclaimed some sense of propriety when he had submerged in the water, but now his discomfort increased tenfold.

Behind him, the younger of the two girls knelt and began pouring sweet oils into his hair. She massaged his scalp, neck, and shoulders, skillfully working at the tense muscles. Daindreth might have enjoyed it if her touch hadn't felt so…wrong. He hadn't asked for this. He kept thinking about Amira and how she might feel about this situation.

Plenty of noblemen, often respectable men in public, frequented the pleasure houses and opium dens of Mynadra, but Daindreth had never been one of them. When he had been young enough to have an interest, he had been too afraid of his demon. What might the creature do to an unsuspecting prostitute?

He'd heard that public bathhouses were common in his mother's country, but his Erymayan sensibilities were not so accepting of the idea. Everything about this seemed improper and, worse, like a betrayal of Amira.

The older girl pulled one of his feet out of the water and began scrubbing at his toes with a stiff cloth. It tickled and he had to resist the impulse to pull away.

Relax, archduke. It's a bathhouse, not a bordello.

Daindreth looked around at the words of Caa Iss, though he wasn't sure why. Had Amira been taken too far away?

At least they are pretty girls, the demon crooned. *Remind me to ask for them later.*

Daindreth swallowed hard, looking past the girl scrubbing his feet to the opposite end of the large bathhouse.

Caa Iss grumbled in annoyance. *Depriving me the view of her won't stop me making plans for her.*

Daindreth focused on calm breathing so as not to disturb his wounded ribs and to keep from flinching as the older girl finished with his first foot and moved to the second. He needed to think. That's what Amira would be doing—planning.

Vesha was here and she wanted him cared for and cleaned up, probably for the sake of the cythraul in his head. If she had all her Kadra'han here, or at least enough of them, that probably meant she was about to try giving him over to the demon again.

For some reason, she wanted Amira this time. And alive, apparently. That thought made him sick.

The only reason Vesha would want Amira alive was if Caa Iss and Moreyne wanted her alive.

The two girls finished cleaning Daindreth. They scrubbed him head to foot, not once showing the least hint of embarrassment at all. Perhaps they did this for men all the time. Were they slaves?

He knew little of Kelamora or their ways. Thadred had never talked about the monastery in detail and Amira hadn't had the chance.

Daindreth had never considered himself a prude—though Thadred had called him as much. Guilt plucked at the back of his mind the whole time, thinking of Amira. The entire bath made him feel as though he owed her a confession and apology at the very least.

Are you excited? I know I am.

Daindreth swallowed. The cythraul didn't have to tell him what he meant. The thing knew Vesha was here and Vesha meant to free him, tonight, most likely. She never was the sort to waste time.

How were they getting out of this? Daindreth looked to his guards. He was fairly certain they had been ordered not to harm him. There were only two of them, but he was naked at the moment. If he'd had a weapon and hadn't still been sore from Bardaka's beating...

Where was Thadred? Daindreth held onto hope that his cousin had escaped with the kelpie. The Kadra'han guard captain had ordered his men to leave the Istovari, but that didn't mean he wasn't sending soldiers back into the forest to destroy the surviving rangers even now.

Daindreth inhaled and exhaled a slow breath so as not to strain his ribs. Amira was imprisoned and Thadred probably had nothing but the kelpie and a few surviving Istovari. It would take an army to break into Kelamora.

Why so sad, archduke? Be excited! You'll be bedding your woman tonight. Or at least I will. You'll get to watch.

Daindreth punched the water at that.

The two servant girls jumped, startled by his outburst.

"Sorry," Daindreth mumbled to them.

Caa Iss chuckled in the back of his mind.

The archduke looked toward the Kadra'han, noting a long knife strapped to the thigh of the nearest one.

Don't you dare, Caa Iss growled. *I know what you're thinking and don't you dare. They'll kill the princess if you do.*

Daindreth considered the cythraul's threat. They might very well kill Amira, but they were going to do that anyway—after Caa Iss tortured her, if the demon's promises were true.

But if Daindreth could get ahold of that knife—any weapon, really—and slit his own throat, Caa Iss would be forced back to the Dread Marches. It would end this whole thing.

Daindreth thought about it until he remembered Amira and Thadred. He'd promised them after Mynadra that he wouldn't try to kill himself again. Circumstances had been different, then. He hadn't been captured by his mother's Kadra'han, but...he'd wait. For now. He'd wait as long as he could, but if they hurt Amira or it looked like it was over...

When they were finished, the girls offered him a robe not unlike the ones they had worn and helped him out of the bath. Daindreth did feel better, though his mind wasn't in a place to enjoy it.

This was pleasant, Caa Iss purred. *I think I want a personal bathhouse in the palace when we are emperor. I know we have one, but I want one adjoining the imperial chambers.*

Daindreth followed the two girls—escorted by the armed Kadra'han, of course—to one of the walls. The wood paneling slid aside, revealing a hallway lined with rice mats.

The reeds felt strange on his bare feet. The wood panel walls were painted with scenes of trees, flowers, and one even displayed a duck pond, complete with ducklings and tiny dragonflies.

It wasn't what he had envisioned as Kelamora at all. For a place dedicated to training the best killers in the known world, this monastery seemed far more a temple to nature than an institution of death.

Daindreth's attendants took him to another one of the sliding panels, one decorated with ferns and spiny trees. Inside was a room with a single stool, several chests, and a mirror as large as any he had seen in the palace back home.

Interesting place. Not quite my taste, but interesting enough.

The girls prompted Daindreth to remove his dressing robe. He hesitated again, coughing awkwardly.

By the door, the two Kadra'han chuckled to each other.

They're laughing at you. I would be too if I had lungs.

The younger of the two girls opened the nearest trunk and pulled out several neatly folded items. She set them down beside the stool while the elder stepped behind Daindreth and began untying his robe without waiting for his permission.

They've already seen you naked. No reason to be shy now.

Daindreth complied with the two girls, letting them smear salves on his many cuts and welts before they dressed him in a heavy kilt and sat him down on the stool. They attended his ribs carefully, wrapping his waist in clean linen and bandaging the more serious cuts on his forearms and back.

They shaved him and Daindreth couldn't help thinking of Amira doing the same thing not so very long ago. He'd enjoyed her fussing and looking after him. Having her care for him had almost made the beating worth it.

Caa Iss never stopped offering commentary the entire time the two girls tended Daindreth's wounds and dressed him.

You act like a silk-covered virgin. But I suppose you are *a silk-covered virgin.*

Daindreth breathed deeply, keeping still as the older of the two girls pulled the razor along his jaw. The cythraul wasn't saying anything he hadn't said a thousand times before.

The two girls dressed him into layers of a long robe that reminded him of what priests wore, red with gold brocade. The silk lining slid against his skin like butter.

They fitted him in soft-soled shoes and combed back his hair. It had grown long these past weeks, longer than it had been in some time.

When they were finished, the older of the two girls offered

him a steaming ceramic cup that had a sharp, clean smell to it. "For your wounds," she said. "It will help with the pain."

Daindreth accepted and drank the mixture, recognizing it as a willow bark tincture, but with something added. "What's in this?"

"It's from our physicians here," the girl said. "It speeds the recovery of wounds."

Daindreth downed the concoction in a few gulps. No point in resisting.

The older girl took the cup back and nodded to the two Kadra'han. "He's ready."

The Kadra'han stepped forward. "Come with us, Your Highness."

Daindreth breathed deeply, looking up to the guards. "Where are we going?"

"The empress awaits you," one of the men said.

It's rude to keep your mother waiting.

Daindreth looked to the two girls in front of him. Regardless of what was going to happen, they would be in danger here. Whether Caa Iss broke free in a few hours or Daindreth and Amira somehow miracled their way out of this, this monastery was about to become a charnel house.

The handmaidens leaned over to help him stand. Daindreth leaned on the closest one for support, bringing his mouth near her ear as he did. "Get out of here," he whispered to her. "Before tonight."

The girl looked to him, startled.

"Take your friend and get as far away from here as you can." Daindreth squeezed her arm. He doubted she would listen, but he prayed to every god that she would.

The older girl stared at him with an odd expression.

She thinks you're insane.

Daindreth turned away from the girl as the two Kadra'han reached him. No one spoke as they led him out of the dressing room and back into the paneled hall.

The wooden slats creaked beneath their feet as they walked. Daindreth's robe rustled and the armor of the Kadra'han jangled, but none of them spoke.

They took Daindreth back through a stone portion of the monastery, low and wide stone walkways barely high enough for Daindreth to walk without crouching. The archduke let the Kadra'han lead him, Caa Iss chattering the entire way.

The cythraul hadn't gotten the chance to speak to Daindreth for days and as he usually did, he had a lot to say. The demon taunted and harried Daindreth, mostly about Amira. The creature seemed wholly convinced that he would be free by tonight and Daindreth was inclined to believe him.

Daindreth knew they were close to his mother when he spotted the pair of Kadra'han guards outside one of the stone arches. He straightened, bracing himself, then stepped through the arch without waiting.

"Your Majesty," one of his Kadra'han guards said, bowing. "We have brought the archduke."

Daindreth found himself in a large, oval-shaped room with one side completely open, overlooking the valley below the monastery. From here he could see the vast swaths of trees, what appeared to be a waterfall near a few slopes, and even the start of the dark tangle that was the Cursewood.

Thadred was out there somewhere. Daindreth wasn't sure what his cousin could do, though. He was half torn between hoping Thadred tried to save him and praying he didn't. What chance did a lame knight with a handful of woodsmen have against a fortress of warrior-sorcerers?

A long table filled most the room. It was some light wood, polished to a shine with gold sparkling in the trim. The entire surface was covered in stacks of papers, pestles and mortars, dried and fresh plants, pieces of animal bones—at least he hoped they were animal—bits of string, knives of different lengths, and a collection of roots.

Vesha stood over the table, directing the work of several young men with shaved heads, dressed much as the two handmaidens had been. It was rare Daindreth saw his mother at work—real, manual labor.

Several strands of her hair hung haphazardly over her face, making her seem frazzled in a way she rarely did. Though she wore a purple robe in a style much like his, fit for an empress, she somehow seemed less intimidating. She looked up when the

Kadra'han announced their entrance.

"Daindreth," she said, pausing. Her expression was odd. Not as serene or resolute as he was used to seeing.

"Mother," Daindreth said, careful to keep the anger out of his voice. "Where is Amira?"

Vesha handed a jawbone to her assistant and her whole body shifted. In an instant, she went from being the overworked witch to the empress. She projected control, mastery, and utter composure. "I see you are well."

Daindreth had played the game of pleasantries in the past. He wasn't going to humor her this time. "Where is Amira, Mother?"

Vesha inhaled, raising her chin. "The assassin awaits judgment for her crimes."

"She's committed no crimes," Daindreth said. "None that haven't been pardoned, anyway." His tone sounded almost taunting to his own ears. "You plan to sacrifice me tonight, don't you? Your goddess would allow nothing less. Is Amira to be offered as well?"

Vesha's composure wavered for just a moment.

"Where are the Istovari children?"

The empress's expression hardened. "They are in the barracks. They are a gift to the grandmaster, to do with as he pleases. He lost many good Kadra'han in the assault on the Haven. The Istovari whelps are my repayment."

Daindreth remained quiet. He had plenty of things to say about his mother using children as currency, but if she wasn't planning to cut their throats to feed her spells, he could concern himself with them later. Assuming later came.

I wonder when they will be for sale. The monastery survives on the sales of trained Kadra'han. Do you remember Amira telling you that? Perhaps we can buy some of them. I do like having Kadra'han.

Daindreth kept his attention on his mother. "You never planned to let them go, did you?"

Vesha didn't even hesitate. "Either the Istovari were going to try trading you to me or you were going to come to rescue them. I saw no way to lose."

So, it had been a trap, just as Amira and Daindreth had

thought. "You're performing the ritual tonight, I assume?"

Vesha, to her credit, at least hesitated to answer. She must feel some shame over it. "Yes."

"Why did you want to see me now?" Daindreth folded his arms across his chest. The wide sleeves of his robe made the gesture awkward.

Vesha was silent for a set of heartbeats. "I wanted to see that you were well. That's all."

"As well as can be expected for a man who's about to be sacrificed."

Vesha's expression hardened. She raised her chin. "Do you...want for anything?"

"I want Amira back." Daindreth wasn't about to let his mother pretend that she was anything but his captor and the captor of the woman he loved. "Better yet, I want Amira freed."

Gah! How you do fret over that woman.

"I can't do that," Vesha replied.

"Why not?"

"You know why," Vesha answered calmly. "I heard you encountered a mudslide near Hylendale. Is that correct?"

Daindreth paused.

"The rains haven't stopped in Hylendale and the north since." Vesha pulled herself to her full height. "In the south, the opposite is happening. The rivers are drying. Many of the crops will fail if we don't have rain soon. We won't be able to feed the people in the Hazar and Dumal provinces."

Daindreth didn't speak for a long moment. How was he supposed to respond to that?

Have you ever seen a person die of starvation, archduke? Caa Iss chortled. *It's one of the nastier ways to go.*

Vesha folded her hands in front of her. "There was an earthquake in Yndra, near the coast. The tidal wave wiped out the entire poor quarter near the docks and damaged many others."

Daindreth had visited Yndra a few times. It was a coastal port near the mouth of a major river, used as a shipping port for wool, lumber, grain, and other inland goods. It was a beautiful place with domed buildings that sparkled like sea glass. The people there had always smiled, even the poor ones.

Vesha took a deep breath. "The death toll is at least three thousand. Maybe more. The marquis estimates it will be."

The ruling marquis was as wide around as he was tall and as magnanimous as anyone Daindreth had met. Despite that, the marquis was a shrewd merchant king who had built a fortune far above his pedigree. He and Thadred had gotten along quite well, even if Thadred had gotten along a little *too* well with the marquis's niece.

"I'm sorry to hear that," Daindreth said quietly. "I didn't know."

Vesha's words came back sharp, angry. "Of course not. You ran away from your people. *This* is what happens when we break a deal with Moreyne."

I might peel apart a few traitors here and there, Caa Iss muttered. *But I wouldn't destroy an entire city like that. Nothing in it for me. Does this make you the real monster?*

Daindreth shook his head, coming back to himself.

"I told you before that this empire would fall apart if we didn't do this," Vesha said, her tone turning sharp. "And you abandoned them."

Daindreth inhaled. "You have no idea what you are doing."

"I am saving our people." Vesha's voice wavered, as if she fought to keep it from cracking. "This isn't a minstrel's ballad, Daindreth. This is reality, and in reality, there are necessary evils for the sake of the greater good."

"As a serpent only begets serpents, so evil only begets evil." Daindreth straightened even as Caa Iss jeered and mocked him in the back of his mind.

"You are young and naïve."

"I am young," Daindreth agreed. "But you are naïve if you think you can trust the demons, Mother. I promise you this—in the end, the price will be far higher than you can imagine. Maybe not at first. Maybe not in ten years, twenty, or one hundred, but in the end, the day of reckoning always comes. Then all the evil we condoned will be repaid to us, with interest."

Vesha was unmoved. "You know nothing."

Daindreth tapped the side of his head. "I have had one of these creatures in my skull for more than half my life. I know them better than you think."

For once, Caa Iss made no comment.

"I won't let you do this," Daindreth said calmly.

"How do you plan to stop me?" Vesha's tone hardened. "I have the girl. If you try to kill yourself again, she will die."

Daindreth nodded. "You have Amira. That's true. But she's dead anyway if Caa Iss breaks free." The archduke looked to the window, the wide-open space and the drop of at least two hundred feet below. "What will Moreyne do our people if I die, do you think?"

Don't you dare, Caa Iss growled. *I will just find a new vessel.*

Despite the demon's threat, Daindreth didn't think it was that easy.

Vesha looked to Daindreth's Kadra'han guards and they moved just a little closer, ready to stop him if he tried anything. "Don't even think about it," she said. "I have your woman!"

Daindreth looked to his mother. "I know."

"What can you do?" Vesha spat.

"I'm not sure." Daindreth furrowed his brow, considering that. "I had best think of something."

Good luck with that, Caa Iss snickered.

"Take him away. I'll send for him when I'm ready."

As the Kadra'han escorted Daindreth out of the room with Vesha, Daindreth had the sick feeling he might have to find a way to kill himself—or worse, his mother.

CHAPTER NINETEEN

Thadred

"**B**ollocks!" Thadred swore as he stepped on a root sideways and his ankle jerked, sending white-hot pain up his hip, spine, and straight to his skull. "Son of a half-pig whore!" He muffled his oaths in his sleeve, not wanting to shout when they might very well have hunters on their trail.

"Thadred?" One of the Istovari rangers leaned over him, sounding concerned.

"I'm fine," Thadred snarled, leaning heavily on Lleuad's glossy black shoulder. He took a few long, deep breaths. "How many of us survived?"

The young ranger—a girl who was probably pretty when she wasn't covered in dirt and blood—answered him with a hesitant grimace. "A little more than half," she answered softly. "The rest are dead back in that clearing."

Thadred nodded, looking around at their forlorn little group. They had only four horses, five counting Lleuad. Even if they managed to somehow break into the monastery, there would be no swift escape.

"It's strange," the girl said, looking around her. "It's been so long since I've seen a forest beside the Cursewood. Not since I was a child. And I was too young to remember then."

Thadred forced a smile, still breathing heavily through the pain in his side. "How are you liking it so far?"

"It's pretty," she said softly, looking up at the canopy overhead. "There's...there's so much green."

Thadred might have chuckled if he hadn't been trying to keep from passing out. "That's forests for you. What's your name, girl?"

"Murren," she answered, blinking at him with large, pale eyes.

"That's a good name," Thadred said. "Can you tell Tapios to come to me, Murren?"

The girl nodded and spun around to find the rangers' leader.

For some reason, the rangers deferred to Thadred as much as Tapios now. He supposed it made sense since none of them had been outside the Cursewood in their adult lives.

They had found their way to a waterfall a good mile or so from the monastery. The large structure was still in sight through the trees, squatting on the side of the mountain like a petulant toad. The red arches leading up the path to the main gate were specks from this distance, but he could see them.

Dain and Amira were in there, and probably with the Istovari children, too.

Thadred ran over everything he knew about the monastery in his mind, trying to recall every drain, servant's entrance, and weakness he could.

"Thadred." Tapios returned with Murren, blood on his hands from where he had been helping to bandage some of the injured.

"We don't have much time," Thadred said. "If I know my aunt, and I do, she's going to try to unleash Caa Iss tonight."

"The empress?" Tapios raised one eyebrow.

"Yes. That fellow who led the Kadra'han in their attack was Darrigan, her captain of the guard. He's never far from her side, so if he's here, she's close."

Tapios shot a look to Murren. No doubt the people were uneasy to hear that the witch of all witches was within walking distance. "If she has the children…"

"She probably hasn't hurt them," Thadred said. "Children with enough power to become Kadra'han are rare these days. They're probably too valuable."

That didn't appear to comfort Tapios. "You think she will have them bound in a Kadra'han's oaths by the time we get there?"

Thadred grimaced. He hadn't thought of that. "Another reason to hurry. She waited for sundown to perform the cythraul ritual last time, so I assume she needs the moon to be out. Moreyne being a moon goddess and all."

Tapios shook his head. "I still can't believe a woman would do that to her own child."

Thadred, for his part, had no problem believing it. "Vesha

203

believes it's in the best interest of the empire."

"Deals with cythraul—"

"Look, I think she's mad. The point is, we need to get in there tonight before she sets Caa Iss loose on the world."

"Do you think the princess is still alive?" Tapios asked.

Thadred shook his head. "I don't know."

The Kadra'han had taken her alive, he had been able to confirm that much from witnesses. As for whether or not they had kept her that way, he had no way of knowing.

"My guess is that the Istovari children are in there, though," he said, jerking his chin toward the monastery. "It doesn't make much sense to take them anywhere else."

Tapios looked to the distant monastery. "How do we get in to find out?"

That was the part that got tricky.

"There are no sewers," Thadred said. "And no entrances save the one by the main gate. There's a secondary escape route that leads out onto the plateau behind the monastery, but it would take us at least a day to approach from that side."

"There are trees and greenery all up along the base of the walls," Tapios said. "Can we get close through that?"

"It's deceptive from this distance," Thadred said. "The ground there is sloped too steep for the horses, probably too steep for most of us." Thadred was too proud to admit that it was too steep for him specifically. Unless Lleuad could carry him, he would be nothing but dead weight.

Tapios blinked at Thadred. "Then what do you plan? You can't just mean for us to sit here, helpless."

Thadred exhaled. He didn't plan for them to sit around helpless, but at the moment it was hard to come up with better ideas. "We'll have to move at dark," he said. "We can't do anything until then, but we will need a plan."

"Why wait?" Tapios pressed. "These trees are so thick, they wouldn't see us approach."

"True," Thadred conceded. "But I'm worried they'll be looking for us."

"How many Kadra'han do you think are in there?"

"Eh." Thadred shrugged. "Kelamora can support

somewhere around two hundred students, teachers, and servants, but short-term, maybe a hundred additional guests."

Tapios nodded. "Not as bad as I feared, but still more than ten-to-one."

"They won't all be fighters," Thadred said. "Even with Vesha. An empress has handmaidens and clerks and to travel here she would have needed coachmen and grooms, too."

Tapios blinked at him. "Then it will only be what? Five-to-one?"

Thadred offered a lopsided smile. "I'll take what I can get at this point."

"How are we supposed to get in there?" Murren asked.

Thadred glanced around. "I need something to draw with." He hobbled to the soft earth along the riverbank, snatching up a stick as he went. He scratched in the ground, trying to recall what he could about the monastery. "A lot of it is dedicated to training courtyards and sparring rooms," he said. "Within the monastery itself, most of it is wooden. The interior is almost entirely cedar and rice paper."

"We can burn it!" Murren offered.

"Slow down there," Thadred said, not looking up from his crude sketching. "We don't know where Dain and Amira are. Not to mention the children."

Thadred closed his eyes, trying to remember the turns and corners of the monastery. He'd drawn a map for Amira when she'd gone to break Dain out of the palace, but that was different. He had spent most of his life in the palace. He'd spent just a few weeks in Kelamora and it had been years ago.

"Ugh." Thadred scratched out the drawing and started again. He looked over to where Iasu was bound hand and foot again, trussed up like a pheasant for market.

Thadred hobbled over to the smaller man, not wasting time. "What were Vesha's orders to you?"

Iasu exhaled out his nose. "I'm not a traitor. I won't help you circumvent her."

Thadred rolled his eyes. "Look here, my friend." He eased down on a rock opposite the smaller man. "Captain Darrigan has served the empress better and longer than anyone alive. You agree?"

Iasu fixed Thadred in a stare that said everything the knight needed to know.

"Even he's trying to stop her folly with cythraul. It's in everyone's best interest, including hers, that Caa Iss *not* be unleashed on the world. That's in keeping with your oaths, right?"

While Thadred had no idea if Iasu had even the slightest interest in being freed, that was how Amira had broken her curse. She'd pitted Daindreth's commands against her curse's intent.

Ironically, Thadred had no chance at breaking his own curse because Daindreth held his leash so loosely. There were simply no commands to pit against each other.

Iasu shook his head. "What game are you playing?"

"Do you want to be free of your curse?" It was a risky game, but Thadred was out of other ways to earn Iasu's cooperation.

"I won't let you hurt the empress." Something in Iasu's tone said he wouldn't help them do that even without his curse.

"I'm not talking about that." Thadred smirked. "What if I told you there was a way to be free of the Kadra'han's compulsions and yet still serve her?"

Iasu scoffed. "Do you think I'm an idiot?"

"An idiot, eh?" Thadred grinned. "How do you explain Amira defying Dain back in Mynadra?"

Iasu hesitated just a few moments and Thadred pressed his advantage.

"He commanded her not to go back for him, you know. Commanded me the same. He ordered us to get as far away from this continent as possible."

The smaller Kadra'han recovered himself. "He gave her ancillary commands."

Ancillary commands—conditional orders that allowed Kadra'han to take different actions under different circumstances. They were a logical assumption, but Thadred had seen the truth.

"No," Thadred said. "The commands he gave us were repeated directly from the empress herself. There was no room for ancillary commands. But Amira still defied him."

Behind Thadred, he noticed that Tapios and Murren had gone quiet, along with the other Istovari. They were listening in. He could almost feel them leaning over his shoulder.

"You see, she put the curse against his commands. Her desire to serve Dain, in her mind, went against his orders. The curse had to kill her or let her serve him." Thadred shrugged. "In the end, it not only broke her compulsions, but it magnified her power overnight."

"You think I'm a fool to fall for such cheap tales?" Iasu snapped.

"It's the truth," Thadred said. "I know Vesha has to be wondering how Amira defied Dain's commands. Now you'll be able to tell her." Thadred looked around him at the bedraggled Istovari rangers, wondering again how he was going to siege one of the most secure monasteries in the world with just this lot.

"Impossible," Iasu retorted. "A Kadra'han's vows can only be broken by death."

"Every curse can be broken," Thadred replied, sounding like Amira to his own ears. "I won't tell you it was easy," he admitted. "Amira almost killed herself in the process. She started riding full tilt toward the palace, direct defiance." Thadred's smile waned at the memory. "The curse nearly choked her to death before breaking."

"You think I'll be killing myself for your archduke?" Iasu's mouth quirked in a mocking look.

"Oh no," Thadred chuckled. "But I am urging you to consider *almost* killing yourself for the sake of your empress."

"I am not so easily manipulated," Iasu scoffed. "You'd spear her if you had the chance."

Thadred wasn't about to deny it. While he'd never thought to kill a woman before, much less his aunt, the idea was becoming less abhorrent by the day. "Keep in mind, my angry little friend, that Caa Iss will do far worse than that if he gets the chance. It's just how cythraul are." Thadred clapped Iasu on the shoulder. "Food for thought."

Iasu didn't have a comeback for that one.

The knight rose stiffly to his feet and turned back to Tapios. "Now. Who could go on a quick scouting mission?"

"Mylva and Godfried," Tapios said. The leader of the

rangers singled out a pair of young hunters—the kids couldn't have been more than sixteen or seventeen. "They're the fastest who aren't injured."

Thadred took note of the two youths, one helping bandage the leg of a comrade and the other wrangling their remaining horses into a picket line. "Good," Thadred said. "Can you have them do a quick pass around the monastery? They have an hour. Tell them not to get too close and not to be noticed, but to see if there are any entrances besides the main one. Can they do that?"

"They're used to prowling the Cursewood," Tapios answered. "Where there are far worse things than imperial soldiers."

Thadred wasn't so sure about that. This was the part of war he hated—putting his own people in danger—but he had no choice. "Good. Send them out as soon as you can."

Tapios jerked his head to Murren, still standing at his side. "You heard the knight. Inform Mylva and Godfried."

Murren nodded. "Yes, Brother Tapios."

Gods, they looked so *young*, Thadred thought. Had he ever been that young? The boy barely had a beard and the girl's hair was still in two braids on either side of her head, like a child. He supposed she looked old enough to be married, and he'd been doing worse things at their age, but...

"Is it true?" Tapios asked, dropping his voice.

"What?" Thadred blinked at the ranger.

"Did the princess break her curse?" Tapios repeated, glancing past Thadred to Iasu.

Thadred could feel the small warrior's glare boring into his back. "Yes." He saw no reason to keep it a secret from the Istovari now. "She hasn't been bound by Dain's commands since we fled Mynadra."

"Why did she not say anything?" Tapios shook his head in confusion. "If the Elder Mother had known—"

"If the Elder Mother had known, they would have kept her imprisoned. As it was, they just had him order her compliance and assumed she had to obey him."

Tapios didn't argue.

The knight wanted to pace and if he had been in a flat palace with his cane, he would have. As it was, the roots and rocks hidden beneath the grass made that treacherous at best.

"Think, Thadred," he ordered himself. "Bloody *think*." He scratched at his beard, trying to come up with some brilliant strategy, but nothing came to mind. Perhaps if he had a week to plan, a month, he could do it. But like this, with the threat of the demon bearing down on them within the next few hours...

"Tapios!" Thadred spun around to the ranger. "My good man, I have an idea."

It was a stupid idea, but stupidity was all they had left at this point.

CHAPTER TWENTY

Amira

The wind whipped up, gusting along the corridor. Amira curled in closer on herself, pulling her knees tighter against her chest.

She'd been here for a few hours as best she could tell from the darkening sky. Birds flew back to their nests beyond her prison and the nighttime animals had begun squawking from the forest below.

Other than the distant animals, she was alone. Or appeared to be, at least. She wondered if Saan Thii or another cythraul might be watching her, waiting for her to expose weakness. The demoness had not appeared to her again, but that meant little.

Footsteps warned her first. She still couldn't sense *ka,* closed off from it as she was in this cell, but she heard the heavy tramp of boots long before a dark figure cast a shadow over her.

Amira raised her chin, glaring up at the captain of the guard. He was alone, to her surprise. He appeared to have changed out of his battle gear and into a less formal, softer uniform. Over it, he had a woolen overcoat that tied in front with rectangular sleeves, after the style of Nihain.

He still wore his sword at his hip, though.

Captain Darrigan looked her over and his expression was hard to read. "How long have you been like this?" he asked.

Amira was humiliated, sore, hungry, cold, and had been crying for at least two hours. All the same, she wasn't about to fall for any of his manipulation tactics. "Since you ordered me down here."

The captain glanced back the way he had come as if expecting someone. He unbuckled his sword belt.

Amira flinched, but instantly steeled herself. She wasn't going to cower in front of him. She *wasn't.* She wouldn't beg for mercy either.

Darrigan undid the sash at the front of his overcoat and slid it off. He bundled the coat and sash in one hand, passing it through the bars of the cell.

Amira stared at him. She'd heard about techniques to break prisoners that involved having one interrogator beat the captive down while another pretended to offer kindness. Was that what this was?

"I know you're cold," the captain said flatly. "And if you like sitting naked on the floor, that's fine, but you look miserable, so here."

Amira gulped, not sure if she should take it or not.

Captain Darrigan dropped the coat inside the bars, tossing it so it landed just at her feet. He rolled his eyes and turned his back. "Better?"

Amira didn't know what to do, but in that moment she was freezing and at the same time burning with the embarrassment of being chained nude in a cell.

She snatched up the robe, hands fumbling with the thick wool. It settled around her far too big, but she wrapped the sash around her waist an extra time for good measure. The chain on her ankle clanked with every motion.

When she stopped rustling, the captain turned back around.

Amira felt like a child in a parent's clothes just then, engulfed by the garment. But she was fully covered again.

The captain of the guard folded his arms across his chest, facing her down. When he didn't speak, Amira got impatient.

"What do you want?" Amira raised her chin. "Don't tell me you came down here to see if I was comfortable."

"I didn't," the captain answered. "Your comfort matters little to me."

"Glad we cleared that up." Amira wrapped her arms around her waist, the massive sleeves of the overcoat hanging from her wrists. "Where is Daindreth?"

"He's secure," the captain replied. "Asking for you constantly, if that's any consolation."

Amira swallowed. "What are you going to do to him?"

Captain Darrigan looked away from her and toward the vast expanse of forest beyond her prison. "How many Istovari do you think survived?"

Amira almost laughed at that, but her teeth were still chattering. "I'm not a traitor."

The captain looked back to her. "When the empress completes the ritual on your archduke, it will be too late."

Amira's nostrils flared.

"I respect you, Amira Brindonu," Darrigan said, his tone calm and surprisingly sincere. "I thought you were a foolish child and I still do, but..." He shook his head and looked away again.

He rubbed at his neck, at the place where Amira had once been able to feel her own curse tightening and choking her every time she disobeyed her father's commands.

"What do you want?" Amira clipped.

His jaw flexed. He inhaled slowly and opened his mouth, then closed it again.

"Darrigan?" Amira waited.

"I love Vesha," the captain said. There was no emotion in the words, just a bland acknowledgement of fact. He frowned, eyes on the wall behind Amira's head.

"I love Daindreth," Amira replied. She wasn't sure if that was a challenge or a commiseration.

Captain Darrigan nodded solemnly. "But she's made her choice," the guard captain said, his words halting and broken. "I...I protect her, but I cannot protect her from herself."

Amira didn't know what to say to that.

Another tense silence passed between them. Amira knew from experience that the captain was speaking carefully, trying to tread around commands Vesha had placed on him. It was a long set of heartbeats before he spoke again.

"You broke free," Captain Darrigan said at length. "You defied your liege and were able to save him. Has he placed any new compulsions on you?"

Amira shook her head even though she was loath to tell the captain the truth about anything he didn't already know. "The curse no longer compels me to obey him."

Darrigan had no visible reaction to that, remaining intently focused on Amira. "There isn't much I can say," he added after another torturously long pause.

"I understand," Amira said. She wasn't sure that the captain was her ally, but he was no friend of Caa Iss. "Are you still going to try and kill Daindreth?"

Captain Darrigan had once, when they first met, strongly implied that Amira should kill Daindreth if she wanted to save him, save the empire, even. He hadn't been able to say it outright because of compulsions given to him by the empress, but he had made it clear enough.

"I would if I could," the captain answered. "But the empress…" He paused again. "She thinks this is the only way."

"Maybe she deserves what's coming to her." In Amira's mind, her future mother-in-law had earned whatever fate awaited her. After all, Vesha was the one who had pressed on, dabbling with demons even when the price was her only child.

Captain Darrigan looked away.

"She's shackled you," Amira said, adjusting the sleeves of the large overcoat. "Met your objections to her choices with commands of silence." She shook her head. "Why do you love her?"

"The archduke dragged you from your home. Forced you into a marriage contract. Why do you love him?" Captain Darrigan's words were sharp. He sounded almost accusing.

"That's different," Amira protested. "Daindreth…he's good. He's kind. And he will do whatever he has to do for his people."

Captain Darrigan nodded again. "His mother is the same."

Amira didn't believe the captain. Vesha might think she was working in the interest of the greater good, but she was willing to do quite a bit of evil to get there. It seemed counterproductive.

"With his last breath, the emperor asked me to protect her. Look after her." The captain's face had gone blank, but Amira wondered if his expression was not *too* blank, as if he were forcing all emotion away for fear of what might show. "And so I will."

Amira pulled his borrowed robe tighter around her. She no longer shivered, but her feet were cold on the chilly stone.

The two Kadra'han stared each other down—both so tangled up in the curse of Caa Iss, the ghost of Emperor Drystan, and the machinations of Vesha's witchcraft. Under different circumstances, they might have been allies. Because of Vesha's power over Darrigan, Amira could never trust his actions even if she trusted his intentions.

"I can do little." Captain Darrigan nodded to his overcoat now wrapping Amira's frame. "But if there is a chance I can do anything to stop this…" He let his words trail off, wincing slightly.

Was he asking for suggestions? Amira dared to ask, "The ritual will be performed tonight?"

"Yes," Darrigan said.

"If Thadred and my Istovari friends are still alive," she began, careful not to say anything that might trigger Vesha's commands. "They might…come pay their respects. To their new cythraul ruler. Who will bring us peace and prosperity."

Captain Darrigan nodded slowly, his eyes brightening. "If they were wise, they would. There will be guards posted, but…" He hesitated. "All the strongest warriors should be with Vesha. To see that nothing goes wrong."

It took Amira a moment to realize that Captain Darrigan was insinuating he would put the weakest Kadra'han on guard tonight—the ones who would be easiest to kill. Was he really willing to sacrifice his own warriors for this?

Of course, he was, she realized. He wanted nothing more than to protect Vesha. These men were sworn to give their lives for the empress anyway.

"Where is Daindreth?" Amira asked again.

"You will be taken to see him," Captain Darrigan answered. "Vesha wants you for the rite."

Amira caught the way his tone changed, shifting into a deeper timber. "I'm supposed to die in this ritual, aren't I?"

"Maybe. If you're lucky," the captain answered.

Amira took that to mean he didn't know.

Captain Darrigan turned away. "The sun will be setting soon. I suggest you do whatever you need to do to prepare for what lies ahead."

"And what lies ahead?"

He looked back to her. "If the empress does what I think she will…" His words faltered again. He paused, grinding his teeth for a moment before he was able to speak again. Vesha's commands were filtering his speech once more. "The empire won't need saving," he said, "because there will be nothing left to save."

"What do you mean?"

Captain Darrigan paused for a long moment, always indicative that he was fighting against some order from his liege. "The last ritual failed. The Fallen Goddess despises failure." His frown deepened before he spoke again. "She wants...restitution."

Amira swallowed as understanding dawned. "You mean she wants more than just Caa Iss in command of Daindreth now?"

"You are..." The captain's head twitched slightly, and Amira realized he had tried to nod, but was stopped. "...cleverer than I thought."

Amira's mind went straight to Saan Thii and the demoness's offer. "Saan Thii made me an offer to betray Vesha," Amira said. "She said she would help me free Daindreth if I became her host."

Captain Darrigan's eyes widened, and Amira saw fear, genuine fear there. "Did you accept?"

Amira shrugged. "I'm thinking on it. If things are as bad as you say..." In truth, Amira had no such intentions, but if her suspicions were correct, the captain probably had some compulsion or other that would force him to tell the empress. If Amira could sow distrust between the empress and her familiar, that was as good a start as any.

"You can't." Darrigan's tone was just a little too like a command. "If Vesha fails again while we still have cythraul—" His voice cut off and he wheezed, choking.

Amira had never seen the captain's curse react that violently before.

"Prepare yourself," he coughed. "I will...I will also prepare." Darrigan left so quickly he seemed to be fleeing.

Amira had never seen the captain of the guard hesitate, much less look frightened. What must he know that she didn't? He would have had a front row seat these past years to Vesha's dealings with the creatures of the Dread Marches.

Sitting back down against the wall, Amira tried to think. She ran over everything she knew in her mind and then ran through it again—starting at the beginning.

Caa Iss had been summoned from the Dread Marches and bound into Emperor Drystan using her blood. But he hadn't been fully possessed as the Istovari sorceresses had intended because the sacrifice—Amira—had survived.

Years later, when Emperor Drystan was dead, the cythraul passed to Daindreth on his eleventh birthday. Eleven was when Istovari boys began their first rites of passage into manhood, so that made sense.

Daindreth had struggled with the demon for control for most his life with general success. As far as Amira knew, though Caa Iss had taken control a handful of times, he had never hurt anyone and Daindreth had always been able to take control again after a brief interlude.

Then came Amira and Daindreth's meeting. Caa Iss had taken control again when the archduke's life had been in danger. They had fought, but when Amira burned the archduke's face with her blood by channeling a blast of *ka*—her own life force—it had suppressed the demon again.

Caa Iss had expressed a desire for her death to Vesha, but Vesha had allowed Amira to be banished. When Amira had broken her curse and come back, Daindreth had been possessed again. But Amira had been able to help him take control again by giving him strength through her Kadra'han bond.

Things had been stable ever since—Daindreth in control, but always hearing the cythraul unless he was with her.

Amira had no reason to believe that anything had really changed beyond that. So why was she still alive now? Did the demon truly just want the pleasure of punishing her? Maybe. He seemed vindictive enough.

Or was she just here to keep Daindreth in line until it was too late?

Amira swallowed. She remembered Daindreth had tried to kill himself the last time Vesha had tried to hand him off to the demon. What if…

But no. If Daindreth were dead, Vesha would kill her immediately. That was probably the whole point.

Pulling on her braid, Amira leaned back against the stone wall of her cell. She was trapped. She was isolated. There was nowhere for her to go and nothing to do.

Her only hope was limping out in the forest somewhere. Thadred had a swamp horse and whatever Istovari rangers might have survived. Not to mention that the monastery would be heavily guarded tonight and expecting an assault.

Captain Darrigan was in command of their defenses and had made it clear that he wanted the ritual stopped. But it didn't matter. He was bound by compulsion to Vesha.

Amira blinked back tears of frustration, fighting anger at Vesha, Cyne, the Istovari mothers, and everyone who had ever bound a Kadra'han.

She thought back to Saan Thii's words about seeing possible futures. Amira could think of no reason for Saan Thii to lie and say that about half of them showed Daindreth crowned as emperor, freed of Caa Iss. If anything, that sounded like a weakness for the cythraul.

Assuming it was true, did that mean they had a one in two chance of breaking free of this?

Amira clenched her eyes shut and fought to envision that— Daindreth crowned emperor at a grand coronation, surrounded by courtiers with Thadred at his side. There would be vassals from across the kingdom coming to bow and scrape and kiss his ring.

He would be emperor. He would be good. His reign would be one of peace, justice, and prosperity—the atonement for the cruelty of his father and the witchcraft of his mother.

She didn't dare put herself in those images. That seemed too much to hope for.

Amira thought about Saan Thii's offer again. Amira had said Daindreth wouldn't forgive her, but she wasn't sure that mattered. If he could be free, if he could be safe...

As she saw it, she had two options—wait to see if Thadred was as much of a miracle worker as she was or try to strike a bargain with the demoness.

Thadred might not even be able to walk up this mountain. He might already have been hunted down by Vesha's scouts. That left Saan Thii.

Amira took a deep breath, closing her eyes. She steeled her resolve, thinking of what she would say. Opening them, she

217

called into the emptiness.

"Saan Thii," she whispered, sure the creature could hear her no matter how quietly she spoke. "Saan Thii, I want to make a deal."

Amira waited. And waited.

Only the chirping of the birds beyond her prison bars greeted her. If Saan Thii had heard, she didn't respond.

"Listen, you bitch," Amira grated. "Do you want a body or not?"

No answer.

Cursing, Amira leaned back against the wall again.

The sun had broken through the cloud cover on its western descent. Though she couldn't see it from her prison, streaks of gold and red shone across the valley below, illuminating the trees as if they were on fire.

Amira had never really had the chance to appreciate the sunsets when she had lived here. Always she had been training or doing chores around this time. Though Kelamora was a serene place, idleness was unforgivable.

"This one's on you, Thadred," she whispered to the emptiness. "Make it good."

CHAPTER TWENTY-ONE

Thadred

Thadred was trying very hard to feign optimism as he listened to yet more bad news.

"So there is no way we could approach from the south?" he said, listening to the report from the rangers who had just returned.

"No," said one, a young woman. "It's too steep and the ground's too soft. I took a tumble just making my way along the foot of it." She gestured to her mud-smeared left knee and thigh.

"And the north?" Thadred looked to the young man who had also been sent out, prompting.

The young man shook his head. "Nothing but a tangle of vines and overgrowth."

Thadred smiled to keep from showing his frustration. "Thank you for confirming that for me."

Tapios looked to him. "Plan?"

When the lead ranger looked to Thadred, so did everyone else. Why was everyone looking to him? Did they think he was a sorcerer?

Well, Thadred supposed he was, in some respects, but that didn't mean he knew what he was doing.

The knight squinted at the fortress of Kelamora in the distance. It sat crouched atop the ridge, scowling down at any who would dare approach.

"There's a lagoon beyond that ridge," the male ranger said. "There are several barges and ships. They appear to be empty, though. Just a few guards."

"Hmm." Thadred considered that. The river was the fastest way to travel to and from Kelamora and was where the monastery got most of their supplies. It made sense that Vesha and her retinue had used the river to get here.

He considered what he might be able to do with this information. Perhaps set the barges on fire? But that would only trap the imperials here and would do nothing to rout them out of the monastery itself.

Thadred suppressed a groan. Small figures marched along the walls of the monastery. They didn't normally have guards posted, but Vesha was no idiot. She would make sure they were guarded. The knight watched, chewing his lip. They expected a rescue attempt, he would guess.

If the Kadra'han knew Thadred was here—which they almost certainly did—they would be waiting for him to make his move to stop them.

But he was in a stalemate.

Thadred swore heartily under his breath, fighting to keep his cool. Losing his temper was the fastest way he knew to demoralize the already stricken Istovari.

They were all looking to him, placing their hope in him, trusting him—for some reason. He had to be the backbone of this ragtag motley. He smeared a hand over his face.

"Thadred!"

Dropping his hand from his face, he turned around. "What?" His tone came out sharper than intended, but thankfully the young ranger didn't seem to notice.

"Defectors, my lord," the youth panted, red cheeks looking all the redder in his pale face. "From Kelamora."

Defectors? Thadred shot a look to Tapios, but the older man seemed just as surprised as he was. "Show me."

The ranger gestured eagerly, bow in one hand.

Thadred limped after the other man, Tapios following close behind. The older ranger could have easily passed him, but waited, letting Thadred have his space.

A few dozen paces down the slope and back through the trees, he found a cluster of Istovari rangers, eyes bright with the excitement of a capture. They held their weapons tightly and turned all their focus toward their captives, making Thadred cringe at their lack of discipline.

Only a few of them should be concerned with the intruders. The rest should be concerned with keeping their makeshift camp protected.

Thadred had to pull back a cluster of over-excited young rangers to see the two figures at the center of their group. If he had been hoping for a guard or maybe even a Kadra'han, he was soon disappointed.

Two girls crouched at the center of the huddle—the oldest one couldn't have been more than seventeen, though Thadred always had trouble guessing women's ages.

The pair had the large eyes and dark hair of Vesha's home country and were dressed in the local style of square sleeves and straight, flat sashes. They looked like servants.

"They're not Kadra'han," Tapios said confidently. "No curse binds them," he added, pointing to their throats.

The knight exhaled a long breath out his nose, clinging to patience by a few delicate threads. "These are scullery maids," he said, measuring his words carefully and deliberately to keep his temper in check. "Not defectors. Probably on their way home after a day's work."

The rangers around him looked crestfallen. "Should we let them go, then?" asked one of them, the young lad who had fetched Thadred to begin with.

"No," Thadred said through gritted teeth. "Now that you've brought them here, they might give us away."

And now he would have to expend resources to keep the girls guarded, unless he was willing to kill them, which he wasn't.

"They might know something," one of the rangers insisted, a young woman, not one Thadred recognized. "They came from the monastery."

"Of course, they came from the monastery." Thadred studied the two young women. "That's the only thing around here."

The younger girl huddled closer to the older one, hiding her tear-stained face from view. The older girl had also been crying, but she tried to face Thadred with a straight face.

"We won't hurt you," said the redheaded Istovari boy. "There's no need to be frightened."

"Don't go making promises just yet," Thadred clipped, as much in annoyance at these idiots as actual suspicion of the girls. "If they are from Kelamora, then they could still be spies."

Tapios looked to the young ranger. He had deferred his command to Thadred easily enough, but when young, helpless-looking women were involved, he seemed to have trouble staying silent. "Where did you find them?" he asked.

"Coming down the slope from the monastery," the young ranger said. "A path near the waterfall."

Thadred shot a look to the redheaded ranger. "There's a path down from the waterfall? Why didn't you tell me sooner?"

"We didn't see it until they came down it," the ranger admitted. "It's overgrown and covered in ferns."

"We are not spies," the older girl said, voice shaking. "We just want to go home. That's it. We just want..." She broke off crying.

"We won't hurt you," the redhead promised.

Thadred scowled at the boy. "Maybe you won't." Even if he doubted these girls were spies and even if he didn't plan to hurt them, what business did this boy have making promises to prisoners?

Tapios shot him a look at that, but Thadred didn't care. Thadred wouldn't dream of hurting random girls in the forest, probably not even if they were real threats, but no one needed to know that right now.

"Please," the oldest girl choked, barely forcing the words out past her whimpers. "We just want to get away from here."

Thadred cocked an eyebrow. Kelamora was in a remote province with few options in the surrounding lands. Though it was not the best employment, it was as close to opportunity as many girls in this rural region would ever have. It was the perfect place to work to save for a dowry or purchase passage to a larger city. Servants tolerated Kelamora for their term of service and then happily left. It wasn't the sort of place they fled.

That these two were running away was... "What makes you say that?"

The older girl looked to the redheaded ranger and then to Tapios, hesitating. "I..."

"Speak." Thadred didn't have time for charm or persuasion and neither did Dain and Amira.

"There are spells being prepared. Dark spells. The masters have done rituals from time to time, but this..."

"Did you—"

Thadred cuffed the redheaded ranger on the back of the head. "Let the girl speak."

The redhead looked to Tapios, but the older ranger just shook his head.

At least one person was on Thadred's side in this.

"Well?" Thadred looked back to the girl. "What's your name?"

"Eda, my lord," the girl said, not making eye contact.

"Eda, do you know how many there are?" Thadred asked.

"We were told to prepare food for one hundred," the girl answered. "We've been working without rest for three days. A great lady brought them. They call her the empress."

The rangers shuddered and even Tapios shifted anxiously. To these people, Vesha was a monster that had haunted their existence for years—a witch that had kept them hemmed into a cursed forest. To Thadred, she was just his aunt.

Thadred kept his tone neutral as he pressed the girl further. "The empress? Were there any prisoners captured recently?"

"There was a man brought to us under heavy guard," Eda said.

"Describe him," Thadred ordered.

The girl gulped, shrinking back at the sharp edge in Thadred's voice. "A little shorter than you. Sandy-colored hair. He was kind."

Tapios shot Thadred a look with brows raised in silent question.

Thadred had no doubt that was his cousin. "Dain was brought to you? What do you mean?"

"They had my sister and I tend his wounds," Eda said, her voice small and frightened and making Thadred feel like a monster.

"Wounds?" Thadred stifled alarm at that. He hadn't seen what had become of Dain after his cousin had been snatched.

Eda hesitated. "He has many bruises and cuts and I think a few broken ribs."

Thadred relaxed just a bit. That sounded like the injuries Dain had already sustained. "Did they bring any other captives?"

The slight girl bobbed her head, her dark hair working free from her bun and falling around her face. "Yes," she said hesitantly. "Yes, they did."

"Who?" Thadred pressed, impatience growing in his chest.

"Did you get a look at her? Is she alive?"

"She?" Eda looked genuinely confused.

Thadred forced down the frustration and fear in his chest, closing his eyes for a heartbeat to compose himself. "Was the other captive a man or a woman?"

He hated to consider the possibility, but Amira might very well be dead somewhere in the forest. The Kadra'han's captive might be one of the missing Istovari rangers for all he knew.

"I don't know," Eda said. "A group of the empress's men took someone to the dungeon after they arrived, but I didn't see who."

Thadred and Tapios shared a grim look. Though they might be divided on rescuing Dain, the Istovari were invested in saving Amira. She was the granddaughter of their leader and their surest hope for getting a foothold back in the world outside the Cursewood.

"Are you indentured?" Thadred asked. "Or hired?"

Eda hesitated. "Indentured. Both of us. I have three years left. My sister has five. They were to pay us each a full dowry when our time was up."

"Hmm. Indentured, so you're breaking your contract with them by fleeing." Thadred rested his hands on his hips. "I doubt the Kadra'han take kindly to runaways, Eda," Thadred remarked. "But you seem afraid enough that you're willing to risk it."

It was true that dark spells were being prepared, but this girl would have been working around them ever since coming here. Magic—or at least the attempt at it—was common enough in places like this.

The girl trembled and for a moment Thadred wasn't sure she had the voice to reply. When she did speak, her voice trembled. "The man…the great lady's guard captain, he told us we were no longer welcome." Eda swallowed. "That if we wanted to live…" She burst into tears, nearly doubled over with sobs.

Thadred wasn't sure he had heard right. Maybe he should have been more compassionate, but he wasn't in the mood and didn't have time. "Darrigan sent you? You were let go then?"

"No," Eda said, hiccupping. "We weren't released, but

he…he frightened us so much and the man they captured, he also said we should run."

"Dain? The archduke?"

"I think so."

"Hmm." Thadred wasn't surprised Dain had tried to get the girls to leave. He might have done the same himself. What he didn't understand was Darrigan. He didn't see what the guard captain had to gain by frightening off a couple scullery maids.

He looked back to the squat shape of Kelamora, mocking him from where it crouched on the ridge. A new thought came to him. "Why did no one stop you when you fled?" Thadred asked. These Kadra'han hardly seemed the sort to let their servants wander free. And the rangers had said that the pair of girls had come down a hidden path. "How did you get outside?"

"They're all busy preparing for tonight," Eda said. "And we used the water door."

"Water door?" Thadred had never heard that term before.

"It's the passage leading down to the river. We use it for fetching water, but you can climb down from there if you go slow."

Thadred's mind whirred, thinking. These were the sorts of sideways and backways he had been taught to seek out during his strategy training as a knight. Excitement pulsed through him for a moment then he paused.

Captain Darrigan had led most of his training and Captain Darrigan was now in command of this monastery. The older Kadra'han would have surely shored up any vulnerable points.

Thadred stared at the dark shape of Kelamora as the sun sank ever farther behind the mountains. Anything they did tonight was a huge risk. Even inaction was a huge risk. If Vesha did what they all expected her to do and unleashed Caa Iss in the world, they would all be doomed.

It was too convenient that these girls had not only fled, but gotten away. They might very well be spies. Anyone who knew the Istovari knew they had a soft spot for young girls.

Yet what if Eda and her sister really were telling the truth? What if they really were a gift from the gods? What if Thadred let his suspicion keep him from accepting whatever tiny advantage they might have just given him?

"Thadred?" Tapios' voice called him out of his reverie.

Thadred realized he had been staring silently at Kelamora for at least a full minute. Everyone was looking at him—the servant girls, the rangers, and Tapios. Even Lleuad now watched him from across the clearing, serpentine eyes fixed intently.

When had Thadred become their leader? He had no idea. As it was, it now seemed he was the last and best hope for Dain and by extension the whole world.

No pressure, right?

He almost laughed at the expectant expressions around him. Did they think he knew the answers to everything?

"This could be a trap," Tapios said. For all his inexperience in war and subterfuge, at least the ranger understood that.

"Oh yes," Thadred agreed. "These fine lasses might be spies sent by Darrigan."

"We're not spies!" Eda said quickly. Thadred hadn't thought it possible, but her face went even paler. "We just—"

"Peace, lass," Thadred said. "Nothing you say will convince me." He looked back to Tapios as the girl began crying softly.

Maybe he should have taken the time to console her, but her feelings weren't on his list of concerns at the moment. If she turned out to be innocent, he would apologize tomorrow. If she was leading them into a trap or even if they just failed to save Dain tonight, nothing would matter.

"I have an idea," Thadred said, looking around the faces before him. "It's risky, but it was always going to be. We will probably die if we try it, but we'll definitely die if we do nothing."

It was not the best before battle speech he had heard, but not the worst he had given. Generally speaking, he'd been taught he shouldn't admit the likelihood of death to troops, especially untrained ones.

But Thadred was tired. He didn't have the energy or the stomach for lies tonight. They were probably all about to die and he was at peace with that. He didn't want to spend his last few hours pretending.

Sair's face flickered before him in his mind's eye—that soft look she'd given him the day they departed the Haven. He hoped she'd remember him fondly. And whatever else happened, he hoped she'd be safe.

To their credit, the Istovari around him didn't back down. If there was one thing these people understood, he supposed it would be self-sacrifice for the sake of the greater good.

"They have our children," Tapios said simply, tone flat. He stood stalwart and determined, ready to face whatever came next. "Tell us what you have in mind."

Thadred grinned at the man. He was starting to consider Tapios a friend. What a lovely chap to die with.

CHAPTER TWENTY-TWO

Daindreth

D aindreth was out of practice when it came to ignoring Caa Iss. He'd gotten so used to the sweet silence Amira brought over the past months that re-learning to stuff down the demon's voice took extra concentration.

Caa Iss chittered constantly about nothing and everything. If Daindreth hadn't known better, he would have thought the cythraul sounded nervous.

What do you think of renaming the royal guard the Black Guard? No, never mind. That's too dramatic, even for me.

Daindreth sat alone in a plush room, back to the brace of a rice paper wall. There was a heap of pillows to one side, some of them large enough for him to lie stretched out, but he didn't go to those. He also avoided the low table set with small plates of dainty morsels and a carafe of rice wine despite the knotting hunger in his stomach.

He had thought about taking the carafe and breaking it to use as a weapon. That was what Amira would have done. But Daindreth didn't see much that could be gained by that. He was still injured, barely able to keep moving, let alone fight. He might manage to injure one of the Kadra'han, but that would be only a minor setback to Vesha.

Closing his eyes, he focused on the sensations of his body— the silk against his skin and the stiff brocade robe over that, the ache in his sore ribs and many bruises. He let that pain ground him, tie him closer to his physical form. He was the one with mastery over this body, not the demon. This body was his, along with its pain, hunger, and various sensations.

Gah! Will that damned sun hurry. Caa Iss rippled through Daindreth's thoughts like a cold draft. *Not long now,* the demon crooned. *Not long.*

Daindreth could sense Caa Iss's anxiety rising. The cythraul worried to and fro like a caged wolf, gnawing at the corners of his prison, just writhing to find a way out.

Daindreth glanced to the silk sash around his waist and then to the crossbrace of the ceiling overhead. He might be able to get the sash around it and then—

Don't you even think about it! Caa Iss snarled. *Try hanging yourself and they will kill Amira.*

"She could already be dead." The words were like stakes being driven into Daindreth's chest, but he forced them out.

She's not! Caa Iss insisted. Daindreth thought he might have imagined it, but there seemed to be a shrill pitch to the demon's words. *She's very much alive, but you doom her if you try anything. Remember your mother's promise!*

Amira was alive. She had to be, Daindreth told himself. If she wasn't...

The door to his room slid open. Outside, he could see the shadows of two guards.

Captain Darrigan darkened the doorway. He was missing the heavy outer coat that Daindreth and the others wore, giving him a battle-ready look.

Finally! Get me to the empress and get this done.

Darrigan stepped inside and slid the door shut. He clasped his hands behind his back, a soldier at attention.

"Captain," Daindreth said, not moving. After sitting here for close to an hour, he was unsure if he could rise on his own even if he wanted to. The slightest motion sent his side throbbing.

The captain coughed and glanced to the side, to the untouched table. "Are you ready, Your Highness?"

"To become the pawn of a cythraul? Never." Daindreth inhaled a long and slow breath, expanding his ribs deliberately so as not to stretch them too fast. "But I doubt that matters."

The captain looked away from him, staring over the archduke's shoulder and not quite meeting his eye.

Daindreth raised one eyebrow. "What do you want, captain?"

Daindreth had always gotten the sense that Captain Darrigan disliked him. The man had loyally served both his parents, but that had been his parents. When Daindreth was around the man, he always felt as if the captain were disappointed in him.

"Your mother wishes for you to join her now."

229

Daindreth almost laughed at that. What a funny way of putting it. "You mean she's ready to condemn me to a lifetime of hell on earth, is that it?"

The captain looked away in...was that shame? He opened his mouth, then shut it again. He made a sharp hissing sound of frustration.

The captain had come to fetch him, but had left the other Kadra'han outside. Odd.

Daindreth studied the captain closer. "Where is Amira?".

"Far enough not to cause trouble," Captain Darrigan answered. "Will you come peaceably?" the captain asked. "Or must I send for soldiers as I did last time?"

Daindreth licked his lips. He was a creature trained for courts and politics, not espionage. If he had been Amira, he would have been able to think of something. He would have concocted a plan to save both himself and everyone he loved simply by taking one of those many knives from the captain.

But he wasn't Amira.

"My fiancée?" he asked quietly. "What will become of her?"

Soon to be my *plaything,* Caa Iss sneered.

"I don't know," the captain admitted. "But if you try to run, my men have orders to—"

"Kill her?" Daindreth demanded.

"No," the captain said calmly. "The empress has ordered they are to start with her eyes."

Daindreth swallowed a tight lump in his throat.

"If you continue to resist, they are to take her left hand, then her right. Her feet next. If you kill yourself, they are to strip her naked and leave her blind, crippled, and handless to crawl through the forest until she dies either of blood loss or exposure." The captain reported it all as if it were perfectly normal, completely expected. "Now I ask again—will you come peaceably?"

Daindreth stifled back a groan of pain and forced himself to his feet. The captain watched patiently as he stumbled upright, every joint and muscle in the archduke's beaten body protesting at every motion. "I will come." His voice was heavy with defeat.

They had found his weakness and they held her captive in a

cell beneath the monastery.

"Come, archduke," the captain said. "It won't be long now. One way or another."

Daindreth wasn't sure what the other man meant by that, but he had the feeling he was missing something.

The dark man didn't touch Daindreth, but never took his eyes off him as he led the way out of the plush room and into the hall. Daindreth was barefoot and considered saying something, but decided it didn't matter. He'd never gone barefoot before, but everything was paved. Outside, the two guards glanced to Daindreth and then to their captain.

"Let's go," the dark man said, taking the lead.

With Daindreth's injuries, they had to move slower than a Kadra'han's usual marching pace. The captain didn't press him to move faster, taking the lead with Daindreth at his back, flanked by guards on either side.

The halls were dark, lit only by torches every so many paces. The whole monastery was quiet, like the very stones feared drawing attention to themselves.

The sick sensation of dread bubbled more and more insistent in Daindreth's chest.

As a particularly large door slid aside to let them in, the guard captain stopped. Behind him, a massive room was aglow with perhaps a thousand candles, making Darrigan look like a fiend of legend.

"May your father forgive me for whatever is about to happen," Captain Darrigan said quietly.

Daindreth wasn't sure what to make of that. The captain had always been an enigma, but tonight he acted especially strange.

Caa Iss growled in the back of Daindreth's head. *Conscience. I have no stomach for such idiocy.*

Before Daindreth could ask the captain what he meant, the dark man turned and marched into the room.

It was large, by far the largest room Daindreth had seen in the monastery so far. Arched ceilings rose at least three times the height of a man. Two columns of wooden pillars divided the room into thirds, perhaps thirty feet wide in total. The room spanned twice as long as it was wide. Rice mats lined the floor, and the room was empty of all furnishing save for the collection

231

of spears, staves, and swords hung along the wall.

A training room, if Daindreth had to guess.

Vesha was there in a simple white robe belted by a blue sash. She wore no adornments or jewelry and might have been mistaken for an ordinary court lady if not for her bearing. That was hard to disguise anywhere. Vesha carried herself like an empress no matter where she was.

The room was filled with robed monks, and men Daindreth recognized as his mother's Kadra'han. They scuttled in all directions, carrying pitchers and correcting sketches of diagrams.

The archduke's gaze gravitated to the center of the room. He'd half-expected a silver chair like his mother had tried using last time, but this time there was a set of chains attached to two of the wooden braces that supported the roof.

When he entered with his guards, everyone looked in his direction.

Under the light of the candles, Daindreth now realized that he was the only one wearing the same white as his mother. Everyone else wore the dark greys, browns, and blues of the monastery's residents.

"Daindreth," Vesha said. "My son."

"Mother." Daindreth kept his tone as cold and cool as he could.

Your mother is a pretty thing, Caa Iss mused. *I've nailed her before, did you know that?*

Daindreth forced himself not to show an outward reaction to the cythraul's words.

I took over your father when he was bedding her. You should have seen the terror in her face when her husband's eyes went red mid-swyve, Caa Iss cackled.

Daindreth clenched his eyes shut, looking away from his mother. "How can you do this?" he demanded. "How can you take his side after everything he did to you? After everything he took from us?"

Vesha's voice was heavy when she answered. "Because I have to."

"My lady." Darrigan shifted. "I urge you to keep your distance."

"He's my son, Darrigan," the empress retorted. "Daindreth?"

Her hand grasped his jaw and he let her tug him around to face her. He opened his eyes and there she was.

Vesha was lovely—her skin pale as the moon, her full lips, and long, dark hair. The emperor had always said Vesha was easy to love, and Daindreth could see why.

"Mother," Daindreth said, anger, resentment, and a deep sadness warring in his chest.

"My son," she said. A sad smile creased her face. "You are the bravest man I know. Your father would be proud of you."

"Would he be proud of you?" Daindreth shot back.

Vesha shut down, a hard mask of determination slamming into place. "Take him to the pillars," she ordered. "Go!"

The captain and the others obeyed, dragging Daindreth toward the pillars at the center of the room. He didn't fight as they shackled him between them, arms stretched apart by chains.

Darrigan and the other Kadra'han withdrew to stand beside the empress some ten paces back. That left Daindreth in the center of the room alone, shackled and exposed.

This was it. In a few minutes, Vesha would finish what the Istovari had started all those years ago.

A commotion from the door of the room drew his attention.

"What is this?" Daindreth demanded.

Monks in the blue and grey robes of Kadra'han residents came, dragging a small girl between them—one of the Istovari judging by her pale skin and homespun frock. She looked to be no more than eight.

Vesha had said that the Istovari children had been taken to replenish the Kadra'han ranks and perhaps the others had been, but...

Why had he not considered this? An Istovari child had been sacrificed to bind Caa Iss. Here, away from the witch's wheel that amplified Vesha's power back in the palace...

"Mother, what is this?" Daindreth shouted, anger and horror rising in his chest.

You didn't think the price of my freedom was free, did you? Caa Iss sneered. *We should have been able to do this without bloodshed, but after what your Istovari whore did to me in Mynadra, it's going to take power.*

Vesha refused to answer Daindreth's demands and she refused to look at the child.

An old man in red robes with a long, braided beard, stepped forward. The grandmaster of Kelamora? He spoke to his acolytes in a language Daindreth didn't know.

The first of the chants began and the force of them knocked Daindreth to his knees.

CHAPTER TWENTY-THREE

Amira

Even being cut off from *ka,* Amira could tell something was wrong. The sensation permeated her like a cold draft, creeping through Darrigan's woolen coat and crawling along her skin like a thousand insects.

She stood, straining to reach the bars of her cell, but the chain on her ankle yanked her back. She cursed, tugging on the chain, but to no avail.

She studied the lock around her ankle. As best she could tell, it was a simple release mechanism that she could probably pry open with a sturdy pin or small nail, but none of those were in reach.

Cursing, she slumped against the wall in futility. No one had come since Darrigan's confusing visit. She didn't want to just wait here until Caa Iss—after overpowering Daindreth—came to fetch her, but what other options were there? She had no recourse and no plan.

Outside the bars of her cell, Amira glimpsed the pale face of the First Moon—Eponine—the one who now ruled the skies since her sister had been cast down. That moon watched, apathetic, not caring that Amira and every one of Eponine's mortal children would be doomed tonight if Caa Iss wasn't stopped.

So often, the Istovari taught Eponine was a loving mother who cared and watched over her children on the earth. But would a mother abandon her children to the mercy of Emperor Drystan? Would a mother have allowed a little girl to be sacrificed? Then again, Amira's mother had done just that, and Daindreth's mother was trying to sacrifice him to a demon, after all.

Footsteps shuffled from the end of the passage. Low voices.

Amira shivered. They were coming for her.

The moon was out, and it was time for the rite to be performed that would free Caa Iss. Amira was terrified for Daindreth's sake, but in that moment, she feared for herself, too.

Whatever Caa Iss planned to do to her, she knew better than to hope it would be quick.

"Let me die well," Amira whispered to whatever deity or supernatural force might be listening. "Let me die quickly. I don't want Daindreth to see me beg."

Amira thought the footsteps were coming closer, but after a moment, she realized they were just louder. And it was more than the pair of guard she'd expected.

Soft-soled boots shuffled, and a pair of male voices exchanged quick words. A female voice interjected something.

Amira strained to reach the bars, but she couldn't get close enough to see down the aisle. What was this?

"This place is strange," muttered the female voice. *"Ka* is dead here."

"What do you mean?" asked one of the males.

"It's blocked," the woman replied. "Like a cave that doesn't let in light. I'm not sure how they did it, but—"

"Quiet!" a new voice snapped. "Do you want to alert the whole monastery?"

Amira froze, heart thundering in her chest. It couldn't be. It was too good to be true.

She opened her mouth to speak, but her voice wouldn't come. Was this a trap? A trick? A taunt?

She swallowed her fear and forced her voice out. "Thadred?"

Silence came from the far end of the hall.

"Thadred, is that you?" Amira's voice nearly choked. *Be real,* she silently begged. *Please be real.*

"Amira?" Thadred's voice came quiet, hesitant.

"It could be a trap," one of the male voices warned, one Amira didn't recognize.

"I can't sense *ka* in that room," the female voice warned. "They might have any manner of spells here."

"Amira, is that you?" Thadred interrupted. The other voices fell silent, and Amira could imagine Thadred gesturing for them all to be quiet—assuming it was him and not an illusion.

"Thadred?" Amira's voice came out as a croaking wheeze.

"Amira." Thadred's tone was soft, but decisive.

A hobbling gait came marching down the corridor.

The male voice protested, and a shuffling came from down the hall. "Sir, I—"

"Move! I have to see." If it was an illusion, it had perfectly copied Thadred's impatient tone.

"It could be a trap!" the female voice said.

"Absolutely. Now move, woman."

A thud was followed by a low squawk of protest.

"Be quiet!" Thadred sounded increasingly irritated. "You might as well start shouting to everyone that we're here."

Amira strained to see, hope and fear of hope warring in her chest. This was too good to be true.

A battered, rumpled figure limped into view, leaning on his cane. His hair was wet, and he looked as if he had just walked through the rain. Thadred gaped at the sight of her, and two rangers appeared at his left and right. "Amira!"

"Thadred." Amira almost sobbed his name.

"What did they—?" Thadred snapped his attention to the door of her cell. "How do we get this open?"

"Is there a key?" the female ranger asked.

"I'm sure," Thadred sneered. "Would you like to go ask one of the Kadra'han for it?"

"They're quad bolts," Amira said. "You don't need a key if you have four hands to open them. You can just remove the whole door."

Thadred cast her a quick look.

"Pins on the top and bottom of the doorframe," Amira explained, pointing. "Do you see?" Amira couldn't reach the door herself, but Thadred and the rangers were another story.

Thadred jerked his chin to the male ranger. "You pull the bottom. I'll pull the top."

The two men fumbled the release mechanism and wrestled the door open. The female ranger stood guard, watching down the passage.

"What's going on?" called another male voice—Tapios—in a hushed whisper.

"We found the princess," the female ranger hissed back. "They're freeing her now."

The door swung open and Thadred staggered inside, nearly falling in his haste to reach Amira.

"Are you alright?" he asked, catching her arms. "Are you hurt? Where's Dain?"

Amira shook her head. "The empress is here. She means to complete the rite and enslave him. They're somewhere upstairs."

Thadred looked down to her ankle. "You're chained." He dropped to a crouch, studying the shackle.

"If I have a lockpick, I can release it," Amira said. "A brooch, a nail—"

At her words, the female ranger pulled a hairpin from the knot at the nape of her neck. "Does this work?"

"Perfect." Amira snatched the quill and knelt, fitting it into the keyhole of her shackle. Kneeling shifted the robe and exposed her bare leg, showing enough to reveal she was naked underneath.

"Amira…" Thadred coughed and looked away. "Can you walk?"

"I can run," Amira said, straightening as the shackle fell off. "This robe makes for poor armor, but I can fight, too."

"You found the princess?" From the hall, Tapios came careening into the cell.

He looked her from head to foot. "Princess Amira. I'm glad to see you alive and standing." The man looked sincere to her. He peered closer at the bruises and cuts that splotched her face, the marks of her capture. "Are you…hurt?"

Amira didn't want to answer that question. No, she hadn't been raped the way these men were probably thinking, but she couldn't bring herself to say she had 'only' been stripped. Just the memory made her throat go tight. "Do any of you have an extra weapon? They took mine."

The female ranger offered a long, thin blade to Amira, one that gleamed with sharpness. "Here."

"What's your name?" Amira asked.

"Jesri," the woman answered. On closer inspection, Amira realized she couldn't have been more than seventeen. Her face still held that youthful softness that had been beaten out of Amira at an earlier age. She was blonde and svelte and made Amira think of a wood sprite.

"Thank you, Jesri. Have you ever killed a witch?"

The girl hesitated. "No, princess."

Amira cast the girl a wicked grin. "Me neither."

Thadred stiffened. "You mean to kill the empress?"

Amira whirled on Thadred, nostrils flaring. "I plan to split her neck to navel and gut her like the sow she is." Amira looked back to Tapios. "You were on your way to somewhere before you came across me. Where was it?"

Thadred stepped past Tapios. "Let's keep moving. We have an archduke to save."

"Sweet Mothers," Tapios gasped, drawing to a quick halt as soon as he stepped outside the cell.

"Eponine's breath," whispered Jesri.

"What is it?" The moment Amira crossed the threshold, she felt it.

Ka swirled through the air in a massive, rotating vortex, taking the shape of a great storm. After the deadness of her cell, it was all the more potent.

It was not quite the noxious stench of the Cursewood, but it was very, very wrong. Instantly, Amira recognized the uncanniness of demonic *ka,* power being manipulated by a witch.

Her heart raced and she let off several hearty curses. "That's the empress," Amira said. "Or her power, at least."

"How do you know?" asked Jesri.

"I've sensed it before." Amira looked to the others. "We need to go."

If there was any advantage to be found, it was that her bare feet moved soundlessly on the stone. The rangers and Tapios followed her and Thadred back into the staircase that connected to the corridor.

Amira nearly ran into another ranger as the man emerged from the darkness. His eyes went wide as he recognized her, though she didn't know him.

Several more rangers followed close behind them. All of them were wet.

"How did you get in?" Amira asked, looking to Thadred.

"The water gate. The one the servants use to get water from the river," Thadred explained. "A runaway servant showed us."

Amira bit her lip, nodding. It was oddly convenient, but she wasn't about to complain. Hadn't she just been praying for a miracle? "Have you seen anyone else yet?"

"No," Thadred answered, gesturing for several of the rangers to take the lead again. "Just you."

"Have you seen any of the children?" Tapios pressed.

"No," Amira replied, feeling a tug of shame. She had forgotten about the abducted in little ones in the chaos and terror of the past few hours. "I haven't seen them at all."

Tapios nodded, jaw grinding in frustration. "You should go back," he said. "If this goes bad, you might be our only hope to—"

"I can't leave Daindreth," Amira said, even as reason told her that he was right.

Tapios nodded solemnly, accepting her answer. He had probably expected as much.

Ahead, the rangers in the lead punched through a rice paper wall with a tearing, cracking sound as the frame gave way.

Amira cringed. "Are we trying to be quiet, or no?"

The leaders of the column didn't seem to hear them as they ploughed through.

Thadred shrugged to her in the darkness.

How strange that this band were silent phantoms in the forest, but could turn into a gaggle of buffoons as soon as one put them indoors. Amira cursed inwardly but didn't comment.

She shouldered her way into the lead, fumbling through the dark of the room. If she remembered correctly from her way down, this was some sort of storage chamber for clay jars, vases, and urns. "Don't knock over anything," she hissed to the darkness. "Follow me."

Not that there was much point in stealth by now. The rangers had already torn through the rice paper door with all the grace of bulls.

Amira slid back the next door and it glided easily aside, opening into a long hall lined with bamboo reeds. "Come," she beckoned. "There's no one here."

No one alive, at least. As best Amira could tell, the passage and the rooms beyond were devoid of life.

The rangers clattered after her, whispering and muttering to each other.

Amira squinted at the rice paper walls. These rooms were dark, but light flooded from up ahead. "Something is wrong."

"Everything about this is wrong." Tapios' tone was tight, sharp. "This *ka* is perverted."

"Not just that." Amira adjusted the grip on the dagger at her side. She slid open one of the rice paper doors and took in the empty space inside—a few abandoned sleeping mats, two chests, and several folded blankets. "There should be acolytes here. Working and studying, if not sleeping. Why is the monastery so empty?" Amira turned to where Thadred's vague outline stood at her side. "Where is everyone?"

Thadred moved closer to her. "They're trying to awaken the demon. The way they failed to do before. You think that's right?"

"Darrigan told me as much, yes," Amira responded. "I don't think he would mislead me about it."

"Unless he himself was misled," Thadred agreed. "But that seems unlikely."

They had never quite understood what Darrigan's plan or goals were besides protecting Vesha. That had involved seeing Daindreth dead before, but since Vesha had ordered him against that, it seemed unlikely he would try again.

Amira stepped inside the empty sleeping room. She opened the nearest chest, groping through it in the dark. She located several pieces of paper, what was probably a leather sheath, and beneath that, found what she was looking for. She pulled out a loose pair of hakama pants and a shirt that folded across itself and tied at the sides in the Nihain style.

"Turn around," she clipped to Thadred.

"Oh." The knight's voice held a note of embarrassment as he turned around, shooing back the rangers who had started to follow Amira.

The assassin was grateful for the dark as she donned her stolen clothes, fumbling them on with unsure fingers. The fabric was soft and well-cleaned, smelling of fresh washing. It felt better against her skin than the rough weave of Darrigan's overcoat, but she pulled the coat over the top.

"They're trying to give Caa Iss full control," Amira said,

241

though that was obvious.

The last time they had tried, the palace had seemed deserted, too. Whatever preparations were involved, Vesha seemed to want to minimize possible distractions.

"What do they need in order to do that?" Thadred asked.

"They used water before," Amira answered. "To amplify the spells. Also…" Amira swallowed, flinching as something shifted in the air.

Ka began roiling under her feet, invisible and undetectable to the body, yet Amira could feel it curling and wisping around her—just as it had that night so many weeks ago.

"Come on!" The assassin raced out of the abandoned sleeping room and back into the hall. There wasn't time for questions. There wasn't time for considering every option or possibility.

She raced toward the heart of the monastery. They encountered no one and in a way that was more frightening than anything else.

As they came nearer, Amira realized that the swirl of *ka* was in the center of the monastery complex, toward the main training room.

"Slow down," Amira called back to the rangers. "Slow down!"

They rounded a corner and Amira could see the lights from the open door to a training room. It seemed to be filled near to bursting with candles, light spilling out even as she could sense power swirling and churning inside.

At least a dozen armored Kadra'han spilled into the hall. Some in the plate of the empire and some in the leather lamellar favored by Nihain warriors.

"Wait!" Thadred ordered, staggering up the rear. "We need a plan!"

The first ranger had already rushed past them, and panic rose in Amira's chest. In tight quarters and against that armor, the rangers' arrows would be worse than useless.

"For the children!" one of the rangers cried.

No one could accuse the rangers of being cowards. Untrained, yes. Stupid, absolutely.

Amira saw the flash of knives being drawn as the rangers charged toward their death. The first ranger crashed into a Kadra'han and was chopped down by a longsword.

Pointless—how pointless.

"Come on!" She grabbed Thadred's arm and yanked him into a side passage as rangers died in front of them. "We need to find Daindreth. And Vesha."

Thadred staggered after her without arguing.

Amira knew what she had to do once she found the empress. She just prayed that Daindreth would forgive her for it.

CHAPTER TWENTY-FOUR

Daindreth

"**M**other." Daindreth shook, fighting to keep control of his voice and his bearing. "Mother, there is a line."

"We need Istovari blood," Vesha said. Still, she refused to look at the child behind her. "Istovari blood bound Caa Iss and Istovari blood can release him."

"Mother, that's a child!" Daindreth shouted, yanking against the chains on his wrists.

Has that ever mattered to me before? Caa Iss sounded genuinely perplexed. *I have never understood that about humans. Why is something considered more precious when it is helpless? Shouldn't the opposite be true?*

Vesha turned and nodded to Darrigan. "Begin the rite." She looked up, at nothing in particular. "Saan Thii? We are ready."

The guard captain stepped forward and gestured to the small girl. "Bring her to me," he ordered. His face was stern, resolute.

Daindreth shook his head. "Mother, there has to be another way!"

Everyone ignored him as Darrigan grabbed the child—a girl with russet curls and pale, delicate arms. Darrigan shoved back her sleeve as she screamed and cried. "Let me go!" she wept. "Let me go. Please! I want my mama. I want—"

See what you are making us do, archduke? See the consequences of you resisting me for so long?

Captain Darrigan stabbed the girl's wrist and dragged the knife back up her arm, slitting her skin like a ripe peach.

The child's screams rose louder and Daindreth couldn't speak, couldn't move, could only watch in sick horror as Captain Darrigan threw her to the ground, a few paces from Daindreth.

The child clutched at her bleeding arm. Her blood soaked the tatami mats, leaving ghastly stains that spread out toward Daindreth like ink splashed in water. It raced like a flood of red worms, slithering around him in unnatural, eerie shapes.

Was this to be the beginning of the rest of his life? Blood of innocents beneath his feet while he could only watch them sacrificed for the sake of…what?

"Mother, please," Daindreth said, voice shaking, reduced to begging. "I know you are not so cruel as this. Please."

Vesha refused to meet his gaze and still refused to look at the screaming child.

A shout and a thud came from outside the room. Darrigan let off a sharp command to the guards by the door and several of them filed out.

What now?! Fury edged the cythraul's tone.

Something clamored in the hallway. People shouted and steel clanged.

Daindreth's heart raced. Was this a rescue? Had Amira and Thadred come for him after all?

"How did they get in?" Vesha demanded.

Let me out, Caa Iss growled. *Let me out and I will deal with this.*

Whether the demon meant that for Daindreth or for Vesha, there was no way of knowing.

Daindreth writhed in his chains. He could still hear Caa Iss. Amira wasn't here. Then who…?

"Protect the empress." Captain Darrigan's tone was unsettlingly calm.

"Kill them all!" Vesha ordered. "Whoever it is, kill them all!"

Save some for me.

Lying on the ground, the little girl with the cut arm wept and cried.

"No," Daindreth pleaded. "Don't let children die for me. Not like this." He wasn't sure who he was begging. Perhaps he was praying, though he couldn't have said to who or what.

Vesha marched forward. Her guards formed a protective gauntlet as a good portion of them charged into the monastery halls to ferret out the Istovari rangers. That was who it had to be. She knelt beside the gasping child and Daindreth thought she would touch the girl, but instead she reached her fingers into the child's blood.

Her hand came away smeared crimson. She traced patterns on the ground in blood, brow pinched in concentration. She stood and searched the room.

"Saan Thii?" Vesha called. "Where are you?" The empress

waited another moment.

Daindreth didn't see if Saan Thii replied or not. He couldn't always see the demoness.

"Captain Darrigan," Vesha said, eyes on Daindreth.

"My lady?" the captain responded.

Vesha's face was a mask of cold indifference to match her voice. "The girl is bleeding out too slow. Cut her throat."

"Mother." Daindreth cast about desperately for some argument, some plea he hadn't used before, anything that might reach her. "It doesn't have to be this way."

"I've already told you!" Vesha snarled, anger twisting her face. "It does."

The empress spoke something in a language that Daindreth didn't know. He could have sworn her eyes sparked, but it might have been the glow of the candles.

Daindreth could feel the demon forcing his way to the surface, clawing and tearing like a parasite ripping free. Daindreth fought back, struggling to maintain control. He clenched and unclenched his hands, proving to himself that he was still in control with that simple motion. His hands shook. His whole body trembled, but he focused on that simple act of will, that tiny, insignificant gesture.

It will be so much easier if you let me do this, Caa Iss crooned, his words a seductive call. *Much less painful, too.*

Daindreth shook his head and crimson flickered across his eyes. "No," he panted. "No, no, no!"

Come now, sweet prince, the cythraul chuckled. *I am inevitable. Why should you suffer through this?*

Past the red haze covering his vision, he watched, helpless, as Captain Darrigan grabbed the girl's hair and forced her head back. Daindreth saw a blade flash and then the girl was back on ground, clutching at her throat while blood mixed with tears.

Stories always made it sound like cutting someone's throat would be quick, but it wasn't. The girl writhed and gasped and wept and Daindreth thought he would vomit.

"Stop!" Daindreth's voice tore through the night, rising even above the clamor of the fighting rangers and Kadra'han.

Your mother wouldn't have to kill children if you wouldn't fight me so much.

"No..." Daindreth resisted, snapping his head from side to side so violently that his shoulders popped. "I can't...I *can't.*"

Daindreth couldn't let it happen. Couldn't let Caa Iss out. This child would be the first of thousands of dead innocents if the cythraul had his way. "No!" Daindreth screamed again. "How many will you murder for this?" he demanded, voice cracking on the words.

Vesha shrieked above the madness. "As many as it takes!"

Daindreth should have prevented this, somehow. He should have done something, made a different choice, chosen—

His mother continued her chanting and Daindreth strayed out of awareness. The words rolled over him in a language unfamiliar at first. Then word by word, he began to understand.

She was making promises to the cythraul, reciting her bargain to the Second Moon Goddess, affirming their contract, offering her apologies for the last failure, and promising recompense.

Daindreth understood her words an instant before he understood what that knowing meant—he was no longer hearing through his own mind.

Something cracked inside his head. Crushing weight slammed into him, knocking him to his knees and snapping his neck back with the force.

Then his vision washed red. His hands gripped his chains, and he couldn't make them let go.

Daindreth's head tilted from one side and then the other and he could do nothing about it. His mouth twisted into a grin as Caa Iss surveyed the carnage and madness around them.

"It is good to be out," Caa Iss purred.

CHAPTER TWENTY-FIVE

Thadred

"S hit!" Thadred cursed. "Son of a half-goat whore."

"That's not helping!" Amira hissed.

"Nothing is going to help this!" Thadred almost yelled the words, but not that it mattered. There was screaming and fighting in the corridors all around them and no one had time to notice an assassin and a lame knight.

Amira grabbed his sleeve. "We have to try!"

Thadred wasn't arguing with that. Of course, he was going to try. That didn't mean he had to be happy about the glaring likelihood of their imminent deaths. "How do we get there?"

The two of them had blundered their way around behind the training room using the hallways and passages within the walls of the monastery. The Istovari—like the untrained idiots they were—were being slaughtered and hunted through the monastery behind them.

Amira dragged him down the corridor.

Thadred spared a moment to be grateful for the monastery's minimalist furnishings—nothing blocked their way as they ran down the tatami hall. Well—Amira ran. Thadred limped.

Amira led him into a dead end, and cursed. Swerving to the left, she found another doorway and fumbled through it.

Up ahead, he spied the glow of candles through the rice paper walls. Amira stepped along the side of that wall, feeling along the edge. She grabbed something and he heard a faint creak as she rolled the door back. These sliding doors looked identical to walls in the dark.

On the other side was possibly the most hopeless situation Thadred had seen.

He recognized Vesha standing in front of him, her hand outstretched and stained in—oh no. The knight glanced to the empress's left and saw the carnage there.

The crumpled body of a child lay at the feet of Vesha's guard captain. The girl's small form bled out, red flowing into unnatural patterns on the floor. The blood circled around where Dain stood as if it had a mind of its own, flowing around him.

How could there even be that much blood in one little girl?

"Oh gods," Thadred gasped. Was this Vesha's "greater good"? That bitch was going straight to the Dread Marches for this. Her and all her cohorts.

Thadred yanked his arm out of Amira's grip.

She whirled back on him, not quite stopping. He couldn't see her face, backlit as she was by the candles, but he didn't need to.

Thadred drew his cane sword and…and what? He had no idea what he was doing, but they were all going to die anyway. The walls were hung with swords, spears, and halberds that were battle-ready steel as far as he could tell, but he couldn't get to any of them without turning his back to their enemies.

For her part, Amira needed no more prompting. She dove for where Dain was chained in the middle of the room as Thadred limped toward the towering figure and the child at his feet.

"Darrigan!" Thadred shouted. This whole thing was probably stupid, but Thadred had no better plans.

The guard captain looked up. He didn't move as Thadred came limping out of the shadows.

Amira reached Dain first, but Thadred marched past them, planting himself between the guard captain and Amira and his cousin.

No one tried to stop him. The remaining Kadra'han in the room formed up around the empress, protecting her and not seeming concerned by the two intruders.

Vesha looked to Captain Darrigan, her face as surprised as Thadred.

The guard captain raised a hand to the empress, as if to tell her everything was under control.

"Taken to hurting kids now, have we?" Thadred asked.

Captain Darrigan looked straight at Thadred, not blinking.

Behind him, Thadred could hear Amira speaking and a deep, rumbling voice that was *not* Dain. Thadred's gut clenched, but he refused to turn around, refused to look. If anyone could save Dain, it was Amira. That left Thadred to try to save the child and hold off the empress's men.

Fantastic.

"Do you mean to fight me, Myrani?" Darrigan asked. The guard captain didn't ask how Thadred had gotten in, didn't ask how he had made it this far. "There will be time enough for that later."

That hadn't been what Thadred expected.

Behind them, Vesha's voice rose to a shrill pitch as she chanted louder and louder.

"Can you feel it?" Captain Darrigan asked, inhaling a deep breath. "The veil is thin. The empress has made all manner of things possible."

Something was wrong—even more wrong than Thadred had thought, but he couldn't put words to it. "What the hell—?"

The guard captain looked to the girl at his feet. "My grandmother was an Istovari. It's how I got my power. Did you know that?"

Thadred frowned. No, he hadn't known that. Darrigan's appearance favored the southern part of the continent. Either way, Thadred wasn't sure why it mattered, especially right now.

"By the law of substitution." Captain Darrigan raised his left arm. His left arm was missing a bracer or any other kind of armor, though Thadred hadn't noticed it before. "A son of Istovar for the son of Drystan."

Pulling back his sleeve, the guard captain made a quick jab with the knife and dragged it up, slicing open his own arm from wrist to elbow. He grimaced in pain for a moment and then he smiled, looking up.

When his eyes met Thadred's they were burning red.

CHAPTER TWENTY-SIX

Amira

Amira couldn't look at the child Vesha had offered as sacrifice. She couldn't. Images of the ruined tower and the faces of the Mothers standing over her flashed in her mind.

"No," she whimpered. "No, please."

Amira raced up behind Daindreth with nothing but the long knife in her hand, no idea what she would do with it. She should have grabbed one of the swords off the wall, but those were out of reach.

Vesha was focused wholly on Daindreth. Her eyes flitted to Amira as the assassin came charging from the dark. Annoyance flashed across the empress's face. "Captain Darrigan!" she shouted, but the guard captain was facing down Thadred.

"Daindreth!" Amira grabbed for his nearest wrist, surveying the shackles. They were simple bolts, not hard to undo if one had two free hands, but impossible for a man with his arms stretched apart.

As she touched him, awareness of his *ka* assailed her senses. She'd been too distracted to notice, but now—

"Look who's joined us," purred a voice that sent a cold chill through Amira's gut.

Amira recoiled instinctively as Daindreth's head twisted around toward her, eyes glowing red with Caa Iss's light.

"You're a fool, little princess," the cythraul sneered. "Couldn't wait for me to come visit you, I see."

"Daindreth…" Amira gasped. She grabbed the back of his neck, gathering her power and trying to feed it to Daindreth— the real Daindreth—as she had done last time.

"It's going to take more than that, little girl." Caa Iss slid his tongue across his teeth. "Did you see how much Istovari blood has been offered me this night?"

This wasn't the end. Couldn't be. Amira refused to accept it.

"No!" Amira screamed. She clung to his arm, gathering power, fighting to focus. "You can do this. We can do this!

We—"

Caa Iss twisted around, snapping the chains that bound him to the pillars as if they were nothing but string. He grabbed her neck with Daindreth's hand.

Amira's knife came up out of reflex, ready to plunge into his side, but she stopped herself, blade hovering just shy of its mark.

Caa Iss grinned down at her with Daindreth's face, a perverted mockery of her archduke's smile. "You won't hurt him, even now, will you?" The cythraul chuckled. "I wish you could hear how he's screaming for you to save yourself." The cythraul dragged her closer.

Amira tried to pry him off with her free hand, but he was too strong. In this form, he was unstoppable.

"You won't, though. Even if it means leaving yourself at my mercy, you won't hurt him." Caa Iss crushed his mouth against hers, hard and rough. Amira tried to shove him away, but it was like trying to shove a mountain.

She tried to kick him off, tried to wrench out of his grip, but none of her tricks worked. He held onto her as easily as if she were a mouse in the claws of a hawk. His feet were bare, and she stomped on his instep, but she had no shoes either and it did nothing.

Amira struggled, her impulse to use the knife, to defend herself, fought with her love for Daindreth. He would want her to protect herself, she knew that. But even with the cythraul in control, it was still Daindreth trapped inside. She couldn't hurt the monster without hurting him. Her archduke was the demon's hostage.

The cythraul's kiss was more of a bite and it left her lips torn and hot with the promise of a bruise. Caa Iss pulled back laughing, licking her blood off his mouth. "Your blood is so *sweet,*" he purred. "The first I ever tasted after a thousand years in the Dread Marches. Yes, you will ever be special to me, little princess. I mean to show you just how special. You will see. Just as soon as—"

Vesha's voice broke off her chants and a cry rose above the screams of the fighting Istovari and Kadra'han in the monastery behind her. "What's happening?"

Caa Iss stumbled, though no one had touched him. Amira's paltry struggles certainly hadn't hurt him either. "What is this?" Caa Iss turned, still holding Amira by the neck.

Amira punched the inside of his elbow, trying to break his hold, but it didn't work. She wrenched her body sideways, toward the weak point in his grip, but that didn't work either. Growing desperate, she kicked the side of his knee, but he barely even seemed to notice.

She was beginning to think it wouldn't matter if she checked her blows or even outright stabbed him.

"What is this?" Caa Iss growled again through Daindreth's mouth. He turned, lips curled, glaring at something, but Amira couldn't see what. "How dare you."

He dropped Amira as if she were an old bread crust. Amira stumbled and fell, scrambling away from the cythraul, clutching at the soreness where his hand had been.

She turned back and her eyes widened in horror. "Two of them," she gasped.

Captain Darrigan stood with his left sleeve soaked in blood. It looked as if it had been sheared open, red still pouring down his arm, though he didn't seem to notice.

His stance was off. His feet arranged at an odd angle, crouched like a creature unaccustomed to the balance of a human body.

And his eyes were the bright, fiery red of a cythraul.

"Darrigan," Vesha said, dropping her hand and spinning around to him. "What...what have you done?"

The guard captain ignored the empress, focusing on Daindreth—now Caa Iss. His mouth moved, but he wasn't the one who spoke. "Hello, brother," purred a familiar voice.

"Oh no." Amira shook her head in horror. This was why Saan Thii had ignored her cries in the prison. The demoness had already made another deal.

"Mother gave this land to me!" Caa Iss roared. "I will lead the horde!"

"Mother is annoyed by your slowness," Saan Thii, now in possession of Darrigan's body, sneered.

"You have stepped out of line!" Caa Iss snarled.

"I will ask forgiveness from Mother when I hand her the

throne of this empire." Saan Thii shaped Darrigan's face into something alien and strange. "I am sure Mother shall forgive me when I give her what you failed to procure for decades."

"What is this?" Vesha demanded. "Saan Thii, you are *my* familiar. This was not the deal!"

"Come now, my *dear* Vesha," Saan Thii crooned. The demoness—in Darrigan's body—marched up to the empress. Saan Thii fit Darrigan's hand against the side of Vesha's face, trailing his fingers down the side of her temple, along her jaw. "You can have us both by your side now. Your trusted captain and me, your dearest familiar."

"No," Vesha whispered, her eyes wide. "Darrigan...betrayed me?"

Out of everything that had happened tonight and everything that had been done, it seemed that this was the thing to truly shock the empress.

From somewhere nearby, Amira heard a long scream echo through the corridor, in the direction she had last seen the Istovari rangers. A shout rose and then a crash.

Saan Thii's mouth twisted into a wicked grin. "He made a deal for your protection," she purred back. "From him." Saan Thii jerked Darrigan's head toward Daindreth—possessed by Caa Iss.

Vesha shook her head. "Darrigan, what have you done?"

"He couldn't protect you from yourself, Vesha, dear," Saan Thii purred. "So he found someone who could."

"Darrigan—"

"Hush," Saan Thii said. Darrigan's hands clasped Vesha's face and pulled her in for a languid kiss. Vesha didn't return the kiss, but nor did she try to pull away.

Watching, it was nothing like the savage kiss Caa Iss had left on Amira, but it was still wrong, somehow. Saan Thii kissed Vesha like an animal licking the marrow out of a bone, like she would drain Vesha dry if given the chance. The blood staining Darrigan's torn sleeve and arm left crimson smears on Vesha's dress.

Saan Thii pulled back and licked at Vesha's lips, grinning at the empress, an expression Amira had never thought to see on

Darrigan's face. "He's in love with you. Did you know that? Of course, you did." The demoness pressed Darrigan's forehead against Vesha's with a smirk. "You want him, too, don't you?"

"Saan Thii!" Caa Iss snarled. "Now is not the time for this!"

In a strange turn of events, Amira agreed with the cythraul. She could still hear fighting in the hallways. The Istovari were lasting longer than she had thought they would, but there was still only so much time that could be bought.

From behind the rice paper wall of the training room, Amira saw a glow. It was faint at first and she thought she might have imagined it.

A figure in armor came racing through the doors of the practice room behind Vesha and the other Kadra'han. He bowed to Darrigan and didn't hesitate when he saw the captain's now-red eyes. "My lord, the rangers are setting the monastery on fire," the Kadra'han reported. "It's spreading fast."

Amira cursed inwardly. That was just the sort of short-sighted plan she had come to expect from these green warriors. The rangers must have found the children and then decided this was their best chance to destroy Vesha and the demons.

Another of the Kadra'han from the ranks surrounding the empress stepped forward. "We can try to help put it out, but that will mean leaving you and the empress."

None of the Kadra'han surrounding Vesha seemed eager to get near the two cythraul and their standoff—but nor did they seem surprised. Oddly, none seemed too concerned about Vesha standing beside the possessed Darrigan, either. Had they known this would happen?

Amira looked to Thadred. The knight knelt beside the sacrificed child, wrapping her still-bleeding wounds in strips from his own clothes. The girl laid motionless.

"Vesha, dear," Saan Thii said, "the other Kadra'han will see you safely back to the barge in the lagoon. I shall join you shortly after we finish our business here."

An old man Amira vaguely recognized stepped forward with a bow. "We will see her safely there, my lord."

Fresh horror shot through Amira. The Kelamora Kadra'han, after generations of neutrality, had chosen a master.

Vesha shook her head. "I want to speak to Darrigan. He

wouldn't have betrayed me like this. He wouldn't—"

"But he did, my dear," Saan Thii laughed. "Now will you try ordering your Kadra'han to defy me, or will you be a good girl and do as you're told?"

Vesha locked gazes with Saan Thii for a long moment. To her credit, she didn't shrink from the demon's gaze.

"You will bow to me," Caa Iss growled, taking a decisive step toward Saan Thii. "You will acknowledge me as your leader. My host is the rightful heir of this empire!"

"Maybe," Saan Thii snickered. "But *my* host has taken the Fanduillion curse upon himself." The red in Darrigan's eyes sparked brighter.

Caa Iss shook his head. "Impossible. He has no authority!"

"The guard captain is a son of the Istovari." Saan Thii twisted Darrigan's face into a wicked grin. "By the law of substitution, he is a valid exchange. A son for a son." Saan Thii glanced to the body of the little girl still clutched in Thadred's arms. "He even made sure to offer me the blood of an Istovari child, everything you were offered when you were brought into this world."

"No!" Caa Iss shook his head violently.

"Do you know what that means?" Saan Thii licked at Darrigan's bloody wrist and raised his eyebrows excitedly, like she had just sampled a particularly good vintage.

Caa Iss took a sharp step forward. "Saan Thii, stop—"

"You are in that body unlawfully, brother." Saan Thii giggled, a sound like broken glass tumbling together. "You have no right to the archduke any longer."

Amira didn't know what was about to happen. She didn't know if this was bad or good, but it couldn't be worse, could it?

A look of utter horror washed over Caa Iss. Then he screamed.

CHAPTER TWENTY-SEVEN

Daindreth

Daindreth felt as if he were being ripped apart. Every fiber in his body burned and white-hot fire sliced through him bit by bit.

Pain lanced through every one of his bruises and fissured bones. He was sure that he was being cracked open like a crab, crushed until he split right down the middle.

Someone shouted and he hit the ground, hot blood soaking his hands, knees, and the sleeves of his robe.

That was why none of the Kadra'han had tried to stop Thadred or Amira. They had known this was coming. They encircled Vesha in a gauntlet behind Saan Thii—formerly Darrigan.

A primal, bestial roar ripped out of Daindreth's mouth. Caa Iss flailed and fought, but he was losing.

Daindreth had once seen vinegar poured over maggots in a festering wound. They'd writhed and convulsed as Caa Iss writhed and convulsed now.

A cracking, snapping sound rent the air like a clap of thunder and Daindreth felt himself *tear*. Caa Iss ripped free of him, yanked out like a thorn.

Daindreth collapsed, body aching and throat raw, but...

The archduke gasped, shocked by how deeply he could breathe and the lightness in his head.

"No!" cried a voice, one not as deep as it had sounded in Daindreth's mind, but still like the rumble of broken glass over granite.

Daindreth looked up and tried to dodge the black and red shadow over him, but the creature was too fast. Onyx claws scraped for Daindreth, grabbing and clutching at him, but the claws passed right over Daindreth as if they were smoke.

Caa Iss in his true form was vaguely humanoid with massive limbs roped in muscle, arms and torso too thick for his narrow trunk. Huge wings hung off his back, crumpled and ragged, as if the creature—when he had possessed his own body—had been mutilated.

He was less impressive than when he had shown himself in Daindreth's dreams, more broken and more feral. More beast than anything else.

Red eyes glinted in a scaly face. His nose had been cut off, giving him a skull-like appearance. His teeth were long and sharp and too close together, reminding Daindreth of a shark's jaw he had once seen.

"No!" Caa Iss shrieked again. "You bitch!" He whirled on Saan Thii.

"Daindreth!"

The archduke looked past Caa Iss and—Amira. Daindreth's heart leapt in his chest. She was alright.

Amira crashed into him, wrapping her arms around his neck and clinging to him so tight, he thought she would pulverize his ribs.

"Amira," he gasped, squeezing his eyes shut against the pain. There wasn't a part of him that didn't hurt, but there was no way he was letting her go.

"I'm sorry." She pulled away and looked him over. "I forgot you're hurt. You—"

"I will make you pay for this!" Caa Iss roared, diving for Saan Thii.

She caught him midair with the guard captain's hand. It seemed that Caa Iss could not touch Daindreth, but Saan Thii could touch him.

Caa Iss's form towered above Darrigan, at least nine feet tall, but Saan Thii held onto his neck easily, as if size and strength in this world had no bearing on either of them. She wore a wicked grin on Darrigan's lips.

Daindreth grabbed Amira's arm, not looking away from the strange standoff before them. "We need to get Thad and the child. Come on."

Amira didn't look away from the two cythraul, either. She clung to Daindreth's arm as they backed away, feet splashing in the blood of the Istovari girl. "Daindreth," she whispered, watching as Caa Iss flailed and fought in Saan Thii's grip.

"You bore me, brother." Saan Thii tossed him away and Caa

Iss staggered back. "Go. Wander the world as I did."

Daindreth's heart beat faster. He didn't want Caa Iss imprisoned in his own head—no that was the last thing he wanted—but a part of him knew that he didn't want that monster loose in the world, either.

"Dain!" Thad cried out to him, kneeling in the blood of the sacrificed child, his cane sword tossed aside.

"Thad." Daindreth dragged Amira back and the two of them crashed to the ground beside the knight. "Oh no."

"Help me!" Thadred held the wounds of the girl, trying to staunch the flow of blood. "I can't—"

Amira pulled the child's small body into her lap, but the girl wasn't moving. "Come on," Amira murmured.

"We're done here," Saan Thii purred.

One of the Kadra'han piped up. "Sir, what of the other Istovari? What of the archduke?"

Sir? The word caught in Daindreth's mind. Had the Kadra'han known Darrigan would make a deal with Saan Thii? They seemed to be deferring to him even now that he was no longer in control of himself.

"Leave them to burn." Saan Thii's red eyes settled on Daindreth.

"Where are the others?" Daindreth demanded. "The other children. Where are they?"

Saan Thii smirked and didn't answer.

"No!" Amira screamed, fussing over the small girl in her arms. "Come on, kid. Live! I did!" Tears fell onto the child's motionless body.

Daindreth put a hand on Amira's back. He wanted badly to make things better, to bring the child back, to soothe that look of torment on Amira's face.

Around them, the fires began licking through the far wall. The air was hot with the flames and smoke began curling above the candles.

Where were the rest of the Istovari rangers? Had they made it out of the flames? Or had they met their ends in the collapsing monastery?

Saan Thii gave a quick command to the Kadra'han and the remaining soldiers surrounded Vesha, almost as if they were

259

taking her into custody.

Vesha looked to Daindreth for a long moment.

Daindreth shook his head. Whatever Saan Thii had planned for Vesha now that she possessed a body, it wouldn't be good. Even if Captain Darrigan had made a deal for the empress's safety, that would only buy her time. It wouldn't truly keep her safe. Daindreth did not know Saan Thii as well as Caa Iss, but Daindreth would sooner trust a starving wolf than one of the cythraul.

Caa Iss lay in a heap on the ground, at least *seeming* to lie on it despite being an incorporeal being. The cythraul pawed at the floor mats and the red blood that ran through them, but it didn't react to his touch. The demon whined in protest, almost pitiful.

Daindreth thought he might have seen tears in his mother's eyes.

"Mother," Daindreth whispered.

Vesha was no longer a witch. She had lost her familiar and she must know it. Saan Thii was in control now—of everything.

The demoness had not saved Daindreth, or any of them. This would only be another kind of doom. Why had Darrigan done it?

"My lord," one of the Kadra'han in lamellar armor spoke. "We shall await you at the boats."

They addressed Saan Thii as if she was still the guard captain.

"Excellent." Saan Thii flexed Darrigan's neck from side to side. She adjusted her stance, looking more human by the moment as she spent time in this new form. "I have just a little business to finish here first." She licked her lips eagerly.

"I ordered you not to harm him," Vesha cried. "I ordered you, Darrigan! I ordered all of you!" The empress looked between her Kadra'han desperately, looking truly afraid for the first time.

"No, my dear," Saan Thii laughed. "You ordered your Kadra'han. I am not one." She waved Darrigan's hand dismissively. "*They* can't deal with your troublesome whelp, but I can."

Vesha whirled on her Kadra'han. "I am ordering you to stop—"

260

Saan Thii grabbed Vesha by the hair and yanked her back. The demoness clamped one of Darrigan's hands over her mouth and leaned down. Vesha struggled, but the demon hissed something in Vesha's ear and the empress went still.

"Good girl," Saan Thii said, loud enough that Daindreth could hear this time. "Now be glad I'm not making you rescind your other orders. I could, you know." Saan Thii laughed. "Now run along."

"Daindreth…" Vesha looked back to him, then away.

"Go!" Saan Thii jerked her chin at the Kadra'han in front of them and the men actually bowed.

The fire was spreading on the other side of the wall, competing with the glow of the candles. How long before it was burning around them?

"Thad." Daindreth spun on his cousin. "Is she alive?" He pointed to the girl.

"Barely," Thad said.

"Then I'm sorry." Dain inclined his head shortly, acknowledging that he was about to do something wrong. "But take her and get to safety. That's an order."

Thadred nodded, accepting the command without complaint. He scooped up the child's limp body, cradling her against one side with his cane sword bracing the other.

He turned and hobbled back the way he and Amira had come, the little girl's head lolled against his shoulder.

Daindreth had to have Amira help him stand. Smoke had begun to sting his eyes and he stifled a cough. He wondered if the flames would reach them first, or the smoke-poisoned air.

Saan Thii ripped a spear from the wall, twirling it in her hands. "It's been a long time since I've wielded one of these," she purred, pacing several short steps to one side and then the other.

"Daindreth!" Amira dashed to the nearest wall and ripped down two longswords, tossing one to him.

He caught it by the hilt, but just barely. His whole body ached, and he wasn't sure if he could do this, much less against a cythraul-possessed opponent. Darrigan was well past his prime, but his years of faithful service as a Kadra'han coupled with his strength from Saan Thii, and the longer weapon made this a bleak situation.

Daindreth looked to see if a halberd or polearm might be in reach, but those were all on Saan Thii's side of the training room. She had been set up to win from the beginning.

Even worse, she didn't seem affected by the smoke that filtered through the walls. She grinned at them, red eyes sparking with something akin to mischief.

"Do you want to attack me?" Saan Thii purred. "Or shall I make the first move?"

A blur of motion to Daindreth's right was the answer. Amira charged, attacking without a second's delay.

CHAPTER TWENTY-EIGHT

Amira

Amira lunged in, swinging her sword with a shout. Saan Thii jerked back a step, bringing the spear head around and jabbing for Amira's chest.

The assassin dodged to keep from being stabbed.

She hadn't expected to hit, but it was enough to make Saan Thii turn and face her, exposing the cythraul's other side to Daindreth.

"Such fight!" Saan Thii crowed. "I do so love a fiery spirit. They're the most fun to break."

With the cythraul facing Amira, Daindreth lunged from the other side, coming forward a quick step.

Saan Thii pivoted to block him. "You think it will be that easy?"

Even with Amira and Daindreth attacking from different sides, Saan Thii had but to pivot to stab at either of them. It was like the cythraul was at the center of a wheel spoke. Daindreth and Amira had to move much farther to reach her.

Amira looked to Daindreth. She could feel the power of *ka* rushing into her, easing the pain in her wounds and flowing strength into her muscles. He was barely standing upright.

Even though they outnumbered her, Amira and Daindreth might very well be outmatched. It wasn't as if they could run, either. Saan Thii was stronger in this form, and she would cut them down.

Amira coughed as smoke filtered through from the other room. All Saan Thii had to do was wait and the two of them would choke to death on the fire's fumes.

Saan Thii stabbed for Daindreth and Amira charged into the opening, stabbing for Saan Thii's exposed shoulder. Daindreth's sword clanged against the spearhead and blocked, but Saan Thii had pivoted again and swung to face Amira in an instant.

The spearhead jabbed for Amira's thigh, and she had to jump back again.

Saan Thii was stronger, she healed faster, and she had the

better weapon, but she was not immortal. Cythraul hosts could be killed—else Caa Iss wouldn't have put so much effort into keeping Daindreth alive.

Amira's eyes watered, but as she blinked, she shook her head. The swelling in her bruised eye was already down. Every moment she spent in this fight, her power increased.

She smiled at Saan Thii and the demon's head cocked to the side, uneasy. That gave Amira the hesitation she needed to charge in, hacking at the demoness.

Saan Thii pivoted again to block, but Daindreth kept up this time. He swung in and Saan Thii had to circle around them both, looping to the opposite side of the room to keep from being cornered.

With Saan Thii now on the other side, Amira turned and dashed for the wall and the polearms hung along it. She grabbed for one and hissed the moment she touched it—hot like coals.

The heat from the other side of the wall was too much already.

Saan Thii was there the next instant, jabbing for Amira while her back was turned.

"Amira!" Daindreth moved to block, but Saan Thii ran around wide.

Amira leapt to the side, not sure she would make it. Saan Thii's spear struck the wall. In the instant before Saan Thii ripped it out, Amira grabbed the spear shaft in her free hand and swung for Saan Thii's neck.

The demoness dropped down and with her free hand grabbed Amira's sword arm.

The two of them locked into a grapple, both with control of the other's weapon, but with Saan Thii having the advantage of strength, size, and speed.

She forced Amira's arm up and bashed Darrigan's forehead into Amira's face. The assassin jerked her head back and the captain's skull crunched into her jaw instead of her nose.

Daindreth had closed the distance again a moment later. He stabbed for Saan Thii's back.

The sword clanged against the demon's armor, scraping as it failed to find purchase. Saan Thii kicked Amira in the knee, sending her sprawling to the ground. She yanked her spear free and jerked it backwards, smashing the butt into Daindreth's chest.

Daindreth staggered, gasping. The strike would have hit his already wounded ribs.

"Daindreth!" Amira jabbed for Saan Thii's torso, aiming for the gap in the armor beneath the armpit.

The demoness leapt to the side, bringing her spear between them again. Amira took a step back as the cythraul dodged for her.

Saan Thii tried to charge in, but she got too close to Daindreth. The archduke swiped at her legs from his place on the ground and something clanged and ripped. Blood splattered the ground and Saan Thii's left leg wavered and she snarled.

Daindreth had drawn first blood. Not enough to debilitate, but enough to be an inconvenience.

The archduke staggered back to his feet and Amira stood there with her sword at the ready, trying to pull back, trying to think.

She could sense Thadred and the child, still moving away through the monastery, though they were barely detectable now. That meant Thadred had succeeded in finding a way out.

In the distance, the empress and her guards were also still moving away, but in a different direction. They headed toward the main gate while Thadred had gone back toward the prison and the waterfall passage.

Beyond them, the *ka* of the forest burned bright and golden. Amira could feel it fluttering and seeping through everything— so alive and ever-changing.

There were still pockets of *ka* scattered through the monastery that Amira took for Istovari and Kadra'han still locked in battle. Some slumped to the ground and Amira feared they would be trapped in the spreading flames.

But what could she do about it?

Around her feet, the *ka* of the child sacrifice soaked the ground, but it was fast dissipating. Too much of the power had been drained by Vesha and then used on Saan Thii.

Power ran down the guard captain's left arm. It dripped on the tatami mats with his blood and pulsed through him red and hot. His *ka* had changed, just as Daindreth's had whenever he had been fully possessed. It was that noxious energy that the possessed had, but beneath it, Amira could still sense Darrigan's Kadra'han power.

That telltale golden band looped his throat. Even now, Darrigan—Darrigan himself—was bound by his Kadra'han's oaths.

As she dodged and parried his blows, Amira watched as his *ka* kept replenishing, never seeming to run out even as it ran down his arm. His Kadra'han's oaths were still making him stronger. The curse still counted this as service.

Saan Thii lunged for Daindreth.

Amira fought the instinct to block and instead rushed in to attack her exposed side.

Saan Thii's spear arched straight for Daindreth and there was no way he could move in time.

Amira jabbed straight for the cythraul's unarmored left arm. Saan Thii reacted at the last possible moment, throwing her weight to the right and ripping back. She skirted out of reach, chuckling.

"And here I was sure you would leap in front of me to defend him."

Amira couldn't get too close to Daindreth. If they were together, Saan Thii wouldn't have to guard herself from two sides and it would only be a matter of time before one of them was struck down.

"Are you alright?" Amira asked, panting heavily.

"Fine," Daindreth grunted, not sounding fine at all. He staggered into a ready stance, raising his sword again.

Darrigan's curse was still making him stronger, so as far as it was concerned, this was all being done in service to Vesha. Yet he had technically betrayed her, so that meant he must have somehow subverted his curse the way Amira had subverted hers.

"What was your plan, Darrigan?" Amira asked, looking to the guard captain's face.

His expression and the light in his eyes belonged to Saan Thii, but he was still in there. According to Daindreth, he had still been able to hear and see everything those times when he had been possessed.

Darrigan had never wanted Vesha to make a deal with the demons. He had been trying everything to keep her from getting in deeper with the creatures. It made no sense that he would make his own deal with one of them, unless...

Saan Thii lunged again, attacking Amira this time.

The assassin retreated a step, then jerked toward the right, rushing for Saan Thii again. She had the advantage until Amira closed the distance and—

The cythraul leapt and pivoted, getting the spear head between them. She jabbed for Amira's shoulder and the assassin felt a tug. She barely had time to realize what had happened before Daindreth attacked Saan Thii's exposed back.

The cythraul was forced to retreat. Daindreth's blows struck against Saan Thii's side and something ripped, but Saan Thii didn't bleed.

A sharp ache spread through Amira's right shoulder. A dark stain flowed over her sleeve, and she swore, more from the inconvenience than the pain.

"You should have killed me today—the moment you found me in the forest," Amira said, looking the cythraul straight in the eyes.

Saan Thii smiled. "Soon enough, dearie."

"I'm not talking to you," Amira spat. "I'm talking to the captain."

Daindreth shot her a look, but Amira's mind whirled.

"You said you were keeping me alive to keep Daindreth under control." Amira didn't take her gaze off the guard captain. "But you kept him under control for years without me."

A beam fell at Amira's back, collapsing in a shower of sparks. It knocked over a swath of candles, snuffing out some, but others only added to the flames on the wooden column.

The assassin edged away from the beam, but didn't dare turn from the cythraul.

"The empress ordered you to be taken alive!" Saan Thii sneered. "You were to be a gift to Caa Iss! A consolation after all the trouble you caused him."

Amira tried not to think about all that implied. Vesha would have handed her over to be Caa Iss's plaything without a thought if it had assuaged some of the cythraul's frustration. "Yes," Amira said, growing surer of her suspicions. "But it was Darrigan's idea, wasn't it?"

Saan Thii let off an animalistic snarl and jabbed for Daindreth with her spear. Daindreth's sword smacked against the spear head.

Amira darted around behind the demoness and sliced the back of Darrigan's neck. It was a clean cut and blood splattered the ground, but Saan Thii still whirled around, teeth snapping like the jaws of a rabid dog.

Through the thickening smoke, Amira watched in horror as the wound to Darrigan's neck closed.

"It's going to take more than that, little sorceress," Saan Thii hissed.

Amira pressed her mouth into a tight line as the heat and fumes of the fire stung her eyes. She fought back a cough, keeping her attention on Saan Thii. The cythraul only needed a single opening to kill both her and Daindreth.

"You posted the guards. So why did you leave me unguarded? Why was there not a single guard between the water gate and me?" Amira said, still speaking to the guard captain. "You knew I'd be here." Darrigan hadn't seemed at all surprised when she had appeared with Thadred. "You *trusted* me to be here."

Daindreth coughed as the air thickened. She didn't think the two of them could survive for much longer, not like this.

They needed to make a move and soon.

Amira thought back to the first time she had fought a cythraul hand to hand, how she had beaten Caa Iss then. Her link with Caa Iss was different—she had been the sacrifice, after all—but...

Her eyes fell on the blood that still dripped down Darrigan's forearm. That wound hadn't healed yet, maybe because it had been sustained before Saan Thii took over.

"Daindreth..." She looked past Saan Thii to the archduke, *her* archduke, on the cythraul's other side. When he met her eyes, there was a tiredness there that told her he was only still fighting because of her. He wanted to lay down and give up, but he wouldn't, not when she was depending on him. The assassin lowered her sword to her side, shifting as if to see him better. She glanced between him and Saan Thii, hoping he understood enough to guess her plan.

Saan Thii didn't give her time to make sure. The demoness rushed in, spear heading straight for Amira's gut. She came fast, the spearhead little more than a blur of steel aiming for the assassin's belly.

Amira dropped to one knee and ducked. Saan Thii saw the feint and corrected, arching her spear thrust down.

Something tugged at the side of her neck and the spear's blade sheared down along her shoulder. White-hot pain shot across her back, but Amira reached up and grabbed Darrigan's left wrist, the one that still bled.

Saan Thii had possessed him, but Darrigan's power was still there. The demoness could control him. She could bend him to her will and take his free choice from him, but there was a piece of him that was and would always be Captain Darrigan—the man who had given his life a thousand times over for the Fanduillion bloodline.

As soon as Amira touched his blood, it was like diving into a pool to find it had no bottom. The power of his decades of service, of his loyalty and devotion, was there at her fingertips.

Amira had wielded massive amounts of *ka* before. She had channeled so much that it had seemed as if the strength of a thousand lives were being shaped by her one. That was nothing like this.

Darrigan's body seemed far too small for the massive reservoir of power that burned beneath his skin.

Saan Thii might inhabit his body, but she didn't belong there. Amira turned Darrigan's power on the demoness as if she were an infection, like a thorn in a wound. Amira directed Darrigan's *ka* against the sickly, noxious presence that was Saan Thii.

The demoness screamed and dropped her spear, but she didn't go down. Saan Thii clamped Darrigan's massive hand around Amira's neck.

Instantly, Amira's vision darkened. She couldn't breathe. Saan Thii forced her head back so far, she was certain her neck would snap.

A shadow appeared behind the cythraul. A tearing, squishing sound met Amira's ears.

Saan Thii's grip released, and a scream rent the air.

Amira yanked Darrigan's hand off her throat.

Daindreth stood behind Saan Thii, his sword rammed through the cythraul's chest. Sweat beaded his forehead and his arms shook, but he held fast.

"No," Saan Thii rasped, blood spitting out her lips. "No, no…" Her voice grew weaker by the moment. She clutched at the sword stuck through her sternum, each motion slower than the last.

The red light in the guard captain's eyes flickered and snuffed out. His body slumped forward and Amira caught him as Daindreth ripped the sword free.

"Captain?" Amira searched his face. "Captain Darrigan?"

The guard captain blinked at her, dark eyes hazy and unfocused.

"They're gone," Amira whispered. "Saan Thii and Caa Iss. You…you did it."

Darrigan's mouth tightened slightly in what might have been a smile, blood dribbling down his lips.

"Captain?" Amira didn't know what else to say.

Captain Darrigan's lips moved, but no sound came out. Without Saan Thii to heal him and keep him alive, blood loss was taking him quickly. Amira held him, not sure if the stinging in her eyes was from smoke or tears.

Daindreth knelt beside her, then, not touching the captain. The archduke wore a strange expression, uncertain, conflicted. As if he were caught between emotions and didn't know what to feel.

Amira realized Darrigan would have taught her archduke to fight, had watched over him his whole life. Despite everything that Vesha had compelled him to do, Darrigan had served the house of Fanduillion faithfully.

This man had saved Amira's life once. He had also tried to kill the man she loved. He served her greatest enemy outside the Dread Marches—Empress Vesha.

But in the end…Amira thought he had just saved her life

and the lives of everyone she loved. And she knew there were many things he had done only under compulsion.

Captain Darrigan's hand clumsily landed on Daindreth's.

Daindreth looked surprised, but he held onto the captain. Daindreth glanced to Amira. She didn't have time to explain to him, to tell him everything she had realized, everything she had pieced together. From his perspective, Darrigan was still their enemy, but there must have been something in Amira's face that helped him understand just enough. "Thank you, Darrigan," the archduke said quietly.

Daindreth squeezed back and the two men held onto each other until the captain's grip went slack and his body slumped forward.

Captain Darrigan, possibly the greatest Kadra'han who had ever lived, was dead. Amira had wanted him dead, *needed* him dead, even. But nothing about this felt like a victory.

"Amira." Daindreth released the dead man's hand. "We have to go." His voice was hoarse, and she didn't think it was just from the smoke. "We have to get out of here."

Another beam crashed to the ground nearby as the smoke thickened around them. Fire spread to the walls along the adjoining side of the room.

Amira nodded quickly. She laid Darrigan's corpse on the tatami mat. They didn't have time to arrange his body neatly as one would for a funeral, but she doubted he would have cared. This burning monastery would have to be his pyre.

Rising to her feet, she caught Daindreth's hand. Both of their hands soaked in the guard captain's blood.

And they ran.

Chapter Twenty-Nine

Thadred

The fire had spread too quickly. With how much this land seemed to rain, Thadred had a hard time believing that this was natural fire. Yes, most the monastery was wood, but it shouldn't burn this fast in such a damp climate, should it?

He found Tapios and several other rangers already waiting outside the water door. A narrow bridge ran under the waterfall, leading to a chiseled alcove where a narrow stream of water had been diverted to make a pool.

Thadred didn't curse at them for pointing their arrows his way before they recognized him. He even held his snarky comments about the rangers setting the place on fire then running.

"Thadred!" one of the rangers, Murren, called to him.

"Yes, hello Murren dear." Thadred staggered across the narrow bridge. The bridge was perpetually damp by virtue of being under the waterfall and a light mist soaked his hair, shoulders, and back. After the heat of the burning monastery, it felt damn good. "A little help?"

Thadred nodded to the motionless girl in his arms.

Murren and another of the female rangers rushed to help him. The child's blood soaked his shoulder and arm. How could such a small body have so much?

Beyond the shadow of the alcove, small, dirty faces stared back. Thadred didn't have time to count, but it looked like quite a few children sheltering in the dark.

"You found her!" Tapios cried.

"You found the others?" Thadred spared a glance to the grungy little urchins staring with wide eyes from farther down the passage. Several rangers knelt around them, consoling them.

Tapios gave a curt nod. "Yes, twenty-five. Only one was missing. Where are Amira and the archduke?"

"Coming," Thadred grunted. He knelt as Murren helped him

lay the small girl down on the ground.

"What happened to her?" Murren gasped, seeing the gashes in the child's neck and arm.

"Sacrifice," Thadred said. "To the cythraul."

Tapios finally seemed to notice the state the child was in and let off a gasp of horror.

Thadred squinted by the poor light. "Someone light a torch or something! I can't work like this."

"Our torches are wet," Murren said, a little sheepishly.

Thadred cursed heartily enough to make a sailor blush. At least the girl's wounds were obvious enough that he could find them in the dark. "Here." He grabbed Murren's hand. "Put pressure on her wounds here. You!" He thrust a finger at the other woman. "Get strips of cloth. Something we can use to tie off the wounds." His pitiful efforts at using his own shirt had done little good.

Tapios hovered over Thadred's shoulder, doing nothing helpful.

Maybe Thadred wouldn't hold back his snarky comments after all.

"Her *ka* is fading," Murren whimpered. "I can't...it doesn't..."

The other woman let off a mournful sound. "Her body's too damaged."

Thadred cursed again. "Pull yourselves together, women!"

"It took at least three Kadra'han to save Princess Amira," Murren said. At least she did as Thadred ordered and was holding onto the child's arm.

Movement at his back made him jump.

"Halt!" Tapios shouted as several other rangers raised their bows. He didn't raise his own and it was then Thadred realized that Tapios wasn't moving his left arm.

"It's us!" croaked a voice that was at least an octave too low.

"Amira!" Thadred called, turning in place. His chest eased when he saw her come stumbling across the bridge with Dain at her side. "You made it. Darrigan?"

"Dead," Dain answered.

"Amira, can you help?" Thadred asked. "She's still alive, but barely."

"I can try." Amira sank to the rocky floor too slowly. Thadred thought she might be injured, but he couldn't tell in the dark. Either way, it was the child who was closest to death. He would worry about the adults later.

Thadred pulled the girl's head into his lap and laid a hand over the wound in her neck. Her blood stuck to him like tar. In truth, Thadred had no idea what he was doing, but so far he had blundered his way through magic. He tried to think, remembering what Sair had said about the spells in his hip and thigh.

He'd spelled himself to survive without knowing it, so he was able to do mending spells. Even if it wasn't a conscious knowledge, he had it.

"Can you put more *ka* into her while I heal the wounds?" Thadred asked.

Tapios looked to Thadred in surprise. "You know the spells?"

Thadred shrugged. "Not like we're going to hurt her *more* at this point." He looked back to Amira. "See if you can just…keep her life force lit." That sounded stupid, but it also sounded right.

Amira laid her hands on the child's cut arm, her hands between Murren's. The blood coming from that wound was thick and sticky. Not a good sign.

Thadred closed his eyes and focused, the way he had done with Sair in the Cursewood. "Come on," he muttered to himself. Anxiety and fear bloomed through him that maybe he would fail, maybe this girl would die in his arms.

Then he reminded himself that this girl was already dead by all rights. The situation could only get better.

"Can you channel power?" he asked the other two women.

"We can sense *ka*," Murren said sounding self-conscious. "We can channel a little, but we don't have enough for spells. We—"

"That's fine," Amira interrupted. "Just channel what you can into the girl, alright?"

Thadred tried to block out their words. Amira could probably direct enough power into the child by herself, but he didn't think she had the skill for the actual healing—the spell itself.

"Amira, you're not leading the spell work?" Tapios asked.

"Thadred knows as much about healing as me, if not more," Amira answered.

Amira's surly confidence was oddly just what Thadred needed.

Thadred rested the girl's head against his lap, her skin cold beneath his hand. Her neck wound was fleshy, raw, and her blood smeared him all over, leaving a thick, crusty sensation on his hands and clothes.

Beneath that, her pulse fluttered. Her heart hammered too fast as her body tried to compensate for blood loss.

Thadred could feel the torn pieces of flesh in her neck and the edges of her wound. They were still alive, still fighting to repair themselves. Her blood congealed and coagulated, trying to stay inside her body, to heal the breech in her skin.

Concentrating, Thadred could see the fibers in her muscles and cartilage, like the threads in a tapestry. The wound was a tear, a gaping hole where the threads had been cut.

He could feel where those threads wanted to knit back together, where they wanted to close. Two fibers of muscle came into his awareness, each on opposite sides of the wound.

This girl's body still wanted to heal. It was still trying. It just needed a little help.

Reaching out, Thadred envisioned those two broken strands of muscle touching, drawing back together. They fused, rejoining and pulling other fibers back together as they did. Some of the fibers rejoined with different pieces than before, but it didn't matter.

"Thad." Dain let out an awed gasp. "Amira."

No sooner had Dain spoken than Thadred felt power rushing up into the girl's wounds. He guided the pieces of her flesh back together, but Amira's wild, unbridled power surged through the child's body, driving it to heal.

"Not so fast!" Thadred protested. "Not so much! I'm still working." He focused harder, trying to keep up with the parts of the girl's body that wanted to rejoin and the spaces he could direct them. "Reach and touch and bind," Thadred murmured to himself. "Reach and touch and bind."

He heard Dain shifting and was aware of the distant crackle of the burning monastery, but he remained focused. He could do this.

The girl's neck knit back together, though Thadred could feel a bumpy, rough line where her skin had been reconnected. Without waiting, he reached for her arm.

"You're doing it," Dain gasped. "It's working."

"Her body is holding *ka* again," Amira said. "But it won't make a difference if she's already lost too much blood."

Thadred shut their voices out. He didn't need Dain's optimism or Amira's cynicism to distract him.

Thadred focused on pulling together the fibers in the wound along the girl's arm. The wound was a clean slice for the most part and convincing the pieces of her flesh to connect was easy. "Reach and touch and bind." He realized he was chanting that under his breath as he guided the girl's body back into wholeness. "Reach and touch and bind."

"Come on." Amira added a curse under her breath.

"I can feel it!" Murren cried.

Another surge of power went through the child and her broken flesh rushed to reunite with itself.

He looked down to see a puckered line both on the girl's neck and her arm, beneath the blood. It was inelegant work, but her skin had sealed and she was no longer bleeding.

Thadred opened his eyes just as Amira grabbed the child's wrists. Power bloomed through the girl, *ka* congealing around her chest as Amira fed straight, raw energy into her small frame. The child's body took it eagerly, soaking it up and drinking it in the way parched ground soaks in rain.

Thadred wondered if it was his imagination, but he thought he saw golden threads ripple through the child's veins. They danced beneath her skin and behind her eyes, her lips glowing faintly gold.

"It's working," Dain whispered. "You're actually doing it."

Amira released the child, panting. "I think it worked," she gasped, looking to Thadred. "She might have a chance."

The child still didn't stir, but Thadred was sure he could see a golden spool of glowing thread in her chest now, swirling around her heart.

Dain put an arm around Amira and rested a hand on Thadred's shoulder. "You did it," he said, kissing Amira's temple.

Thadred stared down at the child. He'd done it. He'd saved her. With Amira's help, but...

"I'm a sorcerer," Thadred whispered, saying the words out loud for the first time. He looked up to Amira, feeling oddly giddy despite everything. "I can use magic."

The assassin nodded. "You're a sorcerer."

CHAPTER THIRTY

Amira

The surviving rangers helped Amira, Daindreth, Thadred, and their gaggle of children back to the camp that had somewhat formed their recovery point. From there, they watched the monastery of Kelamora burn to the ground atop the mountain.

The wounded girl woke up not long after and though she was still weak and tired easily, they learned that her name was Esta.

Her mother was called Jelaine, apparently, and her older brother was a ranger called Rickon. Tapios had known him—he told the others privately that Rickon had been one of the ones killed in the first attack from the Kadra'han.

Esta seemed to have attached herself to Thadred, never straying far. He took to the responsibility surprisingly well, watching over her like a protective uncle.

The other children huddled around Murren and the other Istovari, clinging to the rangers and each other like frightened little birds. None of them appeared harmed besides Esta.

At daybreak, their group went back to the ruins to search for signs of life.

They found one other ranger who was still alive. He had been burned along his scalp and neck, but they thought he would survive, if with a few scars.

They found Jesri's body charred almost beyond recognition beside those of two Kadra'han monks. From the knives in Jesri's corpse, Amira guessed that the young woman had tried fighting them. In the end, all she had done was keep them distracted long enough that they were under a burning beam when it fell.

Tapios and the surviving rangers had all sustained wounds of varying severity. Between Amira and Thadred, they were able to mend the more severe wounds, though Amira found herself feeling drained after. Thadred was able to manage some minor mending himself, but had yet to master the art of drawing *ka* from the world around him.

They collected the bodies of the dead as best they could and wrapped them in what they had—rice mats, rugs, and the cloaks of the fallen. They laid both Istovari and Kadra'han bodies out in the ruined courtyard, not sure what would be done with them.

Darrigan's body was blackened and skeletal, only recognizable by his armor. Amira took special care with that one and Daindreth helped, not asking why. They wrapped him in a spare rug they found downstairs, deciding that they would bury him with the others when the rain stopped.

Amira found a pair of boots and went with Tapios and a few of the other survivors to search for Vesha and her guards. As Saan Thii had said, there were signs that a large group had passed from the monastery, through the forest, and to the lagoon in the nearby valley.

A small dock was there, but no boats. As best Amira could guess, Saan Thii had them all take boats down the river. Where they had gone after that or what the demoness had planned, Amira couldn't guess.

Thadred's kelpie showed up not long after they returned to the monastery. The animal had a gash in his shoulder as if from a blade and an arrow wound to his flank. They guessed he had tried attacking the Kadra'han and Vesha, though gods knew why.

The ragtag group of Amira, Daindreth, Thadred, and the Istovari moved their camp to the lower storerooms of the monastery as it began to rain. Their horses sheltered in the burned out ruins, except for Thadred's kelpie.

That animal paced around the monastery like a mastiff, snorting and resisting efforts by anyone to get close to him, even Thadred.

They traded watches, despite the kelpie's guard and no sign of habitation for miles. Amira took the midday watch, perched in the shade of burned-out watchtower. The stone was scorched black and the wooden steps inside had been burned away, but it still made for useful shelter.

Amira stared down at the valley, sore and tired, but very much alive. Her bruises and cuts weren't entirely healed yet, but she seemed to have done at least a week's worth of healing after last night. Whether it was thanks to her Kadra'han bond or the sheer amount of *ka* she had channeled last night, her power was increasing. At this rate, she might one day be as strong as Darrigan had been.

Footsteps approached from behind and she cocked her head. At first, she thought it was the kelpie pacing back around the monastery, but there were only two sets of feet and not enough *ka*.

"Who goes there?" she called.

"It's me." At Daindreth's voice, Amira's whole body relaxed. He came around the corner, still wearing the robes the Kadra'han had given him and a pair of sandals from the storerooms.

"Hello, love," Amira greeted him, her tone softening. She swallowed, fighting back the hoarseness in her throat from breathing the smoke.

The archduke moved to sit beside her on the ground. Amira moved closer, hooking her arm through his.

"Is everyone alright?" Amira asked out of instinct, though he wouldn't be sitting down if something was wrong.

"Fine," Daindreth said. "That little girl has adopted Thad, I think."

Amira smiled. "He does surprisingly well with children, doesn't he?"

"He does," Daindreth agreed with a grin. "And I think no one is more horrified by it than him."

"What do you mean?"

"Nothing." Daindreth shook his head. He kissed her temple, and she was immediately self-conscious. She smelled of smoke, sweat, and the grease of the road, not at her most appealing.

"I just got back from a walk," he said.

"Oh?" Amira kept her attention on the trees around them, though she could sense nothing but the usual *ka* of the forest.

"Yes. A few miles out with some of the rangers. To scout."

Amira noticed then that his feet were dirty inside his sandals. "And what did you find?"

Daindreth pressed his lips to her temple again, leaving a lingering kiss against her skin before he replied. "Nothing."

There was an odd tone in his voice that made her look up. "Nothing?"

Daindreth shook his head. "Not a thing." His voice hitched. Amira pulled back in concern. "Daindreth?"

"We're alone," he whispered, touching the side of his head. "It didn't matter how far I went. There's no one else here."

Looking into his amber eyes, it took Amira a moment to realize what he meant. The instant she did, her eyes widened. "Dain—"

He caught her face in his hands and captured her mouth in a kiss. Hope burst through her chest as desire swept through her body in a trembling wave.

She returned his kiss eagerly, hands sliding along his sides though she wanted to shove him down and pin him to the grass. He was still hurt, though his kiss made it hard to remember that.

Caa Iss was gone. After all this time, the thing that had stood between them wasn't here.

She pulled herself closer, shifting so she faced him, kneeling on the grass. Her hakama tangled, too much fabric getting in the way. Perhaps she should just take it off.

They were alone. Truly alone. Daindreth didn't have to fear losing control or that he would be sharing her with the cythraul.

His kiss sent shivers skittering down her spine. Something primal and hungry curled in the pit of her stomach. His kiss sent a pleasant dizziness through her head, not unlike being drunk. Heat flared through her whole body and an ache grew between her legs.

She wanted him, craved him like a starving woman craved bread. And here he was in her arms—completely alone on a grassy knoll.

Daindreth's kiss turned slow. He kissed her easily, languorously. No longer did he kiss her like he was giving in to a vice and feared being caught.

Now he took his time, drawing their kiss out, savoring it as one would a fine wine. All Amira wanted was to drink herself into oblivion.

Amira broke away from his mouth and pressed her lips against his jawline. Daindreth's hands slid down to stroke her back, tugging her closer. She left a trail of kisses up the side of his face and he made a deep purring sound of contentment.

She traced her tongue along the shell of his ear and his breath hitched, his fingers digging into her back.

Amira grinned wickedly against his cheek and kissed down the side of his neck, her tongue stroking his skin with each caress.

Daindreth held onto her, his breath coming faster as she reached his collar bone. "Amira," he gasped.

She leaned into him, fumbling for the ties at the front of his robe. His hands slid down her back and she pressed against him, just the barest nudge, asking permission.

He yielded, letting her push him into the grass. She laid him down gently, supporting his head.

Amira found his mouth again, kissing him deep and hard, but trying not to be too rough. He was hurt. She needed to remember that.

She straddled him, careful not to press her weight on his injured ribs. His hands clenched her back, pulling her against him.

"I want to do such wicked things with you," he whispered against her lips.

Amira giggled, catching the ties at the front of his robe. She undid the knots, sliding back his coat and hastily unlacing the shirt underneath. Nihain fashion was much easier to remove compared to imperial styles.

She pulled back, pushing aside the layers of cloth to expose his chest and torso. Purple marks still marred his skin, *ka* pooling around his injuries.

Amira leaned down and caressed the outline of a bruise, measuring more *ka* into him as she did.

Daindreth let off a short gasp.

"Are you alright?" Amira paused, looking to him in concern.

"No, that feels good." He closed his eyes. "It makes it hurt less."

Amira traced her tongue along the edges of another wound. She poured *ka* into him carefully, remembering what Thadred had told her about bodies needing time to accept the healing power.

Daindreth flinched. "Amira."

"Did I give you too much?"

"It's not your magic. It's your tongue."

"Do you like it?"

Daindreth swallowed, hands stroking up and down her back. "Yes. Yes, I think I do."

Amira flicked her tongue over his ear again before nibbling on his lobe. "Where else would you like my tongue?"

"I'm not sure…" Daindreth's breath came fast and shaky. "This is new for me."

It was new to Amira, too, but that didn't mean she was entirely ignorant. She'd overheard enough in seedy taverns and soldier's barracks to have an idea of what to try. "Do you like this?" Amira licked down the side of his neck, tracing the veins in his throat.

"Yes," Daindreth rasped, sounding out of breath.

"What about this?" Amira kissed down the middle of his chest, sucking gently.

"That's nice." Daindreth closing his eyes with a shallow sigh.

Amira's hands feathered over his ribs, careful to slide around the pools of *ka* that marked his injuries. She licked along the planes of his abdomen, earning soft gasps and groans as she did.

Excitement pulsed through her. She enjoyed making him squirm, but she wanted to touch more of him. She wanted to *feel* more of him.

Her fingers went to work on the next tie of his robe, fumbling to undo the laces. Still kissing his exposed skin, she shifted forward, her knee pressed beside his hip.

Amira's mouth found his again and she kissed him deep and hard. She leaned into him, wanting nothing more than to be as close as she possibly could. She leaned too far and over balanced, her weight pressing into him.

He flinched and grunted, breaking off their contact.

Amira stopped and looked up at him in askance. His face was tight, mouth hardened into a line. "Did I hurt you?" She should have been more careful.

Daindreth had fought beside her last night, but that had probably only undone whatever progress he'd made with healing. His wounds weren't cuts and though she and Thadred had infused *ka* into him, they didn't have the skill to heal broken ribs just yet.

"I like what you were doing," he said, voice almost a wheeze. "I do. But yes. That hurt." He touched his side, wincing.

Amira's heart raced and she tried not to show her disappointment. The last thing she wanted was to cause him pain, but the need for him raged against the idea of more waiting. "I'm sorry," she said, guilt plucking at her.

"Marry me?" Daindreth asked, words still strained. Amira must have pressed against him harder than she had thought.

"I signed a contract to marry you." In her mind, this was one thing that had never been in question between them.

"Then do it," he said. "I've spoken to Tapios. He believes that the Mothers will bless our union now that Caa Iss is gone. If they don't, I will sign over a few of my personal holdings to Thadred and make him a landowner, then he can officiate. Tapios and the rangers here are willing to witness."

Amira was surprised Daindreth knew that Hylendale tradition. Most couples in Hylendale had their marriages notarized by the village headman or local baron. Nobles who could afford the compensatory "gift" to the clergy, used the province's bishop, since he was the lawful owner of all the clergy's Hylendale assets. But the only true legal requirement was that the person presiding over the marriage had to own land. It was an old law meant to prevent sailors along the coast from eloping with Hylendale women.

Daindreth watched Amira expectantly. "Marry me when we get back to the Haven?"

"I'll marry you," Amira nodded, realizing her silence had been mistaken for hesitation.

"Good. We'll wait a few weeks to let me get back into fighting condition." A mischievous glint entered his eyes. "And I promise you can ravish me then."

Amira's face heated and she almost smacked his arm before she stopped herself. She raised her chin, returning his devilish look. "Then I have a few weeks to plan all the things I want to do to you?"

Daindreth laughed at that, then grimaced. "It even hurts to

laugh."

Amira touched his shoulder. "I'm sorry, love."

"It's fine." He inhaled slowly and then let the breath out just as carefully. "I have a lot to look forward to now."

In truth, Amira still didn't want to wait another moment, but she could wait a few more weeks if she had to.

As if reading her mind, Daindreth smiled. "Even if I was hale enough to take you now, I don't think our first time should be on the side of a hill in broad daylight."

Amira had to admit to herself that they should probably take more time to get this right—but if he hadn't been hurt, she would have argued. What difference did when or where make so long as she could finally love and know him in all the ways she wanted?

Daindreth's face fell. "It won't be the wedding of an empress. I'm sorry."

Amira grasped his hand, shaking her head. "On the side of a hill, in the hold of a ship, in a cave, on a mountain peak, on a desolate beach, or on the floor in the middle of a grand cathedral. I don't care so long as I can have you."

Daindreth smiled at her then, face breaking into a huge grin. "You'd make love to me in a cathedral? With all the gods watching?"

Amira shrugged. "The gods will be watching anyway, if the priests are to be believed."

He brushed her cheek with his fingertips. "I can't wait to marry you."

Amira leaned in and kissed him again, sweetly this time. Chaste. "We'll get you recovered, and we'll get us married." She stroked her thumb across his cheek. "And then we'll get to work."

Daindreth turned somber at that. "Yes. We have a lot of work to do."

Now that Vesha had lost her familiar and Caa Iss had been excised, the empress would be at her most vulnerable—and probably her most desperate.

If the two of them wanted any real life together, if they wanted to stop the threat of cythraul to the empire, they had to stop Vesha. Daindreth had to become emperor and his mother had to be put down. Deposed at the very least. Amira and Daindreth were too great a threat to the stability and prosperity that the empress prized so highly.

"We'll do it together," Amira whispered.

"Together," Daindreth agreed.

EPILOGUE

Vesha knew Captain Darrigan was dead, though she couldn't have said how. There was an emptiness and a hollowness in her chest that she had felt once before. It had been the morning she'd woken battered and bruised with servants and physicians hovering over her.

Before they had told her, she had known her husband was gone. They had tried to spare her. At the time they had still been hoping to save the baby she was carrying, but Vesha had known it was too late for her unborn child, too.

Her husband had ordered his own death by Darrigan's hand. Vesha had thrown Darrigan in prison and planned to execute him, but she'd allowed him a final audience.

Darrigan had not made excuses in that audience. He had fallen to his knees and begged her forgiveness—not her mercy, her forgiveness. He'd wept at her feet, and it was the only time she had ever seen that man cry. It was then she realized how deeply he too mourned her husband. And no matter how much she hated him for taking Drystan's life, it would never compare to how much the captain hated himself.

Vesha had demanded Darrigan retake his Kadra'han's vows to her, to serve her for the rest of his days. The captain had done it without hesitation.

But Vesha had never accepted his apology and she had still hated him for what he had done. She knew she had been cruel to him for years—cold, harsh, even demeaning.

He had never complained. Never shown a moment's reticence. He had gone far beyond his vows to serve her and protect the empire, even when she had gone against his council.

Now Vesha sat under a brocaded pavilion fit for an empress, watching the shore pass by. Beside her was a tray of grapes, cheese, wine, and seasoned nuts. One of the Kadra'han had come and set it beside her while bowing, almost apologetically. They waited on her themselves since all her handmaidens were on another barge. She ignored them.

When the monastery had gone up in flames and Darrigan had still not arrived, the Kadra'han announced that they were to take her to the barges that still waited at the mouth of the river and back to Mynadra. That was the plan Darrigan had made.

They were all sworn to her and Vesha could have ordered them against that plan. She could have ordered them to storm the monastery and rifle through the flaming timbers until they found Darrigan, but she didn't.

Her longtime confidante, servant, and friend had given his life to enact this plan, so she would follow it. At least for now. It was the least she could do for him.

And Vesha needed time to think. Time to plan. Time to strategize for how she would fix this.

Vesha had known Darrigan was desperate to stop her dealings with the cythraul. She'd known he opposed any efforts at leveraging the creatures, even when the empire had prospered year after year.

She had never thought he was desperate enough to betray her. It had never even occurred to her that he would make a deal with her own familiar.

"Curse you, Darrigan," Vesha swore. "Curse you to the Dread Marches, you bastard." She could still feel the memory of his mouth on hers. It had been his lips, but it hadn't been his kiss—the kiss had been from Saan Thii. Still…the touch of him, the taste of him…it only added to her confusion.

Not that it mattered now. Darrigan was dead.

And he had completely sabotaged her arrangement with Moreyne and the cythraul. Without Saan Thii and the support of the Second Moon Goddess, Vesha had no way to protect the empire. She had no way to stop the floods that now plagued the north or the droughts that crept across the south. She couldn't stop earthquakes along the isles or mudslides in the mountains.

Famine, disaster, and disease would befall the people again and worse than ever before. She was powerless.

Had Daindreth and his assassin had survived?

She thought she might be sick at the thought of Daindreth, her only child, dead and charred in that ruined monastery. But if he was alive, he would challenge her, especially now.

Her son was not vengeful, and he had always forgiven her, even when she had been forced to do her worst. But a man's loyalties changed when he fell in love.

Vesha had seen the way her son looked at Amira Brindonu. It was the same way Emperor Drystan had looked at Vesha all those years ago. The same way Captain Darrigan had.

There were plenty of lords and barons who had questioned Vesha's rule. Some because they genuinely honored the Fanduillion bloodline, but most because they wondered if perhaps Daindreth would be more amiable to their own interests.

Vesha expected to face a civil war by the end of the year, on top of everything else.

It was the worst thing she could imagine and yet Darrigan had died to make it happen.

"Traitor," she cursed under her breath again. But it did no good to dwell on that.

Vesha turned her mind toward what she did have. She still officially had the allegiance of barons, counts, kings, viceroys, and dukes across the empire. She had the support of the clergy, the merchant's guild, and most of her foreign allies. She also now found herself with a new staff comprised of the former servants of Kelamora.

The cooks, hall boys, washer girls, and other servants of the monastery had begged for escape on the barges once the monastery was set aflame and Vesha had allowed it. Not that it was charity. She expected them to serve at least until they reached the next port.

Daindreth had two Kadra'han, one of them being a cripple, and the apparent alliance of the surviving Istovari sorceresses.

Vesha thrummed her fingers on the arm of her chair, thinking. In that light, it seemed Vesha had the upper hand over her son, but she of all people knew not to underestimate a sorceress, much less an entire clan of them.

It must be dark thoughts indeed to shadow so fair a face, purred a voice far better suited to growls and snarls.

Vesha looked up to see the massive, hulking form of a cythraul prince looming over her. He reached for her face. Terror gripped her and she just barely stifled a scream—screams only encouraged cythraul—but then his claws passed through her face, incorporeal.

Never fear, my empress.

"Did your mother send you?" Vesha asked, forcing herself to remain outwardly calm. "Tell her I will find a way to make this right. I will not fail her again. I will—"

Hush, hush, my dear, Caa Iss crooned. He held a talon over her lips. *We have something in common, you and I.*

"Oh?" Vesha glanced past him to where her Kadra'han were still watching the shoreline, where they assumed any threat would come from. "What is that?"

We have both been betrayed.

Vesha supposed they had. Saan Thii had double crossed her just as much as Darrigan had.

Your champion met his end at the hands of your son and his pet sorceress, Caa Iss said, confirming what Vesha had known in her heart. *My sister was dragged back into the Dread Marches by his departing spirit.*

Vesha nodded. "Did he die quickly?"

Caa Iss's tattered wings moved in what Vesha realized was a shrug. *Reasonably. They held him as he died. They didn't leave until he was gone.*

Vesha looked away from the cythraul, blinking quickly to stop the sting in her own eyes.

Darrigan had been held. He hadn't been trapped in rubble and burned alive as she had envisioned. He hadn't died alone.

They both survived, by the way, Caa Iss added, as if he wasn't sure whether Vesha would care. *The archduke and his assassin. Quite a few of the rangers, too.*

Vesha nodded.

You're not surprised by any of this, Caa Iss said. It wasn't a question.

"Darrigan would have found his way back to me by now," Vesha answered. "And Lady Amira is remarkably resourceful."

Yes, Caa Iss agreed. *She is.* He looked back in the direction of the monastery. *Annoyingly resourceful.*

Vesha inhaled a long breath. "Why have you come to me?"

It's funny. But I thought you might need a familiar.

Vesha cocked her brow. "Your sister is my familiar."

Perhaps, but she's in the Dread Marches. You would need to do another

290

summoning to get her back. Of course, after what she did, I'm not sure you'd wish to continue your relationship.

When Vesha had first summoned Saan Thii, it had taken a year of preparation, study, and experimentation to create a bond that would allow Saan Thii to interact with the world. Vesha could probably repeat the process in three months or so now, but that was still three months she didn't have. Disaster was knocking at the empire's door now.

Vesha knew this just as Caa Iss knew this, but it was never wise to appear too eager with cythraul.

"I've done a summoning before," Vesha replied easily. "I can do it again."

Caa Iss exposed his pointed teeth in the ghastly approximation of a smile. *You can,* he said. *If you have time.*

Vesha met the cythraul's serpentine eyes. Her Kadra'han still seemed not to notice, and she wondered if there was some trick the creature had played on them.

"You are out of favor with your mother," Vesha said.

Caa Iss didn't waver. *As are you.*

Vesha held her ground. Cythraul were like feral dogs, they attacked at the slightest show of weakness, but they respected power.

When my sister dragged me from my host, she left me to wander this world, adrift between realities. Caa Iss tilted his head back, horns stabbing at the sky. *That traps me and keeps me from reporting back to my mother with my side of the story, but...* He lowered his head back to Vesha with a grin. *I am not without recourse.*

Vesha looked over the demon, not speaking for a long time. She waited. The river continued to flow by and they passed a group of fishermen who waved at the barges.

When Caa did not break the silence, Vesha said, "My last familiar betrayed me, just as Darrigan warned me she would. I find myself uneager to replace her with another betrayal waiting to happen."

That was a lie. Vesha was desperate to find some method of fixing this great tangle, but how could she?

Caa Iss leaned over her, unperturbed and with an eager glint in his eye. *You need me just as much as I need you.*

That surprised Vesha. She had never heard a cythraul admit

291

to needing anything.

"Do you now?" Vesha countered, doing her best to sound bored.

I want revenge, Caa Iss snarled. *Against my traitorous sister. And against that Istovari bitch.*

Vesha noticed that Caa Iss had not mentioned Daindreth—his host of fifteen years—though he must be foremost on the cythraul's mind. Perhaps the demon feared mentioning vengeance on her son would make her less eager to bargain.

"Keep talking, cythraul," Vesha said, reaching for the untouched wine at her elbow. "Make me an offer."

Caa Iss eagerly slid his serpentine tongue over his lips. *As you wish, my empress.*

Out Now!

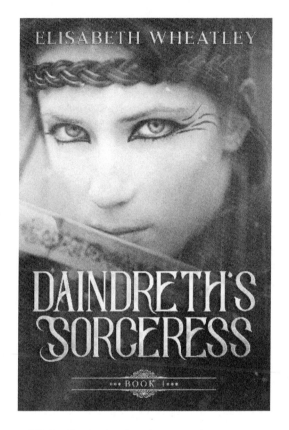

Visit elisabethwheatley.com/sorceress

ABOUT THE AUTHOR

Elisabeth Wheatley is a fantasy author because warrior princess wasn't an option. She loves tea and asking questions.

You can find her at elisabethwheatley.com

Printed in Great Britain
by Amazon

45676806R00169